BAD BLOOD

ALSO BY CASEY KELLEHER

Rotten to the Core
Rise and Fall
Heartless

CASEY KELLEHER
BAD BLOOD

THOMAS & MERCER

Published by Thomas & Mercer, Seattle

www.apub.com

Amazon, the Amazon logo, and Thomas & Mercer are trademarks of Amazon.com, Inc., or its affiliates.

ISBN-13: 9781477827130
ISBN-10: 1477827137

Cover design by bürosüd München, www.buerosued.de

Library of Congress Control Number: 2014944823

For Danny

My Hero.

xx

'*Blood makes you related. Loyalty makes you family.*'

— *Unknown*

Prologue
1990

Bringing his fists up to protect his face, Harry Woods wasn't quick enough. The whirlwind sucker-punch executed by Jake Pinner struck him with as much speed as it did precision. A surge of pain exploded in Harry's skull, the impact almost knocking him to the floor. Harry could feel his right eye bulging as it throbbed in agony, instantly swelling up so that he could barely even open it. Squinting through his left eye, he struggled to keep his focus. He'd taken one too many brutal blows; he was starting to slip.

Jake Pinner was good. Harry needed to be better.

Every part of him ached, but he couldn't give up now. He couldn't lose this fight. He needed to concentrate, but after six gruelling rounds he knew that he didn't have much left in him. This was the most important fight of his career, yet he couldn't shift the niggle of doubt that he wasn't going to go the distance tonight.

'Keep your fists up, Harry, and your chin down.' Raymond Marks' voice echoed from somewhere behind him. His best friend's instructions were dulled down by the roar of the crowd and the intense ringing in his ears, but even so, Harry recognised the desperation in Raymond's tone. Even he was starting to lose his faith in him.

Never one for the sympathy vote, Harry knew that he needed to pull himself together.

This was his shot. His one chance.

Dripping with sweat, he paced the ring, psyching himself back up, all the while keeping eye contact as Jake threw out another blast of powerful hooks. The first blow caught Harry's shoulder, the second missed as he quickly ducked out of the way.

Catching the steely look in his challenger's eye, Harry could see that the man's face was a mask of sheer determination.

Jake 'The Sinner' Pinner was moving in for the grand finale.

The bloke looked set to win, but Harry wasn't done yet. Catching sight of Evelyn out of the corner of his eye, he found the strength to round on Pinner, and go at him with everything he had. Administering a set of brutal body blows, Harry caught his adversary by surprise.

The crowd cheered loudly, egging Harry on.

He was making a comeback.

Suddenly caught up in the moment, everything else in the arena around him just disappeared. The glare of the bright lights, the raucous chanting – all Harry could see was his opponent. As Harry rained his punches with full force, Jake flagged under the unexpected counter-attack.

Pivoting now, Harry put his full body weight behind each blow.

Mercilessly he was back on form. He was nailing it.

Hammering down his fists with perfect execution, Harry annihilated his rival, quickly, ferociously, opening up a large cut above his rival's eye like a crisp packet. Then, he implemented one final, ruthless punch, slamming his opponent to the floor.

Jake Pinner was down. Harry was the last man standing.

'Ladies and gentlemen, tonight's winner by knockout and the new World Heavyweight Champion . . . Harry "The Hammer" Woods.'

Insatiable, the room erupted around him, the audience roaring in celebration of Harry's success.

Holding his head up high, proud of his accomplishment, Harry had never known a feeling like it. In front of everyone, the thousands of people packed inside this massive arena and the rest of the world who were watching at home on their television screens, with much anticipation, Harry had finally done it.

Jake Pinner had fought well, dishing out just as many punches as he was receiving, but in the end Harry had fought stronger, harder, faster. He hadn't backed down.

Standing triumphantly as the sea of cameras flashed around him, blinding him as the press moved in like vultures picking greedily at the fresh bit of meat before them, all desperate to get that much sought-after exclusive quote from the new champion, Harry Woods clutched the large, extravagant prize-winner's belt with pride, lifting it high in the air above his head. This was his trophy. It was what every minute until now had been leading up to. Those endless twelve-hour training days that he'd dragged himself through with monastic devotion, almost to breaking point. The food he'd forced upon himself, enduring a strict diet of six thousand calories a day, without so much as a drop of alcohol. It had been so punishing, so relentless, that at times Harry had almost given up.

Now, though, he knew without a doubt that it had been worth every arduous second. Harry knew deep down in his soul that this is what he was made for. Boxing was in his blood; he was following in the footsteps of his late grandfather, and today he'd placed himself well and truly on the map.

But there was only one person he wanted to share this moment with.

Searching beyond the TV crew, with all their fancy equipment, Harry searched the crowd, looking for his wife. Scrutinising the many faces, his eyes flickered along the rows of people, occasionally catching the eye of a cheering supporter that he recognised, some-one from the industry, or a faithful fan who'd followed him here, halfway around the world to New York City.

Then he saw her: wearing a vibrant purple dress that accentu-ated her buxom figure, how could he not?

His beautiful Evelyn lit up the room.

Clapping her hands she smiled as she caught his gaze. His wife had never looked more radiant than in that moment.

Seeing the tears of joy in her eyes, how proud she looked, Harry blew her a kiss. Smiling at her, his eyes moved down, following the purple fabric of her dress, as it skimmed over the slight curve of her stomach. Concealing her small round bump that only they knew about.

Harry felt a surge of emotions just then, caught up in his suc-cess and love for his wife and his unborn child. Only Evelyn knew just how hard he had worked for this, how much he had wanted it.

What she didn't realise was that he had done it all for her.

For her and their baby.

'You did it, Harry. You fucking did it!' Moving in for a bear hug, Raymond Marks broke the spell; Harry's sentimental moment was over. The two men embraced before Raymond handed Harry a bottle of cold water, then, wrapping a towel around his broad shoulders, Raymond gripped him tightly. 'That was a fight and a half, Harry. You went in there like a warrior. You're the fucking golden boy. Can you hear them all, Harry? They fucking love you.' Raymond was ecstatic. His best mate was a champion. A legend.

And Harry could hear it loud and clear. Standing in the middle of the ring, centre stage in Madison Square Garden in New York City, the chanting, the stamping, the crowd's collective elation. The stadium was alive, the atmosphere electric. The crowd's continual applause was like beautiful music to his ears, to his soul.

He had made it.

As Heavyweight Champion he'd now be fighting the toughest, most notorious boxers in the world.

What's more, now he was one of them.

Looking around him with awe, Harry Woods smiled. With his beautiful wife by his side, and his first child on the way, Harry Woods had the world at his feet, and today was only the beginning.

Chapter One
2014

Walking down the jetty of Wapping's Marine Support Unit's headquarters, Detective Inspector Freya Tompkins braced herself for the task ahead. No matter how often she dealt with dead bodies that had been pulled out of the river, she never ever seemed to desensitise from the initial shock of seeing a gruesome waterlogged corpse. She doubted that anyone ever really remained detached under such horrific circumstances.

Her fellow officers from the Met's Specialist Search and Recovery Team had already warned her that the girl's body they'd pulled from the water was in a bad way, and when those guys said 'bad way', Freya knew that she was about to see something horrendous. As an experienced officer, she'd seen enough decomposing, bloated bodies over the years to know that no matter how hard she tried to build up any kind of constitution to the sights she had seen, the haunting images that were etched on her brain always affected her for weeks afterwards.

Making her way towards the blue tarpaulin-sheeted tent ahead of her, she had a bad feeling in the pit of her stomach. Since she'd got the call twenty minutes ago, she had felt weighed down with a real sense of dread, and her instincts were nearly always right. The press would be all over this case in a heartbeat.

It was a story that the newspapers would deem as of major interest to the general public, like it was the public's right to know every single grisly detail of how the girl had died.

The media was a joke. On average, the Search and Recovery Team pulled a body a week from the Thames's steely waters. Bodies of fated suicides, homeless people or drunks who had accidentally wandered into the water underestimating its dangerous magnitude. The press were never interested in those cases. Most went unreported, in fact, apparently not interesting enough to acquire the public's attention.

Of course, this case was different.

This case was about young girls. Prostitutes mainly. Dead girls who had been stripped naked, beaten and later found dead, floating in the Thames.

The press would be all over this story like white on rice, because it would sell their newspapers.

Freya was already stressed out enough over this case; she could have done without the media circus. So far they had no leads, nothing to go on. And the case going public just added more pressure for her team to get on with finding out who the perpetrator was. People loved reading about this morbid dark side of reality. Especially when it was happening right on their doorsteps.

And this case was as dark as they came.

Lifting up the tarpaulin, Freya carefully slipped inside the cordoned-off area. Holding her breath, she smelled the girl's rotting body before she saw it. Gulping to suppress her gag reflex, she fought to compose herself in front of her fellow officers.

Focusing on the river officers, Freya could see the girl's silhouette out of the corner of her eye, grimly splayed out in the narrow bath that was sunk into the floor, as the body was being examined by forensic pathologists.

'So, what are we looking at?' Directing the question at Officer Blake, Freya had hoped that her voice would sound calm, but even she could hear the iciness in her tone. She sounded disconnected, cold. She was trying too hard, but then, she'd rather come across as cold than show her colleagues her vulnerability. Freya always felt that she had to work twice as hard as her male colleagues to be taken seriously. Even just a hint of unease or emotion from her could jeopardise everything she had worked for. No matter what the Met claimed about equal opportunities in the force, Freya, from experience, knew differently. It was still very much a man's world; give them so much as a hint of emotion, and they would eat you alive.

'We found her down by Masthouse Terrace Pier, over on the North Bank.' Officer Timothy Blake stood up and shook his head solemnly. 'An unfortunate tourist raised the alarm. She was spotted in the water, by the pier. That sharp bend of the river down at the Isle of Dogs has become a trapping point for bodies.'

'Same MO?' Freya asked.

Officer Blake nodded. 'The pathologist reckons she's been in the river for roughly ten days, and going by the fact that she is naked and has ropes around her wrists they suspect that she was already dead when she entered the water. We'll know more once they do the post-mortem.' Glancing behind him to where the girl's body lay in the steel bath, Officer Blake screwed his face up. 'She's taken a battering too. Some of the injuries are consistent with being hit by a large vessel. I'd say she was struck by several of the commuter boats down there; it's a heavily trafficked stretch of water. Seagulls got to her too. But there are other injuries that fit with the killer's profile. The bruising around her throat indicates that she was strangled, and she's covered in bite marks. They're hard to see at first due to the other injuries, but the pathologists have noted numerous teeth marks.'

Freya followed Officer Blake's gaze, finally gathering the strength to look at the girl's mangled body as they lifted her inside the body bag.

'Jesus.' Freya shivered.

The poor girl was someone's daughter, sister, maybe even mother.

And the chances were she had fallen victim to some depraved lunatic.

Some callous perverted monster who had thought nothing of snatching the young girl's life away for his own sexual pleasure.

Just the thought of the girl's final moments made her feel physically sick.

'I think your initial hunch was right, Detective Tompkins.' Officer Blake sighed. 'I think we have a serial killer on our hands.'

Chapter Two

Micky O'Shea shook his head in complete disbelief. The two fucking morons standing before him were either total imbeciles or they both had a death wish. Either way, Micky wanted his money. If these two idiots thought they could fob him off with yet another excuse they had another think coming.

'Did I hear right, Jimmy?' Micky sneered across the room to where his brother stood in the doorway. 'Correct me if I'm wrong, but I think I heard this fat cunt tell me that she ain't got our money. Again.'

'That's what I heard an' all, Micky.' Jimmy, the younger of the O'Shea brothers, sucked his teeth at the predicament. They'd both heard the girl alright. Jimmy could see by the unwavering look on her face that somewhere deep in the back of this bird's thick skull she actually thought that her having nothing to offer except yet another excuse would somehow be acceptable. But Jimmy knew well: excuses wouldn't pay the bills. Only cold hard cash would do that. The blatant audacity of this poncing slag as she tried to palm him and Micky off with yet another excuse as if she just expected them both to lump it like a pair of numpties was grating on him. If he heard, 'We ain't got the money, give us some more time,' one more fucking time he was really going to lose his patience.

In this house the never-ending excuses were beginning to sound like a bleeding scratched record. This pair of cunts had used every excuse in the book, so much so that Jimmy was beginning to think they wrote the fucking thing.

'Look, I promise all we need is a couple more days.' Kelly Stranks flashed a glare at her husband Terry, who so far hadn't opened his mouth to speak so much as a word to back her up. So much for being the man of the house and standing up for her. Sometimes Kelly wondered if her husband had any bollocks, because every time the O'Sheas paid a visit Terry seemed to either lose them, or swallow them. It was bad enough that the O'Sheas were standing in her home, in her lounge as they berated her with their stream of abuse, but the fact that Terry just stood there in silence as they did so, looking like a complete gormless idiot, just added insult to injury.

Terry was a bloody coward. The O'Sheas knew it, she knew it, even Terry bloody knew it.

Still, someone had to deal with these two.

So, of course, as per usual, just like everything else, it was left to Kelly to deal with them.

Micky and Jimmy O'Shea had properly shafted them. That was the way they played the game. Kelly knew that now. She'd been so desperate at the time that she hadn't looked properly at the bigger picture.

She and Terry had only borrowed a few grand to start off with. The O'Sheas had been their last port of call; unable to get credit anywhere else, they were in so much debt that they had no choice but to approach Southwark's most infamous loan sharks. Of course, Micky and Jimmy had been only too glad to help them out.

Friendly, polite, Kelly had thought that maybe she'd heard wrong regarding the rumours about the two brothers. They couldn't have been more charming if they had tried. Even when Terry had been short with the first instalment, they generously offered to top the loan up, without Kelly even needing to ask. They had been so *helpful.* Kelly should have realised right then and there what they were playing at. Instead she'd been so grateful at being able to pay off their debts, put food in the cupboards and to finally get the kids new school uniforms instead of the raggy hand-me-downs they'd both been wearing – castoffs from one of the neighbour's kids – that she hadn't realised until it was too late; that was how they got you.

It had all sounded so simple, so easy.

Of course, it had all been part of their ploy. It was how they sucked people like her and Terry in. The O'Sheas were only making sure that they stuck them with even more debt. Borrowing way more than they could afford, they couldn't make the repayments.

The two brothers had said that they hated to incur late fees, and extra penalties to the unpaid debt, but that they'd been left with no choice.

They'd both played right into the O'Shea brothers' dirty, greedy hands.

The original three-grand debt they'd incurred had somehow very rapidly turned into one of ten grand, and that was when Kelly had realised that the O'Sheas had her and Terry right where they wanted them. Buried up to their necks.

The two brothers had turned nasty very quickly. They were bullies. Turning up at all sorts of times, day and night, it was all just a game to them. Kelly was at her wits' end trying to cope under the strain of it all. They could only afford to pay them three hundred pounds a month, but even that was a large chunk of Terry's wages and it was not only crippling them financially, but it was also proving to be getting them nowhere, and fast.

At this rate they were going to be stuck with the O'Sheas turning up on their doorstep and threatening them forever.

'Terry gets paid tomorrow night. I promise, as soon as we have it, it's yours.' Shooting Terry a dirty look as she spoke, Kelly was fuming with her husband. Terry needed to man the fuck up.

Seeing his wife's face flash with anger, Terry cleared his throat and finally spoke up. 'Two days, max, and I promise, I'll have your money.'

Micky shook his head. Looking around the lounge he was stood in, it was clear that these two didn't have a pot to piss in. He couldn't even remove anything of any value from the property; these two had fuck all worth taking. Their house looked like a dump; they lived in squalor. The carpet was filthy dirty, and Micky could see bits of dried food that had been mashed into the fibres, along with what looked like bits of trodden-in crayon. There were no fancy stereo systems, no game consoles, but that wasn't the O'Sheas' problem. Like other people in this area they were living on the breadline, sponging off the system for help while working on the sly to make ends meet. But it wasn't enough. It never was. These were the type of people that the O'Sheas counted on. Desperate people like these two who had no choice but to borrow from them, and no backup from anyone worth worrying about when they couldn't afford to pay the money back. It was dog-eat-dog out there, and the O'Sheas were hungry for a bite.

'Two more days is a bit of a pain in the arse for us, as it happens. Time is money and all that.'

Then, staring at his brother, Micky raised his eyes questioningly to upstairs. 'Think we need to seek out a bit of insurance for tonight, don't you, Jimmy?'

Jimmy nodded. He knew exactly what his brother was hinting at. They needed to put the shits up these two fuckers, else they'd keep getting fobbed off. Jimmy didn't have time for any more of that shit.

As the younger of the two brothers, Jimmy may have been the shorter of the two, all by a good few inches, but what Jimmy lacked in height he more than made up for in bulk and temper. His body was ripped; his muscles were so inflated he looked like he'd had a bicycle pump shoved up his arse. He was good looking too, the complete opposite to Micky. Rake thin and lanky, Micky had suffered for years with severe acne, and his skin was puckered and scarred.

Looks were the only ways that the two men differed, though. Personality-wise, they were two of the same. Sharing the same volcanic temperament, and zero tolerance for bullshit – it was why they worked so well together.

Jimmy looked at Micky, who nodded in agreement. Micky was right, these two had been coming out with excuses left, right and centre. They needed a warning.

'You, come with me.' Indicating towards the stairs, Jimmy instructed Kelly to go ahead of him. 'Keep that fucker down here.'

Micky nodded and smiled.

Jimmy was a ruthless little bastard when he wanted to be, and these two needed to be taught an important lesson. No matter how skint they were, they owed them money. They needed to pay up.

'Please, no,' Kelly cried. The kids were upstairs, and after seeing the looks that the two brothers exchanged, she was petrified of what Jimmy might do to her. They'd never tried anything like this before, but then, she guessed she had been pushing her luck by not keeping up to date with the repayments lately. Maybe she really had pushed them too far.

'No fucking way.' Terry finally spoke up, as he lurched forward in pure panic, trying to stop Jimmy as he forcibly grabbed hold of Kelly by her arm and marched her out of the room.

Scared, Terry felt out of his depth now. He had two monsters standing in his house.

'Where do you think you're going?' Grabbing Terry by his throat, Micky threw him up against the wall. Pinned up against it, Terry could feel Micky's bony fingers digging into his windpipe as he squeezed. Micky was strong. Too strong for Terry. Even at almost fourteen stone, Terry could feel his feet dangling several inches above the floor.

Spluttering, Terry desperately struggled for breath.

Micky, seeing the man's face turn puce, smiled. He finally let him go, throwing him across the room as he did.

Grinning, Micky stared at him. 'Let's hope your wife don't play so hard to get.'

———⌣———

Yanking Kelly into the bedroom, Jimmy flung her down violently onto the bed. Whacking her head off the headboard, Kelly scampered backwards to get away.

'Please, my kids are in the next room,' Kelly begged now. Huddled in the corner with her knees drawn up in front of her to protect herself, she was wearing one of those cheap velour imitation tracksuits that you could buy down at the local market. Juicy Couture knockoffs that were becoming mandatory uniform with skanks living on benefits in Southwark.

Turning his nose up in disgust at her, Jimmy walked around the room.

The room stank worse than the rest of the house. No wonder it reeked, he thought, as he took in the dirty bed sheets, tinged with yellow stains.

Stepping over piles of dirty clothes and underwear, he couldn't believe that people actually lived like this. Like dirty fucking animals. No-one was too poor to clean. There was just no excuse for it. These people were just pure lazy.

Pulling out the drawers and rooting through the wardrobes, Jimmy ransacked the room, throwing all the contents everywhere as he went, as if he was searching for something.

Though finding anything in this shit pit would be a challenge even for him.

He was working himself up into a rage, dragging all the clothes from the cupboards, and as he leant down, Kelly could see the large protruding vein throbbing on the side of his forehead. He looked like a man possessed. She had no idea what he thought he might find, but she also had no intention of asking either.

She didn't have to wait long to find out.

Sweeping the top of the dressing table with his arm, Jimmy sent her basket of make-up flying to the floor.

There was nothing up here but junk.

Prising open the dressing table drawer, he wasn't holding out much hope of finding anything as he continued to search through all the crap that was shoved inside.

Then he found something. Stuffed right at the back, almost as if it was hidden, Jimmy pulled out the small white jewellery box.

Bingo.

Opening it, he fingered the antique gold brooch delicately in his hand. The chances of the vibrant green gem that sat so prominently in its centre being a real emerald were slim to anorexic, he thought, considering the household he had found it in. But when he took a closer look he thought it was actually a genuine piece. The markings on the gold were a good indication of that, and if it was real then he was sure that he'd get a few grand for it at least. Though he wouldn't tell this bitch that.

'Where did you get this?' he asked.

Kelly shrugged. She didn't want to tell Jimmy that the brooch had belonged to her late mum. It was the only thing she had of hers; Jimmy would love that, wouldn't he? Taking away her last treasured possession to teach her a lesson.

'Just from one of the stalls over at Brick Lane Market. Only paid a couple of quid for it. Just junk, really,' Kelly lied, hoping that he'd fall for her yarn, and put it back in the box. No matter how desperate times had got, Kelly had never once even considered trading her mother's jewellery in. She'd even stuffed the box at the back of the dresser, under the rest of the junk, thinking that the O'Sheas would probably dismiss it as nothing.

She could tell that Jimmy didn't believe her. Instead, he held it up to the light inspecting it more closely. Squinting, he eyed the markings on the back of the brooch by the clasp: eighteen carats. The brooch didn't look like junk, and he could tell by Kelly's stony face that she was lying. Kelly was the type who knew the price of everything and the value of nothing.

Throwing the empty box down on the floor with the rest of the crap, he shoved the piece of jewellery into his pocket.

'Please, don't take it.' Suddenly realising that he was going to take it anyway, Kelly begged now. If Jimmy took it, she'd never get it back. She had no choice but to try to plead with him. 'It was my mum's; it's all I have left of her. Please . . .' Kelly had found it down behind her mum's dresser the day after she'd found out that her mother had died. She hadn't told a soul that she'd taken it. Brooches weren't exactly the fashion anymore, but something about it had made Kelly want to keep it, though she never recalled her mother wearing it. Still, it was beautiful, just like her mum had been, and the little trinket was the only thing that Kelly wanted to remember her by.

Watching as Jimmy turned towards her, for a second she thought that maybe he was considering giving it back, but as she watched him roam her body with his eyes, then lurch forward towards her, leaning on the bed, Kelly's eyes widened in horror. As he leapt across to where she was sitting, Kelly rapidly tried to propel herself away from him, but Jimmy was too strong. Grabbing her by the leg he pulled her roughly across the bed, back towards him.

'No, please don't. Please don't do this . . .' Kelly screamed as she felt Jimmy manhandling her; his grip was strong and she couldn't shake him off.

Hoisting her up, Jimmy snatched at her hands. Grasping them tightly, he wrenched both her wedding and engagement rings off her finger in one swift, rough movement, snapping Kelly's finger back as he did so.

Kelly screamed in pain as the bone cracked.

He'd broken her finger.

Standing up, Jimmy laughed at Kelly in disgust. 'What? You didn't seriously think I was going to rape you, did you? Leave it out! Have you seen the fucking state of yourself? I'd have to be fucking desperate.'

Jimmy reckoned that Kelly couldn't have been more than early twenties, but overweight, and reeking of stale body odour, the girl was a fat lazy slob. He might be a ruthless bastard, but sex to him was all about pleasure, and fucking Kelly would have been about as pleasurable as sticking his cock in a rusty blender.

Kelly and her husband were both scum as far as he was concerned. Popping out kids when they clearly couldn't afford them, and borrowing money that they couldn't pay back, without thinking about the consequences.

They both seemed to be set on learning the hard way.

Well, so be it. Jimmy was happy to dish out their education.

Tapping his pocket, triumphant that he'd at least salvaged something from tonight's visit, Jimmy stood and gave the girl a final warning stare. 'Two days, and if you ain't got our money by then, I'm going to break your husband's legs and burn this fucking house down to the ground. Do you fucking understand?'

Jimmy's cold eyes glistened as he spoke. Nodding, Kelly gulped down the sob in the back of her throat.

She was under no illusions that Jimmy O'Shea meant every word.

Chapter Three

Molly Walters was having a bitch of a day. Not only had Heaven called in sick at the last minute with a tummy bug that was doing the rounds, and royally left her in the shit, but this new girl Shanece was getting right on her tits. The boss had insisted that everything must go smoothly today, but he hadn't factored in lumping her with this brain-dead bimbo.

Molly normally recruited the girls, but there was always the odd exception, especially if her boss Raymond Marks set his eyes on what he deemed as hot pussy while he was out on his travels. That was exactly what she suspected had happened here.

Raymond was as predictable as men come. Shanece looked exactly his type, too. A walking, talking sex doll with the IQ of a goldfish. The girl was easy on the eye and even easier on the brain cells, and Molly would put money on the fact that Raymond would have been in his element with that combination. At least until he'd put his dick back in his pants.

Molly had seen all sorts of girls come through these doors over the years, but this one was so plastic that Molly was surprised the girl didn't have a tag on the back of her neck saying 'Made in Taiwan'. Not only did she have the standard huge breast implants and heavily injected trout pout that Raymond went for, but she also had fake eyelashes, a bright orange fake tan, and bright red fake talon nails. In fact, looking at the girl closely like she was now, it would have actually been quicker for her to list the bits that weren't fake. Raymond must have taken one look at Shanece grinding around a pole in some dingy little bar somewhere and thought nothing of poaching her for himself. Without so much as a second thought, it seemed.

She'd put her wages on the fact that he had probably completely sidelined any kind of interview, and just gone straight in for the oral examination. For quality control purposes, of course. Raymond was always professional like that.

Already bored with the girl, he'd done what he always did and palmed her off here for Molly to deal with. The girl was clueless as to Raymond's way of thinking. Oblivious that Raymond had only wanted her for a quick fuck, and now he was done he was going to get her to pull him in some serious money with the punters, the dappy cow was probably still under the illusion that she was the current flavour of the month. Some girls were always the same. Raymond told them they were special, and they fell for it. Hook, line and sinker. If Shanece hadn't been so annoying Molly might have almost felt sorry for her. Almost.

'I was only gone for twenty minutes, Shanece. How have you managed to double book the diary already? Look. Mr. Sanders and Mr. Dobbs are both due in now at the same time, and it's physically impossible. There are no girls available, and as good as you think you are in the sack, sweetie, you've only been blessed with one fanny. So that leaves us with a problem. And I haven't got any numbers to call them back on, so it's going to be me that deals with them when they both show up.'

Shanece continued to chew her gum loudly as she stared blankly at the computer screen in front of her, trying to figure out how she'd managed to make yet another double booking. 'Oh yeah. I'm not very good with all this "technology" stuff. All these columns in the diary send me into a right tizz. I thought Jasmine or Dahlia were free. Look, it says here that they are both booked in with the same guy. Isn't that a mistake too then?'

'No. There's no mistake. The girls are both booked in for the "Double Delight" package with Mr. Curtis at two o'clock. It's been prearranged especially. But you're right, Shanece, it must have been very confusing for you. Especially as that booking was written in capital letters and highlighted in bloody bold font.'

'Yeah, it should be clearer.' Shanece smiled, Molly's sarcasm totally lost on her.

Molly was beyond pissed off. Raymond would go nuts if she messed things up now at the last hurdle.

She didn't have a clue what her boss was up to, but all she did know was that she had gone above and beyond her normal madam duties with this punter.

And now, finally, after weeks of trying to set it all up, Mr. Curtis was on his way to the parlour for some serious VIP treatment. Raymond wanted the client to be treated like royalty from the moment he arrived; he wanted the girls to make him feel so comfortable that he forgot he was in a brothel. He wanted Mr. Curtis to think he was some kind of a sex god so that he would lose his inhibitions and really get into the whole experience. And other than Molly arranging Raymond to come here and personally suck the guy's dick himself, she'd pulled out all the stops, overcompensating by giving him her two best girls. If Jasmine and Dahlia didn't 'do it' for him, then the guy would have to be either gay or dead.

Even so, just because she was keeping one customer happy didn't mean that she could just forget about all the others. Mr. Dobbs and Mr. Sanders were regulars here and clients like them were their bread and butter. In here like clockwork every week, as were many of the men. Molly needed to sort this mess out, and fast.

Leaning over Shanece, she frowned as she scrolled through the diary trying to see if she could rectify things.

'Well, I don't mind having a bit of double delight myself you know, so if it helps you can always just book them in with me.' Shanece giggled. 'I'm sure that once they turn up and we explain what's happened they'll be fine about it. You know how kinky some sods can be. Having a twos-up on me will probably be a dream come true for the pair of them.'

Molly stared aghast. Not only was this girl vain, but she was also clearly game for anything, yet another much sought-after quality Raymond would have spotted in an instant when he had taken on the girl, Molly surmised.

'Share you? No chance, Mr. Dobbs likes the same routine every time, has done for years. Missionary position with his eyes shut. Poor bugger thinks if he doesn't actually look at the girl while he's dipping his wick, then technically he hasn't cheated. It's bad enough that Heaven has called in sick, because she's the only girl he likes. I'm going to have my work cut out trying to persuade him to go with you as it is. No offence, Shanece, but even just the sight of you will be a gamble enough for him today.'

The girls couldn't be any more different if they tried. Heaven was demure, understated. While Shanece, she was about as understated as a poke in the eye with a flashing dildo. Molly had already heard Shanece with a couple of her punters, panting and squealing like a porn star in the making. Poor Mr. Dobbs was going to have to muster up every bit of self-denial he had today, if he wanted any chance of keeping his mind on his wife while grinding away on top of Shanece. There was no way that she could suggest a threesome with another man; Mr. Dobbs would run out of here faster than Shanece could whip her drawers off.

'Well, how about you take one of them then?'

Molly gritted her teeth as she fought to keep her temper down. She was really trying hard to be patient, really she was. But the girl was pushing her to the limit.

'I run the place, Shanece. I don't lay down with the clients. That's your job.' Molly didn't need to justify her role, but clearly Shanece needed a reminder about who was the boss here. Molly had never bedded a man for money in all the years that she'd worked for Raymond and she didn't intend to start now.

Not that she hadn't had offers. Considering that she was the wrong side of forty, and she was the first to admit that she was no oil painting, Molly was popular with the men. Especially the older ones. They appreciated her gracious curves and her au naturel image. Molly had never even entertained the idea. Raymond employed her for her brains and her loyalty, and unlike the other women here, he treated Molly with a high regard because of that. He respected her, and rightly so. Without her, Raymond wouldn't be able to manage the place, not with the brothel that he had down Wardour Street, opposite the casino.

'Tell you what, why don't you do the missionary guy, what's his name, Dobbs? All you'll have to do is lie back and think of England.' Shanece shrugged her shoulders nonchalantly. 'You can borrow a bit of my slap if you like, got my make-up bag up in the bathroom. Or you could just stay as you are. Don't suppose it really matters what you look like seeing as he'll have his eyes shut the whole time anyway.'

'I tell you what, Shanece,' Molly said grabbing the girl roughly by her arm as she yanked her out of the chair. 'You stick to what you do and let me stick to what I do, yeah? Now get your arse up out of my chair and go and get your room ready. Let me get on with sorting this lot out.' Shanece might have thought she was helping with her useless suggestions but the way the girl was being so blasé about her fuck-up was really starting to grate now.

'Oh and Shanece,' Molly called as she watched the girl totter up the stairs in her six inch heels, just as the main-door buzzer went. 'In future, leave the fucking bookings to me please!'

Checking the security monitor, Molly spotted Mr. Curtis staring hard into the screen. He looked shifty, like he was willing the buzzer to be pressed and the doors to open in case someone spotted him coming in here. Buzzing him straight in, Molly didn't want to give him any reason to complain. He certainly wasn't the usual type of bloke that Raymond associated with, but whatever it was that Raymond was up to, Molly knew that she had to make sure that her end of the plan ran smoother than Shanece's over-preened fanny.

Mr. Curtis was to be given the full works and Raymond insisted that Molly gave the man a fifty percent discount for the privilege.

That alone sent alarm bells ringing as far as Molly was concerned. Raymond was normally so bloody tight, you'd have more luck getting shit from a rocking horse than you would at winging anything free from him. No doubt about it, there was definitely something suspicious going on alright. Raymond Marks never did anything unless there was something in it for him.

Seeing the internal door open, Molly plastered a great big smile on her face, beaming as the man walked up to the desk. He looked nervous.

'Hi, I'm Mr. Curtis. I have an appointment for two-thirty for . . .'

'Your massage,' Molly offered. Though they both knew Mr. Curtis was here for more than just a back rub. With straggly grey, receding hair and a face lined with deep, heavy-set wrinkles, Mr. Curtis looked older in this light, and she could tell by his tone that he was every bit as pompous as he looked. Still, who was she to judge?

'Yes that's right. My massage.' Mr. Curtis nodded, and Molly could see he was on edge about being here. Most blokes were like that the first time they came to a place like this. Reassuring him, she smiled.

'You're in safe hands here, Mr. Curtis. I've organised a real treat for you this afternoon. So if you'd like to follow me, we'll have you all nice and relaxed in no time.'

Molly's voice was professional; she reserved it especially for punters. Guiding the man down the hallway, she pushed open one of the bedroom doors. Then stepping aside, she invited Mr. Curtis in to where the two young oriental girls were stood waiting.

'Mr. Curtis, this is Jasmine, and this is Dahlia.' Molly introduced the girls like they were showpieces, exquisite pieces of art on display purely for him.

They could certainly pull that look off.

Stood side by side next to the massage couch, the girls looked like twins. Wearing only bikini bottoms, they were breathtakingly beautiful. With their long dark hair skimming down over their small naked breasts ending just below their tiny waists, they looked like a mirage.

'Girls, this is Mr. Curtis, and you are both to see that he is made to feel very comfortable.' The speech was purely for Mr. Curtis's benefit; Molly had already told the girls that they were to give this customer an extra special service.

Raymond had been adamant that he wanted the girls to give the man the works. He wanted today to be the best fuck of this man's life, and Molly was in no doubt that Jasmine and Dahlia would fulfil the client's every need. The girls were good at their job. Working as a pair had proved to be a very popular request. Double delight – more like double trouble, Molly thought. If you asked her, sixteen was far too young to be in this game, if they were even that. They may have the bodies of women but these girls were still babies. It made Molly feel sad that they were both already on their way down this very dark path.

What could she do about it? The girls seemed happy enough doing their job, and not only were they coining it in for Raymond, they were making a good earn for themselves too.

All she could do was look out for them, and see that they were treated fairly.

Smiling to Mr. Curtis as she closed the bedroom door and left the three of them to it, Molly walked back to the desk, and picked up the phone. 'He's in with the girls now,' she said quietly into the mouthpiece, keeping her boss up to date, just as he had requested.

———

Placing his mobile down on the table, Raymond Marks smiled as he picked up his whiskey and took a large gulp. Switching on the screen, he sat back down at his desk in his office and watched the kinky sex scene unfold in front of his eyes.

Jasmine and Dahlia were his best little earners, and watching them as they both worked their magic on the guy, Raymond could see why. Smiling, Raymond was enjoying every second of the live show.

This bloke had been getting cocky.

Snooping around trying to dig up shit on him and his business partner. Raymond had taken to trying to pay the guy off. He was greedy, though. The more Raymond gave him, the more he wanted. Just because he'd been given a few backhanders here and there for turning a blind eye, he suddenly thought he was untouchable, lording it up like Raymond was indebted to him.

As if.

Raymond had seen corkscrews that were less bent than this bloke, and it wasn't as if he hadn't paid him generously for the favours that he'd done.

This bloke was cunting him to anyone who would listen, making out that Raymond was in his pocket, when it should be very much the other way around. He was giving him the major hump.

Raymond was smart.

He'd played the long game.

For weeks he'd done nothing but lull the guy into a false sense of security. Raymond let the guy believe that he held all the cards, that he was in control. He let him keep digging his hole, deeper and deeper.

Three weeks he'd spent buttering up this cunt to make him believe that they were new best buddies, and now Raymond couldn't wait to teach the man a lesson.

Right now that ponce was getting his nuts in with two under-age, illegal immigrants and Raymond, having rigged up the room with cameras, now couldn't help but be impressed with his own blinding acting skills.

Under the protection of a false name, Mr. Curtis, or Detective Chief Superintendent Porter as he was really called, had just played right into Raymond's hands.

Having a pig in his pocket would be the best insurance policy that Raymond had ever taken out, he was sure. He had evidence now, evidence that could destroy Porter's reputation at the force. That could lose the man his marriage, his reputation, his job even.

Porter could dig all the way to China for shit on them now, it really didn't matter anymore. Because armed with their very own 'get out of jail free card', Raymond and his business partner would be laughing.

Chapter Four

Terry Stranks was on fire. He'd won almost every bet so far and he was up by well over a grand. He had heard the expression 'on a winning streak', but until now he had never had the good fortune to experience it.

As it turned out, though, roulette was his game. Probably because it was a game where no brains were required. Terry didn't know, nor did he care. All that mattered right now was the euphoric rush of cocaine and tequila that surged through his veins while the pound signs flashed before his eyes. He was on a roll and was pleased to see that it hadn't gone unnoticed by his now growing crowd of onlookers around the table.

Placing yet another pile of chips down Terry felt the hot blonde step in closer, provocatively pressing her ample cleavage firmly against him like she was Lady Luck herself. The pretty girl squealed once more with delight as Terry won the game. He was on to a winner tonight in more ways than one. Grinning, he felt like he was king of the fucking world.

'I do love a man who knows how to play,' the girl purred, her strong Romanian accent making her words sound more like a promise than a statement. She playfully caressed Terry's thigh through his trousers, her hand skimming over his crotch as she eyed up the chips that were piled high on the table in front of them. 'I'm Serena, by the way.'

Terry tried to control the stir in his pants at her obvious touch. She was hot. Wearing a tight black minidress that left little to the imagination, he couldn't help but compare her to the usual desperate dregs he normally ended up getting his leg over down at his local. This bird was in a different league altogether. A league completely of her own. Then, he figured the casino attracted a different class of clientele from the places he usually drank in. Tonight, for once finally up on his luck, Terry felt like this was exactly where he belonged.

'I'm Terry.' Taking the girl's hand, he kissed it noticing how tiny her fingers were in his. 'What's your lucky number, darling?' His words were cheesy, like he was repeating a line he had heard in a film. The girl didn't seem to think so, though; instead, she smiled.

'Nineteen.'

'Nineteen? Okay . . .'

'It's how old I am, so got to be worth a try. Don't you think?'

'Well, that definitely works for me.' Terry beamed. Nineteen. Fucking hell, the girl looked young, but he would never have guessed that she was less than half his age, and clearly by the way she draped herself flirtatiously over him, she was up for a bit of fun tonight. As far as Terry was concerned, he'd just hit the bloody jackpot.

Pulling a bird like this one proved that he still had it.

Winking, he placed a hundred pounds' worth of chips on red, number nineteen.

A straight bet – just like the girl.

Clenching his fists tightly in anticipation, he watched as the ball left the dealer's hand, hitting the wheel and bouncing a few times before rapidly spinning.

It was a thirty-five to one, and if this came in he'd be laughing.

As his gaze chased the ball, he watched as it whirled around the wheel. His stomach was in knots; the adrenaline mixed with the cocktail of alcohol and drugs he had taken was starting to really take effect.

The tension in the air was electric. He could feel everyone's eyes around the table burning into him.

The ball slowed.

Thirty-two, fifteen, then a slight wobble and Terry couldn't believe his eyes.

Red, lucky number nineteen.

Hearing Serena's loud screech of pleasure as the ball came to a halt, Terry stood dazed. He'd just pocketed three and a half grand. Combined with his early winnings he was looking at almost four and a half K in total. What a touch. No matter how pissed off Kelly would be that he had gone off on another bender tonight, the money he'd bring home would soften the blow, he was sure. Especially if it meant that they could keep the O'Sheas from their door for a while.

All women were the same. Whoever said money didn't make the world go round was a mug. Money always talked and it was the only language that most of the women Terry knew were fluent in, especially his Kelly.

'Very impressive, Terry,' Serena said, as Terry gathered up the pile of chips he'd won. 'How about we get ourselves a bottle of something from the bar and go back to mine? Celebrate in style. Unless you have to be somewhere else?'

'That sounds good, hang on.' Terry checked his phone briefly – it was 3 a.m. and not only did he have fifteen missed calls but his voicemail was flashing too.

No prizes for guessing who that was.

The way that Kelly harped on at him, you'd think she was his personally assigned parole officer, not his wife. It hadn't been long into their seven-year 'life sentence' that Terry had worked out the reason some men referred to their other halves as 'the ball and chain'. He was firmly weighed down now himself, only there was no chance of getting out early on good behaviour. Together forever, until death do us part, that alone was a grim enough thought.

When he'd met Kelly she'd been just seventeen years old, almost thirty years his junior. That had been her main appeal if he was honest; young girls generally just did what they were told, and were grateful for what they got, unlike the women his own age who were so bitter and saddled down with enough baggage they could fill a luggage belt at an airport. The last thing Terry wanted was to end up stuck with some old nag.

Kelly had been a safe bet, or so he had thought. But as it turned out the girl could moan for England. Talk about hard work.

Despite all that, he did love her, in his own way. Sometimes, though, he just wanted to go out by himself. Be his own man. Not a husband, or a dad, or a bloody dogsbody at work. Just him. Terry Stranks.

Hovering his fingers over the mobile phone's keypad, he thought about sending Kelly a text. Then he quickly thought better of it.

She would have spent the night pacing the house like the bleeding antichrist with a bad dose of PMT as it was, and she'd see right through his text messages. Kelly could spot one of his lies from a mile off. Fuck it! Switching the phone onto silent, Terry shoved it deep inside his pocket. He was entitled to go out and have a bit of fun if he wanted to and seeing as the nagging cow was going to go mental at him no matter what he did, he figured that he may as well make tonight's bid for freedom worth his while. Besides, he justified, girls like Serena didn't come along that often – actually, in his world they didn't come along at all. He had a pocket full of cash and a stonking hard-on to contend with, so it really was a no-brainer.

'You know what, babe, that sounds like a fucking blinding idea. I tell you what. I'll go and sort the readies out, and pick us up a bottle of bubbly, and I'll meet you outside, yeah?' Terry watched

Serena as she left, wiggling her pert little arse as she walked; she was a stunner alright.

The night may no longer be young but the girl he was about to fuck was, and Terry – never normally this fortunate – intended on enjoying every minute of it.

———⌣———

'Not what you expected?' Serena asked, seeing Terry's expression as he scanned the bleak bedroom. 'I'm sharing this place with some other girls, I won't be here forever,' Serena reasoned as she flicked her hair over her shoulder and pouted her lips.

Terry shrugged; splayed out on top of the duvet he had noticed that the room was bare, impersonal even. Just a double bed and a rickety looking bedside cabinet where Serena had placed the half-drunk bottle of Moët down next to a brown threadbare lamp. The décor was the last thing on his mind; the only reason he had even noticed how bleak the room looked was because against the bland surroundings, Serena only looked more striking. She was so stunning, so beautiful that she lit up the room.

'Trust me, interior design ain't really my thing. There's only one thing on my mind and that's you . . . Now come on, get your kit off and get that tight little arse of yours over here pronto.' Terry patted the space next to him. He'd just snorted his last bit of gear and he was dying to see Serena naked so that they could start having some fun.

'Terry! You bad boy.' Serena giggled at his enthusiasm as she bent down and retrieved the pink silk ties and handcuffs from the cupboard next to him. Jiggling them in front of him, she raised an eyebrow. 'But you know what happens to bad boys, don't you, Terry?'

Terry grinned cheekily, as Serena expertly tightened the handcuffs around his wrists, attaching him firmly to the bedstead, as she placed her mouth over his. She kissed him, slowly. Teasing him.

'I take it that you are about to enlighten me?' Terry could barely contain his excitement. Nor the prominent bulge in his underpants.

'Bad boys need to be taught lessons, Terry, and you seem like a very naughty boy to me.' Serena still had her dress on, but seeing as he copped an eyeful of her beautiful pert breasts every time she leant over him, Terry wasn't complaining. If she wanted to play kinky games with him, then he was more than up for it. God, young girls really were a different class altogether these days.

Slipping her hands inside the waistband of Terry's boxer shorts, Serena let her fingers gently brush against his bare skin before she slid his underpants down over his legs, leaving him completely naked.

Taking in the view as Serena then bent over at the end of the bed, while she tied his feet, Terry caught a flash of her skimpy red knickers as her dress rode up. If she didn't hurry up, he was going to go off like a fucking starting pistol in a minute.

'Me? A bad boy? You ain't seen nothing yet . . .' Terry moaned in pleasure when Serena finally turned and climbed on top of him, straddling his body as she wrapped her taut limbs tightly around him.

Terry could feel the heat between them with her grinding on top of his naked body. Still wearing her dress, she let the sharp points of her stiletto heels dig into his thighs. It was such a turn-on. She was teasing the fuck out of him, and it was all he could do not to come there and then.

As she swung her long blonde hair playfully down so it brushed against his chest, Terry closed his eyes and inhaled her sweet, fruity perfume. He could feel her warm breath on his cheek as she leaned down towards him. Eagerly awaiting her next move, the anticipation was driving him crazy. She lifted his head gently and placed the blindfold over his eyes.

Physically stopping a groan from escaping his mouth, Terry couldn't hide the disappointment he felt when she got up and moved away from the bed a few seconds later.

'I'm taking off my dress . . .' Serena whispered provocatively. 'And now my panties . . .'

Terry grinned, he couldn't wait for her to get back on top of him. All this kinky shit the girl seemed to like was giving him the raging horn.

Suddenly confused at what was taking her so long, Terry listened for a few more seconds to the commotion at the end of the bed. He could hear the zip being opened on the inside of his jacket, as his clothes were being searched.

'What the fuck . . . ?' Writhing around, he tried to break free from the handcuffs, while the girl was rifling through his belongings.

'What's the matter, bad boy? I thought you liked games, Terry?' Serena searched Terry's wallet, and spotted the typical tell-tale photograph that she had obviously been expecting. 'Oh how sweet. You never mentioned that you were the dutiful family man.' Serena scoffed. Men were all the same as far as she was concerned. She had yet to meet the exception. Any man who was unlucky enough to come in contact with her got exactly what they deserved.

'You know what they would call you in my country? They would call you a filthy pig.' Serena grabbed the pile of money, and counting the notes she smirked. There was just over four and a half grand.

Not bad for a night's work, if she did say so herself.

Every single penny of it belonged to her. Today she was finally breaking free. Raymond would go ape shit no doubt, but by the time he realised that she'd done a runner she would be long gone. And so would tonight's earnings.

Wrapping her black faux-fur jacket around her shoulders, Serena glanced around the cold, dirty room. The place had been a roof over her head, but it was far from what she would call home. It was squalor and she wouldn't let a dog live here.

Her eyes, full of contempt, rested on Terry. Spread-eagled on the bed, his pale skin and fat rolls jiggled as he thrust his body about angrily, trying unsuccessfully to force the restraints. Tonight had been the first time she had brought a man back here. Normally, she went back to the men's hotel rooms, or their cars, luring them in under false pretences just like she had done with Terry. Then she'd fleece the pervy bastards for whatever she could get.

It didn't matter that Terry had seen where she lived tonight, because she would never be coming back. Tonight, thanks to Terry's winnings, she was finally able to get away from here.

Smirking as she pictured Raymond's face later, when he came to collect his money but would instead be faced with a naked and bound punter, Serena felt empowered.

Terry would be her parting gift.

It was true what her mother once told her: if you lie down with dogs you will get up with fleas, and Raymond was infested. Serena had been used as a pawn. The only things that talked in that man's world were money, sex and violence. She had been tricked into coming to England by men from her own country. Fellow Romanians with their false promises of a job, a home, a future. It had all been lies. Sold to the highest bidder. Raymond had taken her passport and forced her to earn her keep, just like the rest of the girls he had working for him. What Raymond hadn't sussed out, though, was that instead of using her body to earn her money, Serena had only ever used her brains. Ripping off drunken lowlifes in the casinos had earned her a fortune. Not only had she managed to keep Raymond off her back by becoming his best little earner for the past two months, but she'd also managed to save almost enough to escape.

Serena smiled as she pushed the large wad of money deep into the purposely torn lining of her handbag along with the rest that she had hidden away.

She didn't have a fortune by any means, but it was enough to give her a good start. Somewhere away from London. Away from the dirty men here who controlled her life. Finally she could send for her daughter and her mother; they could come to England and Serena could start afresh.

'You must be delusional. Look at you, old and fat. Why would I want to have sex with you?' Serena's lip curled with disdain, her rich Romanian accent stronger now as she felt her temper get the better of her. 'You disgust me.'

'You fucking bitch!' Terry spat, defeated. He couldn't believe that the girl had set him up. Fleecing him of everything he had, and insulting him while she did it.

'Well, unfortunately for you there will be no fucking. But "bitch" I am happy to wear.' Serena sneered as she shook her head, chucking his empty wallet onto the floor. Serena couldn't resist picking up Terry's mobile phone. 'Why don't we send your wife a little picture, Terry? Show her just what a bad boy her husband really is.'

Capturing a picture of Terry in all his naked glory, Serena pressed send to the number that had been ringing him all evening. The irate wife, she guessed.

'Naughty boy, Terry, very naughty boy.' Serena pocketed the phone before gathering up all of Terry's belongings and marching out of the room, slamming the door behind her.

Listening to the sounds of her footsteps as they faded to silence, Terry waited.

She was gone.

The smell of Serena's perfume lingered in the air; the heady aroma now smelt bitter, making him feel sick.

'Fucking cunt.' Tugging his hands and kicking out his feet, Terry threw himself around the bed with as much force as he could manage, frantically trying to yank the metal cuffs from the bed posts. It was no good. All he'd managed to do was slip his blindfold off.

'Fuck's sake!' he shouted. 'Can someone fucking help me . . . ?'

The cocaine had worn off and the chill in the room prickled his bare skin. He had no idea how long he was going to be stuck here for and he was fuming.

The thought of all that money, gone, just like that, made Terry want to cry.

Humiliated, he'd just fallen for one of the oldest tricks in the book. Royally stitched up by a fucking brass.

Once Kelly got hold of him she would string him up by his balls.

Chapter Five

Slamming her cup down on the breakfast bar, Kelly Stranks gritted her teeth in annoyance, sending her hot tea flying all over the table and all down the front of her fluffy pink dressing gown. Leaping out of the chair she grabbed a tea-towel from the worktop and mopped up the spillage as the sound of the shouting coming from the next room rattled through her brain. It was barely seven o'clock in the morning and already she'd had an earful.

'Can you two bloody kids quit with your bleeding racket? I've got a banging headache as it is without listening to the pair of you squabbling like a bleeding cat 'n' dog. Half the bloody street can probably hear you,' she screeched. 'One more word from either of you and there will be trouble.'

Kelly waited, silently counting to three. She wasn't joking either – another sound and she was ready to slap the legs off the pair of them.

Something in her voice must have warned them that she really wasn't going to put up with their usual obnoxious behaviour today, because to her surprise both of her children immediately took heed to her warning and instantly fell silent.

Sitting back down, Kelly lit another cigarette. The seconds of satisfaction that she felt as she inhaled a long slow breath were short-lived. Glancing once more at the clock above the kettle she was instantly reminded of why she was in such a bad mood in the first place.

Her good-for-nothing bloody husband!

It was always the same. Every payday without fail, Terry did his usual disappearing act. Going on a bender, and spunking the only money they had coming in on God only knows what, or who. Well, last night was the fucking end. They say that pictures can speak a thousand words, and the one she had received of him stark bollock naked at four-thirty this morning had left her physically reeling. She didn't know what the hell he was playing at but when she finally got hold of him she was going to castrate the cheating bastard.

Stubbing her cigarette out, she got up and switched the kettle on to make herself another cup of tea, before immediately lighting up another.

She peered around the kitchen looking at the dark mouldy patches in the corners of the walls trailing up to the ceiling, hovering above her like black murky clouds. The house was rotten, just like their life, and Kelly had had enough.

Fighting back her tears, she refused to cry.

She would not shed another single tear for that bastard. No way. He didn't fucking deserve them.

She shook her head as she thought of the promises that he had made her. Promised her the world he had; what a joke that had turned out to be. She'd been so young and naive, and blinded by the idea of making her own way in the world, and proving her father wrong, that she had stupidly hung on to Terry's every word.

Terry Stranks, her knight in shining armour, though as it turned out the man was no more than a liar in cheap tinfoil. Now, seven years later Kelly was finally under no illusions that her husband's idea of giving her the world was in fact a two-up two-down council house in one of the shittiest, most poverty stricken streets in Southwark.

From day one everything about Terry had been a front. Not only had his promises been as empty as the bed she had slept in last night, but his pockets had been too. The fancy sports car he had first picked her up in on their first date, the lavish gifts he had wooed her with. It turned out that Terry had had a big win on the horses just before he met her. It was a one-off, a lucky fluke she had since learned.

Terry was a massive gambler, and a shit one at that. After getting a bit cocky with his winnings, he had frittered away the last of it trying to win more. His riches had dried up quicker than one of Kelly's Revlon nail varnishes and by the time she realised that Terry wasn't all he made himself out to be, it was too late. She was already pregnant. Seventeen years old, and up the duff.

Her dad had gone mental at her of course, having already taken an instant dislike to Terry, due to the fact that he and Terry were almost the same age. He'd been fuming. Spouting off at her about how he'd warned her about men like Terry. Kelly was so caught up in her new life with Terry and she had been so determined to prove her dad wrong, that after one row too many with her father, Kelly had left home and moved in with Terry.

She'd been stuck with the bastard ever since.

Pulling deeply on her cigarette, Kelly's hands shook with anger.

Seven years she'd given to that man, and what had he given her? A belly full of stretch-marks, and two kids that gave her nothing but grief all day long. She'd sacrificed everything for that man. Even her family.

Her dad had warned her. Like they said, she'd made her bed and, being too stubborn for her own good, Kelly Stranks was going to have to lie in it.

So much for living the fairy-tale.

Stubbing out her cigarette, her mouth felt dry and she was no longer in the mood for it. Why did it feel that, with every passing day, life was becoming more and more of a struggle?

Terry knew that they had been counting on his wages; if he'd pissed it all up the wall again she was going to cause murders. She just couldn't work out what the man was playing at. He must have a bleeding death wish if he thought the O'Sheas were going to let them off again when they turned up here for the money they were owed later, and he didn't have it. Staring down at her broken finger, Terry had seen what they were like, how angry they'd been. Jimmy had even taken her mother's brooch, the bastard.

He was a fucking let-down. Instead of anger now, Kelly was feeling numb.

This really was the last straw.

'Muuumm . . .' Billy screeched as he tore into the room, his eyes blazing with anger, bringing his mum's thoughts abruptly back to the present. 'Miley drew on my shirt.' Billy spun around to reveal the bright red felt-tip scrawl that covered the back of his white school shirt. 'What does it say, Mum?'

Kelly put her hand to her forehead in despair at the sight of her daughter's artwork. It looked like a drawing of a penis.

'Miley!' Kelly shouted as she spotted Billy's bottom lip start to quiver and his cheeks turning red in anger. She knew Billy was going to start lashing out at his younger sister. Kelly had never known a six-year-old to have such a bad temper. He reminded her of her brother Christopher at that age. 'Where is she?'

'Dunno.' Billy shuffled his feet and stared at the floor defiantly.

'Billy?' Kelly could see by her shifty son's face that he had done something he shouldn't have.

'Billy?' she shouted, her patience wearing thin.

'She's in the shed,' he said in a small defiant voice. 'She said she was going out there to feed Thumper, so I locked her in. It serves her right, Mum, she's a little bastard.'

'Oi, watch your mouth.' Kelly clouted Billy around the back of the head.

'What? You call us that all the time,' Billy whined.

Losing her patience, Kelly took a deep breath before she really said something that she would regret.

'For fuck's sake! Get that shirt off and see if there is another one in the laundry basket, will you? Hurry up or we'll be late for school.' Marching out to the shed, she tried to keep her cool. 'You two kids are going to be the death of me, do you know that?' Kelly shouted as she approached the shed and struggled with the padlock, whilst Miley kicked the wooden door repeatedly, crying and screaming at Billy to let her out.

Pulling the door open, Kelly shook her head. Miley's bright red face, twisted in anger at her brother, quickly turned to one of upset. Five years old, and with a mop of gorgeous blonde curls, she looked the innocent. Miley was more than capable of winding her brother up, and thinking that she could manipulate her mother the way she did her father, she sobbed now.

Kelly wasn't having it.

'This is what happens when you wind your brother up . . .' Just before Kelly could scold the girl further, she heard her son's shouts from the house.

'Mum . . . quick, Mum. It's Dad . . .'

'Right you, inside. And no more drawing pictures like that on your brother. What the hell are they teaching you down at that school, huh?' Kelly said before turning on her heel, and going in to sort her husband out. The mood she was in now, she was going to let the dirty stop-out bleeding well have it.

'Oh the wanderer returns, eh? Where the fuck have you—'

Stopping dead in her tracks as she reached the lounge, Kelly saw her husband crouching over the sofa, naked, wrapped in nothing but a cream bed sheet and holding his side in agony. Kelly gasped. Terry looked like he'd been attacked.

Seeing the congealed blood, cuts and swelling that covered her husband's face, Kelly put her hand over her mouth. Then, remembering the kids were in the room, she quickly shooed them out.

'Go upstairs, kids. Billy, put the telly on in my room. See if you can find something to watch for a few minutes with your sister.' Kelly ushered her terrified looking kids out of the room. Closing the lounge door, she turned to Terry.

'Oh my God, what's happened? Was it the O'Sheas?' Kelly asked, confused.

Shaking his head, Terry raised his hand up in protest, clearly in pain as he did so. 'No, it weren't them, Kel. I got fucking mugged. I was walking home from work last night, and three blokes jumped me, three big Nigerians. Held me hostage in some bloody squat,' Terry said as he slumped down into the chair. 'I tried to fight them off but they beat seven shades of shit out of me. Tied me to a bed, and took all my wages . . . and my bloody phone.'

'Oh my God, Terry. I've been calling you all night. I thought you had gone on a bender. They sent me a photo of you stark bollock naked. I thought you were . . . Well it doesn't matter what I thought.' Kelly felt guilty now. She had left numerous messages on Terry's voicemail telling him exactly what she thought of him and the whole time he'd been kidnapped and held hostage by a bunch of violent thugs. 'I was so worried about you, babe.'

Terry pulled the blanket tightly around him, groaning as he did. 'Did they take it all?' Kelly asked.

Terry stared at his wife incredulously. Here he was battered and bruised and still her only thought was about the poxy money.

'Well, I'm only thinking about the O'Sheas . . . What are we going to tell them, Terry? We said we'd have their money for them.'

'They took every penny, Kelly, and right at this moment in time I have no fucking idea what we're going to say to them. I'm in agony; they're the least of my worries.' Terry moaned in pain. The last thing he wanted to think about was the O'Sheas. They would be after his blood when they turned up here later, and Terry knew that there was nothing he could do now to stop them. The only way out of it as far as he could see was to do a runner. Get Kelly and the kids over to his mum's and hopefully buy himself some more time until he could figure out what the hell he was going to do. The fact that Kelly and his mother could barely be in the same room together without nearly killing each other was beside the point. Kelly would have to lump it. They were desperate after all.

'Cor, fucking hell, I think I'm dying.' Terry exaggeratedly flung his head back on the sofa, deciding to enjoy Kelly's calm disposition for a few more minutes before he brought up the subject of his plan for them all to descend upon his mother.

'Can I get you anything?' Kelly was racked with guilt for thinking he had been with some tart last night.

'I'd murder a sausage and egg sandwich, Kelly?' Terry asked sheepishly, wondering how much he would be able to milk his predicament.

'A sausage and egg sarnie?' Kelly asked. 'I meant a bloody ambulance, or some painkillers at least.'

Terry shook his head. 'No, I'll be fine. It's only a few bruises. A sandwich is all I want, my sweet. I haven't eaten since yesterday lunch time. I'm starving.'

'Right, well you just put your feet up and I'll go and whip you something up. I'll make you a tea with a few extra sugars too. You probably need it for the shock. Then we need to work out what the fuck we're going to do, Tel. That fucking Jimmy meant what he said about what he'd do if we didn't pay up this time. So we're going to have to figure something out.'

As Kelly busied herself in the kitchen, Terry leaned back against the sofa and closed his eyes. He was knackered. It had been a long night and an even longer morning.

Finally, after bashing the bed post against the wall for what seemed like forever, another dozy tart from the bedroom next door had come to his aid and released him. But not until she had pissed herself laughing at the sight of him, figuring rightly that her friend Serena had done a proper number on him.

The Romanian bitch had taken his belongings and, left without his clothes, Terry had had no choice but to wrap himself in the bed sheet he'd been lying on. He'd been shitting himself about coming home. Kelly had warned him last time that the very next time he cheated on her, she was going to have the locks changed, and Terry knew that she meant it. Terry had to really put his thinking cap on if he wanted to get out of this mess, and the little brainwave he'd had en route about throwing himself down a concrete stairwell by the river and claiming to have been mugged seemed to be working a treat.

The fall had been harder than he had anticipated, and he hadn't meant to do quite as much damage as he had, but every bump and scrape that covered his battered body had been worth it.

Kelly looked riddled with guilt at thinking the worst of him and Terry was glad that he had got away with last night's antics.

He'd been fuming that the conniving slag had taken his money, and that he was once again back at square one, but at least he didn't have Kelly in his ear giving him grief too, on top of everything else. That really would have been the icing on the cake.

Kelly was right about one thing, though.

The O'Sheas would turn up here later expecting their money, and Terry had a feeling that, unlike his unsuspecting wife, they wouldn't be so easily fobbed off.

Chapter Six

Evie Woods frantically tried to hide her modesty as the group of girls dragged her naked from her bedroom into the communal hallway. Hitting the floor roughly as the girls flung her down onto the coarse grey carpet, Evie tried to scamper away. But the girls pulled her back, laughing. They were enjoying the fact that Evie Woods was mortified.

'Please, leave me alone. Get off me,' Evie shrieked as tears filled her eyes. Kicking out, Evie was desperate to break free. They'd ambushed her just as she'd been about to get into the shower, and had set upon her.

Shouting at the top of her voice, Evie's distressed calls for help were of no use. Instead of persuading anyone to help her, Evie's cries were just making the whole ordeal worse: they alerted all the other students in the dormitory to her attack, and now crowds of her classmates ventured out of their rooms to investigate the commotion. The group of girls holding her were delighted to have so many onlookers.

'Please leave me alone. Get off me.' Tears stung her eyes as she begged and pleaded, but like a pack of excitable hyenas laughing in her face, the gang were relentless.

Curled up into a ball, Evie felt her legs being wrenched apart as one of the girls grabbed her arms and held them flat to the floor above her head.

'Please.' Evie was unable to control the heavy, pathetic sobs that escaped from her mouth.

Evie had tried so hard not to cry, but now, how could she not? Lying spread-eagled on the communal hallway floor completely exposed, she was vulnerable. Completely humiliated as everyone stood around her laughing.

'Hold her legs there.' Madeline Porter, the group's ringleader, squatted down on the floor as she shouted out instructions to the others. Her plump face was twisted with hate as she peered down at Evie's skinny frame with scrutiny.

'Let me go,' Evie begged, but she could see in Madeline's face that the girl was only just getting started.

Madeline Porter had been making her life hell since the day Evie started at the school seven long years ago. Evie had barely had time to grieve for her beautiful mother, for whom she'd been named, when her dad had packed her off to board at Walborough Girls' School.

He had the best intentions, she knew that. The Buckinghamshire private school was said to be one of the most exclusive in the country. He wanted her away from the morbidity of the house, so that she could still have a chance not to let her mother's sudden death overshadow the rest of her life.

But Evie had hated it from the very first moment. Just nine years old, Madeline had set upon Evie, singling her out. She'd seen Evie for what she was – an easy target – and the girl had taken great pleasure in spreading rumours about Evie and her family. Turning the other girls against her, by telling them that the only reason Evie was able to attend the eight thousand pounds a term school was because Evie's father wasn't just a boxer, he was a gangster. Madeline told everyone that Evie's dad had robbed a jewellers in Mayfair. Her family were crooks, and everyone believed her. Madeline's dad worked for the Met, after all.

Evie had quickly landed the nickname of Dodgy-Goods-Woods, a name she had carried around for years. And the other girls, influenced by Madeline, had distanced themselves from her.

Slowly, over the years, the bullying had got worse. Now, instead of just name calling, it had turned more physical. The girls purposely destroyed her belongings, pulled her hair, tripped her up.

But today, Madeline Porter was taking her assault to a whole other level.

Evie screamed in terror as she felt something metal and cold between her thighs. 'Ahh what's the matter, Evie? Bet you wish you had your daddy here to protect you now, don't you?' Prising Evie's legs open even wider with her knees Madeline Porter held the can up and sprayed Evie's groin area with the coloured hair spray.

Laughter erupted from the group once more.

'The colour suits you,' Madeline taunted. 'Mouldy green, for little miss prissy knickers. Bet this is the first time your minge has seen the light of day, isn't it?'

'What in God's name is going on out here?'

Hearing the house-mistress's voice, Evie felt relief wash over her, as the girls immediately sprang to their feet, feigning innocence when Mrs. Parks neared.

Staring at the group of girls, then at Evie, who had her hands strategically placed, covering her tiny breasts and spray of pubic hair, Mrs. Parks could clearly see what had happened here.

'Girls. Get yourselves down to the hall immediately. The end of term assembly will be starting shortly,' Mrs. Parks scolded, her voice stern. Then watching as the group of girls sauntered off, sniggering quietly amongst themselves, Mrs. Parks turned to Evie. 'Look at the state of you, Evie Woods. Go and get yourself cleaned up this instant,' Mrs. Parks reprimanded, haughtily. 'There are only two days left of term and I really haven't got time for such immature nonsense.'

Evie felt dumb-founded.

Searching Mrs. Parks's face for even so much as a hint of compassion, Evie knew that her teacher must know that she'd been deliberately set upon. Mrs. Parks must know that she was being bullied by Madeline Porter and her so-called cronies – everyone knew.

Yet they chose to turn a blind eye.

Even now, Mrs. Parks seemed set on playing down the vicious attack, almost insinuating that Evie being dragged naked from the shower, and publicly mortified was somehow her own fault. Like she'd taken part in some kind of silly game.

'Go on.' Mrs. Parks clapped her hands, forcing Evie out of her stunned trance-like demeanour as the girl looked at her teacher questioningly. Surely Mrs. Parks should help her? Surely she could see that Evie was the victim here?

But instead, Evie was met with a look of contempt.

'And if you're late for assembly I'll be putting you on litter duties at lunch time, so chop chop.'

Standing up, baring her small naked breasts and her splay of bright green pubic hair, which Madeline Porter and her cronies had just inflicted on her, Evie wanted the ground to swallow her up.

'You've got five minutes.'

Walking back into her room, Evie felt numb. Not once had she told a single soul about the excessive bullying that she'd suffered here at Walborough Girls' School. It'd just make things worse. Yet on the few occasions that Madeline and her disciples had been caught red-handed, the teachers had chosen to ignore it.

Standing under the scalding hot water as it cascaded down her naked body, Evie scrubbed herself vigorously with a flannel.

Lathering the soap up between her legs, she tried to scrub away not only the bright coloured dye, but also the humiliation she had endured.

She could still hear the chorus of laughter the girls had made, mocking her as they got their kicks.

For years she'd endured the countless torment. The vicious threats, the name calling. Lately, though, the bullying was escalating beyond any form of control, and today had been the worst yet. What was to come?

Unable to get all the remnants of the dye off, Evie gave up. Stepping out of the shower, she wrapped a towel around her naked body, and walked back through to her bedroom.

She could hear the cluster of doors slamming one by one down the corridor as the other girls all made their way down to the assembly hall and Evie knew that she was going to be late now. Another reason for them all to laugh at her again, when she got chastised by the headmistress in front of them all for her poor timekeeping.

Throwing on her uniform, she was determined to walk in there with her head held high. She wouldn't let them see that they had made her cry, that it bothered her. She was an expert at hiding her true feelings. She'd been doing it for years.

Even when she went home for the holidays she had to put on an act, and pretend that she was happy. She'd be mortified if her dad found out just how weak and unpopular she was.

She swept her hair into a tight bun on top of her head, and left her face devoid of make-up as always. She'd slip her glasses on, and if she ran she might just make it. But she couldn't find them.

Lifting up the damp towel she searched underneath, then chucking it back down she remembered that she'd left them on her bed.

She couldn't see them.

Pulling back the cover she put her hand over her mouth to stop herself from gagging. A dark brown trail of excrement had been smeared all over the inside of her bed sheets, the rancid odour making her retch. Her glasses had been purposely covered in shit too, and placed in the middle of the mess.

Evie wanted to cry.

She was trying so hard to stay in control, to not let them break her, but they were so persistent, so mean.

After years of suffering the constant torment of Madeline Porter and her cronies, Evie Woods had had enough.

People only treated you how you let them, and Evie had been letting these girls belittle her for far too long. It was time that she stood up for herself.

The girls probably thought that what they'd done was hilarious, but it was the final straw.

Evie wasn't going to take their shit anymore.

Chapter Seven

Resting the cue just under his chin, Raymond Marks effortlessly lined up his next shot. Gently tapping the white ball he sank the black into the pocket, finishing off the game in one swift, smooth movement.

'I don't know why you put yourself through it, mate. You know that I'll thrash the arse off of you every single time.' Flashing Harry a triumphant smirk, Raymond loved winding his friend up. Snooker was about the only thing that Harry wasn't much cop at, and knowing how competitive he could be, Raymond couldn't help but feel smug at his win.

'Not every single time actually,' Harry countered as he placed the cue back in its holder on the wall and walked the length of his games room, back over to his stall at the bar. 'You seem to forget about that one time down at The Manors. If my memory serves me correctly, I was on fucking fire that night, wiped the floor and the snooker table with you.'

Raymond shook his head then and laughed. 'The Manors? The youth club? Jesus Christ, Harry, we were fourteen years old. I'm surprised that you can even remember that far back. Still, I suppose you have to hang on to your one and only victory, eh? And we both know the only reason you beat me was because I was otherwise occupied that night. I had a handicap. Don't you remember that Karen? Two years older than us and tits to die for. She spent the entire game eyeing me up. I couldn't concentrate at all.'

'Yeah she was a distraction, wasn't she?' Harry laughed now too. Karen Wards had been one of the best looking girls down at The Manors and it was common knowledge that Raymond had had a massive crush on the girl. 'She wasn't cheap either. Cost me two Curly Wurlys and a packet of Black Jacks to get her to agree to my little plan.'

'Plan? Oh have a laugh, you mean to tell me that you set me up?' Raymond shook his head. Why didn't it surprise him? Harry always was a crafty sod, sharp as a knife even back when they were kids.

'It's only taken you, what? Just over forty years to work that one out. Anyway, from what I remember it didn't work out too badly for you in the end? I asked her to distract you from the game; the rest of it had nothing to do with me.' Harry raised his eyebrow. His plan to have Karen Wards drape herself at the opposite end of the snooker table and pout seductively at Raymond had worked out better than he'd anticipated, and had most definitely gone in his friend's favour.

'Fair enough, mate, I'll let you off. I may have lost the game, but I certainly won the prize that night.' Raymond grinned again at the memory of the fumble he'd encountered, as the experienced girl had hitched her miniskirt up and let him have sex with her up against the wall at the back of the youth club. Losing his virginity to Karen Wards had been a consolation prize and a half for losing out on a snooker game to Harry.

'So, what was it you were going to tell me earlier, about the casino? Did you have some trouble?' Harry asked as Raymond took a seat next to him.

'No, no trouble. I just ran into your old mate Terry Stranks. Thought you'd wanna know that the philandering toe-rag has been up to his old tricks again.'

Harry felt himself clench up. Just hearing Terry's name got his back up. But Raymond was right: whatever that man was up to, Harry wanted to know.

'That bloke is a first class cunt. Did he know that you'd clocked him?'

'Nah, he was off his fucking rocker, Harry. Coked up to his fucking eyeballs and all over one of my girls. He left with her too. Little Romanian bird called Serena.'

Raymond watched as Harry let the information sink in. He hated being the bearer of bad news, but he knew that as much as Terry Stranks' actions riled Harry, Harry was adamant that he would rather know what the bloke was up to than not, and if Harry insisted on keeping tabs on the bloke then Raymond was happy to oblige. Yet he could see by Harry's face that he was nevertheless fuming at Terry's latest shenanigans.

'Anyway, don't you worry. The cocky bastard already got his comeuppance as it turns out.' Raymond took a swig out of his drink. 'There I was, sat on my tod outside the house in my motor keeping an eye out for the prick, when who comes out not fifteen minutes later? Serena. The cheeky bitch had only fleeced Terry for every penny and then tried to do a runner, hadn't she? She got the shock of her life when I collared her.' Raymond shrugged. 'Anyway, by the time I'd dealt with her and got back to the house, Terry had cleared off.'

'Fucking joker.'

'Tell me about it. Still, I got a nice little earner out of it,' Raymond agreed. 'You want to do anything about it?' he asked. He could see by his friend's face that Harry looked fit to kill, but he also knew that Harry wouldn't do anything to retaliate.

Harry shook his head.

Raymond didn't know why Harry put himself through the pain of wanting to know. If it were him he would have washed his hands with the guy long ago. Either that or stuck a bullet in the bloke. Changing the subject, Raymond sat down opposite his friend. 'Now, enough of the chit-chat. What's going on with Christopher?'

'Don't even get me started on him.' Rubbing his temples, Harry sighed. 'The boy is like a time bomb just waiting to go off. I'm at my wits' end with him, Raymond.'

Raymond knew exactly what his friend was going through. The last he'd heard, Christopher had had his boxing licence revoked. His fearsome reputation was not only spiralling out of control but it was also preceding him: forever in the papers, it hadn't taken long for the British Boxing Board of Control to get wind of the chaos that Christopher was creating outside of the ring, and they had quickly withdrawn his licence, unwilling to be associated with someone so volatile. The boy had fucked up his career before he'd even started.

As Harry's friend, Raymond had seen the boy's erratic behaviour go from bad to worse over the years but he knew that it wasn't his place to say it. Harry didn't need him to point out the obvious. Christopher had more issues than *Vogue* magazine, and they both knew why. Raymond was just glad that Harry had finally pulled his neck out of the sand and was admitting that he could see it for himself.

'I'm pulling him off the job.' Harry stared at Raymond now, waiting for him to say something. To tell him he was overreacting, or that he was wrong.

But instead Raymond nodded his head fully in agreement: Christopher was too much of a wild card to be involved with the business. 'It's been a long time coming, Harry. I think you're right.' Raymond nodded.

'The boy's too much of a risk. His head is all over the fucking place.'

'What's he said?' Raymond asked, wondering how Christopher had taken the news that his own father couldn't trust working with him.

Harry shrugged again. 'Told the kid that I'm going to sort him out with an unlicensed fight. That gig that I'm promoting next week, I've told him that he's going to be the main attraction. He seems keen too, so who knows? All I do know is that the boy needs to vent, and I need to keep him focused. You know what he's like, his ego's the size of this fucking house, thinks he's going to be the next Muhammad Ali. He didn't even question my decision.'

Downing his drink, Raymond could see where Harry was coming from. It was best to pacify Christopher sometimes, otherwise they could end up with a shitstorm on their hands and neither of them wanted that.

'Anyway, it's done now. So, we're a man down. But I reckon we can more than cope.'

It was a big job coming up, and really they needed all hands on deck. But not wanting to worry Harry, Raymond changed the subject.

'Right, how's about one more before I hit the road?' Raymond held up his glass. 'And then I think we should have a rematch. But I'll tell you what, let's make it fair. Let's square things up so that we're equal this time.'

Getting up to get the drinks, Harry looked at his friend questioningly. 'Oh yeah, and how are you going to do that then?'

'I'll give you a thirty-eight point handicap to start you off . . .' Then, kicking off his shoes, Raymond chuckled. 'And I'll play using only my feet.'

Chapter Eight

'Fuck me sideways, this bloody driveway is almost as long as the M25,' Kelly moaned as her stiletto heels sank down into the gravel as she walked. The place was stunning, though, she couldn't deny that.

Making her way up the plush road in Hampstead Heath, Kelly found it hard to believe this was the same city she lived in. All the houses around here looked grand, expensive. Lined with huge wrought iron gates that led onto long winding driveways, and facing out onto the Heath. The views were magnificent. It was like being in the countryside; acres of protected land, dotted with woodland and pretty ponds. The place was a far cry from the grey depressing council house that she and Terry were used to back home in South-wark; it was a completely different world in fact.

Even if she wanted to, there was no hiding how impressed she was. Flicking her long blonde clip-in hair extensions over her shoulders and pouting her heavily glossed lips Kelly glanced round at her surroundings excitedly.

So, this was how the other half lived, eh? She opened her eyes wide in awe at the grand house that stood up ahead of them. The sheer size of the place was incredible, and lit up against the dark evening sky the house looked breathtakingly beautiful.

'Cor, check out his motors.' Terry whistled as he eyed up the collection of cars that lined the driveway like ornaments. 'An R8, a Bentley and a Range Rover.'

'Jesus, Terry, put your tongue back in, would you? You look bleeding gormless.' Kelly failed to suppress the flicker of annoyance as Terry gawped at the cars longingly. It was wishful thinking on her husband's part; Terry wouldn't be able to afford the valeting on these motors let alone the log books. 'I bet you're glad we got a bleeding Tube now, aren't you?' Kelly added smugly. 'Imagine if we'd have turned up in your shitty little Astra, we'd have probably been laughed all the way back to Southwark. They'd have loved that, wouldn't they?'

Kelly hated their Astra. It was a rust bucket on wheels, and if she was given the choice she'd have rather crawled through the streets of London on her hands and knees than be seen dead sitting in that heap of shit.

'His last place was incredible, but this gaff is like a fucking castle in comparison,' Terry murmured, ignoring Kelly's comment as he mentally added up the value of the motors. 'He must have money coming out of his ears.'

Terry stared straight ahead, pretending to focus on the detailing of the Edwardian stained glass doorway that towered above them as he secretly wondered if coming here today was such a good idea after all.

'It is a bit plush, though, ain't it? Like one of those houses you see in magazines, you know, the sort of place you'd imagine Posh and Becks living in,' Kelly cooed. 'Here, Terry, imagine if David opened the door to me wearing those skimpy little pants that he wears in those adverts. How funny would that be. Hung like a bloody stallion that man is.'

Chuckling to herself, Kelly checked her reflection in the door's glass panel before tugging down her silver sequined miniskirt that had ridden up to reveal the huge unsightly control knickers. Magic knickers my arse, she thought. Jiggling about to adjust her outfit, she couldn't help but think that her lumps and bumps had been shoved so far up her pants that some of her belly was now occupying space in her bra.

Kelly had gone to a lot of effort today, but no amount of make-up or hair spray could prevent her hands from shaking like they were.

Giving Terry a final once-over, Kelly pursed her lips. The shock of seeing him in such a state this morning was gradually subsiding now. She had thought that he looked a right mess when he'd turned up this morning, but now he looked downright awful. The bruising had started coming out now, covering his face in dark lesions of black and blue. His right eye was so swollen that he could barely open it. It was no wonder everyone had stared at them on the Tube on the way here.

'Do your jacket up, Tel,' Kelly said as she pointed at his check shirt that stretched tightly across his protruding stomach. 'You look smarter with it done up.' She was going to mention that the buttons on his shirt looked like they were struggling under the strain of his wobbly gut, but as a generous size fourteen herself Kelly decided to keep her thoughts to herself on the issue of her husband's expanding beer belly. She'd got her dress in the sale, and even though it was only twenty quid, she felt a million dollars wearing it, and she wasn't going to give Terry any opportunity to tell her otherwise.

'Do you reckon he's had a win on the lottery or something?' Terry asked as they waited patiently for someone to answer the door.

Kelly shrugged. 'Fuck knows, but he is obviously doing something right,' Kelly said, plastering a big smile on her face as the door was opened by the housekeeper.

'Staff.' She turned to Terry and raised her eyebrow. 'This really is the life, eh?'

Following the housekeeper down the long corridor, Kelly couldn't take her eyes off the exquisitely beautiful décor as they went. The spectacularly high white ceilings were splayed with huge chandeliers and Kelly was hypnotised by the shimmering beads of light that rained down above them from the teardrop shaped crystals. Even the marble floor twinkled, illuminated by tiny gold speckles as they walked.

Wrinkling her nose, Kelly spotted a large vase of fresh lilies.

She had been able to smell the sickly sweet aroma from the minute they'd entered the house. The overpowering smell made Kelly feel nostalgic, instantly reminding her of the blanket of lilies that enveloped her mother's coffin as it was lowered into the ground.

Kelly hated them.

Shaking off the memory, Kelly focused on the fancy artwork that lined the walls: huge white canvases splayed with abstract streaks of colour. No doubt these pieces had cost a bomb, but Kelly just didn't get it. She had similar paintings stuck to her fridge at home that the kids had done at school. Anyone could splodge paint onto a piece of paper and call it art. But then what did she know? The only decorations that lined their walls at home, she thought irritatedly to herself, were the sticky hand prints from the kids, and a couple of framed Millwall photos that Terry had picked up from the local market. She could have killed him when he'd brought those bloody monstrosities home. She'd asked him to sort out the rising damp, not hang fucking pictures over it and pretend it wasn't there. By choice she'd rather look at the mouldy wall than that tat.

'Mr. Woods, you have guests,' Rita the housekeeper announced as she opened the door to the games room.

Standing up, Harry looked perplexed. Rita knew not to interrupt him, and he had made that perfectly clear when she had shown Raymond in, not even an hour ago.

'Rita. You'll have to tell whoever it is that I'm in a meeting.' Pissed off that his housekeeper had interrupted him, Harry wasn't in the mood for niceties. He hadn't been expecting anyone. 'Now isn't convenient.'

Pushing Rita aside Kelly strutted into the room, followed by her husband.

Speaking with more bravado than she felt, now that she was standing in front of the notorious Harry Woods, Kelly smiled. 'Hello, Dad. You missed me?'

Chapter Nine

'Kelly?' Walking the length of the snooker table, Harry was gob-smacked to see his estranged daughter standing in front of him, and her waste-of-space husband lurking behind her. Still, she was here, and it was a sight that he hadn't thought he'd see again when she left home seven years ago.

'I thought it was about time we sorted things out, Dad.' Kelly spoke softly, unsure of her dad's reaction. Kelly could see that he looked confused. Turning up here out of the blue was obviously a bit of a shock for him. But even so, she could gauge by his face that he was genuinely pleased to see her.

'Come here and give your old dad a hug, of course I've bloody missed you, girl.' With his arms outstretched, Harry pulled his daughter to him, hugging her close. He had thought this day would never come. Kelly had made her choice years ago when she'd so brutally cut him out of her life like a cancer.

As painful as it had been, seeing her now made the years that stood between them suddenly seem like just seconds.

'You all right, Raymond?' Kelly could see his lip curled in distaste, clearly not finding the reunion as moving as her father did. Well, fuck him. She wasn't here for him. Raymond Marks had never been overly fond of her and the feeling was most definitely mutual.

The bloke was an arsehole. Just some skanky pimp who whored out girls for a living. Why her dad even tolerated the man, let alone classed him as a best friend, Kelly would never know. Knowing that she had a lot of making up to do, Kelly decided to keep her opinions about the man to herself.

'I'm good, Kelly,' Raymond replied bluntly, then stood up to leave. Kelly looked every bit the tramp he'd imagined her to turn into. She looked brash, cheap. Everything about her, from the skanky hair extensions to the tacky blue eye shadow, screamed attention seeking. Kelly hadn't changed one bit. Raymond had never liked the girl. She'd always been all about herself – a real selfish mare – and since she had cut Harry out of her life, and off from his grandkids, Raymond liked her even less.

'Shall I leave you to it, Harry? You've got a lot of catching up to do.'

'No, don't be silly, Raymond. We're all family here,' Harry said as he ushered Raymond to sit back down before turning to the man they'd just been talking about.

'You all right, Terry? Blimey, what happened to your bonce?' Harry finally addressed the elephant in the room: a dishevelled looking Terry Stranks, standing awkwardly in the background like a spare part, and judging by the state of Terry's bashed up looking face now, Harry could see that Raymond's girl must have done a right number on him.

Still, he deserved it. Terry Stranks would never change. Once a scumbag, always a scumbag. Though why Kelly couldn't see it, Harry really had no idea. 'Bloody hell, I've done twelve rounds in the ring and come out looking prettier than you.' Harry laughed, then gripping Terry's hand firmly, he shook it, purely for his daughter's benefit.

'Oh it's nothing,' Terry said, playing down his injuries. 'I got mugged last night.'

'Mugged, bloody hell. Well, I wouldn't say that was nothing,' Harry said, feigning sympathy. 'Did you manage to get a good look at the bastard?' Harry spoke calmly, but underneath the surface his anger bubbled away. So that was his story, was it? The only one around here who was still obviously getting mugged was his Kelly. Mugged off by her lying, cheating, no-good husband.

'Three of them there was, Dad, can you believe it? You can't even walk home from work anymore without fearing for your life. They were all foreigners too. Bloody disgusting, isn't it?' Kelly hated that she'd had to turn up here today with Terry looking such a state; she'd wanted to try to give off a good impression. Last night had been a one-off. It certainly hadn't been Terry's fault.

'See, Raymond, I told you that it couldn't have been Terry that you saw last night down at the casino.' Harry smirked at his estranged son-in-law before he continued. 'Convinced it was you, he was. Said you were on a win 'en all.'

'Definitely wasn't Terry then, Dad, he never bloody wins.' Kelly's laugh was forced. She was trying to lighten the mood as she looked at her husband, whose face was quickly resembling that of a slapped arse. If her dad was being civil, then why couldn't Terry? The least he could do was try.

'Nope, definitely wasn't me,' Terry muttered quietly, his cheeks burning.

What were the chances of him being clocked last night by Raymond Marks of all people? If Kelly copped on to what Harry was implying and realised that he had been lying to her all along about last night's escapades, she would string him up.

'I knew it weren't you.' Harry shot Terry a sly wink when Kelly wasn't looking.

'Even you weren't sure, were you, Raymond? Said that the bloke he saw had a bit of a podge on. Almost a dead ringer for you actually, only this guy was fat as fuck.' Harry held his hand about a foot away from his stomach, emphasising Terry's protruding beer belly.

'Dirty git was pawing all over one of my toms too,' Raymond added, his steely cold glare transfixed on Terry. 'Devious little bitch tried to do a runner. Caught her with a nice wad of money on her, which I pocketed. Whoever the poor bastard was that she ripped off must have been seething.' Raymond continued to stare, but his face was expressionless, he gave nothing away.

Terry could feel himself getting hot under his collar; sweat was forming across the back of his neck and he could feel Kelly's eyes boring into him, as she watched his reaction.

Harry and Raymond were laying it on so thick that Kelly was bound to catch on in a second. Nervous about how the conversation had turned against him, Terry felt sick. That bitch last night had been one of Raymond's girls? Fucking hell, what were the chances? If these two thought they were clever by trying to stitch him up they had another think coming. No matter what happened, Terry was sticking to his story. He was mugged. He wasn't at the casino.

Sensing that the conversation was going off kilter, Kelly tried to change the subject. She needed to get to the point of why she was here, but she felt too embarrassed to ask now.

'You're looking really well, Dad.' The tension in the room was so dense you could almost see it, and the last thing she wanted was for everyone to start focusing on Terry and his recent spate of bad luck. Not after all this time. It was going to be hard enough as it was, without reinforcing her dad's belief that Terry was still up to no good just because he'd been mugged. 'You haven't aged a day.' Kelly smiled warmly. Her dad had always been a handsome man – even his career as a boxer hadn't put paid to that. In fact, if anything, Kelly thought that the crook on his nose and scar above his left eyebrow had always made her father look even more handsome. The older he got, the more handsome he became. Even now with his hair flecked with grey and the deep set laughter lines framing his eyes, he still had that lovable rogue quality to him.

'Must be that Oil of Olay stuff.' Harry winked. 'And so are you, Kelly, darling, it's like time has stood still.'

In truth Kelly looked awful. She looked older than her twenty-four years. Pale and bloated, the puffy bags under her eyes gave away how tired she looked: like she had the weight of the world on her shoulders.

'How rude of me, I haven't even offered you both a drink. What do you fancy, Kelly? How about some champagne? That okay for you, Terry?'

Terry nodded as he watched Harry stride to the other side of the bar, place four glass flutes on the counter and pop the champagne cork loudly – Harry was a flash bastard. Terry felt his gut twist with jealousy as he looked around the plush room that reflected the man's vast wealth. Everything in the room screamed money; Harry even had the family crest displayed proudly in the centre of the bespoke snooker table. Terry would bet his life that even the cream plush carpet he was standing on cost more than his and Kelly's entire worldly possessions. Everything about this gaff oozed expense. Watching him now, dishing out expensive drinks like he was lord of the manor, Terry felt like a proper mug for coming here. Raymond was still shooting him daggers and he could tell by Harry's stilted tone that he wasn't really welcome here. They were putting up with him for Kelly's sake. Nothing had changed, except that maybe Kelly was too dumb to see it. Too dumb or too desperate.

'The house is amazing, Dad.' Kelly smiled. The sheer size of the place was incredible and secretly Kelly was blown away by the wealth of it all.

'Well, it's a far cry from the old house in Ealing Common, huh?' Harry said sadly. 'Sold it shortly after you left. What with your mother and everything . . . it just didn't seem right to stay there.' Kelly nodded, leaving her dad's words to hang in the air. She had fond memories of the old house, the house they had grown up in. It hadn't been anywhere near the scale of this place, but it had been beautiful all the same. Kelly had many happy memories from back then. Her dad was right: nothing had felt the same after her mother had died.

'How is everyone? How's Evie?' Kelly asked cheerfully, convinced that she probably wouldn't even recognise her younger sister now.

'Oh you know our Evie, always good as gold that one. She's an angel.' It upset Harry to think that Kelly didn't really know her sister. Evie had only been nine when Kelly had run off with Terry. Kelly knew nothing about her. Just like he didn't know anything about his own grandchildren. 'Unlike your brother. Now he is a whole other story.' Harry laughed, lightening the mood, as he passed around the glasses of champagne before necking half of his in one go.

Taking her glass, Kelly nodded knowingly; he was talking about Christopher.

Her oldest brother, Nathan, had been the only one that had actually kept in touch with her over the years, albeit in secret, when Terry was at work. Nathan had visited her and the kids a handful of times. He'd pop in with sweets for the kids, and often gave some money too before he left. He had been the one to give her their dad's address, and he had kept her up to date with all the family news. Kelly might have been the eldest of all her siblings, but Nathan, just two years younger than her, was by far the most level-headed and sensible.

He was the total opposite of their younger brother Christopher, who had flung his weight about as though he was untouchable, even as a child. When Evie had come along and taken his place as the baby of the family, Christopher had become a right terror. He would gain attention any way he could, and even now as an adult, he was still at it. Old habits die hard and all that, she guessed.

'So, how are my grandbabies?' Harry couldn't hide the emotion in his voice as he asked after his grandchildren. It broke his heart that he'd yet to meet them both. He prayed that now Kelly was here, offering an olive branch, maybe that would finally change.

'God, they're far from babies now, Dad. Billy's almost seven going on seventy and Miley is six in a couple of weeks.' Cutting her dad off from seeing the kids had been the only thing that Kelly had felt truly guilty about over the years. Like she and Terry had agreed at the time, if Harry couldn't accept Terry as her husband then it was all or nothing. Kelly had chosen her husband. For better or for worse. 'They're good, though, thanks. Bit of a handful at times, but you know kids . . .'

Harry smiled. 'Oh I remember. You lot used to try to run rings around me when you were that age. Wasn't a thing that I begrudged giving any of you back then. Your mother always warned me not to be so lenient on you all, but I never listened. Thought I knew best . . . Probably where I went wrong. Spoilt the lot of you.' Harry sighed. 'No wonder Nathan and Christopher grew up to be such stubborn little bastards.' Harry laughed, speaking fondly of his boys. It went unsaid that Kelly was in fact more stubborn than both her brothers put together. 'You wait until yours fly the nest, it's a shock to the system, I'll tell ya. Evie's back from boarding school next week, and I tell you what, I can't wait to have her home. The boys are always out and about, so most of the time I'm left rattling round this big old place on my own.'

Harry was pleased that Kelly had turned up here like she had today, but he also knew that the girl wasn't just here to make small talk. If she wasn't going to get to the point then he would. 'So, what is this visit really all about, Kelly?' Harry asked as he topped up his daughter's glass. 'Don't get me wrong, it's lovely to see you. Just, why now?'

'Everything is fine, Dad, I just thought it was about time.' Embarrassed, Kelly could tell by the way her father was looking at her that he could see right through her, just like he had always been able to.

Harry had always been able to read his children like books. Sometimes, growing up, it had felt like their dad had known them better than they had known themselves.

'Really?' Harry looked at Terry now. The pair of them coming here out of the blue after all this time . . . Something was definitely up.

Suddenly tears of humiliation stung her eyes. Kelly felt foolish now. All these years she'd acted the 'big I am' and now here she was, back home with her tail between her legs.

'Actually, Dad, everything's far from fine.' Kelly choked, suddenly unable to hold back her tears. Surprising even herself, she broke down sobbing. 'We're in the shit, Dad. Terry got mugged last night and the money that they took, we were counting on it. We owe it to some people, you see . . .' Kelly trailed off. She'd said it now. Placed her cards on the table for all to see.

She needed money.

Terry stared at Kelly, mortified as she blurted out her sob story. The earlier speech she had given him before they had left the house about not acting desperate had been clearly forgotten. Terry felt like a right dip-shit, standing here while his wife laid it on thickly.

'So . . . what? You thought after seven years of not seeing me, of keeping my grandchildren from me, that you could just waltz in here and ask for a hand-out?' Harry asked as he sat back down on his bar stool, stung. He was beyond angry, but worse than that he was hurt. No matter how calm he tried to remain, he couldn't hide the genuine pain in his eyes.

Kelly was a piece of work.

'This ain't the "Bank of Harry," you know,' Raymond spoke up, unable to help himself; he was gobsmacked at the cheek of the girl.

He knew it.

The second she had skulked in here, with Terry trailing behind her, he had known that she was on the ponce.

Not five minutes ago, Harry had held his arms open to welcome his daughter back, and now his friend sat there looking like he'd had the wind knocked out of him. He'd clearly believed that Kelly had come to make peace with him because she missed him. Like the girl had had some sort of an epiphany and suddenly wanted to make things right between them both.

She had just wanted the money. Of course. The girl had always been all about the money. Well she could put on the water works as much as she wanted, Harry wouldn't fall for that crap.

Glaring at Terry, Harry frowned as he shook his head.

'I thought you were working?' Harry himself had worked his way right to the top with his bare hands. So men like Terry, he just couldn't comprehend. How he could just stand here and let Kelly beg like this, Harry couldn't fathom. It was a fucking insult. Terry should be providing for the girl. He was her husband.

'I am working, I'm down at the refuse depot still. But you know how it is, we have more money going out than we have coming in . . .'

Raymond rolled his eyes at the man's blatant audacity. Terry had a fucking nerve. Terry was a bin man as and when, for a bit of cash in hand on the side of his benefits. Yet for some reason the bloke frittered money away like he had his very own money tree growing in his back garden, and then had the cheek to turn up here and let his wife beg for a hand-out.

'Who do you owe money to?' Harry asked now as he fought to keep his temper.

'The O'Sheas. Some firm over in Lambeth. Two brothers,' Terry said. 'I only borrowed a few grand here and there, to help us get by, but they keep adding interest and late payment fees . . .' Terry's voice dwindled off. He could barely look Harry in the eye.

'How much?' Turning back to his daughter, Harry couldn't look at Terry for another second. The bloke was a fucking joker.

'Twenty grand,' Kelly said without missing a beat. The money that they owed the O'Sheas was half that, but seeing as there was the smallest chance that her dad might just help them out, and seeing as he was clearly good for it looking at this place, Kelly, as always, was in for a penny, in for a pound.

Whistling, Harry nodded his head and stood thinking for a moment.

He knew the O'Sheas. They were a right shady pair. A couple of times they had tried to arrange a meet with Harry so that they could talk business with him. Harry wouldn't even entertain the pair of them. They'd tried to muscle in on Harry's setup in Soho, trying to turn the Turks against Harry by stirring shit up between the two camps. Luckily Harry was too respected in the game for even the Turks to fall for the O'Sheas' botched attempt at causing a turf war. Harry had made no secret of the fact that he didn't want the O'Sheas anywhere near him or his growing empire. The O'Sheas worked the South East, and as far as Harry was concerned, grotty Southwark suited the pair of them to a tee. The men were wasters, ponces, and Harry's intuition had proven once again to be spot on, merely reinforcing his belief about only working with people he trusted explicitly. His boys and Raymond were his right-hand men. It didn't surprise Harry one bit that Terry would get caught up with that calibre of people. He was on the same level. And by the sounds of it, he was dragging his daughter down there with him.

'Shall I have a word with them?' Harry knew that with just one word of warning from either him or Raymond, the O'Sheas would quickly crawl back under whatever rock they'd just come from and that would be the end of that.

They were small fish, in a very big pond.

Terry shook his head. 'No, we want to sort out our own mess. We don't want any more trouble from them and we don't want a hand-out from you either, Harry,' Terry finally spoke up. 'All we're asking for is just a bit of help. Me and Kelly, well, we've been talking and we thought that maybe you could help us out. Let me work it off for you. I'm happy to do anything at all: DIY, gardening. Anything you need doing . . . I'll be good for it,' Terry added, desperately regretting coming here now as he watched Harry's eyes twitch with irritation. Then he played the trump card, going along with what Kelly had told him to say. 'And well, we are family and all that . . .'

'I've heard it all now.' Raymond laughed. Terry Stranks really did like a gamble and the way he was going Raymond was surprised that Harry hadn't knocked him on his arse and used his flabby body to clean the floors as he turfed the man out. 'That was a fucking good one.'

'Oh, do you know what? We'll just leave. I'm sorry we even asked now.' Kelly got up and slammed her glass down on the table. 'Come on, Terry. This was a mistake. Let's go.' The way that Raymond was sitting there looking down his nose at them was getting right on her nerves. Terry was really trying. They really needed some help. Raymond looked like he was loving every second of this.

'Hang on,' Harry said as he too stood up. Clenching his fists tightly at his sides, Harry could feel how tense his shoulders were. He hated Terry with a passion. They were almost the same age for fuck's sake. The bloke had hooked up with his daughter when she had been only seventeen years old. She had been just a child in Harry's eyes. To him, Terry was near on a paedophile.

His dislike of Terry all those years ago had overshadowed everything. Harry had demanded that Kelly end the relationship. When she had refused to, he'd come down hard on her. He knew that now, but at the time he'd been like a man possessed. She was his daughter, his baby, he was trying to protect her. Harry had learnt the hard way in the end that he'd gone too far. Despite his threats and his ultimatums, Kelly had chosen Terry over her own family. Terry had won.

Now that she had finally turned up at his door once more, there was no way Harry would give his daughter any reason to cut him out of her life again. If there was even the slightest chance of sorting things out with Kelly and finally seeing his grandkids, Harry was going to do everything in his power to take it. If that meant he'd have to suffer Terry, then suffer the man he would. This had gone on for far too long.

'Course I'll bleeding help you, Kel. I ain't going to see my girl struggle, am I? I just thought that you'd come here to see me. To sort things out . . .' Harry trailed off. It saddened him that she was only here for the money. That she hadn't realised the error of her ways and just wanted to see her old man.

'I do, Dad. I guess the money is the excuse I needed to give me the courage. I really have missed you, Dad, and I really need your help. We ain't asking for a freebie. We want to pay back what we owe. Then get ourselves straight, Dad. Do things properly . . .'

'Okay,' Harry said, ignoring the glare that Raymond had just shot him. Then thinking for a few seconds he added, 'The twenty k, it's yours. And do you know what, Terry, there might just be something that you can help me out with . . .'

Pausing, Kelly and Terry stared at Harry, unsure of where the conversation was going. He'd already said they could have the money, and by the sounds of it he was also offering Terry an in.

'That job we were just talking about earlier, Raymond. We could use an extra body, couldn't we?'

'Hang about . . .' Raymond started to object, but he was silenced by Harry's raised palm. They might be one man down for the job, but Terry was a fucking joker and Harry must be mental to even consider letting the bloke get involved, family or not. Christopher may be a loose cannon, but Terry was an outright liability.

Harry must be going soft in the head.

'Whatever it is, I'm your man, Harry,' Terry immediately butted in, hoping that Ray wouldn't talk Harry out of his decision. As much as Flash Harry irked him, he was clearly doing well for himself, and Terry fancied a slice of the pie. If Harry was going to let him on board, then Terry was going to grab the opportunity with both hands.

'Right then, that's settled. Take a seat and let's talk business,' Harry offered.

'You really mean it, Dad?' Feeling giddy with champagne and excitement, Kelly smiled at her father like he was made from twenty-four carat gold.

If her dad was offering Terry an in, then who knew where it would lead? Her father might keep him on and give him more regular work. They'd all be laughing then. No more value range supermarket shops, no more hand-me-down clothing for the kids, and no more hiding behind the frigging sofa from the likes of the bloody O'Sheas.

'Course I mean it, silly. Now come here . . .' Harry hugged his daughter close to him once more, kissing her forehead. 'And you. Don't you ever go leaving your old man out in the cold again. Do you hear me? I've bloody missed you, Kelly.'

Kelly's voice was small when she finally spoke. 'I'm sorry, Dad. It's just everything that happened—'

'Sshh.' Keeping his own counsel on his daughter's relationship Harry squeezed Kelly tight. 'It's all water under the bridge now. You are home and as far as I'm concerned that's all that matters.'

Hugging her dad back, Kelly had forgotten how good it felt to feel her father's arms around her. Glancing around her father's extravagant games room, Kelly wished she'd come home years ago.

Things were going to change for her now, big time.

Grinning at her husband, Kelly felt happier than she had done in years.

Her dad was right. After all these years, Kelly was finally home.

Chapter Ten

Taking the huge bouquet of flowers from her boyfriend, Cassie Wright smiled. 'Ahh, thank you, babe. They are gorgeous.'

'Only the best for my girl.' Nathan Woods winked, before sniffing the air. 'So, what culinary delights do we have in store for us tonight?' Nathan grinned, as Cassie rolled her eyes.

He was winding her up. The first time she'd made him dinner, they'd been so engrossed in each other that neither of them had noticed the black smoke billowing out from the kitchen until it had been too late. Sending the alarm beeping loudly, the shepherd's pie Cassie had made had been cremated, and Nathan had never let her live it down. She'd been trying her hardest since then to improve her cooking skills, and despite a couple of bouts of dodgy guts here and there, she was slowly but surely getting better.

'Actually, Cass, whatever it is smells quite edible for a change . . .'

'Hey!' Cassie laughed. 'If you must know, I've made you your favourite.' Cassie grinned again as Nathan kicked off his shoes and made himself at home. 'Beef bourguignon, and I did it in the slow cooker this time, so it's almost impossible to burn. Though you are a bit late, so if it is mullered it will be your fault, not mine.'

Nathan laughed then. Cassie was a tonic. He'd turned up almost an hour late as it happened and unlike other birds who'd have thought nothing about giving him an ear-bashing for his slap-dash timekeeping Cassie hadn't so much as batted an eyelash. But then, he figured Cassie wasn't like other birds. With a busy career herself as a senior nurse, she understood that Nathan was busy with work commitments of his own. She just let him come and go as he pleased. Their relationship was easy, natural. Neither of them made any demands of each other, or held any expectations.

It was a first for Nathan, meeting a girl who was so at ease with herself, and he couldn't seem to get enough of the girl. She was almost perfect. Almost. She did have one massive flaw, as Nathan was quickly finding out: the girl couldn't cook for shit.

'Don't worry, Cass, I took the liberty of organising a couple of fire engines to be on standby this time.' Nathan laughed as he poked his head out of the open balcony doors and shouted down to the imaginary fire crew. 'It's all right, lads, she's made it in the slow cooker. The coast is clear.'

'Ha ha! Very funny. Pour yourself a drink, and I'll go and put these in a vase, and then see if I can salvage the dinner.'

Opening the bottle of wine he'd bought, Nathan poured Cassie a glass, and then poured himself one too. He didn't normally drink Sauvignon – he was more of a Jack and Coke drinker – but it was Cassie's favourite tipple, and tonight he fancied making an exception and joining her. Placing her glass down next to the neatly folded napkins, and the cutlery that had been laid out just-so on the small black table, he couldn't help but smile. As always Cassie had everything looking just perfect.

The flat was pokey, but somehow Cassie, as with everything, just made the best of it. She liked the place, said the perks of living in staff accommodation meant not only did she get the rent discounted but she was also just a stone's throw away from the hospital, directly across the road in fact.

Stepping out onto the balcony, Nathan sipped his drink as he took in the view of Great Ormond Street Hospital opposite. With her career as a nurse, Cassie really did come from a totally different background to him, but somehow they worked.

He remembered the first night she had told him that money meant nothing to her. How they had both been lying in bed together and Nathan, disbelieving her, had laughed at such a notion.

Money was a way of life to him. It was every bit as essential as the air he breathed. Up until meeting Cassie, Nathan had never met a woman who didn't lap up the lavish gifts, the extravagant nights out. The money, the status, it was a major part of his appeal. Or so he had thought.

Cassie had been adamant and had spoken with such conviction about her job, that he knew she was speaking the truth.

'Trust me, Nathan, if you saw what those families go through, what those poor kids go through day after day . . . It's soul destroying. I honestly couldn't give a rat's arse about money. As long as I have my health then as far as I'm concerned I'm a very rich woman.'

Nathan hadn't believed her at first. He'd been spun that line before.

'You do know who my family is, don't you?' Nathan had laughed, as he hugged her tightly, softening the mood.

The Woods were notorious in London, and Nathan had made no secret of who he was when he'd met Cassie. He was the son of the famous Harry Woods. Ex-champion boxer and a local celebrity. And – on the side – a man who didn't let the law stop him earning. Nathan and Christopher had naturally followed in their father's footsteps, although Nathan had never really felt that a life in crime was his calling. He'd just gone along with it all, like it was expected of him. Now he'd met Cassie, something about her made him want to do better for himself, and for her.

'So what?' Cassie had shrugged as she had lain snuggled in his arms, her naked body pressed against his. 'I'm not interested in your family, or your surname, nor what's in your wallet. It's you I love, Nathan. You as a person. If you turned up here tomorrow completely skint and wearing only a bin bag, nothing would change that.' Cassie had meant every word.

'So?' Nathan had laughed too, as he pulled her naked body back on top of him. 'What you are saying is . . . you're only using me for my gorgeous, toned, Adonis-like body then, are you?'

'Too bloody right.' Kissing him on the neck, Cassie had disappeared down under the covers to show him exactly how much she appreciated him.

Hearing an ambulance whizz past brought him back to reality, its blues and twos blaring loudly down on the main road. Nathan smiled at the memory. He took another sip of his wine before lighting up a cigarette.

He finally understood what she was saying. Cassie was right: money couldn't put a price on what they had.

Shaking his head, he laughed as he listened to Cassie singing off key to herself in the kitchen as she dished up, feeling a million miles away from the usual world he inhabited. It felt good. It felt like he was truly at home here. He was turning into a soppy sod, but he liked it.

'Right, grub's up so take a seat. I hope this is okay. I haven't got any red wine in, so the sauce might be a bit bland . . .' Cassie apologised as she placed Nathan's plate down on the table, and then sat down opposite.

Nathan stood in the doorway watching as Cassie sat down and immediately took a bite of her food.

'What? I'm starving. Why are you just standing there gawping at me?' Cassie laughed, placing her hand over her mouth politely as she spoke.

Nathan walked towards the table. 'Come here.' Nathan held Cassie's hand. Pulling her up out of the chair, he held her to him. 'You are gorgeous, do you know that? I wish I didn't have to shoot off later. If it weren't for Dad having this job on tonight, you know you wouldn't be able to get rid of me, don't you?'

Nodding, Cassie grinned.

Inhaling her familiar scent as he held Cassie close to him, they kissed passionately.

Feeling Cassie pressed against him, her mouth over his, Nathan's appetite for food had suddenly disappeared. Scooping Cassie up into his arms, Nathan threw her over his shoulder.

'Hey, what about the dinner?' She laughed as Nathan made his way towards her bedroom.

'No offence to your cooking, babe, but if it's a choice between you and that . . .' He nodded over to the plate of watery looking food, slopped in the middle of the plate on the table behind them. 'Then it really is no contest. The only thing I want to devour tonight is you,' Nathan said as he threw her down on the bed and playfully started to undress.

Throwing her head back, Cassie laughed.

Nathan Woods was making a habit of sweeping her off her feet and Cassie was loving every minute.

Chapter Eleven

'Ahh come on, Keith, how about one more for the road? What do you say?' the man slurred, unsteadily holding out his empty glass in the hope that he could persuade the landlord for just one last refill.

'No, sorry, no lock-in tonight, lads. I'm knackered; I need my bed. And I'm sure you both have homes to go to? Won't your old ladies be waiting up for you back home?' Taking the glass from the man, Keith Ryan ushered the last two staggering punters out of the pub's main doors.

'It's the thought of our old ladies waiting up for us that makes us want to bleeding well stay here,' the second man muttered bitterly.

'Ah go on, get home. They must be angels putting up with the pair of you . . .' Shivering as the cold night air swept in, Keith just wanted the men to piss off so he could lock up for the night.

'You might need to get that looked at.' The first man indicated the cut on Keith's forehead, tripping down the front step as he spoke, grabbing at his friend's arm to steady himself. 'You're lucky that scumbag didn't take your eye out. You don't think he'll come back, do you?'

'No, he'll be long gone. Don't you be worrying about me, this is just a scratch. It's all part of the territory.' Keith shrugged. 'I'll see you in the week, lads.'

Finally closing the main door of the pub, Keith bolted it and leant back against the oak frame, breathing a sigh of relief that the night was finally over and the pub was empty. After the shitty week he'd had, his only thought tonight was crawling into bed. His head was throbbing but he wasn't going to let on to the punters that he was in pain, and besides, it was probably nothing a few paracetamol and a couple of temazepam wouldn't sort out.

Irritated by the jukebox that was still playing in the background, Keith walked over and yanked the plug from the wall, forgetting for a second about his hand. Until a sharp jolt of pain shot down his fingers, throbbing at his quick movement. Cursing as he spotted fresh blood seeping through the bandage that he'd hastily applied earlier, Keith had a feeling he'd probably need stitches. The gash didn't seem to be healing too well, and pressing the material firmly against his skin to stem the bleeding, he decided he'd just have to make do. There was no way he was going down to A&E at this time on a Saturday night; the place would be full of the likes that frequented this place, drunkards who'd had a skinful cluttering up the walk-in centre with their self-inflicted injuries as if they had nowhere better to be. If his hand was still giving him grief in the morning when the girls arrived for their shift he'd go then.

The cut was deep, he knew that because the shard of glass he'd pulled out of it earlier had been so imbedded he'd practically had to dig it out.

Still, it was only a cut, it wasn't going to kill him. Keith Ryan considered himself lucky that he'd walked away with just a slice to his hand and a banging head. Considering that he'd had a glass whacked in his face.

Technically, he hadn't come off too badly. The irate druggie that attacked him had been so fucking high, he barely knew what he was saying, and if Keith hadn't been so quick to protect himself by putting his hand up in self-defence, the attack could have been a whole lot worse.

Checking his reflection in the mirror behind the bar, Keith wiped the crusty trail of blood that had trickled down his forehead. He noted the bags that hung loosely under his eyes. Running his fingers through the dark shadow of stubble that lined his jaw, even without the gash on his head he looked a mess. In just this past week he felt like he had aged an entire decade. All he had tried to do was be a good landlord and keep his pub in order, and this is what he'd got in return for his efforts.

Punters around here took the right piss, coming in on a daily basis to use his toilets, most of them snorting more lines of coke than you'd find on the average barcode. The Railway used to be a lovely pub, but lately it was getting such a bad reputation that even the locals had started calling the place 'The Main Line' because of the amount of gear that was knocking about. And now he not only had the cokeheads sniffing about the place, but the Old Bill were keeping tabs on the place too. So tonight Keith had decided that enough was enough. Taking matters into his own hands, before he ended up getting his licence revoked, he'd spent the best part of the evening barring anyone who even so much as looked suspicious, and on top of that he'd also taken to using the old landlord trick of coating every surface in the public toilets in a thick layer of WD-40.

He'd hoped that once the skanky dregs saw their lines of gear literally disintegrating before their very eyes they'd take the hint, and fuck off elsewhere.

Of course, there would always be some nutcase who would kick off, and tonight Keith had suffered the wrath of one of the disgruntled users.

Blaming Keith for his loss of a high he'd forked out on, the bloke had gone loopy. After a violent scuffle, and some help from a couple of the locals, Keith had managed to finally turf the bloke out. But not before the bloke had tried to wrap a pint glass around his head in the process.

Feeling the alcohol-sodden carpet sticking to his shoes as he half-heartedly traipsed around the tables collecting empty glasses, Keith gritted his teeth. This place had gone to the dogs, he thought, grimly, as he slung the glasses onto the bar next to the glass washer. Leaving them for the girls to sort out in the morning, Keith couldn't be arsed to do any more tonight.

Opening the till, Keith counted the small pile of notes and loose change. The takings were so low that he wondered if it had even been worth opening up at all this evening. Bang in the heart of London's gay community, The Railway pub didn't even try to compete with the vast array of flamboyant, fancy gay bars that neighboured this end of Soho. With real local ales, and a homely atmosphere, The Railway was just a traditional working man's pub, and Keith had been banking on its simplistic appeal for the place to have any success. He had thought that it would be a welcomed change from the theme nights and cabaret shows that were offered by his competition. The place was proving to be a gamble that wasn't paying off.

His pub was run of the mill, and in a street full of competition, the realisation that it just wasn't working was finally starting to hit home.

Hearing a bang from down in the cellar, Keith swore under his breath.

Those bloody rats.

Grabbing the bag of traps that he'd meant to put out earlier, he was suddenly very much in the mood to go and sort out the vermin that had infested his cellar, once and for all. The basement was overrun with the buggers, and bloody enormous they were too. He'd seen one run behind the barrels that morning, almost the size of a cat it was. There was no way that he was going to let the disease-ridden bastards loose to do any more damage, not after one of the little bastards had already somehow managed to chew through one of the pipes down there, flooding the whole cellar as a result. If he hadn't been so hard up, he'd have paid pest control to come in and sort it out for him; as it was, like everything else, he was going to have to sort it out himself.

Switching the main bar lights off, Keith made his way to the basement door, unsure of how much more he could take.

This week had been a fucking nightmare. Not only had the pub been targeted by vandals, leaving Keith to fork out money that he didn't have to replace the two windows they'd smashed, but some fucker had nicked the two patio heaters he'd invested in for the smoking areas out the front. Then finally, to add insult to injury, a gang of kids had used the front of his pub as a canvas for tagging their graffiti all over.

This place was haemorrhaging money left, right and centre. He already owed the Woods brothers almost a hundred grand for taking out the two hefty loans with them. He could barely pay it back – he'd been late with the past two payments, which had financially crippled him, so there was no way he could borrow any more.

He just needed to keep his head above water but it was proving easier said than done. Lately it felt like no matter what he did, he was barely treading water let alone staying afloat.

Opening the door, he made his way down the creaking steps.

The damp smell of mould wafted up his nose. Shivering in the dark as he heard tiny feet scurrying around him Keith hit the light switch. His skin was crawling at just the thought of the flea infested vermin hiding behind the beer kegs, with their evil beady eyes peeping out, watching his every move.

Deciding to get on with the task of eliminating the rodents, he placed the traps down in the corners of the room.

Hearing a loud creak, he jumped. He'd caught a movement out of the corner of his eye.

The black shadow was too big to be any sort of rodent.

With a look of dread on his face, Keith turned around as the realisation hit him. He wasn't alone. 'What the fuck?'

Stepping out of the shadows, Christopher Woods loomed a good foot taller than Keith. His smirk was full of malice and his mocking tone matched it. 'Now, now, Keithy-boy. That ain't no way to greet a guest, is it?'

Keith looked to the stairs, trying to work out if he could make a run for it.

Christopher was already one step ahead. Pulling out the knife, he held it up. Challenging Keith, daring him to give him a reason to use his weapon.

'Not having the best of weeks, are you, mate? Burgled, flooded and now an infestation . . . What are the chances?' Christopher smiled, kicking the box that was down by his feet so that it tipped up. Releasing more scurrying rats into the room.

Keith gulped as he realised how much of a coincidence his run of bad luck had been. He felt suddenly very foolish. He should have known that the Woods brothers wouldn't just walk away so calmly from a blatant rejection. It all made sense now. The only bad luck Keith had really had was the day he had been brainless enough to get involved with these boys.

'You had any moments to reflect on my brother's offer?' Christopher narrowed his eyes, grabbing the wooden chair at the edge of the room and dragging it between them. Then pointing the knife in Keith's direction, Christopher indicated at the man to sit.

Keith shook his head, confused.

Since Nathan and Christopher had paid him a visit last week, their offer had been all that he'd thought about. Though 'offer' was perhaps not the best choice of words. They wanted this place in return for the debt to be cleared. Keith would have to walk away with nothing. As desperate as he was, he just couldn't do it. He'd put everything he had into this place.

Gulping as he watched Christopher step closer, staring through him with an evil glint in his eye, Keith prayed that Nathan Woods was lurking about somewhere nearby. Out of the brothers, Nathan was without a doubt the more reasonable of the two. At least if he was here too, Keith might stand some kind of chance of walking out of here unharmed tonight.

'Grab a pew, Keith. I've got a feeling we're in for a long night. Nathan made you a good offer too. Personally you must be some kind of a thick cunt to even think about turning him down.' Christopher reached inside his long leather coat, pulling out the rope he'd concealed. 'Two loans you've taken out. Not once have you made the repayments on time. So it makes sense really, don't it? You give us this place and we'll scrub your debt.'

Keith's eyes were wide with fear as Christopher tied him to the chair. Petrified, Keith didn't struggle. He didn't want to antagonise the man any further. Instead he silently prayed that Christopher was just trying to put the frighteners on him.

His debt was a hundred thousand pounds with interest, but the pub was worth five times that. He knew it and so did they.

But they were persistent.

'I said I'd make the payments and I will . . .' Keith was so scared that his voice quivered when he spoke.

Christopher laughed at the man. He was scared shitless and so he should be. 'Well, you know, dribs and drabs ain't how we work, Keithy-boy. And we're a bit bored of waiting for you to get your act together. My brother has his sights set on this place, and what Nathan wants, he gets, do you understand?'

Christopher yanked the bandage from Keith's hand, purposely disturbing the cut. Then placing the sharp point of the knife against the cut on Keith's forehead, Christopher scored the blade down the man's cheek. Opening up his face as Keith screamed in agony.

'Right fucking nasty gash that is. Dripping claret all over the floor, you are . . .' Christopher reached into his pocket and pulled out a roll of thick black gaffer tape; the last thing he wanted to do was have to listen to the man's pitiful screams all night long.

'Please, you don't have to do this. It's yours, take it . . .' Keith cried before Christopher wrapped the tape tightly around his head, covering his mouth.

The pub had fast become a noose hanging around his neck. And now, tied up in the basement with this psychopath, Keith was certain that no business was worth this amount of grief. It was just bricks and mortar; if the Woods brothers wanted it so badly, he'd let them have it.

'I'd love to believe you, Keith, really I would. But your sudden decision sounds a bit hasty to me. So I'll tell you what. You sit here and have a proper think about it yeah? I'll go up to the bar to have a few drinks. Bit parched I am, you see. You don't mind if I help myself to your rum, do you? At least you won't be lonely down here while I'm gone, you'll have some company.'

Keith shuddered as he saw the evil glint in Christopher's eyes, as he bent down and tugged at the rope, checking it was tightly secured.

'Misunderstood little bastards rats are. Naturally shy creatures they are 'en all, more scared of you than you are of them. But I'm not so sure. See, I've seen what these little fuckers are capable of when they're hungry,' Christopher sneered. 'You lock these little fuckers away in a box for a couple of weeks and they get so fucking hungry that they start eating each other. How fucked up is that?' Turning the lights off, Christopher slammed the cellar door behind him.

Whimpering all alone in the darkness, Keith could feel the scuttling rodents sniffing around his feet. Only a few at first. Then more and more surrounded him. Terrified, he tried to kick his legs out as he felt one crawl onto his shoe, but he had been tied so tightly he could barely move.

Persistent, the rats continued to climb up his body. Keith could feel the creatures' sharp, wiry nails digging into his skin as they began scampering up inside his jeans, scratching and clawing at his legs.

Writhing around in a bid to shake the rodents off him, Keith tried to scream, but the thick tape that masked his mouth muffled his cries. Jolting backwards, his panicked movements caused the chair to wobble, and then topple. Impacting with the cellar floor, his jawbone crunched as it whacked against the cold concrete.

Feeling the warm trickle of piss escaping down his leg, as the rats prevailed over him, Keith blacked out.

Chapter Twelve

Accelerating the motorbike at lightning speed, Raymond's adrenaline was pumping as he sped down the Essex dual carriageway. Even the roar of the bike's engine couldn't muffle his thundering heartbeat. Going full throttle, the bike soared despite battling against the bad weather. Pushing through heavy sheets of rain, Raymond was adamant that the downpour was not going to hinder their getaway.

Glancing around to check that his two accomplices were still there, Ray saw that Nathan was steaming up directly behind him, hot on his trail.

Unfortunately the same couldn't be said for Terry Stranks.

He was lagging much farther behind, and was closely followed by the persistent flashing blue lights that were tailing them.

Raymond gritted his teeth, hoping to God that Harry knew what he was doing letting this muppet on board.

Cursing again loudly Ray turned his attention back to the road in front of him, just in time to see the large puddle covering his lane. Skidding, the bike swerved dramatically as it aquaplaned across the lay-by. Ray tightened his grip and fought to gain some control. The second that he felt the bike's tyres hit some traction, he expertly pulled himself and the bike back up level and managed to somehow steer himself back over to the other side of the road.

Seeing the roundabout up ahead, he signalled with his arm so that Nathan would know to follow.

They needed to get off the main roads, and lose the police as quickly as possible.

———

The two police cars roared behind Terry. He could hear them screeching up behind him, just a few feet away from the back of his bike. Raymond and Nathan were both up ahead in the distance, but he knew there was no way he was going to catch up with them now. As thick black smoke billowed out from the back of the bike, Terry was scared to go any faster. It rode like a sack of shit, and with the lashing rain impeding his view he was already zigzagging all over the place.

Terry was fast losing hope of being capable of outrunning his own shadow let alone the police cars that were quickly gaining on him.

It was supposed to have been an in and out job. Raymond had assured them that it would be a piece of piss. The warehouses down on the docks were manned by two security men, and all they had to do was pick up the shipment that had just come in. It all seemed legit.

Harry had a massive warehouse at the back of his house filled to the rafters with all sorts of foreign merchandise that he'd had shipped in – Woods Enterprises, he called his little empire. It was obviously making him a shit load of money.

Terry was only too happy to help; all he had to do was help Raymond and Nathan deliver the goods. Talk about easy money, twenty grand just to courier a couple of parcels.

Terry should have known that it would never be that cut and dried, and thinking about it now, with the police hot on their tails, he didn't actually have a clue what was inside the packages, nor had he given a shit until now. That had been a mistake.

Harry had been so vague when he'd arranged everything, and though he'd mentioned exported goods, he hadn't once even hinted about what they were picking up.

Three men on bikes, riding around Essex in the middle of the night. How had he been so stupid? Of course the whole operation had been suspect. Everything was so hush-hush, and Terry had a sneaky feeling now that whatever it was they had stowed away in their bikes, it was far from kosher.

He'd even let Raymond's words of wisdom go straight over his head when he'd warned Terry not to stop for anything. Even if the police gave chase, he said, you put your foot down and keep going. Don't stop for nothing.

Terry had been so keen to comply, he'd just nodded like a prat at whatever they said. Seeing Nathan's tail lights up ahead in the distance, just as they went out of view as the bike turned off at the roundabout, Terry cursed loudly.

He'd fucked up. He should have never got involved in this.

The police were gaining on him, and if they caught up with him the proverbial shit would well and truly hit the fan. Terry knew the brief. He was lagging behind and now he needed to split off from the rest of them.

He felt a trickle of sweat running down his forehead under his helmet. He'd have to take a different route, to try to throw the police off track so they'd at least lose Raymond and Nathan.

Moving over towards the left-hand side of the road, Terry veered to the left of the roundabout to make it look like he was following the two other motorbikes.

The police car behind him was so close now that it almost skimmed his back tyre. The fuckers were trying to box him in.

Wobbling now, as he leaned into the curve of the roundabout, Terry swerved unsteadily, dodging in between the two cars. Tipping the bike hard, he bolted to a sharp right in a bid to lose them.

The transit van came out of nowhere, the full beam blinding him.

Before Terry even had time to register where the light had come from it was too late.

Pulling its brakes, the van skidded on the wet road surface. Terry heard the screech of metal on metal just seconds before he felt the force of the impact. The van hit him head on, sending his bike in an upwards spiral into the air, his weightless body following closely behind like a floppy rag doll.

Landing heavily with a thud, Terry felt the wet ground around him soaking him up. His body screamed in pain. Everything ached. As he gulped in bursts of air, he tried to control his breathing. He was badly winded and a sharp pain ripped through his chest.

He heard the police cars screech up next to him seconds later, and the officers leapt from their vehicles. Terry tried to move, but it was impossible. There was no escaping them now.

'Stay down,' the officer ordered as he neared Terry's limp body, before checking that he was okay and more importantly unarmed. 'What's your name?'

'Terry, Terry Stranks.' Moaning in pain, Terry couldn't do anything but stay down. He felt battered. Lying there silently as the police called in an ambulance, Terry closed his eyes.

Harry had warned him of the worst case scenario, and this was it.

Staring up at the dark night sky, he gazed at the stars twinkling above him as if they would somehow give him his 'get out of jail free card'. He knew that no matter what happened now, he'd have to keep his mouth shut. Harry's name was to be kept out of it no matter what.

Fuck!

Hearing the emergency sirens blaring as the paramedics grew closer, the officer's stern tone of voice broke Terry's thoughts. 'Terry Stranks, we're taking you into hospital under police custody,' the officer instructed as he peered down at Terry with clear scrutiny, as the paramedics arrived on the scene.

'It's all right, you're going to be okay,' the young paramedic reassured him, as she and her colleague carefully checked Terry over before hoisting him up onto the stretcher.

'I'm far from fucking okay,' Terry grunted, in no mood for niceties, his mind whirling from trying to figure out what he was going to do.

'Judging from the state of your bike over there, you are one very lucky man,' the paramedic said with a smile as they wheeled the spinal board over to the ambulance.

'Guv. We found this on his bike. Must be three kilos of cocaine in there at least.'

Terry closed his eyes as he listened to the two police officers.

Cocaine?

No wonder Harry had been cagey about telling him what they were picking up.

He had three kilos of the stuff on him? He was royally screwed now.

Grimacing in pain as the orthopaedic stretcher was pushed up the ramp and into the back of the ambulance, Terry couldn't agree with the paramedic.

Tonight had been a total fuck-up.

He was alive, yes.

Lucky? Terry Stranks?

Not a fucking chance.

Chapter Thirteen

'How did it go?' Walking into the dining room and seeing three of his four children sitting together around the table as they ate their breakfast, Harry would have normally been full of beans, classing the occasion as a rare treat. But this morning the only beans he needed to be full of were coffee beans and plenty of them. He was knackered. He'd hardly slept all night, worrying about the three of them. Between the fire at Evie's school yesterday, and the job he had sent the lads out on last night, Harry was frazzled. He needed to snap out of it, though. Tonight was an important night. He was hosting a massive boxing event over in Hackney, and Christopher was all set for the main attraction. It was true what they said: it never rained, but it poured. Harry felt rushed off his feet.

'It went okay, I guess.' Nathan shrugged. He'd managed to get in about 3 a.m. and there had been no sign of Terry. Raymond had told him to go home and get some kip. Terry was probably just lagging behind. Nathan wasn't sure, though. Still, he knew not to discuss anything around the breakfast table, especially in front of Evie. 'Uncle Raymond said he'd fill you in. Said he'd be here for breakfast, so he's probably on his way.'

'Good.' Harry sighed. 'How about you, darling, did you sleep alright?' Harry looked at Evie, sat between her brothers, like a rose between two thorns. Unlike him with his bags and dark circles under his eyes, there wasn't a trace of Evie lacking any sleep. In fact, sporting a pair of pyjamas, a messy bun and not a scrap of make-up the girl's stunning beauty somehow managed to light up the whole room. She was the image of her mother.

Harry had obviously lain awake last night and done enough fretting for the both of them. He'd thought that Evie would have been petrified after the school catching ablaze like that, but she looked perfectly okay.

He'd been worried sick when he'd got the call from the school yesterday about the fire that had broken out. He'd jumped straight in his car, driven to the school at break-neck speed, but of course, when he'd finally got there Evie had been absolutely fine, just as the headmistress had said. One of the girls had apparently left a cigarette burning in her bedroom, and the whole place had gone up in flames. Luckily, everyone had got out unharmed.

'I always sleep like a baby when I'm home, Dad.' Evie shrugged as she tucked into her plate of scrambled eggs. She really was glad to be home. The smell of the place, her soft cosy bed. Right now it was the only place she wanted to be. Especially after the past few days.

Sitting here now with her family, everything else that had gone on felt surreal. She still couldn't believe that she had done it. Lighting Madeline Porter's cigarettes and throwing them down on the girl's bed, Evie had managed to set the whole school on fire. She could only hope that Madeline got the comeuppance she deserved for the damage.

Harry smiled. He was pleased that Evie seemed better than yesterday. When he'd picked her up she'd been adamant that she didn't want to go back to the school. Harry had nodded understandingly at the time, putting her words down to the shock and trauma of the fire, and decided to leave the subject for the time being. Evie could probably do with a bit of a break for now anyway. The school would be closed for months due to the extensive damage, so Evie would have no choice but to stay at home with him now, and Harry was secretly pleased. He loved having his Evie at home with him, and with everything that he had going on at the moment, it was perfect timing.

'Ha, slept like a baby . . . tickles me that saying does. Between shitting their nappies every five minutes and waking up crying for a bottle, the little brats don't really get much shut-eye, do they?' Christopher snorted at his sister, before continuing to shovel food greedily into his mouth, unaware that his dad's eyes were now boring into him.

'Oi,' Harry warned, raising his brow. 'Have some manners when you speak to your sister. She means that she slept well, you bloody moron. Contented.' Irritated, Harry could tell that Christopher was in a wind-up mood again today. After everything that Evie had gone through yesterday he didn't want anyone upsetting the poor girl. Especially Christopher. 'And bloody slow down, will you? You're eating like you've never seen food before, no-one's going to nick your bleeding plate,' Harry scolded. 'And should you even be eating that shit before the fight tonight?' Remembering his strict diet and regime before a match, Harry didn't know how Christopher had managed to wing his fights up until now. It was a good job that the boy was a natural fighter, and clearly he had a lot of luck on his side. Because 'discipline' to Christopher would have sounded like a foreign word.

'Don't you worry about me, Dad,' Christopher muttered. 'My body's a machine.' He'd forgotten how tetchy his father got when his precious Evie was home. The way he acted like the kid was fucking royalty or something. Princess Evie, sat on her throne at the head of the table. The only regal thing about her as far as Christopher was concerned was that she was a royal pain in the arse.

'Here, Nathan, guess who rang me last night. Only bloody Keith Ryan. Asked me to pop over, said he'd been mulling over our offer. Said he'd had a change of heart.' Christopher grinned smugly. He'd been dying to tell Nathan the news all morning.

'Really? Great, we can nip over and see him in a bit.' Nathan wiped his mouth with his napkin, surprised that Keith had changed his mind, and even more so that out of the two of them, Keith had decided to contact Christopher. The more he'd thought about it, the more he had decided that if they did take on that pub he'd want to do it on his own. The only person he'd spoken to about it was Cassie, and she agreed with him. Nathan wanted to set up on his own. Do things legitimately. Without his dad or his brother getting involved. But he'd yet to tell Christopher that.

'No need, Nath, I popped over there myself. Strike while the iron's hot and all that. Had a little chat with him over a few rum and cokes, you know? Anyway, the upshot was that he wants rid of the place as soon as possible. Said he wants to go off travelling. Said he'd been mulling over your offer, and you'll never guess what?'

Christopher stared at Nathan now, his eyes wide as he tried to create some suspense. 'What?'

'He only signed over the place to me right there and then. Put both our names on the paperwork, he did. It's great, isn't it? We are officially joint partners.' Christopher smiled. He was so smug that Nathan couldn't help but eye his brother suspiciously.

Keith Ryan had looked shit scared of Christopher the last time they had paid the bloke a visit. From the off it had been Nathan that he had dealt with. Nathan had been the one that had laid the deal on the table, Nathan had been the one to approach with an offer. So why Keith would have called Christopher up out of the blue, Nathan really couldn't fathom. Everyone knew that when it came to doing business with the Woods brothers, Nathan was the more diplomatic of the two.

'Travelling? Where is he going?'

'Well, I weren't really listening to his bloody life plans. Said something about some family stuff, and that he had to leave today. Was it New Zealand he said? Oh, I dunno. Anyway, who gives a shit? The place is ours. I've got the paperwork here, it's all legit.'

Seeing the tension between his sons and betting his life that there was a lot more to it if Christopher had been involved, Harry couldn't help but interrupt. 'Is this the pub you were talking about the other day, The Railway on Wardour Street? That place has been a dive for years. The landlord must have been struggling. Are you sure it's a sound investment, Nath . . . ?' Seeing Nathan's scowl at his words, Harry knew that he was overstepping the mark interfering in the boy's business. But, he couldn't help himself. He had given his boys not only his backing, but also some hefty funds to get them both up and running. Christopher was earning well from his fights, and Harry could tell that Nathan desperately wanted to find his niche too. Nathan was adamant that he wanted to get into property, and Harry respected that.

After the lifestyle that Harry had given his kids, the fact that one of them wanted to make their own way was commendable. Nathan was astute in his thinking, and Harry got where he was coming from. Harry didn't want to piss on the boy's parade, really he didn't. He just wanted him to invest his money wisely. But at the same time, what sort of a father would he be if he just sat back with his trap shut, and let them both invest their money in some shoddy venture that wasn't going to get them a decent return? He also wasn't sure that partnering up with Christopher was the wisest of decisions – the boy had been a nightmare lately. Still, Harry kept his own counsel on that matter. 'The landlord must have bitten your bleeding arm off to get out of there?'

Christopher grinned at his dad's turn of phrase. He couldn't have been more apt if he'd tried. The memory of Keith Ryan's blood-soaked skin, punctured with teeth marks, was still fresh in his mind.

If only his father knew the half of it. The rats had gnawed one of the bloke's fingers down to the bone, and taken a large chunk out of his face too. If Christopher hadn't woken up from his booze fuelled session when he had, the furry little fuckers would have had themselves a real feast.

Finding Keith bitten to shit, and hysterical, Christopher had done the human thing and, using his knife, he'd kindly finished the bloke off. After he'd made him sign all the appropriate paperwork of course.

As much as Christopher would have loved to let the rats maul the man to death, he couldn't be arsed with the mess of it all. The greedy bastards had had more than a nibble, and that was good enough.

Right about now, Russ Hollins, Christopher's trusted mate and number one man for clearing up his mess, was in there doing the clean-up op. Russ was a grimy bastard. Blood, guts, shit, piss – nothing fazed the lad. His job at the crematorium just outside of London was turning out to be a real touch for them both as it happened. Russ was coining it in. By helping renowned gangsters 'get rid of evidence', not only was he making a shit load of wedge, but he was making a fair few contacts amongst real criminal faces.

Russ had stuck Keith's body in the cremation casket of some old boy in the early hours of this morning. Right about now, the unsuspecting family would probably be singing 'Kum Ba Ya', or something equally mind numbing, oblivious to that fact that poor old Keithy-boy was also cooking away nicely inside the incinerator with their loved one.

Christopher had opened the cellar hatch before he had left the pub too, and smoked the place out. The little bastard rats would have shat bits of Keith Ryan all over Soho by now. He had everything covered.

Christopher knew how much his brother wanted that pub and now, after his quick thinking, it was his.

'Ahh, well you see, that's where you're wrong, Dad. Nath thinks it's a great investment, don't you, Nath . . . Said that we're going to make a killing from the place.'

Nathan rolled his eyes as he watched his brother ram a whole sausage into his mouth, slopping ketchup down his chin as he spoke.

'Oh yeah, what's your plan then, son?' Harry asked Nathan, intrigued.

Nathan pushed his plate away. His appetite was gone, what with Christopher sitting opposite him, shovelling food into his mouth like he was some kind of scavenger.

'Have you seen the massive development they've built just up the road from the pub? Over two hundred high-end apartments. Real fancy ones too. Security gated, plush kitchens, private hot tubs. Not your average first-time buyer kind of place. The property developer on the job said that nearly all the units have already been reserved. Do you know who's snapping them up? Single, gay men. Soho's gay scene rakes in the money.'

Harry nodded. Harry should have known that Nathan would have done his homework before he'd made any kind of an offer. The boy was shrewd when it came to business, just like him. Harry knew Soho like the back of his hand; it was his territory. Nathan couldn't go wrong investing in property there. 'So you are going to turn the pub into apartments?'

'No. We are going to totally revamp the place. Completely gut it, and turn it into a swanky little wine bar, cash in on the pink pound.'

'Pink pound?' Christopher stopped eating and gave his brother his full attention. Nathan had said they'd make a killing on the place, but until now he hadn't actually gone into detail about how. 'You mean you want to turn that place into a wine bar for poofters? Are you having a laugh?' This was the first he had heard about a gay bar, and he wouldn't have been so keen to go to so much effort last night if he'd known.

'I knew you'd be like this.' This was exactly why Nathan had wanted to go it alone on this place. His brother was reacting exactly as Nathan had known he would.

'Knew I'd be like what? The Woods brothers running a fucking gay bar? We'll be the fucking laughing stock, mate. People will think we're a right pair of fucking fairies.'

'We won't be running it, Christopher, we'll get someone else to manage it. It's going to be really classy. No theme nights, no gimmicks. Just a swanky upmarket bar. Look at the bigger picture: we're investing in property, we won't be hosting wine soirées . . .'

'Soirées? Fuck me, you're even talking like a faggot now. Are you sure there's not another motive as to why you wanna open a bar just for benders? If you're bored with your Cassie already you can just put yourself on one of those dating sites. Much cheaper and a lot less effort than opening up your own fucking pick-up joint.'

'Oi, rein it in, boys,' Harry ordered, just as a knock on the dining room door stopped him from further berating the boys for talking so crudely in front of Evie. Evie, who had been sitting as quietly as ever, was now staring down into her coffee cup looking uncomfortable, as her brothers argued about their new bar.

Harry had made it a rule never to talk business in front of his youngest daughter. Evie didn't need to know their business dealings, and he'd thank the boys to follow suit by remembering that.

'Sorry to disturb you, Mr. Woods, but Raymond is here . . .' Before Harry's housekeeper could continue, Raymond Marks marched into the room.

'Morning,' Raymond addressed the room. 'You got a minute, Harry?'

'Of course, Raymond.' Harry excused himself from the table. 'Evie babe, we've got some bits to do this morning, but if you fancy it we can shoot over to Westfield later on? We can put a dent in my Coutts card and get you a nice dress or something for tonight?'

Unable to hide her excitement, Evie grinned. 'Tonight? Really, Dad? What, you mean I can come?' Harry could see that Evie was made up that he was letting her come to Christopher's big fight tonight. Normally he'd have no intentions of taking her to a boxing event held in a dingy nightclub, but seeing as she was home from school two days earlier than expected, and after everything she'd been through, he could hardly leave her behind.

'Yes, really, sweetheart. But remember, when it gets nasty you can always leave, okay?'

Then, leading Raymond and Nathan across the hallway to his office, Harry wanted to finally get down to some business. He could tell by Raymond's face that something had happened last night.

Taking a seat in the office, Harry sat back in his chair and stared at Raymond. 'So, did it all go to plan?'

Leaning forward in his chair, Raymond rubbed his chin. 'Terry got a capture.'

Harry sat forward now too. His huge frame mirrored his friend's as he spoke, this time quieter. 'Where is he now?'

'Your man Mansell rang me first thing, gave me the heads up. Terry's been placed under police arrest, and taken to Broomfield Hospital, over in Chelmsford.' Raymond was tense. He and Nathan had made it back from the job in the early hours, and he'd told Nathan to go home. That he'd wait for Terry. He had a sneaky suspicion that Terry had taken a tug, but until he'd got the call from Harry's guy, he hadn't been a hundred percent certain.

Staring at Harry now, Raymond wondered how his friend managed to stay so calm, because unlike him, Raymond had a really bad feeling about all of this.

One word out of Terry's mouth and they were all going to be up shit creek without a paddle. The man had taken a massive gamble by letting Terry do the drop, and Raymond had tried and failed to share his reservations with him.

'He won't talk,' Harry said, as if reading Raymond's mind.

Raymond nodded but he wasn't so sure.

Harry was treading a very dangerous line. Terry knew too much.

'He won't,' Harry said again, this time with conviction. 'He knows he'll be a dead man walking if he does.'

Chapter Fourteen

'The only reason I didn't come down there, babe, is so that you wouldn't say something that would land yourself in even more trouble.' Pulling a handful of toilet roll out from the dispenser on the wall, Kelly had waited all day to hear from her husband, hoping that somehow he would manage to call her. She knew he'd have the hump with her for not going straight down to the hospital to see him, and she wanted to explain. Though typically caught out by Terry's bad timing, her phone had finally rung while she was sitting on the bog in the nightclub's toilets with her knickers around her ankles.

Kelly had already had a heads up on Terry's predicament. Her dad had called her first thing this morning to tell her Terry had been caught. He wanted to put her mind at rest that he would get it all sorted and that she wasn't to worry, but Kelly had been left fuming after she hung up.

One bloody job, and Terry couldn't even do that right. It was like the man was destined to fail. Terry had fucked it up. She should have bloody known.

Her dad had promised her that he would sort it, and Kelly had no doubt in her mind that he would. Her dad was a man of his word after all. He'd told her that it was all in hand, and that she wasn't to worry. So she'd taken her dad's advice and steered clear of visiting Terry. He was right, if she went down there she'd only be giving Terry the opportunity to incriminate himself. He had a right temper on him, and if he had spouted off when she got there about being caught, he might drop her dad and Raymond in it. That was too much of a risk. As long as Terry didn't open his mouth, the situation was salvageable. Trying to explain that she was only staying away for his sake was proving near on impossible. Terry was raging with her and she was struggling to get a word in.

'Of course I want to see you, Tel. But I'm doing what's best for us both. Don't get the hump . . .'

'The hump?' Terry laughed incredulously. 'Are you having a bloody laugh, Kel? Did you hear anything I just said? I've been holed up in hospital with my neck in a cunting brace. They're sending me down for an MRI scan in a minute. And to top it off the Plod reckon that they're going to throw the bleeding book at me. Five years they reckon I could get. I've been here for sixteen fucking hours, and where the fuck is my wife? Nowhere to be fucking seen, that's where!' Terry shouted now, and Kelly could imagine her husband's face, contorted with rage as he gritted his teeth in anger.

'Five years? Have a laugh, Terry, you'd have had to have tried to murder someone to get five years . . .' Kelly tried to calm him down. He really was making a big fucking fuss out of nothing. She'd never known a bloke to be such a drama queen – talk about melodramatic. 'What have they got on you? Speeding and failing to stop?'

Aware that the nurse was looming a few feet behind him and probably earwigging at his rant to his wife, Terry lowered his voice to almost a whisper. 'You do know that when your dad asked me to pick up a few packages for him, it wasn't a fucking audition for Postman Pat's postal round, don't you? He needed mules to do his dirty work. The police found three kilos of cocaine on my bike, Kel, they are trying to do me for possessing with intent. Do you know what that fucking means? They think I'm some big time fucking dealer.'

'What?' Kelly's head throbbed as she tried to make sense of what Terry was telling her. 'Are you sure? My dad isn't involved in drugs. Why would he be? It's not like he's short of money.' Thinking about it, when Kelly had asked what they'd be picking up when they did the job, her dad had swept over what the items actually were. She'd been so caught up in the money, and the fact that Terry had been given an in, that the smaller detail had somehow become irrelevant. Import and export, he'd said.

'Use your loaf, Kelly. I've seen palm trees less fucking shady than your old man. Flash Harry had us on a drugs run,' Terry whispered, snarling.

Kelly could hear Terry growling in frustration at the other end of the phone but she didn't let his anger deter her from continuing. This was going to be okay. Her dad had promised her.

'Look, there must be a mistake.' Kelly was sure that Terry was wrong. Her dad had assured her that he was going to sort it, so Terry just needed to calm down. 'My dad said that he is sending his solicitor down to the station as soon as you get there. Some bloke called Paul Davis. He'll fill you in on everything once he gets there.' Pulling her knickers up, Kelly held the phone against her shoulder with her jaw so that she could open the door to the cubicle.

'He'd better be good, Kel, cos unless the bloke can pull a magic wand out of his fucking arse, I'm looking at doing a stretch inside.' Terry gritted his teeth.

'According to my dad he is meant to be the best brief in the business.' Walking over to the sink, Kelly pressed her free hand under the soap dispenser only to find that it was empty. Eyeing the scum around the top of the tap, she grimaced, settling on holding her hand under the running water. This place was a shithole. 'Just sit tight until you speak to him, yeah?'

'Whatever,' Terry muttered. He was done with trying to argue the toss with Kelly. The woman didn't have a clue what sort of a nightmare he had ahead of him.

It was all well and good telling him to calm down, but Kelly's dutiful caring wife act wasn't fooling him; all she cared about was the money, he wasn't stupid. Flash Harry had dished out twenty grand and Terry knew full well that she didn't want him to blab his mouth off in case he jeopardised it.

Drying her hands on the last paper towel, Kelly moved aside as a group of young women burst into the toilets, laughing and joking loudly, clearly all merry from having a few too many. Kelly placed her fingers over the mouthpiece to muffle the noise so that Terry wouldn't hear.

'What the fuck is that racket?' Terry asked.

'Oh it's nothing, babe, just some crap on the telly. Listen, you just keep positive, babe, okay? You'll be home before you know it.' Kelly tried to change the subject.

Silent at the other end of the phone, Terry listened to the sound of squealing girls echoing in the background. He could hear the thumping bass of music in the background now too. Un-fucking-believable!

Here he was laid up in hospital and that bitch was out on the fucking lash.

'Listen to you? Are you fucking taking the piss or what? It was listening to you that got me fucking where I am now.' Terry was fuming.

'For Christ's sake, Terry, will you calm down?' Aware that the girls were eavesdropping at the sound of her husband bellowing down the phone at her, Kelly kept her cool by rolling her eyes at the group of girls, making out that she was more than in control of her conversation.

'Calm down? Calm fucking down? Do not treat me like a fucking cunt, Kelly . . . You're out on the piss, aren't you . . . ?'

'Look, if you must know I'm at the fight night that Dad organised. He thought it would keep my mind off things . . .' Kelly justified.

'Oh I bet he fucking did. Well, as long as you lot are all okay. Don't fucking worry yourselves about me, eh?'

'Oi. My dad was only trying to help us out. He gave you an in, Terry, a chance. You want to remember that.' Kelly had had enough of pacifying her husband. Her dad had given him a chance to step up to the plate and prove himself. 'You were the one that fucked up. Not him, you. As per fucking usual!'

'Fucked up? I was hit by a fucking transit van, Kelly . . .' Terry spat. 'Ah, do you know what? Go and fuck yourself.' Gripping the handset tightly Terry smashed the hospital phone down repeatedly onto the receiver, abruptly ending the call. His wife's whiney voice was giving him a belter of a headache. That selfish bitch was quids in no matter what the outcome. No wonder she sounded so bloody calm, it wasn't her that was going to have a fill of porridge every day for the next five years.

Popping her mobile phone back in her handbag, Kelly sighed before reapplying her lipstick. Talk about narky. It wasn't her fault that Terry had gotten himself nicked. It wasn't as if he hadn't been pre-warned that the job had its risks. Import and export was a risky business, and her dad had told him from the start: if he got caught, he mustn't implicate anyone else. Her dad didn't want the tax man on his case.

That had been the deal. Plain and simple.

Why Terry was spouting off about drugs she had no idea. There was no way her dad would be involved in that. But then, Terry always was dramatic.

Staring in the mirror at her reflection, Kelly looked as stressed as she felt. Even the bathroom's dingy lighting couldn't disguise her blotchy skin. Taking her face powder out of her bag, Kelly coated another layer of foundation on. Sitting next to her younger, beautiful sister Evie all evening didn't help her confidence either. Unlike Kelly, Evie had been blessed with the same natural beauty as their mother, God rest her soul. Though unlike their ever glamorous mum, Evie was totally understated. Like she didn't even realise how stunning she was. If Kelly had those looks she'd be flaunting herself to everything with eyes.

She didn't. She wasn't ugly by any standard, but her looks were just average. Like everything else in her life, they required effort. And a lot of it.

Pouting her lips and flicking her hair, Kelly knew that Terry would be fine. Her dad had promised her that he'd sort it, and he would. She was sure of it.

Stepping out of the grotty nightclub toilets, Kelly Stranks put all thoughts of her disgruntled husband to the back of her mind.

Sod Terry.

Tonight she was out with her family.

A few more glasses of wine would soon sort her out.

Chapter Fifteen

'He's up next.' Nathan grinned across the table to where his father and Raymond sat. They both looked a lot calmer than he was. Christopher hadn't even got in the ring yet, and already Nathan could feel his heart beating nineteen to a dozen.

His adrenaline was soaring. He loved watching his brother fight.

Christopher could be hard work a lot of the time. His loud and obnoxious temperament, combined with his aggressive foul temper, made him bloody hard work as a rule, but in the ring, his volatile disposition was Christopher's making. He was a machine, and with all eyes watching him Christopher loved nothing more than to put on a spectacular show, and Nathan along with every other boxing fan in the room had been eagerly anticipating this fight all evening.

'Jesus, this place is heaving. I had to fight my way back here through the crowds,' Kelly said as she pulled out her chair next to Evie and re-joined her family at the table.

Kelly had secretly loved walking through the packed out venue, aware that she was the centre of attention. Everyone in the room knew who her family were, and she had seen how people had stared over at her, gossiping. So they should be. She was Harry's long lost daughter after all. Well, tonight she was back in the fold and she had forgotten how good that felt. God only knew how many of these events she must have missed out on over the years. Well, never again.

'It's a good thing your old man's a boxer then, ain't it, Kel? It's in the blood. Give 'em a right hook when you need 'em to move out the way, eh?' Dressed in his finest Armani suit, and sporting his favourite diamond encrusted Rolex watch, Harry winked at his daughter. Just like Christopher, as the promoter of the fight, all eyes were on him tonight too, and as always Harry Woods had set the bar high with his event. As a former pro himself, Harry knew what worked, and because of this his boxing events were legendary. Unlicensed, but run with the utmost professionalism, the tickets were sold purely by word of mouth, and Harry could fill a venue with just a few hours' notice. Be it a pub basement, social club hall, or like tonight, a grotty nightclub dance floor, people didn't give a shit where it was. It was common knowledge that everything Harry touched turned to gold, and if Harry Woods held up an envelope, these people would want to be invited to its opening. By the looks of the heaving room tonight, Harry knew that there was no doubt he'd exceeded himself once again.

Packed with celebrities, and faces from all over London, the dingy Hackney nightclub had been transformed into a venue brimming with high status and vast wealth.

Harry couldn't have felt happier, because tonight in front of thousands of observers, it was Christopher's night to shine, and God knows the boy needed this.

If Christopher proved himself tonight, it might put him back on the right track. The boy was so full of aggression, and Harry secretly hoped that if he won tonight, he'd focus more of his energy on what went on inside of the ring, rather than all the shit he was intent on doing outside of it.

'Everything all right?' Harry asked, as he watched Kelly stare into space, daydreaming as she swished her champagne around her glass. The girl had been miles away all day.

'Yeah, Terry just rang. One of the nurses at the hospital let him use the ward phone. He didn't sound too happy, Dad. I told him what you said about sending your brief . . .'

'Yeah and what did he say?'

'He said that the police told him he could be looking at five years . . . He said that he thinks the packages they picked up . . . were dodgy.' Kelly took a sip of her drink, unable to stop her hand from trembling as she waited to see her dad's reaction. If Terry went down, she didn't know what she was going to do. As much of a useless shit as the man could be, he was still her husband, and Kelly couldn't face the thought that she might end up bringing the kids up on her own for the next five years if there was even so much as a grain of truth in what he had told her.

'Dodgy packages? The police are obviously winding him up. Did you tell him what I said about not talking to anyone?' Harry was sure that Terry wouldn't open his mouth, it would be more than his life was worth, but you just never knew how someone would react when faced with the possibility of getting a capture. If Terry did start singing like a fucking canary just to save his own arse, Harry would make sure it was the last song that bloke ever sang.

'He won't say a word, Dad. He knows the score.'

'Don't look so glum then, girl, Paul will do the best he can. In the meantime, no matter what happens, you and the kids will be more than looked after. I will personally make sure of that. Terry won't go short either.'

Kelly smiled. It was what she had been hoping to hear. At least with her dad looking out for her and the kids, things wouldn't be so bad, and her dad seemed positive that it wouldn't come to that anyway. Terry would be fine. 'Thanks, Dad.'

'You're welcome, my girl, now cheer up yeah.' Harry smiled, pleased that his daughter had perked up a bit.

'Excuse me, Mr. Woods,' two young women interrupted. 'Could we have your autograph please?'

The ladies all loved Harry, and flattered as always, Harry was only too happy to oblige. Flashing the pretty women one of his most charming smiles, he asked each one their name, before scribbling down a message on the front of tonight's boxing programme.

'Tell you what, let's do a swap. I'll show you mine if you show me yours . . .' one of the women said cheekily as she slipped Harry a piece of paper with her name and phone number, boldly winking at him before they walked off.

'Jesus Christ, Dad, that bird was younger than me.' Nathan laughed, enjoying the view as he watched the two girls sauntering off.

Harry grinned. 'What can I say, son? The price of fame, huh?'

'Dad!' Giggling, Evie rolled her eyes, though she was secretly proud of him. Her dad lapped up the attention. Always had.

'Ladies and gentleman, good evening once again.' The ring announcer's voice boomed in the microphone as the lights went down and the flurry of noise around the ring quietened. 'Please take your seats for tonight's main event, eight rounds of boxing in the heavyweight division.'

Nathan leant over to Evie, aware that this would be the first fight his younger sister had ever witnessed. Wanting to reassure her, he was apprehensive of how she would react.

'You going to be okay watching this, Evie? It could get messy.'

'I'll be fine.' Evie smiled at Nathan's thoughtfulness. She clearly looked as nervous as she felt about watching her brother fight tonight. After begging her father to let her attend, she knew that no matter how brutal the match was, she'd have to brave it out. She wasn't a little kid anymore, and the sooner she made her father and brothers see that the better.

Overhearing Nathan, Raymond leant over and offered Evie some support. 'Stop mollycoddling the girl, Nathan, she'll be fine.

Jesus Christ, you'd think Evie was six, not sixteen, the way you all carry on. It's just another fight, and it's what you lot do. She's a Woods too, you know, so give the girl a bit of credit, yeah?' Seeing Evie smile back at him gratefully, Raymond winked.

'In the blue corner, and weighing in at two hundred and eleven pounds is Christopher "The Aggressor" Woods,' the ring announcer continued as a roar of chanting and cheering erupted in the crowded room.

As Christopher paced the ring, the crowd roared. They loved him.

Christopher Woods was fifteen stone of pure, lean muscle. His body was ripped, and raising his arms in the air, he basked in the praise that he received as he jumped from one foot to the other.

He had a reputation to upkeep. Nicknamed 'The Aggressor', Christopher was known for predominantly going in for the attack, instigating the first punches. Christopher honed in on his rage, attacking his adversary with as much speed as force. Tonight, Christopher was in the mood to pummel the fuck out of his opponent. Psyching himself up as he punched the air dramatically, he showed the crowd he was more than up for it.

'And in the red corner, weighing in at two hundred and eight pounds . . . Tyler "Tornado" Walker.'

The tall, black boxer slipped under the ropes of the ring in one swift movement. As he held Christopher's glare bravely, the two men sized each other up.

'Wow, if looks could kill.' Evie felt her stomach knot in apprehension as the two fighters glared at each other with menace, causing the referee to step in between the two men before the fight had even started. The atmosphere in the room was electric, and judging by the obvious animosity in the two boxers' faces, Evie had a feeling that the fight was going to be ruthless.

'That Tyler Walker has been gunning for Christopher for ages. Reckons if anyone is going to put "The Aggressor" down, it will be him. The bets are sky fucking high on this one. Walker's never lost a fight yet. But my money is on Christopher.' Nathan took a swig of his Jack and Coke.

Walker was undefeated, and if Christopher won tonight, he'd be firmly on the map.

Nathan knew how much his brother needed this. He'd fucked his professional career up good and proper when he'd been arrested for fighting outside that Chinese restaurant in Canning Town. The board had revoked his licence, but somehow Christopher still wanted to make a name for himself. With their dad's backing at this type of event he still could. There was more than one way to climb a mountain, and just like their dad always said: Where there's a Woods, there's a way.

Their dad wasn't known as one of the best boxing promoters in the business for nothing.

Unlicensed or not, Christopher was born to fight, and if there was any chance of keeping their brother out of trouble then their dad was adamant that he would do all he could to keep his son firmly in the game.

Evie was seemingly clueless as to just how ruthless their brother could be, but he knew better than anyone that when she did witness Christopher unleash hell in the ring tonight, it would at least be somewhat contained. Something their brother was incapable of being outside of it.

This was the fight that everyone had been talking about. If Christopher did win, their dad stood to make a shit load of money from it too. Walker's supporters were here in droves, and the crowd were split fifty–fifty, so the stakes were high.

Hearing the bell sound, Harry watched proudly as his son threw out punches in such quick succession at his opponent. The boy fought fearlessly, like he was on fire. Just the way Harry had taught him: Keep your guard up, and get in there hard and fast. Take no prisoners.

And his words had clearly been heard.

Harry watched, impressed, as his son executed each blow like a true pro, effortlessly raining down fist after fist.

Walker threw a few punches back, but they were weak, and already the man was wobbly on his feet, his earlier bravado gone now that he was faced with Christopher's immense fury in the ring.

Christopher was out for blood.

Only two minutes into the fight and in spectacular style, Christopher administered an almighty uppercut.

Walker's head snapped back.

Christopher sneered.

He had the glint of the devil in his eye, and he felt superior. Walker was nothing. He was no-one.

Hitting out with a lightning left hook, Christopher inflicted some true Woods-style boxing on the man. Watching in fascination as his opponent's legs buckled beneath him, Christopher nodded his head triumphantly as the man crashed to the floor. He was unable to get back onto his feet; Christopher had successfully finished the man off. The referee counted Walker out. He was defeated.

'In the record time of two minutes and eight seconds, the winner by knockout victory is Christopher "The Aggressor" Woods.' The referee held Christopher's arm high. Victorious as the crowd got to their feet and cheered mercilessly, Christopher Woods smiled broadly at his adoring fans.

Put him down? Looking at the state of the fucker splayed out on the floor, Walker wouldn't be capable of putting a toilet seat down now.

The gobby fucker had been well and truly put in his place, down on the floor where he belonged.

Christopher Woods was a champion in the making and no fucker was ever going to put him down.

Chapter Sixteen

'If you can just keep really still now, Terry. We're almost done, I'm just going to check the area at the back of your neck once more.' Terry jolted awake as the radiographer's voice echoed through his headphones, cutting off the calming classical music that must have sent him to sleep.

His eyes flickered as he focused, familiarising himself once again with where he was: stuck in a poxy MRI machine at Broomfield Hospital in the middle of Chelmsford, Essex.

Feeling claustrophobic as he remained completely still, grateful for the slight breeze that swept through the machine, Terry was feeling fed up with being poked and prodded by half the NHS, and he just wanted the whole thing over and done with now.

Hearing the final beeps from the scan, he was relieved when the nurse pulled the couch out from the tunnel.

'Bloody hell, how much more of this is there? I must have been under for hours . . .' Disorientated, he grunted ungratefully as the nurse did her best to make him comfortable as she helped him back into his wheelchair.

'Actually, it was only an hour.' The nurse tried to be sympathetic but from the moment she had come on shift, Terry had done nothing but gripe and moan at her. Difficult didn't even come close. 'And I appreciate that this is trying for you, Mr. Stranks, but we have to do everything in our power to work out what's wrong. You've had a nasty accident.'

Officer Mansell stood up. Having been sitting in the corner of the room, keeping a watchful eye on his prisoner, he was getting fed up too. Hopefully they'd find out the extent of Terry Stranks' injuries sooner rather than later, because sitting on his arse for the best part of the day and listening to this prisoner whinging and moaning was doing his head in.

'Cor, bleeding hell, at this rate I'm gunna need another bloody X-ray with the way you're manhandling me,' Terry shouted in agony as the nurse carefully tried to reapply Terry's neck brace.

'I'll send the results straight over to Mr. Stranks' doctor,' the radiographer informed the nurse sympathetically, as she dealt with her disgruntled patient. Then glancing up at the clock on the wall, he added, 'Though I'm guessing that it will probably be first thing in the morning now.'

Terry felt exhausted. All day he'd been in this poxy place. They weren't exactly treating his injuries as a priority. This would have been over and done with hours ago if it wasn't for the victim of a car accident taking priority over him. There had been talk of his MRI scan being put off until tomorrow, but the radiographer had agreed to fit him in as his last patient of the day.

'Oww! God it fucking hurts. I want some more pain relief, I'm in fucking agony here.'

'Mr. Stranks, I think it would help if you stopped fidgeting. Let's get you back to the ward, then I can check your chart and see when you're due your next lot of meds.' Curtly ignoring Terry's whines, the nurse smiled gratefully as Officer Mansell held the door open for her and the hospital porter.

As the lift doors opened, Officer Mansell watched as the porter wheeled Terry inside. Just about to follow, he pulled his mobile phone from his pocket. Seeing as Terry clearly wasn't capable of going anywhere, Mansell decided to meet them up on the ward.

'Actually, I'm just going to make a quick call to my governor. Won't be a minute, okay?'

The nurse nodded and the lift doors closed.

Mansell desperately needed a cigarette. He'd only be a few minutes.

He'd already been filled in on what a sorry sack of shit Terry Stranks could be, and after spending the day with him, he'd seen it for himself first hand. Hopefully, by the time he'd had a quick smoke and re-joined his patient, the nurse would have had time to administer Terry's pain relief and sent the moaning git back off to a deep and, most importantly, sound sleep.

Making his way to the hospital's main entrance, Mansell pulled out his packet of cigarettes, and lit one up as he huddled underneath the porch that covered the main doorway entrance.

The sky had turned black, and the rain was just starting to fall.

Right about now his wife would be putting the kids to bed. Another night that he could have spent with his kids, lost because of some lowlife like Stranks.

Thinking about the long night ahead of him, Mansell ignored the steely looks he was getting from the elderly woman standing next to him, as she exaggeratedly wafted the smoke cloud that hovered around her to express her obvious irritation at him smoking.

Mansell took one last pull, savouring the last bit of nicotine, before he stubbed his fag out, and purposely flicked the butt down on the pavement next to him to wind the old busybody up.

'Here, you should be setting an example,' the elderly lady piped up, pointing at Mansell's uniform with disgust. 'That's littering that is.'

'So it is.' Mansell smirked as he made his way back through the main doors. 'What are you going to do about it, sweetheart? Arrest me?'

Chapter Seventeen

Reaching the second floor, the porter steered Terry along the busy corridor, the nurse following closely at his side.

'I need a piss.'

'Well, another few minutes and we'll be back on the ward, and we'll get you sorted out. Okay?' the nurse replied tartly.

'I don't think I can hold it. I'm busting.' Terry shook his right knee erratically, desperately trying to hold it in.

'Well, I'm afraid you're going to have to wait, Mr. Stranks. You're still in police custody and I'm under strict instructions to take you straight back to the ward.'

'What, so you're happy to just let me piss myself? Don't I have any basic human rights? I need a piss, and if you don't let me go to the toilet in the next two minutes I'm going to piss myself.' Terry purposely spoke loudly, so that the people they passed could hear him. This bitch was a proper jobs-worth. Out of all the nurses in the hospital, trust him to get stuck with the one that had a face so sour, she could curdle milk. Where were all the tasty Essex birds when he needed one?

'Well, of course you have rights . . .' the nurse said, feeling uncomfortable as the porter flashed her a look, in obvious agreement that the nurse was indeed being too harsh on the patient. 'I'm just saying that you will have to try to hold it.'

'I really can't. Look I'm sorry for being an arsehole today. Really I am. I'm just in so much pain. And I have been holed up in that horrible machine for ages. I just need a wee. Look at the state of me . . . It's not as if I'm capable of wiping my own arse at the moment, let alone doing a runner if that's what you're worried about.'

Seeing the disabled toilet up ahead, the nurse reluctantly gave in and nodded at the porter to stop.

'Okay then,' she resigned. 'But you have two minutes, and the porter is going to go in there with you, in case you need some help. Is that okay with you, William?'

The porter nodded.

'Thank fuck for that,' Terry said, relieved that the nurse had finally seen sense.

Wheeling Terry inside the cubicle and closing the door behind him, the porter offered Terry his arm so that he could help him get up.

Grabbing it gratefully, and gritting his teeth as he eased himself out of the wheelchair, Terry hauled himself up onto his feet.

'You okay?' the porter asked as Terry let go of his arm and stood up unaided.

Terry nodded. Resting his hand on the wall, he leant up against it, wobbling unsteadily on his feet as he did so.

As he stepped forward to help, Terry shrugged the man off.

'I'm fine, thanks.' Pulling his gown up so that he could take a piss, Terry turned abruptly to the porter who stood beside him now. 'Do you wanna hold my tonker as well as stand there bloody gawping at it?'

Terry smirked as the porter, clearly embarrassed by his insinuation, finally stood back and let him have his piss in peace.

'You want a hand getting back into the chair?' the porter asked apprehensively once Terry had finished, not wanting to antagonise the patient any further by being overly helpful.

Terry shook his head. 'What's the point in plastering these posters everywhere if you lot ain't going to practise what you preach, eh?' Terry said as he nodded over to the boldly written notice about patients washing their hands in order to prevent the spread of germs. 'I gotta wash my hands, ain't I? This place is probably crawling with all sorts of contagious shit.' Carefully stepping past the porter towards the sink, Terry turned on the tap. The water spurted out loudly.

Terry knew that if he got back in that wheelchair he was done for. As soon as the doctors and the Old Bill realised that there was fuck all wrong with him, he'd be carted off straight down the police station. If he had any chance of escaping then it was now or never.

Grabbing the porter by his collar, Terry dragged the man down with a fast, swift movement that shocked him just as much as it did his poor unsuspecting victim. Smashing the man's head against the sink, Terry felt the man struggle, before he did it again. This time even harder, with full force. The man's skull cracked loudly as it whacked against the steel tap.

Mesmerised, Terry stared as the porter flopped to the floor unconscious.

The attack was over in just seconds, and the poor bugger hadn't known what had hit him.

'Is everything all right in there, William?' the nurse called, hearing the commotion. Quickly locking the cubicle door now, Terry wheeled the chair over to the far wall directly under the window, and ripped off his neck brace.

He ignored the nurse; the snooty bitch probably had her ear up against the door, listening in.

'Mr. Stranks? What's going on in there?' Banging on the door now, the nurse sounded flustered and Terry couldn't help but smile as he hoisted himself up onto the window ledge. He almost wished that he was sticking around, so that he could be a fly on the wall when this jobs-worth bitch explained to her superiors how she had let a police guarded patient abscond from her care.

He'd played a blinder with his acting skills too. Surpassing himself.

Not only had he managed to fool the police and the paramedics, but he'd even duped the doctors and specialists into believing that he'd been badly injured. Apart from the odd scrape and bruise, the paramedics had been right. He had been lucky. He was totally unharmed.

He'd waited all day for his chance to escape from the watchful eye of the police officer, and now, while the copper was nowhere to be seen, Terry was grabbing the opportunity with both hands.

Hearing the snooty cunt of a nurse as she persistently banged her fists ferociously on the door, Terry grinned as he ducked his head down and managed to squeeze himself out of the tiny window and onto the grass verge. Finding himself down a secluded alleyway at the back of the hospital, Terry smiled again. He couldn't have planned his getaway better. Squatting down on the floor, he could see in through the office windows, and the lights were all out. This late in the evening, the coast was clear.

This was his chance.

Terry ran as fast as he could, but the wet sludge beneath his feet together with his eagerness to get away proved too much of a hindrance. Slipping, Terry fell backwards. Lying on the grass with his hospital gown clinging to his body, already drenched from the pouring rain, Terry couldn't help but laugh. Once he started he couldn't stop. Roaring with laughter, he couldn't help thinking what a sight he must look. Sporting a hospital gown and no under-crackers, and covered head to toe in mud. Who cared? He'd escaped. That was all that mattered.

Getting back up onto his feet, Terry ran for cover to the woodland that ran down the side of the hospital.

Blanketed by the dense overgrowth he ran so fast that his chest felt like it would explode.

He was free.

Chapter Eighteen

'Any excuse to crack open another bottle, eh, Dad?' Nathan laughed. He often wound his dad up about how much champagne he drank. Lately he'd been drinking even more than usual. 'I reckon you must bathe in this stuff going by the amount of bottles you manage to get through.'

'It ain't a crime to have a taste for the good stuff, son. Life is short, so bloody enjoy it. And besides, tonight we are celebrating,' Harry reasoned as he proudly raised his glass in the air and toasted his youngest son's success.

'To our very own champion, Christopher.'

'To Christopher,' everyone chorused.

Christopher beamed, cherishing the moment of rare praise from his family. He'd earned it. With Harry Woods as his father, Christopher always felt like he had a lot to live up to, and tonight for the first time ever he really felt like he had. He had surpassed himself. Tonight, with the world and his wife watching, Christopher had more than proved his worth as a fighter.

'Walker went down like a hot sack of shit, didn't he? Knocked the fucker out in just over two minutes. I'm a fucking legend.' Knocking back his drink in one go, his adrenaline surging and heightened by the coke he'd been doing all night, Christopher was still buzzing.

'You made a right mess of him,' Raymond agreed.

'Bet it's a long time before he thinks about getting back in the ring with anyone after tonight, eh?' Nathan was impressed; his brother had beaten the man senseless.

'Well, it ain't like the bloke's got to worry about brain damage or anything. He must already have that if he thinks he can go around spouting shit about taking me down. That's what they call a punch-out. Someone who spouts their shit, but can't back it up in the ring,' Christopher snarled.

He hated blokes like Walker. As far as he was concerned, if you were tough enough to walk the walk, then you didn't need to back it up with chat. And chat was clearly all Walker had.

'He'll be fine. Getting knocked out is an occupational hazard. Walker knows that. Or at least he does now.' Harry grinned.

As always Harry's event had been a roaring success. Tonight, Christopher had given the attendees exactly what they had wanted: a fight to remember. Every influential person in Harry's orbit had been there, and the boy had made his name in front of them all.

Harry had made a fairly decent earn from it all too.

'Poor Evie, you geared yourself up for nothing. I think you blinked and the whole thing was over.' Nathan laughed as he hugged his younger sister to him.

'To be honest I'm glad it finished as quickly as it did. Don't think I could have stomached much more,' Evie admitted as she swept her long dark hair behind her ears before taking another sip of her drink, the bubbles fizzing up her nose as she did. Christopher had fought like a wild animal and she had been left unnerved by the entire experience. She had seen the evil glint in Christopher's eyes as he fought. Even afterwards when he had coldly stepped over his opponent who was sprawled out on the floor like a wounded animal, Christopher hadn't shown even so much as a flicker of remorse. Evie had searched his face for it as he stood there victoriously, but she had only been met with a look of triumph. Maybe that was the whole point, though. What did she know about boxing after all? Her brother was the fighter.

Placing her glass down on the side, Evie sat on the sofa next to her sister.

'Well, I for one couldn't be prouder,' Kelly slurred. 'That was the best night out I've had in bleeding ages.' Grinning from ear to ear proudly at her brother, she hiccupped loudly before bursting out laughing. After the amount of booze she'd knocked back tonight, she was feeling more than a little bit tipsy.

'Shall I order us in some pizza or something?' Harry rolled his eyes, and then laughed too. 'You look like you could use a bit of grub, Kelly, to soak up some of that alcohol.'

He was glad that she had managed to put Terry out of her head for the evening. Tonight, surrounded by his kids, and of course Raymond, Harry was thoroughly enjoying himself. So much so that he didn't want the night to end. This was exactly what he needed.

'I'm stuffed, Dad,' Evie said as she kicked off her heels and sat back on the sofa, hugging a cushion to her. The excitement of the evening, combined with the couple of glasses of champagne her father had allowed her to have, had left her feeling shattered.

Ray sat down next to her. 'Stuffed? You barely ate anything,' he teased. He had watched Evie during the meal and the girl had picked at her food and pushed it around her plate as if it was contaminated.

'I think it was nerves. I didn't really know what to expect,' Evie said honestly.

'If you think that was nerve-racking you should have seen your dad back in his day. Now *he* was a force to be reckoned with. They didn't call him Harry "The Hammer" for nothing, you know. Your dad could knock his opponents out cold in one almighty strong blow.' Raymond winked at Harry. 'Where do you think Christopher got his technique from? Your dad taught you everything he knew, didn't he, Christopher?'

Christopher smiled, masking the fact that Raymond was getting his back up.

Tonight was about him, not his dad.

All he ever heard about was how great a fighter his dad had been. Times had changed, and his dad was retired for a reason. If he got in the ring now, there was no doubt in Christopher's mind that he would wipe the floor with his father. He may have been a force to be reckoned with back in his day, but it was Christopher's turn to be in the limelight now.

He was intending to enjoy every second of it.

'Don't order any in for me, Dad. I'm off out,' Christopher said as he checked his phone. He'd been bombarded with messages after his win tonight, and he was determined to go and celebrate in style. He'd worked his nuts off for tonight's victory and now it was time to bask in the glory.

'I'm meeting Russ and Darren for a few drinks in a bit,' he said, standing up as he smoothed down his grey suit trousers. His crisp white shirt, almost bursting at the seams, clung tightly to his torso, enhancing his muscly physique. 'You coming, Nath?'

Nathan glanced at his watch. It was half eleven, and the night was still young, and normally Nathan would have gone with Christopher without so much as a second thought, but right now the only person Nathan wanted to see was Cassie.

'Nah. I think I'm going to go over and see Cass.'

Christopher rolled his eyes. Nathan had turned into a right soft cunt since he'd hooked up with that bird. The girl was stunning, there was no denying that. Nathan had always had impeccable taste when it came to women. They might look like classy birds, but nine times out of ten, they were just fame-hungry slappers. Nathan never bothered getting close to any of them. This Cassie seemed different, though. She'd somehow wormed her way inside his brother's head. It was like Nathan could only focus on her now, and her alone. Christopher could admit that the bird had tits to die for, but she was still just a bird and they were two a penny. Great for a ride, but they came with far too much grief. Since Nathan had hooked up with Cassie, Christopher had seen him change right before his eyes.

'Be careful, Romeo . . .' Christopher leaned over to where Nathan was sitting and playfully swept his hand through his brother's hair. 'That massive thumbprint on your head might leave a bald patch.'

'Oi. Leave it out,' Nathan said, annoyed. 'I ain't under the thumb. I just really like the girl that's all. There's no harm in that, is there?'

'Fair do's,' Christopher said, holding his hands up. He couldn't be arsed to say any more on the subject. Nathan got so touchy about her. Tonight was his night, and if Nathan didn't want to join him in celebrating then that was fine by him. 'I'm off then.'

'Don't get wankered, though, eh? We've got to be over at The Railway first thing tomorrow morning. The decorators are meeting us there at ten.'

'God, I'm so bloody excited.' Kelly beamed. Nathan had asked if she wanted to manage the new bar and, of course, she'd jumped at the chance. Sure that her Terry would be home in no time, Kelly knew that he'd be a hundred percent behind her. Managing a fancy wine bar would be a great opportunity for them both. They could put all this rubbish behind them and both start afresh.

'Hang about, Christopher, do you want a lift?' Raymond said as he stood up and got his keys. 'I'm heading off now myself. I can drop you at Cassie's place too if you like, Nathan.'

'Yeah, great,' Nathan said gratefully. Just about to call a cab, he put his phone back in his pocket.

Shaking the boys' hands, Harry said goodbye before turning back to his daughters. 'Well, looks like it's just me and my girls tonight then,' Harry said turning back to his youngest daughter. 'Are you sure I can't tempt you both with a slice of pizza? Just so your old man doesn't feel like a gluttonous pig eating it all by himself.'

'Oh go on then, Dad. But only if I can have pepperoni.' Evie smiled.

'I will too, I'm starving. Then I'm going to hit the hay.' Kelly yawned. Her dad had set up the spare room for her and while she was knackered, it would be a shame to go to bed so early. The kids were over at Terry's mum's house for the night, and Kelly wanted to make the most of her very rare night of freedom. Besides, sleeping here would be like staying in a five star hotel compared with going home. Kelly knew as soon as her head hit the pillow she'd be out for the count. Heaven. Before that, a slice of pizza and one more drink was just what she needed.

'Dad. You've got a visitor.' Nathan showed Officer Mansell in and then stood in the doorway with his brother and Raymond, observing.

'I'm so sorry to bother you this late at night, Harry,' Mansell apologised profusely. Turning up at Harry's place at this time of the night was a liberty, he knew, but he didn't have any choice. 'I've been trying to get hold of you all evening. I just wanted to give you the heads up before some of my colleagues turn up.'

'Your colleagues? What do they want?' Harry asked coolly. Shocked that Mansell had showed up unannounced like this, and aware that his youngest daughter was in the room, Harry hoped that whatever it was that the officer had to tell him was bloody worth the rude interruption.

'It's Terry . . .'

'Terry?' Harry felt himself stiffen at the mention of his useless son-in-law's name.

What had the dipstick done now? If Terry had dropped him in it, there was going to be a world of shit.

'Terry? What's happened to him?' Hearing her husband's name, Kelly sat bolt upright in her chair, suddenly feeling sick with trepidation. Staring from her father to the officer, she felt a flutter of panic rise up inside her.

Their conversation earlier suddenly sprang to the forefront of her mind. He had sounded really upset. Irate even. Maybe she had underestimated just how angry he actually was. God, what if he'd done something really stupid. She'd never forgive herself.

'I'm afraid that Terry is missing, Mrs. Stranks.' Mansell had half hoped that Terry had headed straight here after he'd escaped. But he could tell immediately by the surprise on everyone's faces that neither Kelly nor Harry was aware that Terry had even bolted, so there was no chance that they were hiding him.

Unfortunately, Mansell's governor wouldn't be so believing. Already, half the squad had their money on the fact that Terry would be lurking around here somewhere, hidden under the false security of his notorious father-in-law's shady wings. They were going to be turning up any minute.

Terry had actually done right by Harry, and kept his trap shut since he'd been brought in. Mansell's colleagues had no evidence that Harry was even involved, only hearsay and a strong suspicion. They'd thought that they'd get Terry to talk too; they'd even managed to put the shitters up him by threatening him with a hefty prison sentence.

Terry looked like a man that they could easily break down, and just a few choice words could have led them to the man they really wanted to catch.

Harry.

Now he'd done a runner and Mansell was in deep shit because of it.

'What do you mean, Terry is missing? How can he be? You lot only nicked him yesterday. He's in hospital under bloody police arrest.' Kelly narrowed her eyes accusingly. She had only spoken to Terry a few hours ago. This officer had obviously got his facts wrong.

'I'm afraid that he absconded from the hospital earlier this evening. We are doing everything in our power to locate him. We've got one of our units watching out for him over at his home address – your home address – and we've just sent another to his previous address, which we believe is his parents'.' Mansell turned to Harry apologetically. 'But the governor wants this place searched too.'

'Why? Terry ain't bloody here. What does Porter think he's playing at, huh? He knows not to come sniffing around here.' Harry shook his head. The last thing he wanted was the pigs round, tearing his place up. Not that they would find anything. That wasn't the point. They couldn't just turn up here as and when they felt like it.

'It ain't him, Harry. The order came from higher up. Porter tried to hold them off, but they ain't budging on this, and they can't just take your word on it, Harry, they want to see for themselves. My head's already on the chopping board because Terry did his little Houdini routine under my watch, and not only that but he's gone and caused a whole world of shit for himself too. He's a wanted man. Even more so after tonight's antics. Gone and caused murders he has.'

Harry raised an eyebrow, questioning Mansell.

'He battered one of the hospital porters. Left the bloke in a bad way too. Smashed the poor guy's skull in . . . He's in the ICU and he's critical,' Mansell added, just so Harry would realise the seriousness of the situation.

Putting her hand to her mouth, Kelly gasped in disbelief. 'No, not Terry. He wouldn't have done that . . .' Kelly's hand shook as she tried to take everything in.

'Fucking hell.' Harry shook his head. Terry had just made the situation a million times worse. There would be no coming back from this. He was a wanted man now.

'Well I think me and the boys should get out there and have a look for him too,' Raymond chipped in as Kelly broke down crying. 'Better that one of us finds him than the Old Bill.'

Harry nodded. Raymond knew everyone, so once word got out that Terry was on the missing list it wouldn't take long for someone to come forward with an idea about where he might be holed up. Harry would put money on it.

'I better ring Freda, she's got the kids for the night. She'll be having a fit if the police have turned up and told her what her precious bloody son's gone and done now. She'll be a nervous wreck.'

Harry nodded as Kelly went out to the kitchen to phone her unsuspecting mother-in-law.

'Like I said, Harry, I'm sorry to disturb you. I knew you'd want a heads up. The governor is shitting bricks over all this as it is.'

Harry nodded. He appreciated that Mansell was risking himself further by personally coming here to deliver the news himself. 'I'll walk you out,' he offered, as he led the way to the front door.

'If you spot him, I want to be the first to know, you got me?' Harry said sternly as he thanked Mansell for his services by slipping some notes into his hand.

Mansell nodded. It went without saying that Harry would be the first person he called. Harry knew that.

Look after Harry Woods and Harry Woods would look after you. That was always Mansell's priority.

People who said crime didn't pay talked out of their arses as far as Mansell was concerned.

'You can count on it.' Mansell nodded gratefully.

Watching as the officer crossed the driveway through the pouring rain and hurriedly got into his car, Harry let out a long, controlled breath.

Terry was now a wanted man, with a list of offences that were getting longer and more serious by the second. If Terry got caught now, he'd be looking at doing a real stretch.

Which meant that the chances of him opening his trap to try to wangle himself a deal had just soared sky fucking high.

Staring until the officer's rear lights had shrunk in the distance, and slipped out of view, Harry stood for a few more seconds. Savouring the calm before the storm.

Raymond was right. They needed to find Terry before the police did and make sure that he didn't open his mouth. Before they disappeared off to look for him, Harry wanted to speak to Raymond and the boys alone.

They needed to sort this shit out once and for all.

He'd worked too hard for too long building up his business for someone like Terry Stranks to fuck it up for him now.

If Terry was already playing games in order to save his own arse then there was no telling what he might do next.

Chapter Nineteen

Soaked through, Terry pulled the sopping wet hospital gown up and over his head and slung it over the stable doors. Standing there naked, his body shook uncontrollably as he unclipped the horse's worn looking blanket.

'I'm sorry, mate, but I need this more than you do. I'm freezing my nads off here.' Terry eyed the horse as he pulled the blanket from his body, but if Terry's presence was causing the animal any unease, the horse didn't show it.

Huddling in the corner, Terry wrapped the blanket tightly around himself, tucking his freezing cold feet deep into the bale of hay. The barn was damp and the stench of horse shit and piss was so strong that he couldn't help but gag. Seeing as it was pissing it down outside, Terry was just glad of the shelter.

'Fuck,' he grimaced as a prick of brambles hidden amongst the dry straw plunged into the open gash on the sole of his foot. Pulling his foot back out from the bale, he saw that his feet were cut to ribbons. The small areas of exposed skin that hadn't been shredded were covered with large red welts.

He had run for miles tonight, through the dense woodland. He'd felt the jagged branches and twigs crunching beneath his bare skin as he had run, slicing viciously through his skin like jagged knives penetrating hot butter.

Still, he had continued. He had no choice.

Now, carefully wrapping the blanket around his feet, Terry winced in pain.

Knackered, he clawed big handfuls of hay in around his body, surrounding himself in a mock cocoon.

The horse stood watching, then as if bored by his unexpected visitor, he turned and stood at the other end of the stable, his back to Terry.

Closing his eyes, Terry lay his head back against the dry straw that he'd scooped behind him as a makeshift pillow. His mind was racing as he wondered how many police officers would be searching for him. He'd heard the sirens as he darted through the trees. On foot and hidden in the undergrowth, no matter how big the search party was they'd have their work cut out if they wanted to find him.

He'd knocked that porter clean out.

It was all that sour-faced bitch of a nurse's fault. If she hadn't sent the poor guy in to escort him while he was taking a piss none of this would have happened. The bloke wouldn't have got hurt.

Just thinking about that sickening crack he'd heard as he bounced the man's head off the tap still made him feel physically sick. He could still visualise the bloke's body, slumped lifelessly on the toilet floor.

It had been an accident, hitting him that hard; Terry's strength had surprised even him.

Still, it was done now. He'd escaped, that was the main thing.

When Terry had spotted this place, he hadn't believed his luck. He was exhausted, and this little old barn was a perfect place to hide out in while he got some well-earned rest.

Terry had seen an old farmhouse a couple of hundred metres away in the distance, where a lonely porch light shone out indicating that there were signs of life, but otherwise the house stood in darkness. He figured that he'd be safe to hide out here for at least a few hours.

Closing his eyes, Terry listened to the sound of the raindrops dripping through the hole in the roof, as he tried to figure out what his next move would be. The police were bound to have his house covered, so he wouldn't be able to go back there.

If he tried to call Kelly, she'd more than likely tell her dad. Right now Harry Woods getting wind of his whereabouts was the last thing that Terry wanted.

Kelly might be gullible, but he wasn't. He didn't trust that man an inch.

Terry was stumped. He didn't have a clue what to do next.

All he did know was that he couldn't get caught.

He wouldn't survive five minutes in prison, let alone five years. Not a chance.

His plan had been to escape. After that he had no idea what he was going to do next. He hadn't thought that far ahead.

Right now, alone and exhausted, all Terry Stranks wanted to do was sleep.

Chapter Twenty

Yanking down the tight red miniskirt that had ridden up around her waist as she had crouched down, exposing her minuscule thong and her pasty white arse cheeks, Paige Carter continued to brush her hand through the grass scouting for discarded dog-ends. She was on a come-down and desperately needed some nicotine to take the edge off. The heroin-induced high she had experienced earlier had long worn off, and already she was clucking for her next fix.

'Shit.' Knocking her bag over, Paige watched as the contents tumbled out; a lip gloss and a pound coin rolled off the small stone wall and dropped down into the water with a small splash.

Sighing, she shoved the remaining contents roughly back in her bag. The lip gloss she could live without, but she had planned on using that last pound to buy a pack of Rizla on the way home. She'd been picking up manky cigarette ends for the past ten minutes so that she could make herself a couple of decent sized smokes.

She'd have to try to ponce some money off someone on the way back home now, but at just gone three in the morning she'd be lucky if there was anyone around. Anyone worth talking to anyway.

She should be kicking herself for spending all her money on her hit earlier, but even she knew that if the chance to score came up again and she had the money, she wouldn't think twice about going for it. Shooting up, she had waited eagerly for the initial hit to get her, willing the rush to take over. She lived for that rush.

When it had come, it came hard and fast.

She was no longer slumped up against the dirty wall in the secluded cold underpass, just a skanky druggy with vacant eyes and a deadened soul, with a dirty needle sticking out of her arm.

No, instead Paige was transported a million miles away from the shithole that was her grim reality.

Flying high for those few short hours, she felt the warmth that she longed for, that she craved. Right down to her bones. The rush she got from it was one of the best feelings in the entire world. The hit had been just what she needed. Mind-numbingly potent, she had surrendered her mind and body to it completely, embracing the oblivion that it gave her.

It was euphoric, but as always it hadn't lasted nearly long enough. Her habit was getting worse.

She lived and breathed for her next hit. Even the threats from her pimp, Rusty, about what he would do to her if she rocked up back home with nothing to show for her night's earn didn't scare her nearly enough anymore to be seen as a deterrent. Heroin was all she could think about, from the minute she woke up until the minute she finally slipped into her bed at night.

She needed the drug like she needed oxygen.

Rusty would go ape shit later, and he'd probably beat the hell out of her like he had last time. The memory of him dragging her around their flat by her hair as he whacked her head off every surface was still fresh in her mind, but so was the feeling of her last hit.

And that recollection was far stronger.

Out here on the streets, touting for business and getting into cars with strange men, it was soul destroying. She earned her money the only way she knew how: by letting men paw her body as they made her perform countless shameful acts.

Heroin helped her to forget all of that. It helped her to survive.

Her hunger for her addiction far outweighed any promises she had made to Rusty. It wasn't him who had to lie down with his legs wide open, while vile disgusting men used his body for their own sexual satisfaction. It wasn't him who was humiliated and violated on a daily basis.

Picking out one of the fag butts that she had stowed away in her bag for later, Paige sat back down on the wall, and lit it. Ignoring the acidic taste of what could have been dog piss on her lips, she relaxed as she took a long pull of the fag.

As she cast her eye over the Thames, she thought that the river always appeared so breathtakingly beautiful at night. Paige felt the familiar sadness inside her as she took in the glistening lights from the bridges and buildings as their reflections shone down like mesmerising pools of colourful magic, dancing on the water's surface.

She was too old to believe in magic, and too cynical. She knew better than most that the world was really a cruel and unforgiving place. Shaking her head at her naivety, she knew that like everything, the river's beauty was just an illusion. If she looked closer she could see the thick film of scum that floated up against the wall where she sat.

Shivering, Paige wrapped her arms around herself; hugging her body, she tried to keep warm.

A car had just pulled in slightly further up, catching her attention, and Paige stared suspiciously as it parked on the grass verge.

Her patch was a notorious working girls' spot, but the other girls had gone home now. The chances of someone driving out here looking for business at this time of the morning were slim.

Watching as the big burly bloke got out of his flash motor and started to walk down towards her, Paige took in his immaculate suit and his well-groomed appearance. He was massive. His huge frame looked even bigger than Rusty's, and Rusty was one of the biggest men that Paige had ever seen.

He was a punter, she was sure.

The Old Bill wouldn't have been so conspicuous. They would have turned up wearing a stereotypical anorak or something; they stood out a mile off and Paige could always tell a copper from a genuine paying customer.

Getting up as the man neared, Paige stuck out her tiny chest, and plastered one of her irresistible smiles on her face. It made a change to see a decent looking fella out looking for a lay. Especially one as good looking as this guy; he couldn't have been short of offers from girls. Still, Paige knew how it worked. He was probably married, and fancied a bit of strange to relieve himself from the boredom of monogamy.

'You looking for something in particular?' Paige called out. 'Or someone?'

The man had stopped now. Standing a few feet away, he was wavering.

Still unsure of the man's intentions, Paige quickly decided that she'd take her chances in approaching him. If he was a copper and she did get thrown in a cell for the night for soliciting, it would be a welcome punishment compared to going home and facing Rusty's wrath. At least then she could make out that the police had fleeced her for her nightly earn. Rusty would believe that too. He knew that there were more bent coppers than there were straight these days. She'd seen to a couple of the dirty bastards herself. They were the worst kind. Dressed in their uniforms, demanding freebies in return for them not taking her stash or nicking her. Most of them were a law unto themselves.

Still, this bloke looked like he was sniffing around for a ride, and her money, if she had any, would have been on the fact that he was definitely a punter.

Smiling as the man gestured with his hand for her to go to him, Paige didn't have to think twice.

Grabbing her bag, she stepped away from the wall.

Desperate to earn a few bob, she was going to give this fella the ride of his life.

He was her only chance at making some money tonight. Going home to Rusty with at least a few quid in her pocket was a million times better than turning up completely brassick.

Who knew? If she gave this bloke the full on VIP treatment she might even be able to wangle a lift home afterwards too.

———

Leaning over the wall Christopher threw up. Overwhelmed with nausea, he felt weak. Dizzy.

The feeling was intense, but he welcomed it wholly.

If he didn't feel like this, he'd question whether maybe he was some kind of a monster.

Because only a monster would be left numb after what he'd just done.

Standing here throwing his guts up, he had managed to sicken even himself with his depraved actions.

He was only human after all.

Spitting out a mouthful of pungent phlegm, Christopher wiped the corners of his mouth and then stood back from the water's edge.

He'd have to get rid of his clothes, which were splattered with blood; he'd have to burn them when he got home.

He could still smell the girl; her sickly sour scent was all over him. He could smell her skin, her hair. How she'd masked her bitter body odour with cheap, heady perfume.

It was a shame she was dead really. For a whore she had actually seemed quiet sweet. Young and eager to please. She had been willing to let him do anything he wanted, though all for a price of course.

Christopher, with the victory of tonight's fight overshadowed by having to look for that prick Terry, had still wanted to celebrate, and spotting the girl touting for business, he had gladly taken her up on her offer.

The girl had thought she was on to a winner, spotting Christopher all dressed up in his smart clobber, with his expensive car. Pound signs must have flashed before her eyes; blinded by the idea of earning herself some money, she'd been ignorantly unaware that she'd inadvertently just sold her soul to the devil himself.

Christopher had taken her with force; bending the girl over he had fucked her with such fierce brutality, all the while the intense rage building up inside him just as it always did. His desperate need to hurt her escalated so quickly, the pressure inside him became explosive.

He could feel it again. The same feeling as before. Building up inside him as he pounded away against her naked flesh.

He couldn't just release himself like a normal bloke.

He needed to give in to it, to really hurt the girl.

His head throbbed, as he tried his hardest to suppress the strong urge that overcame him to throttle the girl. The need overwhelmed him, becoming so intense that he had no other option but to give in to it.

Caught up in a vicious frenzy Christopher had lost control, lashing out at the girl every way he could. Biting her, punching her, and finally, with his hands wrapped around her throat, he had squeezed the very last breath out of her cold, still body.

Then, pushing himself back inside her lifeless body, he finally reached his climax.

Shuddering, it was all over.

The girl was dead, and Christopher's rage had subsided as quickly as it had emerged.

Mesmerised as the girl's body was dragged down into the dark, gloomy water, weighted by the rocks that he'd tied expertly to her scrawny, battered limbs, Christopher watched until she disappeared from his sight.

Until the water became still once more.

She was gone. Disposed of like she was a piece of unwanted rubbish.

Turning, Christopher heard a noise. Worried that someone had seen him, he grinned as he spotted another skanky whore lying on the floor of the underpass behind him. He caught the girl's eye, but even from this distance, Christopher could tell that the girl was so drugged up she'd be lucky if she knew the time of day let alone be capable of recounting anything that she may or may not have witnessed tonight. Deciding that she wasn't any kind of threat, Christopher shook his head at her before he continued to walk. His mood was almost sombre, reflecting on his actions as he made his way back to his car.

These girls were all the same. Even the one that he'd just killed may have looked young and naive, but deep down she had known what she was doing. Degrading herself for money, offering herself up on a plate to strangers.

He hadn't really done anything wrong.

The girls was obviously destitute, broken.

All he'd done was help rid the world of yet another piece of undesired litter.

She was nothing but a whore.

Just like all women were deep down, and Christopher had done the humane thing by putting the girl out of her misery.

Chapter Twenty-One

'After you, ladies. Welcome to . . . "Destiny's".' Nathan proudly held the pub door wide open as he showed his two sisters inside. Watching their faces as they looked around and then at each other, giggling, Nathan didn't know why he bothered.

He was trying to help Kelly out, but all the girl did was throw it back in his face.

'Destiny's? Are you are fucking kidding me? Dusty's more like.' Kelly peered over the top of her sunglasses as she walked the length of the bar, wrinkling her nose up at the strong sour smell that filled the air.

Nathan rolled his eyes. Kelly never had been one to hide her true feelings, and in typical Woods style she had no qualms about saying it how it was. His sister clearly couldn't see the wood for the trees – once the decorators had been in this place would be transformed.

'Are you sure you know what you're doing taking this place on?' Kelly asked. Boozers like this place were ten a penny. From the way Nathan had been talking last night Kelly had been under the illusion that her brother had bought a swanky wine bar. But this, well, it was anything but. Nathan must be losing it.

'It does have potential,' Evie offered, seeing disappointment flash across Nathan's face. 'Can I go and have a nose around?'

'Go for it.' Then, turning back to his churlish sister, Nathan glared. 'Oi, I'm doing you a favour, don't forget.' Kelly was an ungrateful mare turning her nose up at the place, and his patience with her was starting to wear thin. 'Don't let how it looks now fool you. Trust me, after a lick of paint and a bit of TLC this place is going to be a gold mine. You won't even recognise it.'

'I should hope so too. I don't mean to sound rude, Nathan, but even you must be able to see that this place is bloody rank.' Kelly was unconvinced by her brother's optimism and as her eyes swept over the dated floral curtains and matching wallpaper that violently clashed with the garish carpet, she couldn't help but think that the place looked like a psychedelic throwback from the sixties. Retro might be making a comeback, but this place was beyond a revival.

Nathan bit his tongue. He knew Kelly was just stressed out. Terry doing a runner had set the girl on edge, and if what the police had said last night about what Terry had done to that hospital porter was true, then he couldn't blame her for being so het up. 'Are you okay?' he asked.

It had been a tough night. He, Raymond and Christopher had driven around for hours looking for him, but to no avail. They'd asked about too, but no-one had seen or heard anything of Terry. It was like the bloke had just disappeared completely off the radar. It had been almost 3 a.m. by the time Nathan had finally got into bed. Caught up in it all, he hadn't even had a chance to call Cassie.

'Yeah, I'm fine. I'm just knackered, that's all.' Unable to stifle the yawn that escaped as she spoke, Kelly covered her mouth. 'I just couldn't sleep.'

She was hung-over and exhausted. Everything seemed to be happening all at once. Back in the fold of the family, she had thoroughly enjoyed the evening up until they'd gone back to her dad's and that bent copper had turned up.

Hearing about Terry had knocked her for six. The police had no sympathy towards her either. They'd all but interrogated her.

Kelly had spent hours just lying in bed and staring up at the ceiling once they'd gone. Her mobile phone hadn't left her hand, she was that desperate to hear that he was all right.

Terry had only made his situation worse. He was so far in the shit now that he had practically buried himself in it. Kelly couldn't stop thinking about that poor man that the police said Terry attacked. Terry could be looking at attempted murder on top of everything else, and if the porter didn't pull through then . . . Well, Kelly just couldn't even contemplate it.

By running, Terry not only made himself look more guilty, but he had gone and made everything a million times worse.

Hung-over and knackered, the enthusiasm that she had felt last night when Nathan had asked her if she would like to manage their new spangly wine bar had long since dwindled. She knew that she was being a bitch to Nathan, and he didn't deserve it.

She was trying to put on a front. Trying to hold herself together.

'Eww. Can you smell that?' Changing the subject, she decided that she'd rather sound like a moody cow than look like an emotional wreck. Kelly, feeling the bile rising at the back of her throat, bent down and helped herself to a bottle of Coke from the fridge underneath the bar. Taking a swig, she tried to suppress the nauseated feeling that had swept over her, as the much needed sugar and caffeine hit kicked in.

Nathan shrugged. There was a strong chemical smell about the place.

'I think it's bleach or something?' Evie offered, as she came back through to the bar and caught Kelly's comment. 'I think someone must have cleaned the cellar. I opened the door, but the smell was so strong that it made me gag. Shame that whoever had the OCD cleaning frenzy down there stopped when it came to the rest of the place, eh? The place is filthy.'

'Can't bloody win with you two, can I? One minute the place is too dirty, next it smells too clean.' Fed up with his sisters' incessant moaning, Nathan opened one of the windows to let some air in. 'Look, I know this place is old, and yes it bloody stinks. The decorating firm will be here soon and once they get started this place is going to look the nuts. This place needs some hard graft. And I need your help. But if you ain't interested in taking me up on my offer, Kelly, then you just let me know. Cos there are loads of people that would bite my bleeding arm off to work somewhere like this. Especially if it means they get to live upstairs rent free as part of the privilege.' Taking out the notepad from his pocket, Nathan busied himself making notes. He was bored with trying to convince the pair of them of the pub's potential.

'Rent free?' Kelly's ears pricked up as she worked out how much money she would save herself and Terry each month without forking out for living expenses. A bloody fortune, that was how much. 'I'm sorry, Nath, I don't mean to sound ungrateful. Really I don't.' Kelly sniffed as she realised her brother was fast losing his patience with her. 'It's just, what with Terry and all that, my head is all over the place.'

'Well, like I said, Kel, I ain't forcing you to come on board with this, it's your decision.' Nathan chewed his pen as Evie sat on the bar stool next to him. Both staring at Kelly now. Waiting for her answer.

It really was Kelly's decision now. Solely hers. The way the police had spoken last night, once they caught up with Terry he could be looking at going down for years.

She would be on her own raising the kids.

She needed to think about the bigger picture and pull herself together.

She had nothing left to lose. She'd spent her life waiting for Terry to come up trumps for her and give her the life that she wanted so badly, and the way things were going now she'd be left waiting for all bloody eternity.

Maybe it was time to make her own fortune. This place was huge, and if they did move in here the kids would be able to have their own bedrooms, with their own double beds.

All completely rent free.

It was a life changing opportunity.

It would all be down to her.

Peering down the long wooden bar, Kelly tried her hardest to visualise the place once it had been tarted up. 'Kelly Stranks, Landlady.' The title did have a nice ring to it. Nathan wasn't stupid, he was far from it in fact. She'd be a fool to pass it up.

'Would I get a say in the décor?' Kelly asked, as Nathan carried on jotting down his design ideas ready for the decorator's arrival. Kelly's brain suddenly went into overdrive.

'Well, down here is all sorted. But upstairs, that would be totally up to you. If you wanted it . . .' Nathan smiled, knowing full well that it had been the mention of rent free accommodation that had finally swung it for her. 'Just say the word, Kel, and I'll get the decorators to discuss what you want when they get here. We can get the whole place done in one go.'

'Okay. I'll do it,' Kelly shrieked, suddenly feeling excited.

'Great.' Nathan smiled. 'I'm glad you've said that, Kel, as I've already taken the liberty of booking you on the training course to get your personal licence. Rang them first thing.'

'I could help out too,' Evie offered, feeling a bit left out of the conversation. She was happy for her sister of course, but sometimes she felt like she was invisible.

'We'll see.' Evie was desperate to get involved, Nathan could see it in the girl's face. 'I don't want her to lose her bloody licence before she's even got it, Evie. You're only sixteen remember.' Then feeling mean he added, 'But I'm sure if it's alright with Kelly, then you could help out collecting the glasses and doing a bit of cleaning around the place every now and again.'

Evie smiled.

'Well, it's fine by me, Evie love.' Kelly smiled. Over the past couple of days her little sister had really started to grow on her. Kelly had thought that Evie would be stuck up; stunningly beautiful and attending a posh private school Kelly had expected her to be full of herself, but in fact she was the complete opposite. Evie was quiet, shy. She seemed happy to blend in to the background and not make a fuss, unlike her and her brothers who were often all fighting for attention. Kelly could see that Evie was genuine too. She wanted to help her, with the kids, with the bar. As much as Kelly wanted to dislike the girl, she couldn't. Evie was lovely inside and out. 'Tell you what, why don't me and you go and have a mosey around town later? We can have a look at some bits and pieces for the flat, take the kids out for lunch too, yeah?'

Evie nodded. She could see that Kelly was desperate for company, and no wonder with her husband disappearing off like that. 'I'd love to.'

'Alright, losers.' Christopher stepped out from the doorway behind the bar, enjoying the fact that he'd just made his siblings jump out of their skin in fright. 'Thought I'd use the back entrance, being a gay bar and all that.'

Nathan shook his head and then continued writing, ignoring Christopher's immature comments, refusing to bite.

'You must be knackered after last night,' Kelly asked, noting how tired Christopher looked. 'You look almost as knackered as I feel. Did the fight take it out of you?'

'Yeah, something like that.' Christopher grinned. 'Here, give us a sip, Kel, I'm gagging for a cold drink. My mouth's drier than a nun's fanny.' Taking Kelly's bottle from her hand Christopher took a swig. He was dog tired. By the time he'd got rid of his clothes and got into bed it had been almost 7 a.m. He'd only had a couple of hours' kip and he could have done with at least another eight, but he knew if he didn't come down here in time for the decorators Nathan would have copped the right hump.

'Hey,' Kelly moaned. 'Get your own.'

'Alright, moody,' Christopher said as he bent down to help himself to a drink from the fridge. 'I take it by the look on your sour moosh that you still haven't had any word from that wayward husband of yours?'

'No.' Kelly flinched at Christopher's insensitivity; her youngest brother had no tact. 'Here, and you can make that your last free drink.' Kelly nodded to the bottle that Christopher held in his hand as he took a seat at the bar. 'Landlady's rules!'

'Have a fucking laugh, Kelly, you dozy cow. Drinks ain't freebies to us, me and Nathan fucking own them. They're already bought and paid for.'

'I could have you barred, you know.' Kelly grinned.

Christopher was so easy to wind up. Such a stroppy git, he could dish jokes out, but he could never take them, and seeing the frown etched on his disgruntled face, her riling him up about being in charge was clearly working. Christopher hated anyone telling him what to do.

'What's the point in having a bar if we ain't going to get some fucking benefit from it? Free drinks should be standard . . .' he continued.

'Of course we can have free drinks, you mug,' Nathan sighed. 'But other than that, this place needs to be run tighter than two coats of paint. I don't want the Old Bill round here poking their noses in. This place has had a bad reputation for years, and I want to start a clean slate with it. There'll be no lock-ins, no fights.' And then glaring at his brother he added, 'And no drugs.' Nathan had watched his brother closely last night during the fight. Christopher had been coked out of his head, and it wasn't a one-off occasion. How his father hadn't noticed was beyond him.

'What are you looking at me for?' Christopher feigned innocence at Nathan's implication.

Nathan held Christopher's stare. He could tell he'd pissed his brother off. He could also tell that even now, having just rolled out of his pit, Christopher was high as a fucking kite. Nathan knew his brother better than anyone, even better than Christopher knew himself.

'Paranoia is one of the effects, you know.'

'Funny fucker.' Christopher shrugged his brother's comment off. It was none of his brother's business what he did.

'Where's Dad and Uncle Raymond?' Christopher thought that they would be the first people here – his father would have been itching to get a glance at his sons' new investment and put his two pence worth in.

'Think he said something about clearing some business thing up. I'm sure they'll be here in a bit.' Nathan checked his watch. Now that the police appeared to be keeping an eye on them, his dad and Raymond didn't want to take any chances. They'd gone down to the warehouse first thing this morning, and Nathan had a feeling they were going to be a while clearing everything out. 'We may as well make a start and crack open the champagne. You know what he's like, he'll be expecting a glass of the good stuff at the ready when he does turn up.' Nathan grinned as he pulled from the fridge the bottle that he'd put by especially for the occasion. He wanted to celebrate. He was determined to prove to his whole family that this place was going to be the first in a very long line of smart investments.

Destiny's was going to be a tidy little earner. Nathan was happy to leave the boxing and promoting to his dad and the fighting to

Christopher. He'd learnt a lot from working for his dad, but Nathan wasn't cut out for crime, his heart wasn't in it. He had just gone along with it all until he figured out what he really wanted to do. Now he had. He wanted to deal in property; that was where the real money was, and more importantly it was what Nathan felt most passionate about. His only regret was that he'd taken Christopher in with him on this development. Already there was friction. And, though his brother didn't know it yet, it wasn't a mistake that he intended on repeating.

'Shall we make a toast?' Nathan popped the cork and poured the drinks, before passing them around.

'I think Kelly should do it, being the new landlady and all that. You need to give the place your blessing, Kel.' Evie clapped her hands together excitedly for her elder sister. From what Evie had seen since she'd been back home, this place was exactly what Kelly and her nephew and niece needed. A new start.

'Yeah, go on, Kelly, what do you say?' Nathan grinned.

Slipping her sunglasses back over her eyes Kelly dramatically flopped her head down on top of the bar, before speaking the words she never thought she'd hear herself say. 'What do I say?' she laughed as she half-heartedly raised her champagne flute in the air, her forehead still resting on the bar. 'I say, please God, no more bloody champagne.'

Chapter Twenty-Two

'You did lock them, didn't you, Raymond?' Unscrewing the concealed compartment in the floor of the Volkswagen Caddy, Harry glanced back to the main warehouse doors making sure that the bolts were securely on. 'I wouldn't put it past the Old Bill to have followed us.'

'It's locked, Harry. Chill. Even if they had followed us, they would have lost us when we switched the cars. The gormless twats are probably sat in the multi-storey car park eyeing up your Bentley right as we speak.'

Raymond could see that his friend was on edge. He'd been like this since he'd arrived at his first thing this morning. It wasn't like Harry to get so het up about this kind of shit. Normally things like this wouldn't rattle him. Harry had been in this game for too long to start quaking in his boots over someone as insignificant as Terry Stranks.

So the police had searched his house . . . So what? Harry knew that they would never find anything. It was how he worked. Harry lived by the rule that he would never leave so much as a skid on his doorstep let alone shit on it. It was his family home.

Passing the brown paper parcels to Harry, Raymond could tell that Harry had more on his mind than he was letting on.

'Yeah, you're right. Here, what about DCS Porter?' Harry reasoned. 'Did you see his face last night as he apologised for having to search my gaff? He looked like he'd shat his pants.' The police were convinced that he was hiding Terry and that just proved to him what bloody imbeciles they were. 'If the pigs owned a brain cell between them they would have known that I fucking hate Terry with a passion. And if that cunt had turned up at my place looking for help, I would have handed him in quicker than that lot could have identified their arses from their elbows.'

They had gone about searching his house like the blind leading the blind, and Harry had been determined to hide the fact that them turning up at his house had seriously rattled his cage.

'Don't you worry about DCS Porter. Like Mansell said, he was just keeping up appearances and making sure that he looked like he was doing his job, Harry. Trust me. Porter won't fucking do a thing to either of us. Not unless he wants to make his Internet debut as a dodgy fucking porn star who likes giving it up the arse to underage girls.' Raymond grinned. As far as he and Harry were concerned they were both as safe as houses.

Raymond loved the fact that he had Porter over a barrel.

The bloke had had a right bee in his bonnet, ever since he and Harry had turned over that jewellers in Mayfair eight years ago. Talk about a bone of contention. Porter was convinced that Harry was involved, so much so that he'd been digging around for dirt on Harry for years.

Finally, with the help of Molly, Raymond had managed to put paid to all that, by getting his own form of collateral damage in the form of filmed evidence. Porter wouldn't dare touch them now. It would be more than his life was worth.

'I wonder where that fucker Terry is, though?'

'Fuck knows, but wherever he is, I would put my money on the fact that he hasn't travelled via a motorbike.' Raymond shook his head now, laughing. 'I tell you, Harry, it was the funniest thing I ever saw. I turned round to make sure that Nathan was still behind me and spotted Terry about two hundred metres behind, caught in a cloud of thick black smoke. If his bike had been going any slower, it would have been in reverse.'

Harry couldn't help but laugh then.

Harry had always said that the devil was in the detail when it came to executing a plan, and with Terry's bike purposely rigged, and Officer Mansell at the ready to pull him in, Terry getting caught red-handed with three kilos of the purest calibre cocaine on the market had been a dead cert. Harry wanted to tuck the fucker up for a few years at least, and keep him as far away from Kelly as possible. As for the transit van that had materialised out of nowhere and knocked the fucker off his bike, well, as far as Harry was concerned that had been genius timing. A pure coincidence, money couldn't buy that kind of bad luck; it was just a shame that the collision hadn't killed the cunt.

It was all sorted, and Harry had even got his brief all geared up to go and advise Terry to take the rap once the police had him.

Harry had thought that Terry, being the divvy cunt that he was, would just go along with it all and do exactly what he was told. Harry had truly believed that by the time that twat realised that he'd actually been shafted it would be too late. He'd already be locked away in an eight by six cell, on his holidays courtesy of Her Royal Majesty.

The only thing Harry hadn't figured on was Terry doing a runner.

So as it turned out, Terry had a bit more clout than Harry had given him credit for.

He'd underestimated his son-in-law.

'You should have just had him done, Harry. We could have made it look like an accident so that Kelly would have been none the wiser that we'd been involved . . .' Raymond didn't want to state the obvious, but he couldn't understand why Harry hadn't just done that in the first place. He'd have happily done the honours if it had come to it. In fact nothing would give him greater pleasure than to put Terry Stranks down like the dirty dog that he was.

'What, and watch Kelly bury her husband?' Harry stopped and stared at Raymond now. 'You saw what that did to me when I had to bury my Evelyn. I couldn't do that to Kelly, no way.'

'Yeah, but that was different, Harry. It wasn't as straightforward as that.'

Raymond trod carefully as he spoke.

They barely mentioned Evelyn's name anymore.

Harry just shrugged it off, as if she never existed. Heartbroken and racked with guilt over what happened.

Packing the parcels down tightly in the compartment, Harry purposely ignored Raymond's direction of conversation and closed the lid down. Then he pulled the board of ply lining back in place, and screwed the panel back down to the floor.

Raymond took the hint. He knew more than anyone how hard it had been for Harry. To bury his wife, and carry the secret of her death around on his shoulders each day. He'd been there for him every step of the way of course. He'd helped Harry to cover it all up, and he'd helped Harry ever since by picking up the pieces.

'Kelly loves him,' Harry reasoned. As much as they both hated Terry Stranks, Kelly, for some godforsaken reason, really did love the man, and Harry couldn't be the one who took that away from her. Not permanently anyway. Not like that.

Feeling his chest constrict, Harry took a deep breath. He could feel the dull familiar rattling forming inside his chest again. He was stressed out and it was starting to take its toll. Jumping down from the back of the van, he knew that he needed to be honest with Raymond. Well, as honest as he could be.

He'd been thinking things through for weeks now, and Harry knew that he was going to have to start facing the reality of his situation sooner rather than later. He just couldn't find the right words.

'Do you know what? I'm getting too old for this shit.' Harry stood facing Raymond. 'I've been doing some thinking and it's time that I stepped back from all this. I'm done in from it all.'

'What do you mean?' Raymond sat down on the edge of the van. The warehouse was stuffy, and Raymond pulled at his shirt collar to loosen it.

'Look, we both knew that this wasn't going to be forever. Fuck me, since we started out we've made a fortune. We're quids in from the Dubai account alone, we're set up. I just feel like it's time to step back now.'

A feeling of immense unease swept over Raymond, something that he had rarely experienced when it came to thrashing out business with one of his oldest friends. Harry had just dropped an almighty bombshell. He wanted out. Just like that. It didn't make sense.

'I don't get it, Harry.' Confused, Raymond was trying to digest Harry's unexpected announcement.

'There is nothing to get, Raymond, I'm just tired of it all.'

Raymond screwed his face up. Without a shadow of a doubt there was more to all this. As the saying went, you can't bullshit a bullshitter, and Raymond Marks could smell the stench of crap from a mile off.

Harry, seeing that Raymond wasn't convinced, shrugged as he continued. 'You've seen yourself what we're having to deal with now. The fucking Turks are taking over Soho, flooding the market with their gear and selling the shit so cheap that we just can't fucking compete anymore. We've already had to drop our prices to accommodate the Mancs in case they decide to go elsewhere. It won't be long until the Turks move in on our deal.'

'Compete? Jesus, Harry, can you hear yourself? Our gear is the fucking purest shit out on the streets. Even if those oily eyed cunts try to undercut us, you get what you pay for. Their shit is so bulked up with fucking Levamisole, just one baggie could deworm a fucking herd of cows. People are wising up to buying from those fuckers.' Raymond was telling Harry what he already knew. It wasn't just the Turks that had been basking in the limelight lately. The Russians had been all over the press recently too. News of their latest contribution, 'Krokodil', a fast becoming 'poor man's heroin', had hit the streets too. That shit was so toxic it could rot people's flesh right off their bones. The bigger firms didn't want anything to do with it. It was a fucked up world out there and the foreign gangs were ruthless. They didn't seem to have any morals when it came to what they used to cut their shit up with. There may be honour among thieves, but there was none amongst dealers, that was for sure.

'You know as well as I do that the foreign gangs are fucking ruthless, Harry. They just want the highest return for their investments. Once they've had their money they don't give a flying fuck about the aftereffects. People are wising up to that. No-one with half a brain cell wants to associate themselves with that lethal shit. Look at our contacts. They're willing to pay a premium for the purest cocaine on the market. And we have the best supplier going, Harry. There is no competition.'

Raymond stared at his friend defiantly. If Harry walked away now, he was a fool.

With his supplier in Holland providing them with a steady influx of the purest of gear and regular monthly shipments, all they had to do each month was deliver the shipment to their contact up in Manchester. Harry cut out all the middle men and made a fortune. Raymond did the drops, and the rest was history.

Harry couldn't just walk away now. The market was theirs for the taking.

'Let the Turks fucking sell to the fucking scum out on the streets. They ain't got shit on us. We're wholesalers, Harry, fuck being the middle man. That's their role.' Raymond knew that he was fighting a losing battle; once Harry made his mind up there was no room for persuasion and he knew by the way that Harry was talking that this hadn't been an overnight decision. Even so, Raymond knew that he had to try to make Harry see sense.

'Don't you just feel fucking tired of it all, though, Raymond?' Harry asked. 'I am. My head's done in. I'm going to be fifty-five this year. My kids are all grown up and I just want to sit back for a bit and enjoy my time with them.'

Raymond caught the tilt to Harry's voice as he spoke. There was something else going on here. Whatever it was, Harry wasn't going to let on.

'In case you're forgetting, we're the same age. And I ain't being funny but fifty-five is a long way off from being fucking eighty-five, Harry. What do you want to do, eh? Fucking retire? Sit watching *Cash in the* fucking *Attic* while you do the sudoku puzzles in the back of the paper? Fuck me, Harry. That ain't you. You ain't ready to give all this up.'

Harry laughed now, despite himself.

A real belly laugh. Raymond always had such a way with words. He always hit the nail on the head.

'You're a fucking baby in the grand scheme of things. We both are. And you're as fit as a bleeding fiddle . . . You could run rings around me.'

'Look, I hear you, Raymond. Really I do. But like I said to you before, this wasn't meant to be forever and it's time for me to take a step back.'

Silence fell between them. Raymond could see by the stern look on Harry's face that his mind was made up.

'Okay then, mate,' Raymond sighed.

Harry wasn't budging and Raymond knew by the finality in the man's voice that the conversation was over. 'Whatever you say. But I really hope that you don't regret this decision a few years down the line.'

'You know me, Raymond, I don't do regrets.' Harry shrugged, glad that his friend was finally backing down.

Life was far too short for regrets and Raymond, as much as he cared, didn't know the half of it.

'Now come on, let's get this shit out of here.'

Chapter Twenty-Three

Walking into the room, Cassie picked up Jacob Mulligan's notes. 'Hey, my little man, how are you doing today?'

Staring out from under his skull and crossbone bandana, the little boy shot Cassie a cheeky grin. 'Hello, Nurse Wrong.' The three-year-old giggled loudly.

'Excuse me, little mister.' Cassie put her hand on her hip and pouted her lips playfully. 'I think you'll find it's Nurse Wright.'

Giggling even more now, Jacob shook his head. 'Nurse Wrong, Nurse Wrong,' he sang.

Jacob was a little star in the making. For the past couple of weeks caring for Jacob had become a highlight of Cassie's day. He never failed to make her smile. Cassie had taken a real shine to the boy, just as he had her. Though she knew that professionally she needed to keep her distance – working on the oncology ward meant that she had long ago learned the hard way about getting too close to patients – there was something very special about Jacob, and Cassie, like the rest of the nurses on Elephant Ward, couldn't help falling in love with the child.

Smiling over at Jacob's mother, Cassie could tell that the poor woman was out of her mind with worry. Cassie couldn't blame her.

Today was going to be one of the toughest days the poor woman had ever endured.

'You didn't sleep again, Sally?' Cassie asked sympathetically. The guest bed looked like it had been slept in, but going by Sally Mulligan's puffy eyes and ghostly white complexion, Cassie would put her money on the fact that the woman had lain awake again worrying. Another sleepless night.

'Not a wink.' Sally shook her head.

Cassie moved around the bed so that Jacob was just out of earshot. 'You are in one of the best hospitals in the world. I know you're going to be worried out of your mind when he goes down to theatre, but he is in safe hands and he's a strong little man.' Cassie felt awful that her shift had finished and she wouldn't be here when the anaesthetist finally came to fetch Jacob for his surgery. She guessed in a way it was for the best. They had no idea how long he could be down there – it could be just a matter of a few hours, but more than likely it would be a lot longer. 'He's going to be just fine.'

'Thank you.' Sally clutched Cassie's hand tightly, appreciating the nurse's sentiments in trying to put her mind at ease. They both knew that Jacob's operation was set to be a complicated one, as brain surgery always was. Jacob had a Rhabdoid tumour. And it was aggressive. The child hadn't responded well to the chemotherapy he'd been having and, after six long weeks of persevering, the surgery today was his last option.

'I think one of the other mums has just filled the percolator up in the kitchen if you fancy a nice strong cup of coffee?' Cassie suggested.

'No. I'm fine, ta. I'll get one later, when Jacob goes down . . .'

Nodding, Cassie could already see how hard today was going to be for Jacob's mum. She'd seen it so many times before. It actually surprised her how it was always the mums that worried themselves sick, while the children that were going through the actual physical surgery often took it in their stride. But then, ignorance was bliss, she figured. Normally the mums did more than enough worrying for everybody.

'How about you, Jacob? Have you got everything you need?' Jacob was colouring in a picture in his bumper colouring book, scribbling with his crayons, and surrounded by so many cards, toys and teddies that the room could have passed for the hospital gift shop.

'Can I have some Coco Pops, Nurse Wrong? Mummy says that I'm not allowed as today is my properation,' Jacob answered.

'Op-er-ation.' Quietly, and with a weak smile, Sally corrected her son. Though just the mere sound of the word, spoken out loud, made her feel sick to her stomach.

'I'm afraid Mummy is right, Jacob. You are going down to theatre shortly.' Checking her watch, Cassie knew that Jacob would be collected soon. Spotting the look of disappointment on the small child's face, Cassie couldn't help herself. Sitting down on the empty chair next to him, she winked at Sally before lowering her voice and relaying to Jacob a very important secret. 'I'll tell you what though. You tell me something special that you want to eat later on and I'll pop back as soon as you come out of surgery and bring it for you especially. McDonald's, pizza, giant chocolate chip cookies . . . Anything in the whole wide world!'

Cassie watched as Jacob opened his eyes wide at the thought of being able to have anything he wanted. Taking a few seconds to think Jacob shrugged his shoulders.

'I just really, really want some Coco Pops. Maybe I could have two bowls?'

Laughing now, it never ceased to amaze Cassie how selfless some of the children that came in here were. After everything they had gone through, how they suffered, they were always so selfless. Her job was so humbling.

'Then Coco Pops it shall be. I've got to go home now. So you be a brave boy for your mummy, won't you?'

'I am brave, Nurse Wrong. Look, I'm a pirate today.' Jacob pointed up to his bandana. Then doing his best pirate impersonation he let out a loud, 'Ooh arr.' Just like he'd seen in the cartoons. Jacob's hair had fallen out from all the chemo sessions that he'd endured, and the boy was obsessed with his bandanas. Every day he had a different one to show Cassie, but he'd worn this two days in a row now so Cassie knew that it must be his favourite.

'Shiver me timbers,' Cassie laughed. 'Wow, you really are a very brave pirate. I'll see you later, Captain Mulligan.' Cassie curtseyed before walking to the end of the cubicle and blowing Jacob a kiss.

The boy smiled, then putting his small chubby hand up in the air he pretended to catch it. Just like Cassie had shown him.

Chapter Twenty-Four

'Well, it ain't the usual type of place I'd go for a pint, but you certainly know your market.' Raymond sat back in the booth as he scanned the busy bar. The place was packed to the rafters and he was impressed. Taking in the groups of trendy, well groomed men and women that filled the room, Nathan had certainly done a good job of honing in on the pink pound, just like he had said that he would.

'You've done bloody amazing,' Harry said proudly. Nathan was bang on the money. He'd had his work cut out for him. The place had been a dive when Nathan had first taken it on and if Harry hadn't seen it with his own eyes, he would never have believed the transformation was possible. In just one short week the place was completely unrecognisable.

Destiny's was every inch the upmarket wine bar that Nathan had promised it would be. The place was outstanding. The rickety old bar had been ripped out and replaced with a rustic French oak, which complemented the new wooden flooring perfectly. One end of the bar was dotted with leather upholstered stools while opposite, lining the entire side of the room, were a cluster of luxury velveted booths.

'How the bloody hell did you get it all done so quickly?' Raymond asked. 'Even *DIY SOS* would have struggled with this size project in a week.'

'I paid the decorating company double bubble, Uncle Raymond, and we all worked around the clock. I haven't seen Cassie all week.' Raymond and Harry laughed at how sullen Nathan looked at his sacrifice.

'Where is she tonight then? Working?'

'No. Well, kind of, I guess. It's her night off but she's gone in to see one of her patients. A little boy with cancer. He's been in theatre all day. I spoke to her earlier on the blower and she felt bad that she couldn't make it tonight, but she had sounded quiet worried about the little fella. So I insisted that she go and see him. Honestly, Dad, the things that girl deals with, I don't know how she does it. She's amazing.'

'Well, I tell you what, son, she's in good company with you then. And I hope it works out for you both.' Harry smiled at his son. He was so proud of how the boy had turned out. He didn't want to start getting all slushy on the kid, though. 'You've done a blinding job on this place. Proper top notch it is. And I hate to admit it, but as much as I love that brother of yours, thank God that he didn't have too much input when it came to the décor.' Harry chuckled.

'This place would have been kitted out with strobe lights and a bleeding disco lamp if he did.' Nathan laughed as he nodded over to the state-of-the-art DJ booth that he had invested a fortune in. 'What do you think of the new bit of kit? Bit better than the other one?'

'It looks perfectly understated, unlike that bloody monstrosity your brother ordered.' Harry laughed. 'Raymond, you should have seen the state of it, had me in fits it did. Bright bloody pink and covered in glitter, I ain't ever seen anything like it.'

'Don't, Dad, it wasn't bleeding funny.' Nathan shook his head at the thought of it. Apart from the odd unhelpful bit of inspiration from Christopher, it had been Nathan that had put his heart and soul into the place. 'Honest to God, Christopher ain't all there. He actually thought that it was a stylish feature. He probably had the Village People's "YMCA" all set up on the playlist too.' Listening to Christopher's stereotyping of the gay community all week had actually left Nathan gobsmacked. Somewhere in his tiny, ignorant mind Christopher truly believed that anything remotely camp or tacky in his eyes was technically classed as 'gay'.

'How come you know so much about what "gays" like?' Christopher had sneered at him earlier, miffed that not only had Nathan made him return the dodgy-looking pink DJ booth, but he had also constantly dismissed all of his design ideas. 'Are you sure Cassie isn't just a cover story to hide the fact that you're a secret ring snatcher?'

Nathan had ignored his brother's snidey jibe, too busy sorting out the last minute details himself to get into another row with him. He wanted every detail to be chic, and stylish. Whereas Christopher wasn't capable of going beyond cheap and nasty tat.

He had been glad when Christopher had finally gone home to get changed and left him, Evie and Kelly to finish up getting the place ready. The girls had worked flat out today with the cleaning and organising. Thank God they had, or else this place would have never been ready in time. His sisters had both been a million times more helpful than his so-called business partner.

They'd only opened the doors half an hour ago, and Nathan felt a surge of pride as he looked around. His first investment looked like it was set to soar.

The place was exactly how he'd envisaged it, right down to the very last detail.

Not only had Nathan lined up some of the best DJs in town and given them regular slots, but he'd also invested in a top notch menu too. Fresh local produce, with lots of fancy dishes. With good food on offer, drinks flowing, and top tunes playing, once people came through the door, Nathan wasn't going to give the punters any reason to want to leave.

'Where is your brother, anyway?' Raymond asked, looking about the place. He had thought that Christopher would be here by now, lapping up some of the praise on their grand opening. That boy loved the limelight.

'I think that's him there . . . Yep, talk of the devil.' Peering out of the window, Nathan spotted his brother's huge frame getting out of the taxi that had just pulled up outside, along with his two sidekicks, Darren and Russ.

Glancing out, he was pleased that his brother had at least made an effort. Kitted out in a suit so fitted that it contoured the outline of almost every muscle, Christopher looked as dapper as always, towering above his two mates. Nathan had a sneaky feeling that Christopher could probably dress in a bin bag and still receive the same recognition. He radiated the vibes of a man who could more than handle himself.

'Looks like Christopher has a few admirers.' Raymond laughed as he watched Christopher swaggering along the pathway outside the pub, past the packed tables that were overflowing with smokers. His enormous physique demanded presence and people moved out of the way as he walked towards them.

'Fucking hell,' Nathan sighed, noting that he was indeed receiving a steady stream of captivated stares following his broad frame as he went. 'I hope no-one's stupid enough to crack on to him.'

Going on how homophobic Christopher was, Nathan had been in half a mind to try to put him off from coming here tonight, but how could he? They were business partners. This place was a joint effort. Or it was supposed to have been.

'Too late for that. Look, he's pulled . . .' Harry laughed as they all watched as a nerdy looking guy, dressed in white skinny jeans and a baby-blue pullover bravely approach Christopher.

Even from this distance they could see that Christopher had a face like thunder on him at the thought of being chatted up by a gay man. His eyes flashed with malice, and Nathan could see his brother's neck turn puce, a sure warning sign that Christopher was going to kick off.

'Oh fuck!' Nathan abruptly stood up as he recognised the man that Christopher was now glaring at. 'I'll be back in a minute,' he called as he began making his way to the main door as quickly as he could before his brother put them out of business before they had even started.

'Hi there. It's Christopher, isn't it? Wow, it's so hot in there that I needed to come outside just to get some air.' Wayne smiled. He knew he was babbling but he couldn't help himself. Christopher Woods was a beast of a man and standing in front of him, Wayne, not normally so easily unsettled, suddenly felt nervous. Just the sheer size of the man was intimidating. The bloke didn't look too friendly. Faced with Christopher's icy cold stare, Wayne tried to remain unfazed as he offered out his hand. He'd heard how volatile Christopher Woods could be. He was almost as famous for his short fuse as he was for his boxing. 'I'm Wayne, Wayne Barnes.'

'And?' Ignoring the geeky looking bloke's extended hand, Christopher leaned back. This bloke was in way too close proximity for his liking. He must have a death wish if he thought for even one second he could try it on.

Christopher turned to his mates and raised his eyes trying to make light of the situation to save face.

'You certainly know how to draw a crowd.' Ignoring Christopher's rudeness, as he sipped from the long cocktail glass, Wayne persevered with his conversation. 'Must be the cocktails. Cucumber Daiquiri this one is, it's gorgeous.'

Wayne was doing everything in his power to keep his cool. Christopher Woods was known for his abruptness, in fact that was all part of the man's charm. It's what people loved. His fiery temper, his strong physique. Like his father, Harry Woods, Christopher was fast becoming a celebrity face in London, with a bad boy reputation to match. Wayne could see the attraction; there was just something so delicious about taming a bad boy. 'I can see you're a busy man, so shall we just get straight down to business. Do you want to go inside? It would be great if I could get a body shot of you standing up against the bar.'

'Er, I don't fucking think so, mate.' A body shot? Christopher rubbed his temples. This poncy cunt was starting to infuriate him now. These fucking gays were more upfront than he had anticipated. This one clearly had balls of steel thinking that he could just swan right up to him and try his luck. If this bloke was aware of who he was, then he'd also be aware of the fact that Christopher wasn't gay. Blatantly being chatted up by this mincer in full view of his mates, and before he'd even got his foot in the door of the bar, Christopher was raging. What was this bloke? Some kind of a cunt?

Incensed, Christopher leaned in and spoke loud enough so that the man could hear him clearly. 'Unless you're hiding a tight little pussy and pair of titties under that fucking clobber you've got on, I ain't fucking interested. I'm straighter than a fucking ruler, you get me? You've got more chance of me shoving that Cucumber Daiquiri up your arse fucking sideways, than anything attached to my anatomy!'

Christopher had warned his brother that everyone would start to think they were both a pair of benders, but had Nathan listened? No, he hadn't. Nathan always thought he knew best. But not this time. Christopher had been right. He'd barely been here more than two bleeding minutes and already he had been propositioned by one of the dirty bastards.

Christopher knew that this would happen. He was a good-looking fucker, so he couldn't really blame the gays for trying their luck. They probably thought he was a prime bit of meat ready for the taking. The only thing this bloke would be riding tonight was a fucking ambulance if he even so much as put his slimy hands anywhere near him.

'How dare you . . .?' Indignant, there was no way Wayne was going to stand here and be spoken to like this, no matter how threatening Christopher Woods may think he could be. No-one spoke to Wayne like that.

'How dare I?' Christopher laughed now, joining in with his mates that were stood behind him. He could see that his words had had the desired effect as he watched Wayne's face flash bright red with anger. The bloke looked like he was going to have a bitch-fit and Christopher was enjoying making the slimy bastard squirm.

Hearing Darren and Russ both laughing behind him only spurred Christopher on some more. That and the crowd of onlookers who were gathering around on hearing the heated argument. Christopher revelled in being on show once more, and this dirty bastard needed to learn a few rules on etiquette around here. 'Here you go, cunt-chops. How's this for a dare?' Grabbing the bloke roughly by his top, Christopher pulled the man in closely before head-butting him hard in the face.

Wayne's nose exploded as he fell backwards, landing awkwardly on the floor. Sprawled out on his back at Christopher's feet, he writhed around the floor in agony, cupping his hand under his nose, as he tried to catch the stream of blood that poured out. The blow had been unexpected and the pain that had exploded in his head was making him feel disorientated.

Christopher sneered down at him as he snorted up a mouthful of mucus from the back of his throat, which he spat straight into Wayne's blood splattered face.

Darren and Russ roared with laughter now. Christopher was like a man possessed when he copped the hump, and rolling up his sleeves now, it looked like he was just getting started.

'What the fuck are you playing at?' Shoving his way through the crowd that was now standing around Wayne, Nathan had just come steaming out of the pub.

'For fuck's sake, Christopher. What is your problem?' Nathan berated his brother before squatting down on the floor and turning his attention to Wayne.

The man looked a sight. With blood all down his shirt and tears of humiliation filling his eyes, Nathan knew that there was no way he was going to be able to smooth this over.

Once again, Christopher had gone too far.

'Jesus. I'm so sorry, Wayne. There seems to have been some kind of misunderstanding. My brother . . .'

Christopher didn't feel that he needed to justify himself, but seeing as Nathan was so het up about it, he would. 'Don't apologise on my account, Nath, there was no misunderstanding, trust me. This cunt was trying it on and just got himself a much needed reality check.'

Flashing his brother a warning glare, Nathan turned his back on Christopher and tried to salvage the situation as best as he could with the injured man. 'Do you want to come inside and we'll get you all cleaned up?' Nathan wanted to calm the situation down, but he could tell by the look on Wayne's face that the last thing he wanted to do now was go into the bar.

He could murder Christopher for this.

'I'm not going anywhere near that Neanderthal.' Wayne was shaking. In all his years, he'd never come up against someone so vile and offensive. 'A gay bar owned by a gay-basher. Is this how you get your kicks?'

'Oi, watch your mouth. Don't forget who you are talking to.' Christopher was getting severely pissed off now. He could see the crowd of people around him whispering and looking at him with disgust. It had been this little prick who had started it, and as far as he was concerned he'd done the decent thing and finished it. If the bloke wanted to get gobby and go in for round two, Christopher was more than happy to oblige. No matter how annoyed Nathan was. No-one was mugging him off.

'It might pay well for you to realise who you're talking to actually.' Wayne glared at Christopher bravely now as he picked up his bag and checked that his camera equipment inside was still in one piece.

'I couldn't give a flying fuck if you were George Michael,' Christopher sneered. Then seeing his brother's stern look he shrugged. 'What?'

'This is Wayne Barnes.'

'Yeah, thanks for that, Nath. Big help that is, but he already told me his name before I nutted him one.'

Nathan gritted his teeth. If Christopher had just listened for once this week, instead of being so off his face on gear, then none of this would have happened. 'Wayne's from *GT* magazine. He was the one I told you about last week! He's doing a big feature for us on the big opening night.' Nathan couldn't be bothered to elaborate any more than that. What was the point? The night was ruined, and now thanks to his brother so was Destiny's reputation.

'Correction. I *was* doing a feature,' Wayne said as he flung his rucksack over his shoulder. 'But don't you worry, you're still going to get your column inches. In fact, once the police pay you a visit you might even make front page news.' Wayne leaned in to where Nathan was standing, not quite brave enough to go nearer to Christopher, but still determined to save face. 'I'll be making sure everyone knows exactly what kind of people run this place. And as for you claiming to be straight . . .' Wayne pointed his finger in Christopher's direction. 'You're not straight, you're narrow . . . Narrow-bloody-minded.'

Picking up his bag, Wayne stormed across to the other side of the street.

The small crowd of people who had gathered around gradually wandered off. Nathan watched as some of them put down their glasses and left too in unity, and Nathan couldn't blame them. Christopher had been bang out of order. The attack was completely unprovoked.

'Do you realise what you've just cost us? That man was the fucking key to getting our name out there.' Nathan glared angrily at his brother. Now up close, he could see the tell-tale signs that Christopher was off his face again. His bloodshot eyes were like saucers and his pupils were dilated.

He looked like shit. Christopher had always been jittery and paranoid, but lately he had become more so, and Nathan was starting to feel that he was getting more and more out of control. He was sick of having to pick up the pieces where his brother was concerned.

'Shit, Nathan, I didn't realise he was from the magazine.' Christopher knew instantly that his apology was too little, too late.

Glaring at Christopher, Nathan was beyond furious. He was physically seething. Even Darren and Russ had the good manners to shut up now.

Shaking his head in dismay, Nathan was disgusted.

'Stay off the fucking gear, Christopher. It doesn't fucking suit you. And while you're at it, stay the fuck away from me tonight 'en all. If the Old Bill turns up, you're going to get pulled, so do me a favour and fucking well do one. You've already caused enough trouble for one night.'

Walking back into the bar, Nathan slammed the door behind him.

Christopher was a liability. There was no way that this bar would work out with him involved. As of tomorrow, Nathan would be running Destiny's alone.

Christopher was out.

Chapter Twenty Five

'Oh. My. God!' Kelly grinned as she strutted up and down the shoe shop swinging her hips dramatically, before spinning around and planting her hand on her waist in front of the mirror. The second she'd spotted the black patent leather stilettos through the shop window, Kelly had made a beeline straight for them. Dragging her sister in with the pretence that they'd 'just have a look', she knew instantly that she just had to have them. 'I bloody love them. What do you think, Evie?'

'Not many girls can work a pair of heels like those and I must say they do look exquisite on you.' Before Evie had a chance to answer, the eager shop assistant standing nearby interrupted, throwing yet another compliment in Kelly's direction, clearly desperate to make a sale.

'Yeah, it's a little problem of mine. I make everything look so damn good. Bit of a trend setter, ain't I, Evie?'

Evie sniggered and Kelly rolled her eyes now. The assistant was trying just a tad too hard to put on the hard sell, and he really didn't have to. The deal had been done the second Kelly had clapped eyes on the shoes when she'd peered in the shop's window as they were passing.

'Oh I don't know, Kel, I mean they're lovely and all that, but I'm not sure they are going to be very comfy for working behind the bar.' Evie stared at the gold pointed studs that lined the entire heel. 'They look more like lethal weapons than shoes. You'll end up breaking your neck going up and down the cellar in those, they have to be at least six inches high. What about some ballet pumps like mine?'

'Ballet pumps?' Taking her eyes off her reflection, Kelly turned to her younger sister and stared down at Evie's plain grey suede pumps. Pursing her lips Kelly wriggled her nose. 'Evie babe, no offence. But if I had to choose, I'd rather wear sandwiches on my feet than those things. One thing in life I don't do is flat shoes. I'm five foot two; without my heels I'm barely able to see over the top of the bleeding bar. Besides, there is something about a nice high shoe that just makes me feel, I dunno . . . sexy.' Kelly shrugged.

Taking in her reflection in the mirror once more, Kelly looked herself up and down, admiring how the high heel transformed her figure. Her legs looked instantly longer and thinner.

Turning to the shop assistant, Kelly smiled. 'And these bad boys scream sexy. I'll take them.'

Evie rolled her eyes playfully as the shop assistant led them both over to the tills.

'Well, we both knew the second I clapped eyes on these little beauts that they were coming home with me, didn't we? Ballet pumps? What are you like, eh? Still, I guess at least you can get away with them, being so tall and skinny. You're just like Mum, do you know that? She had a gorgeous figure too.'

'You're joking, Kelly. I'd love to have some of your curves.' Evie smiled meekly now. 'Plus, I haven't got a clue about fashion really. Never really bother much with dressing up when I'm at school. The girls there don't really . . . I don't know . . . include me in things, you know.'

Evie blushed as she spoke and Kelly could tell that there was more going on with Evie than met the eye. Taking the bag from the shop assistant, Kelly linked her arm around her sister's as they walked back out of the shop.

'Don't include you? Why not?' Kelly could feel Evie tense up as she answered.

'They don't really like me,' Evie offered, and then saw Kelly's look of concern.

'Don't be silly, how can anyone not like you?' Kelly laughed.

Shaking her head, Evie finally opened up. 'Honest, Kel, no-one does. There is this one girl, Madeline Porter. She's the ringleader I guess. She's been making my life hell for years. I guess everyone else just follows suit.'

'What do you mean? That this Madeline bullies you? Why haven't you said anything, Evie?' Kelly stopped in the middle of the shopping mall, and looked Evie right in the eye. She could tell by her sister's burning red cheeks that Evie felt uncomfortable opening up to her about the situation.

'I didn't want Dad to worry about me. You know how he can be. He'd end up going down to the school all guns blazing and make things a million times worse for me.' Evie shrugged. 'And I guess I just felt a bit embarrassed. I'm not like you or the boys. I'm a coward, Kelly. I hate confrontation.'

'Listen to me, Evie. You're far from a coward. You're just too bloody nice, that's all. And you're bloody gorgeous to boot. If those little bitches down at the school are picking on you, it will only be because they're jealous of you. So you don't take any notice, okay?'

Nodding, Evie felt a solitary tear slip down her cheek. Her sister didn't know the half of the torment she'd endured over the years and

Evie really couldn't bring herself to tell her. She had no intention of going back to the school ever again, so as far as she was concerned it was over now. But even so, it felt like such a relief to finally tell someone.

'If you ever need anything, you come straight to me from now on, yeah? Us girls need to stick together. You can tell me anything, Evie. Here . . .' Rooting through her handbag Kelly grabbed the spare key that she had intended on giving Evie anyway. Kelly could have kicked herself for getting Evie so wrong. Her sister wasn't stuck up at all, nor did she think she was above everyone because of her stunning looks and expensive education. In fact, as she had now just found out, none of that could be further from the truth. Evie had a heart of gold, but years of being bullied and feeling lonely had clearly left their mark.

Kelly wanted to help her. 'This is for you. I was going to give it to you anyway.'

Looking down at the key, Evie cried even harder. Kelly was being so nice. Evie had never had that before.

'Here, don't cry. We're sisters. That's what we do, we look out for each other. If you ever want to talk about it, or anything else for that matter, you know where I am, okay?'

Ignoring the hordes of shoppers that passed them, Kelly wiped her sister's tears away with her thumbs, before hugging her sister close. 'Here, I've got just the thing to put a smile back on your face. How's about you let me give you a make-over, huh? You said you want some help with fashion, and well, hunny, you are looking at the Queen of the High Street. I read *Heat* magazine like it's the friggin' Bible.'

Evie laughed now. She could see that Kelly really was genuinely trying to cheer her up, and after spending the best part of five hours trawling through all the shops at Westfield, there was no denying that Evie really was having a great time.

'Nathan gave me an advance on my first month's wages.' Kelly raised her eyes. 'What do you say? We can go and get your hair and make-up done, my treat. Go on, it will be a right laugh.'

'Okay.' Evie smiled again

'Good.' Kelly beamed. 'First, thing's first, though. If I'm going to sex you up Kelly-Stranks-styley, those ballet pumps have got to go.'

Chapter Twenty-Six

Nathan didn't know what to say. Cassie was putting on a fairly convincing act of being okay, but he knew from her phone calls this week that she was anything but.

'I didn't know if I should bring a bottle of wine with me or not. I wasn't sure how you'd be feeling. If you'd even want a drink?' Nathan placed the bottle down on the table; he wished he'd brought flowers and chocolates now instead. He'd figured Cassie could probably do with a drink, so he'd picked up a nice bottle of wine.

'I won't, thanks.' Cassie shook her head. 'I couldn't . . .'

'I won't either then.'

'Don't be silly, have one. The world doesn't stop turning just because I'm an emotional wreck.' Cassie smiled, but Nathan could see by the sadness in her eyes she was just doing what she always did – she was pretending not to let things bother her. He could see that she'd been crying again too.

'You look beautiful.' She did. As always. Cassie was perfectly understated, like she didn't even have to try. A simple black dress clung to her tiny figure, and her hair was twisted into an up-do just the way he liked it. With a few loose curls cascading down, softly framing her beautiful face, Cassie was naturally stunning.

'Don't. I feel like shit warmed up.' Cassie was convinced Nathan was just being kind. She knew that she looked awful; she'd barely left the flat for days now. She'd not even been in to work. No amount of concealer could cover up her blotchy skin, or her puffy eyes. So tonight she hadn't even bothered. Instead she'd just chucked on a plain black dress and shoved her hair messily up on top of her head.

Having respectfully given Cassie the space she had asked for, Nathan was glad that instead of facing her demons alone, she was finally letting him in.

'How are you feeling?'

'Ah, you know, I'm up and down.' Cassie shrugged. She'd spent near on the entire week sobbing her heart out, and now she just felt numb. She couldn't get little Jacob Mulligan out of her head. She knew that she had let her professional guard down, but how could she have not? Jacob was a real character, and she couldn't help but fall in love with him.

All she kept thinking about was how she'd walked into the hospital, clutching that stupid box of Coco Pops that she'd promised him. Cassie's timing, as ever, had been infallible. It was like her sixth sense.

As soon as she had seen poor Sally Mulligan talking to the surgeon, Cassie had known.

Jacob was dead. He hadn't survived his operation.

Cassie didn't remember dropping the box of cereal, or how she had run to be at Sally's side as the woman collapsed to her knees in a heap on the floor, her howling screams echoing loudly down the corridor, like a fatally wounded animal. Cassie would never forget the turmoil she'd seen in the woman's eyes. Sally was inconsolable. She was trapped inside herself, overwhelmed by her uncontrollable grief, completely distraught – until the doctor administered the sedative.

'I just can't believe it, you know. I can't get my head around it all. I know it's my job but God, this just feels so hard. I can't believe that the poor little lad is gone. I can't get the image of Sally out of my head. She was devastated, Nathan. It's like she's an empty shell. It's like the lights have gone out in her eyes.'

'Have you spoke to her today? How's she doing now?' Nathan asked seeing Cassie's eyes glazing over as she spoke.

'She's doing better, I guess. As well as can be . . .' Cassie had spent hours with Sally over the last few days; they'd both sat and drunk coffee like it was going out of fashion, while Sally had relayed every story she could recollect about Jacob.

They'd laughed and cried together, and Cassie had been enthralled as she listened. It was as if their words and thoughts were keeping Jacob there with them.

'I should never have let myself get so attached to the boy,' Cassie said sadly. Unable to suppress her tears once more, she broke down. 'I need to pull myself together, Nathan, but I just feel so sad. Life is so bloody cruel.'

'Come here.' She was sobbing now, and Nathan hugged her to him. 'You're only human, Cass. You'd have to have a heart made of stone to not let your feelings get in the way sometimes.' Nathan hugged Cassie hard as he spoke, feeling her body shake with emotion. He'd give anything to take her pain away.

'Do you want a drink, Cassie? Shall I pour you a wine?'

Cassie shook her head.

'How about something to eat?'

'I can't, Nathan. I can't keep anything down.'

Cassie pulled away then. Wrapping her arms around her, she took a step back.

All day she had waited to see Nathan; after almost two weeks apart and endless phone calls, she'd been dying to see him tonight. Now he was here, she wasn't sure anymore.

All day she had told herself that everything would be all right. All day she had rehearsed what she was going to say. Now, with tears streaming down her cheeks and the feeling of nausea in the pit of her stomach, Cassie didn't know how she was going to tell him.

So she just blurted it out.

'There's something else, Nathan.' Cassie spoke quietly.

'I'm pregnant.'

Chapter Twenty-Seven

The words had barely left Cassie's lips when they heard the loud rap at the front door.

'It's a bit late for visitors, isn't it? Shall I get it?' Snapping out of his trance, Nathan looked at Cassie questioningly. He felt numb with shock at Cassie's revelation, unable to find the right words to say how he felt. Whoever it was at the door had just given him an extra few minutes to digest everything.

'Yeah it is late, isn't it? No, don't you worry, I'll go. It might be Sally. I told her to pop round any time, night or day.' Wiping her eyes, Cassie went to open the door.

Stepping back as she saw Christopher's huge frame looming in her doorway, Cassie tried to remain composed.

'Oh, Christopher? Is everything okay?' Cassie asked. Nathan's unruly brother was the last person she expected to see at this late hour.

'Yeah, not bad, Cassie. Just thought I'd pop over with the takings. I did try and call first, but Nathan still ain't answering his phone, so I'm guessing that he still has the raging hump with me. Is he here?' Having just snorted another line of gear, Christopher tried his hardest not to ramble. The girl had a stupid look on her face, staring at him like he had two heads or something.

'Yeah, er, why don't you go on through.'

Walking through the flat with Cassie traipsing behind him, Christopher entered the lounge where Nathan was still sitting. Clocking the look on his brother's face, Christopher knew instantly that his presence wasn't welcome here.

'I won't stay.' Christopher nodded to Nathan, then glanced around the room. He couldn't help but notice how pokey the place was. It wasn't up to his brother's usual high standards of living quarters. Still, his brother would probably be happy to live in a shed if it meant that he could spend all his time with his so-called precious Cassie. 'I only brought you the money from the bar. Tried to call, but . . . Well, you know. You ain't answering my calls.'

'My phone's off for a reason, Christopher. I'm kind of in the middle of something here.' Getting up from his seat, Nathan picked up his packet of cigarettes and then, walking over to the balcony, he stood just outside the door and lit one up.

'Look, Nath, if you're still wound up about the opening night, I said I'm sorry. I didn't realise that the bloke was a journalist, did I? I would never have fucking nutted him one if I'd have known. What more do you want me to do, huh? Go round and personally kiss the bloke's feet?'

'No.' Nathan shook his head, angrily. The word 'sorry' rolled off Christopher's tongue far too easily, and far too often. 'I've already cleared up your mess. I stumped up fifteen grand so that Wayne Barnes wouldn't slaughter us in *GT* magazine. That bloke could have shut us down. You go so much as within fifty feet of that man and he said he's going straight to the Old Bill. It's sorted now, so don't you go anywhere near him, you get me?'

Sensing the tension in the room, Cassie tried to intervene. 'Do you fancy a cuppa, Christopher?' she asked, then catching Nathan's glare she shrugged. The last thing she wanted was to be stuck with

Christopher when they still had so much to discuss. But she was only being polite.

'Nah I won't, ta. Seeing as you're both so busy and all that . . .' Christopher scowled at his brother now. Nathan hadn't even offered him so much as a seat let alone a brew.

Slinging the bag of cash down on the table, Christopher had taken the hint. Not wanting his brother to realise that his indifference was starting to bother him, Christopher did what he always did and got his hackles up.

'I'll get off then, yeah? Let you two lovebirds get back to whatever it was you were doing. Don't bother seeing me out.'

Nathan stood with his back to his brother, inhaling the smoke from his cigarette down deeply into his lungs.

Hearing the front door slam, Nathan stubbed his cigarette out and came back inside.

Christopher could be such a disgruntled stroppy shit sometimes. Ah well, he was a big boy, Nathan was sure that he would get over it. Besides, he had bigger things to think about now. Like the fact that he was going to be a dad.

Perched on the edge of the sofa again, Nathan stared ahead at the floor. He could feel Cassie's eyes burning into him as she waited for his reaction to her news.

'Well? Are you going to say something?' Cassie asked, feeling anxious. Standing by the dining room table, she fiddled with her hands awkwardly. The room had been silent for what felt like forever and suddenly Cassie felt uncomfortable.

Maybe she had read the signs wrong after all.

Maybe Nathan didn't feel the same way about her as she did about him?

She'd said it now, there was no taking it back. She was pregnant.

She was in just as much shock as Nathan was, having only had the day to get her head around the notion herself.

So caught up in her anguish, she had thought that the sicky feeling that had overwhelmed every day this week had been grief. It was only when she had been lying in bed late last night, unable to sleep yet again, that she had figured out that she had missed her period. She was late.

She'd racked her brains to try to work out how it could have happened. She and Nathan had always been so careful.

First thing this morning she'd nipped out and got herself three tests. After doing them all she got the confirmation that she knew she would: PREGNANT. Spelled out right there in bold, dark letters.

She'd since spent the day pacing her flat, rehearsing what she was going to say to Nathan when he got here tonight. In fact, she'd been dreading how Nathan was going to react, but now, Nathan sitting there speechless, it was a bit of an anti-climax.

He hadn't responded at all, and she was feeling sick to her stomach that maybe she'd read it all so wrong.

'I just . . . don't know what to say.' Finally finding his voice, Nathan ran his fingers through his hair. This had been the last thing that he'd expected to hear tonight.

But now, with just one short sharp sentence, everything had changed. Just like that, in a heartbeat. Glancing up at her, he could see the anxiety written all over her face as she waited for his response. He was still in shock, still trying to digest Cassie's words.

'How? We've always been so careful. And you're on the pill.'

Cassie nodded. 'I know, Nathan, but no protection is guaranteed as a hundred percent. It just happened. It was an accident. Trust me, Nathan, I had the next five years all mapped out for myself too, this wasn't part of my plan either.'

Her career was everything to her and she'd worked so hard to get her promotion as senior staff nurse. Now pregnant, everything would change.

Casey Kelleher

'Look, I know we've only been together for six months and it's not the ideal situation but, well, I guess we have to look at it as a blessing in disguise.'

Feeling calmer now that she had told him, Cassie sat down next to him. Placing her hand on his knee she searched his face, serious now. 'I want you to know that I'll understand if you don't feel ready for this. If you don't want this then you can still walk away. It's not some sort of a trap.' Cassie stared at him hard in the eyes. 'It is what it is. But I'll understand if you don't want it.'

She meant it too. There was no way that she expected anything from Nathan. If he wanted to walk, then she'd let him. Men had that luxury; it was always the woman who was left holding the baby, who had to shoulder the responsibility no matter what. Whatever happened tonight, Cassie needed to know that if Nathan wanted to stand by her and the baby one hundred percent, he was doing it because he wanted to. Not because he felt like he should.

'But I want you to know, Nathan, that there is no way that I could even contemplate getting rid of my baby, so you just let me know where you stand. Because I can either do this with you or without you. I'm strong. Independent . . .' Cassie stopped herself; everything that she had rehearsed earlier was coming out wrong. She sounded cold, harsh. Like she was giving some kind of a speech. She couldn't help herself. She hadn't expected Nathan to react like this. It unnerved her.

He was just sitting there staring at the floor.

Saying nothing.

She'd been pacing the flat all day, worried out of her mind that Nathan would want to run a mile. She wouldn't blame him, but if he was going to bail on her, she'd rather he do it now than further down the line.

She would understand. Six months into a relationship was nothing really in the grand scheme of things, and time-wise they

184

were still just getting to know each other. This was a lifetime commitment.

It was a lot to take in, she knew that herself. Still, she had hoped that maybe, somehow, they would work it out together.

Nathan got up.

Mirroring her own footsteps earlier that day, he too paced the room, digesting the news just as she herself had. He was in shock. She had been exactly the same. All this silence was making her feel on edge. Looking at him, she willed him to speak. To say anything, she didn't care what. As long as it was the truth, as long as he meant it and she knew where he stood.

'Jesus! I'm going to be a daddy?' Pulling himself together, staring Cassie straight in the eyes, Nathan grinned now as the news sank in.

'You are.' Cassie smiled back.

He was smiling. Thank God. He looked happy.

As relief swept over her, Cassie couldn't help but let her tears escape now. 'God, Nathan, I've been dying to tell you all day.'

'Come here.' Nathan held her to him. 'Seeing as this seems to be a night for revelations, I've got something I need to tell you too.' Nathan looked serious. Staring her in the eyes, his hands on her cheeks.

'What?' She knew it.

Her mother had always said if it seemed too good to be true then it probably was. Here it was. The punchline. Bracing herself, Cassie waited.

'I love you, Miss Wright. And that little baby in there is going to be the most loved little thing on this earth. I'm bleeding over the moon, girl.'

Nathan meant every word.

Hugging him hard now, Cassie had never felt so relieved. Nathan had worked so hard these past few weeks to prove to her that he wanted to leave his family's firm and set out on his own.

Legitimately. Cassie knew that he had meant it. He'd promised her that he was going to make a success of himself, and make her proud. He already had. There was no doubt in her mind that she loved the bones of this man. Now he'd said it too.

'Shhh,' Nathan soothed, as he wrapped his arms around her tightly. 'So, in here . . .' Nathan moved his hand down, placing it on Cassie's stomach, 'there could be a very strong, independent girl.' Repeating her own words, Nathan couldn't resist winding Cassie up. 'With a beautiful smile and a full head of wild curly hair?'

Cassie smiled and then added, 'Or an outspoken little boy, with piercing blue eyes, who gets moody when he's tired and is a very fussy eater.'

'Fussy eater?' Nathan jibed. 'Ah, he'll only be fussy if his mummy is cooking,' he teased.

'What's up?' Cassie asked seeing Nathan suddenly looking all serious on her again.

'Well, actually, now that I've let the news sink in a little bit, there is something that I'm not very happy about.'

'What? Tell me.'

'I'm not happy about not having a ring for you . . .'

As Nathan got down on one knee, Cassie sucked in her breath. 'Nathan, you don't have to do this . . .'

'Don't,' he insisted. He didn't want anything to spoil their moment.

'I know it wasn't planned and I know that I haven't got you a ring . . . yet. And I know that this is going to sound cheesy as hell, but you make me feel like one of the happiest men alive.' Nathan was tearing up himself now. He meant every word that he was saying.

Meeting Cassie had changed his life.

She showed him the good in people. She made him feel like he wanted to be a better person too.

'Cassie Wright, will you do me the great honour of being my beautiful wife?'

Crying now too, Cassie couldn't speak. Nodding she leant forward and kissed him hard on the mouth.

Cassie felt overwhelmed with love.

Nathan Woods was her everything, and them being a family made her feel like the happiest person alive.

Chapter Twenty-Eight

Having just been made to feel less welcome than a dose of the clap, Christopher slammed the car door and slumped down in the driver's seat of his Audi.

Whacking his fist against the dashboard, he was seething.

Nathan had muttered something about it being late and that they were 'busy'.

Busy? At this time of night. Busy at it like a pair of rampant rabbits more like.

Nathan had asked him for the poxy takings, so if he had a problem with him turning up at Cassie's with them, he should have stopped being such a stubborn twat and answered his phone to him. Instead of bloody ignoring his calls.

All of this over a poxy argument with some fucking queer. The bloke couldn't have been that traumatised if he'd accepted Nathan's hush money. Nathan was just being pathetic.

And his brother wasn't the only one with a life; Christopher had better things to do than run around for his brother like a fucking delivery boy.

Christopher had spotted the look on that stuck-up bitch's face when she'd opened the door tonight. How she'd quickly plastered a forced smile on her face and had half-heartedly invited him inside.

Christopher hadn't been fooled by Cassie's fake niceties. Even buzzing from the coke, he hadn't missed a trick. He'd seen windows less transparent than that bitch, and not only could he see right through the girl, he'd also clocked the look that she had shot Nathan.

Of course, Nathan couldn't have shooed him out of the place quickly enough after that. The bloke was so blatantly pussy-whipped, it was almost as if Cassie had placed some kind of spell over him. If it had been any other bird that his brother was shagging Christopher would have had no qualms in telling the bitch to stick the kettle on regardless of how late it was, or how unwelcome she tried to make him feel.

Now Christopher was physically reeling. He was his brother for fuck's sake, what did he need to do, book a fucking appointment?

So, Cassie didn't like him. Christopher didn't really give a shit to be honest. He'd never been concerned about whether any of Nathan's previous little tarts had liked him, and he had no intention of starting now.

Nathan was so loved up it was laughable, only now the joke was wearing thin as it was becoming more and more apparent with each passing minute that all the while Nathan had Cassie, he didn't need Christopher anymore.

That girl had Nathan wrapped around her finger and it was starting to really get on Christopher's tits.

'Fucking women always fuck everything up. Cunts.' Christopher spat the words out.

Agitated, he drummed his fingers on the steering wheel. Staring out of the window, he glanced up towards Cassie's shitty flat. He could see Nathan up at the window, drawing the curtains that led out onto the balcony.

Christopher sneered.

He was making a point of purposely shutting him out. Shutting everyone out.

Well, if Cassie thought she could keep Nathan all to herself, she was in for a shock. Because Christopher wasn't going anywhere. He was his brother. He'd been there for him all his life.

Nathan was a mug to allow himself to get blind-sided by a fucking woman.

They couldn't be trusted.

Christopher would never, ever be that weak.

Placing his hand down under his seat he felt around for the small plastic bag that he had carefully concealed earlier. Ripping it open, he poured a small line of powder onto the back of his hand, before snorting it quickly and rubbing the small powdery remainder into his gums. The drug hit the back of his throat and instantly his mouth went numb.

The gear always took the edge off his moods, and instantly he felt himself gain some control again.

Gripping the steering wheel tightly, Christopher took a long deep breath. It was late, but he didn't want to go home, he was too riled up. Revving the engine, he decided to make his way back over to the wine bar.

His wine bar.

It had just gone closing time, and Kelly would have fucked off up to bed by now, so he'd be left free to sit and drink himself into oblivion without anyone getting on his case.

Yeah, fuck it, why not? It was his bar too.

Nathan might swan about acting like he was the head-honcho, but Christopher's name was also on the deeds; he was a legal partner, they were equals.

Waiting for the car that was coming along behind him to pass, Christopher pulled out, driving carefully; after the amount of nose candy he'd been snorting, he didn't want to give the Plod any reason to pull him over.

Nathan would love that. Then he'd have even more ammunition to use against him.

People were quick to notice his fuck-ups, he realised. It had always been that way. Like it was almost expected of him. His dad in particular. He treated him like he was a fucking no-mark sometimes. The way he talked down to him, as if Christopher needed to be told. His dad had this way of looking at him sometimes, with such disappointment. He didn't even need to say anything, Christopher just knew.

He was a fuck-up, a let-down.

Having lived in both his dad's and Nathan's shadows all of his life, Christopher was used to being overlooked.

Nathan was the brains. He was the smart one. With his business head and his astute ways. Christopher was just fucking brawn.

The only thing he really excelled at was getting inside the ring and pummelling the shit out of people. He loved fighting, and it came so naturally to him that it actually required little effort.

Of course, he'd managed to fuck even that up, hadn't he? He'd stunted his career before it had even taken off. He'd never even come close to being the boxing legend that his father had been.

Fighting was in his blood. Battling it out in the ring was his only real release. He had a raging temper on him, and very little room for tolerance. It would pay for people to remember that.

Especially his family, it seemed.

If Nathan wanted to act like a prick and keep holding a grudge against him over the opening night, then so be it.

He'd fucked up. He could admit that.

Nathan had always forgiven him in the past, but just because he had Cassie now, he was treating him like he was nothing.

Like he was only good enough to collect the takings and run pointless errands.

Well, it was about time everyone realised that Christopher Woods was no-one's fucking errand boy.

Least of all Nathan's.

Chapter Twenty-Nine

As she cashed up, Kelly's feet throbbed; squashed into her new black stiletto heels, the skin on her ankle was raw from where they'd been rubbing all night, and she could feel the start of a whopping great big blister forming. Still, no pain no gain, she thought to herself, and tonight, dressed in all the new clobber she'd bought when she'd gone shopping with Evie, Kelly knew she was looking good. She'd lost a few pounds this week too, and tonight three punters had bought her drinks. And they'd been straight.

'Blimey, don't know about you, Kel, but I'm cream-crackered.' Monica, one of the barmaids, was standing by the door, pulling on her jacket. 'Can't wait to get in me bed.'

'Tell me about it.' Grabbing the keys so she could see the girl out and lock up for the night, Kelly nodded in agreement as she walked across the pub. 'I'd say that was probably our busiest night yet. Looks like things are picking up a bit now, thank God.' Christopher had already picked up tonight's takings. He hadn't stopped long, and Kelly put that down to the fact that Nathan had probably warned him off hanging around the bar because of his Neanderthal display on the opening night.

Talk about giving the place a bad name. Luckily it hadn't seemed to stick. As a new venue, Destiny's stood out. Its plush décor and prime location drew punters in.

'I'll see you tomorrow, darling.' Closing the door behind Monica, Kelly had just put the key in the lock when she felt it being forced back open.

'What you forgotten now?' Kelly laughed thinking Monica had come back. The girl was so bleeding forgetful that she'd leave behind her head if it wasn't attached.

'It's me, you doughnut. Open up.'

Hearing her brother's familiar voice, Kelly sighed. She was exhausted after tonight's shift and the last thing she wanted right now was Christopher on her doorstep again.

'You've had the takings already.' Kelly twisted her key back out of the lock; she felt uneasy about protesting, especially as she could tell her brother was wired. It was all well and good Nathan putting a ban on Christopher being here, but it wasn't him who had to instil it, and now she was faced with him on her own.

'I know that. I ain't got bloody dementia.' Christopher rolled his eyes. 'I want a drink, don't I.'

Stepping back as Christopher pushed his way in through the half open door, Kelly sighed as Christopher threw her a deliberate wink, knowingly trying to piss her off.

'Fucking hell, Kelly, the fucking face on you! You got PMT or something?'

'If I had to be bleeding every time I found you annoying, Christopher, I'd be frigging anaemic,' Kelly shot back sensing that her brother was clearly in one of his wind-up moods.

Christopher laughed despite himself.

His sister was a hard-faced bitch at times and whereas most people would shit their pants faced with him in one of his moods, Kelly gave back as good as she got.

'Here, I hope your sour moosh ain't been putting off the punters. You gonna get us a drink then or what?' Christopher sat down at one of the tables ignoring Kelly's stroppy mood. He knew he wasn't wanted here, but he didn't give a shit.

Pulling his phone out of his pocket he checked it for messages, half expecting at least some kind of apology from Nathan for being so short with him. There was nothing. Not so much as a fucking word. Throwing his phone down on the table Christopher was fuming. How long was he going to have the nark?

The wine bar was supposed to be their investment. He and Nathan had gone in on it together. Nathan seemed to have forgotten the fact that they were partners in this.

In fact, if it hadn't been for him getting rid of Keith Ryan, Nathan would have never even secured the place at all. So if anything, Christopher had even more rights than he did. He may not have a smart mind or mouth like his brother, but his methods had gotten him results. Forget flattery, it was violence that got you everywhere in his book.

'Go easy, yeah,' Kelly said warily as she placed the glass down in front of her brother, noting how miserable he looked, and judging by the frown on his face, she thought that something, or someone, must have severely pissed him off. Kelly wasn't sure if plying him with alcohol was going to make him feel better or worse, but knowing how unpredictable he could be, she was putting her money on the latter.

'I tell you what, Kel, you just do what you're paid to do, yeah? Pour the fucking drinks, and keep your opinions to yourself.' Then looking down at his own massive frame he added sarcastically, 'Last time I checked I was a big fucking boy, yeah. So just keep them coming. Go on. I'll have another.'

'Look, I'm just looking out for you, that's all . . .' Kelly placed another rum down in front of him.

Downing his drink, Christopher slammed the glass down on the table arrogantly. 'I think you forget, Kelly, that this is my bar, not yours, so I'll say when I've had enough. Now, get me another.'

Taking his glass, Kelly had a bad feeling.

Picking her phone up from behind the bar, she pretended to be busy filling her brother's glass with ice as she quickly dialled Nathan's number. Nathan had expressly told her that he didn't want Christopher hanging about the place causing any more grief than he had done already, so she thought she'd call him.

Only he'd switched his bloody phone off.

So now it seemed that she was going to be stuck here on her tod, trying to pacify her brother and his almighty temper by herself, and already on his third drink, she had a feeling that the way things were going she could be in for a long night.

'Does Nathan know you're here?' Kelly enquired, hoping that the mention of their brother might make Christopher think twice about starting any more trouble. The only good thing was that there were no punters here if he did.

'I don't need Saint Nathan's fucking permission, you know,' Christopher sneered as he watched Kelly slam about collecting the glasses from the bar. 'This is my fucking bar too.'

'I'm not being funny, but I'm sure he won't be too happy if I keep pouring drinks down your throat. And I don't want him to think that I'm not doing my job properly. Being the landlady 'en all . . .'

'Landlady?' Christopher roared with laughter as he banged his hand down on the wooden table. 'Fuck off Kel, you did a one day fucking training course that even a bloody monkey could have done. You're just a glorified barmaid. You're only here because Dad asked Nathan to put you on the payroll to keep you from pining over that prick of a husband of yours. He felt sorry for you and wanted to give you something to do.' Christopher grinned now, slurring as he spoke. He leant back on his chair. 'It was all part of his great plan, so stop chatting shit to me and do as you've been told. Fetch me another drink.'

'What do you mean, plan?' Christopher was talking shit, but his words had instantly got her back up. He was really pissing her off now.

'Stranks in name, Kel, but you're a Woods by nature and Dad was bang on.'

'Bang on about what? Dad was just trying to help us out. What are you talking about?' Christopher was obviously trying his best to rattle her, and it was working. Slowly losing her patience, Kelly knew that she was playing into his hands by asking him to elaborate, knowing how her brother got a kick out of winding people up. But she wanted to know what he meant.

'Fuck me, Kelly. Have a day off, would you! I'll get my own fucking drink, shall I?' Snorting now, Christopher stood up and made his way to the bar, taking great pleasure in leaving Kelly hanging.

'Tell me what you meant.' Kelly's heart pounded in her chest as Christopher filled his glass from the optic. Pouring a double measure of rum into his glass, he didn't bother with the ice or Coke this time.

'Fucking hell, Kel, I thought I was supposed to be the thick cunt of the family. Dad weren't trying to help you. Him and Raymond planned it all, didn't they? They gave you the money to get yourself out of debt, and they set Terry up. Except they didn't plan on your divvy bastard husband doing a runner, did they?' Downing the drink in one, he smiled. Going by the look on Kelly's face, his bossy sister wasn't feeling so cocky now, and Christopher was thoroughly enjoying himself.

'You're lying!' But Kelly knew that he wasn't.

'Am I?' Christopher grinned. Kelly was close to tears now. 'You're not seriously telling me that you believe Dad had some sort of an epiphany and wanted to welcome Terry back into the family and the firm with open arms? Fucking hell, Kel, they must have seen the pair of you coming.'

Christopher was really enjoying himself now. He could see by Kelly's face that his words stung her, and he was glad. He was so close to really fucking losing his rag tonight, why shouldn't he set the cat among the pigeons. His dad and Nathan treated him like a moron, so he may as well play up to it.

Fuck them. Fuck them all.

'Dad wouldn't do that to me.' Kelly's voice was quiet now, as she tried to piece together all the conversations she'd had with him since. He'd been trying to help her, trying to help Terry, hadn't he?

'You know that for a fact, do you? You know Dad so well, don't you? You have no idea about the shit Dad keeps from you,' Christopher sneered. 'And what about your cunt of a husband, huh? Do you know where Terry was the night he claimed to have been mugged?' Christopher waited now.

Kelly had shut up, and he could see that for the first time this evening he had her full attention. 'He was holed up in Raymond's brothel trying to get his leg over with one of his Romanian whores. The girl was only a little bit older than our Evie apparently.'

Kelly looked like she'd been slapped in the face. Holding onto the bar, she felt humiliated that Terry had cheated on her yet again. The fact that her entire family knew about it made it even worse.

'Get out.' Her voice remained stone cold as she spoke.

Suddenly she no longer found Christopher's huge frame intimidating, nor was she wary of his quick temper. Suddenly she no longer cared.

She could see through his big bad boy persona.

Christopher was just plain nasty.

He was heartless.

Stood here rubbing her nose in it, he was clearly loving every minute of her anguish.

'Oh don't worry, Kel, I'm going.' Slamming his glass down on the bar, Christopher couldn't help but put on the campest wave he could muster. 'Toodles.'

Sauntering out of the bar, with a massive smile on his face, he felt so much better, having rendered Kelly silent with his revelation.

His sister wasn't so fucking full of it now.

Chapter Thirty

Cowering in a newsagent's doorway, Terry pressed his body up against the pane of glass, keeping out of sight as a group of lads walked noisily past. Shouting and cheering, the group sounded drunk, and in their high spirits they probably wouldn't have even noticed Terry skulking about, looking like another of London's homeless. Still, Terry didn't want to take any chances.

It was the early hours of the morning but Soho was wide awake. Wardour Street was busy, and people were bustling out of the late night bars and strip clubs around him.

They were ignoring him, he realised, and he felt almost invisible. Finally he could relax.

Taking a deep breath, Terry scanned the length of the street before stepping out from where he had been hiding. He double checked his mum's scribbled handwriting; he'd been round there before he'd come here, at a loss as to why his house was stood empty. Unwilling to contact Kelly in case she told Harry his whereabouts, Terry had come here to see for himself if his mother had her facts right.

Kelly? Landlady of a bar in Soho? It just didn't add up.

Now he was here, he was convinced that his dear old mum must be going doolally.

Peering over the road, she'd been right about the address. The bar did say 'Destiny's'.

It was plush too. Terry had been half expecting some kind of shithole. He thought that the place would look as cheap and tacky as it sounded, but standing here now, eyeing the fancy signage and the poncy looking bay trees that lined the main entrance, Terry was baffled.

Making his way over to the main door, he looked up to the gold plaque that hung above it. There printed on the metal sign was his wife's name: 'Kelly Stranks, licensee'.

How was it possible?

Two weeks he'd been on the run. Just two. As it turned out, you could do a lot in that small amount of time, just as his wife had clearly proved.

In all the years Terry had known Kelly she'd never failed to surprise him with her selfishness. But this . . . This one had topped them all. All the time he had been on the run, clawing his way through bins for food, and slumming it in derelict squats, he'd expected Kelly to have been out of her mind with worry for him.

Had she fuck!

As always she had been looking out for number one.

Somehow the selfish bitch had managed to move her and his kids out of their home, out of the place that they had lived together in as a family for the past seven years, without so much as even waiting to consult him.

It was a complete liberty.

For all Kelly had known he could have been lying dead in a ditch somewhere.

The self-centred bitch obviously hadn't agonised over his whereabouts for too long. Maybe a few minutes at the most, Terry thought, because make no mistakes, there were no flies on that fucking woman.

Seeing a young couple walking towards him, arms linked as they laughed loudly together, Terry moved quickly back down to the sanctuary of another shop doorway, still paranoid that he might be seen.

Staring back at the bar, Terry thought that Kelly's name might be hanging over the door, but that place had Harry Woods' name written all over it. Terry would put his life on the fact that it was Harry's way of sticking his two fingers up at him.

He must have had it all planned from the start. How would he get his hands on this place so quickly and move Kelly in otherwise?

With Terry out of the way, Kelly would conveniently forget all about him. That was Harry's plan. It must have been. The bloke clearly knew his daughter well.

Once a Woods, always a Woods.

Kelly obviously didn't give a flying shit about him. Lording it up here, like the lady of the manor. Terry could just imagine it.

Well. Harry could try to tempt that selfish mare of a wife away with promises of a better life, but there was no way that he was keeping him from his kids. There was no way he was going to stand for that. Harry's plan was about to go tits up once more.

Billy and Miley were his life. They had his name. They were Strankses. There was no way that Terry was going to leave them here with that bitch.

No way in hell.

Chapter Thirty-One

Jolting bolt upright in bed, Kelly took a few seconds to gain her bearings as she stared around the dark room, her eyes focusing on the small slither of light that seeped in from under the door.

She'd heard something. She was sure of it.

Listening out against the silence in case one of the kids had stirred, she couldn't hear anything now.

She hated sleeping on her own at the best of times. Tonight even more so. Her head was all over the place. Since Christopher had left she hadn't been able to get his words out of her head. She replayed them over and over. Terry had broken her heart.

He'd done it a thousand times over since they'd married. The randy bastard was always cheating on her. He had promised her after the last time that he'd never do it to her again. Except he had. Kelly knew that he'd never change his ways. He couldn't. It just wasn't in him.

As for her dad and Raymond setting Terry up, they had no right.

Her dad had made out that he was helping her, but all along he was settling his own score, getting his revenge. She wished with all her heart that Christopher had been shit stirring, doing his usual and winding her up. But as she recalled her brother's complacent tone, she knew that what he said had been true.

It had taken her ages to fall asleep after he'd left. When she finally had, it was only because she had cried herself to exhaustion. Then the bad dreams had come.

Hearing another bang, Kelly felt her heart quicken.

She'd definitely heard the noise this time.

A loud bang, from downstairs.

Wiping her eyes, she wasn't sure what to do. The last people she wanted to call out were her brother or her dad, especially after what Christopher had said. She felt foolish enough as it was, and calling them out because she'd heard 'a bump in the night' would only reinforce the fact that they thought she couldn't fend for herself. Plus, she was fuming with them all.

She'd have to check it out herself.

It was probably just one of the kids anyway. This place was still so new to them all, every noise, every creak. It was bound to be unfamiliar.

Throwing on her dressing gown, Kelly wrapped the fleece material tightly around her, and then switched the bedroom lamp on.

The bare floor was freezing, and she tiptoed carefully so that she didn't step on any more nails from the exposed gripper rods. She'd stood on so many nails tonight that her feet felt like pin cushions. The carpet fitters were due in the morning and that couldn't come soon enough. The decorators had been in and made the place look lovely, but it wouldn't be until the carpet was all down that the place would properly feel like home and she could start putting all their stuff away.

Making her way down the hallway, Kelly peered in through the crack in Miley's door. Feeling relieved when she saw her daughter all tucked up under her covers, Kelly couldn't help but smile. Miley had spent the evening being looked after by her Auntie Evie, and instead of being in her pyjamas the girl was wearing her Tinker Bell dress-up outfit. Kelly had put Evie in a cab before she had locked up for the night, and as it turned out she was beginning to think that her dad was right. Evie was an angel. Kelly would have been lost without her helping out with the kids this week. Smiling as she saw that Miley, ever the little fidget, had somehow turned right around in her sleep and had her foot wedged up against her night light, Kelly crept back out so as not to wake her.

Moving on to the next room, Kelly peered in and saw Billy fast asleep too. Cocooned under his duvet, snoring his head off, he was out for the count.

Kelly felt relieved that the kids were okay, but then, as she wondered what had made the noises, she began to panic once more.

She was going to have to check downstairs.

Every house had its strange noises at night, and this place being so large and prominently placed in the middle of one of Soho's busiest streets was no exception.

She knew that she wouldn't be able to sleep again unless she found out what had woken her.

Tiptoeing down the hallway, Kelly's heart was beating fast in her chest as she heard the noise again.

A loud tapping, coming from the main bar.

If it was bloody Christopher again, she was going to kill him. He couldn't just keep turning up here whenever he felt like it. Especially in the middle of the night when she was here alone with the kids. It wasn't fair.

Quickening her pace, Kelly was starting to feel angry now. Christopher may have a temper on him. So did she. She wasn't going to put up with this shit, especially after the way he had spoken to her earlier. She was going to nip it in the bud. Tonight would be the last time he turned up here unannounced and uninvited, that was for sure.

Nearing the bar door she could hear the inconsistent banging, much louder now. Cowering in the doorway, she listened, and berated herself for feeling so scared. She was being stupid and she couldn't just stand here all night. Taking a deep breath she mustered up all the courage she could find and went in to investigate.

Switching on the main light, Kelly felt a rush of relief sweep over her as she scanned the room. There was no sign of Christopher and as her eyes followed the banging sound, she realised that she'd stupidly left one of the small top windows open. She must have missed one when she was locking up.

Climbing up on the chair, the window swung in time with the wind and bashed against the pane once more. Kelly reached out and pulled it shut, securing the latch tightly.

Then she groaned as she noticed the window farther down by one of the booths. The carpet was covered in shattered glass where it had been smashed. Probably bloody kids. The little buggers didn't have a clue about respect anymore. Getting their kicks from destroying other people's property. If her Billy ever went round behaving like that she'd personally pull his pants down and give him a good wallop, no matter what age he was.

Wide awake now, she'd have to get some boarding from somewhere and block it up for the time being. The window led out to the side alleyway of the bar, so the chances of any opportunists walking by and trying their luck getting in here to steal something were slim enough. Again, Kelly didn't want to give her dad or her brother any opportunity to think that she couldn't cope by herself. They already seemed to think she was incompetent by the way they had all purposely gone behind her back.

Walking over to the bar, Kelly grabbed herself a glass and held it up to the optic. She'd go down to the cellar and get some cardboard in a minute. First she needed a drink.

Her nerves were shot to pieces at having to come down here and investigate what the noises were, and her brain had played out all sorts of scenarios, all of them wildly dramatic and totally over the top.

Still, she'd earned herself a drink by being so brave. She felt proud, in fact.

Who needed Terry, or her dad? Not her.

Besides, a nice stiff brandy was probably her only hope of getting any more sleep tonight.

Drinking it back in one large gulp, the burning feeling numbed the back of her throat, warming her instantly.

Then she heard another bang directly behind her. This time it was twice as loud and definitely deliberate.

It was the exact sound that she'd heard when she'd been upstairs.

Feeling her skin prickle with goose bumps, Kelly had an awful feeling in the pit of her stomach.

'Terry?' she called out, almost dropping the glass in fright.

Turning around, Kelly Stranks realised that she wasn't alone.

Chapter Thirty-Two

Keeping low to the floor, so that he would remain undetected, Terry's hands were shaking uncontrollably as he pressed them against the cold concrete. Creeping along on all fours, he swept the pavement with the palm of his hand as he went so that he wouldn't get cut. There was barely any light down this alley, and he could hardly see the tiny shards of glass that were scattered beneath the broken window. He could feel them, though, crunching under his feet with every movement.

Standing completely still directly under the sill, Terry waited. Crouching down in the shadows he could hear voices. Men's voices. They were muffled at first, but then there was shouting. He thought they sounded familiar, but he couldn't be sure.

Taking a deep breath Terry knew what he had to do. He couldn't just stand out here like a spare part. He needed to go in. Reaching his hands up onto the thin metal pane, he hoisted himself up onto the concrete sill. Then, perched awkwardly, he listened again.

This time it had gone quiet.

Trying to work out what he was going to do, Terry peered down inside the window. Directly beneath him, there was a booth.

He could lower himself down into that, and somehow keep down. Maybe then he might just be able to stay undetected, until he knew what he was up against.

Lowering his leg down, Terry silently moved his body farther inside, careful of the long pointy shard of glass above him.

The voices were back, louder now.

Terry's stomach churned, as the realisation hit him.

He did recognise them.

Before Terry had the chance to do or say anything else, he felt the strong grip of a hand grab him roughly by his neck and yank him back out to the alleyway.

Thrown viciously to the ground, Terry's heart lurched. He'd been so caught up in trying to get inside the bar undetected that he hadn't realised that he'd been seen.

'Well, well. Look who we have here,' Terry heard the voice say in the darkness.

Terry opened his mouth to try to explain what he'd been doing. His voice disappeared as quickly as the almighty blow to the top of his head had been inflicted upon him.

Feeling just seconds of the excruciating pain, he slipped into unconsciousness.

Lying on the cold floor of the alleyway, Terry Stranks was out cold.

Chapter Thirty-Three

'Oh here he is! The wanderer returns . . . Harry "The Hammer" Woods, Champion of the fucking world.' Evelyn Woods slurred her words as she staggered out of the bedroom, slopping her gin and tonic all over the carpet as she lunged towards her husband, who was making his way up the stairs. Unsteady on her feet she lost her balance, and fell to her knees on the carpet. Laughing, Evelyn caught the disappointed look on Harry's face.

'For Christ's sake, Evelyn, it's three o'clock in the afternoon. Where are the children?' Having just driven straight from the airport, excited to see his family and laden with gifts as always, the sinking feeling inside his chest was quickly replaced with anger as he realised that Evelyn was wasted yet again.

It was becoming a reoccurring event. Harry went away on business while Evelyn stayed home and drank herself into a paranoid stupor.

This was the worst he'd seen her, though. She looked like she could barely stand up. It was partly his own fault for always turning a blind eye: he'd been as much in denial over the years as she had. But now, seeing her in this state yet again, he was starting to feel out of his depth. The more depressed Evelyn got, the more she drank. It was a vicious circle and it was happening far too often for his liking. It wasn't fair on the children. Evie was only nine. And a sensitive soul she was too.

'The kids? They're out. With their friends like always, they don't need me anymore. Wonder where they get that from? So I had a few drinks . . . So what? What do you expect me to do, huh, Harry? Sit around sipping green tea like some kind of trophy wife, while you're off gallivanting all over the world, probably getting your leg over with anything that breathes. You must think I'm bloody stupid.' She held out the beautiful emerald brooch that she had found hidden away deep inside one of Harry's pairs of trousers. Evelyn stared at her husband's face for his reaction.

And it was there.

The flicker of being caught out. Guilt had flashed in her husband's eyes, only fleetingly, but it had been there all the same.

Groaning silently inside, Harry looked down at the jewel. He'd thought that he or Raymond must have dropped it after the Mayfair robbery, and he'd resigned himself to the fact that it had just disappeared. After a week of searching everywhere for it, all Harry had been able to do was pray that it didn't turn up in the wrong hands and incriminate them somehow. Evelyn finding it had been the last thing that he'd expected.

'Where did you find it?'

'Where did I find it? What the fuck has that got to do with anything?' Evelyn screeched. 'What is it? Some kind of gaudy fucking present for one of your whores?'

Harry rubbed his head.

He couldn't tell Evelyn where he'd got it from. He never told her anything that related to his business. All she needed to know was that the bills were paid and Harry had more money than she could spend. And Evelyn could spend money like it was an Olympic sport.

He was going to have to think fast if he wanted to convince her that he hadn't hidden it from her on purpose.

'I bought it for you, Evelyn.'

'Oh how lovely, Harry. Silly me. Oh I feel so foolish now. Why didn't you say?' Tossing the jewel behind her into the bedroom, as if it was just some cheap crappy toy out of a Christmas cracker, Evelyn turned back to her husband. 'What do I look like, huh? Like I was born yesterday?'

Harry shook his head. Evelyn was wrong. The more she drank, the more insecure and suspicious of him she became. And that's all she had, suspicions. Totally unfounded, completely untrue.

Only Evelyn was too busy draining bottles of gin to realise it. They'd been having the same row now for years. Fuelled with drink, Evelyn's constant accusations were grinding him down. He had told her until he was blue in the face that she could trust him, that he'd never hurt her. God knows, he'd spent years trying to prove to her how much he meant it too. What more could he do? When Evelyn had complained that she was finding it hard to manage the house and the kids without him, he'd hired a gardener, a chef and a housekeeper. When Evelyn had complained of being lonely, he'd surprised her with a puppy to keep her company. When he was away, he always made a point to ring her first thing in the morning and last thing at night so that she would know that she was his first and last thought. Other than give up his career and stay home with her, Harry was all out of ideas as to how to make her see that she was his world.

'Evelyn, please don't. We've been through this a thousand times. The brooch was for you. I was having it cleaned. It was a surprise. I wouldn't even so much as look at another woman. You know that.'

'Well you're hardly going to come home and bloody confess to it, are you?' Evelyn shrieked before downing another huge gulp of her drink.

'I'm not going to confess anything, because it's not bloody true. The drink is making you talk shit. We can't go on like this, Evelyn. You need help.' Harry had tears in his eyes now. His wife's face was twisted with anger and bitterness.

Harry knew that she was depressed, that she was an alcoholic, and it pained him so much that he couldn't help her. That he didn't know how to help her.

'Help? Help!' Staring over the rim of her glass, Evelyn screeched now, indignation filling her voice at Harry's accusation. 'I'm not fucking ill, Harry. I'm lonely. Lonely, bored and fed up of our shitty life.'

Evelyn could see her husband's crestfallen face as she spoke: he looked shocked, defeated. But she didn't care.

She wasn't falling for his bullshit.

He was a man, and they were all the same.

She'd painstakingly watched her own mother turn to the bottle after finding out that her father had cheated when she was a child, and now history was repeating itself.

Only she hadn't caught Harry at it yet.

Unlike her mother she would be dammed if Harry thought for one second that she would put up with his lies and betrayals. She'd never let any man humiliate her. She was too strong for all that.

'You might think I'm the fool, Harry, but the only real fool here is you.' Evelyn laughed now, a loud forced cackle escaping from her mouth. 'You're not the only one who could go off and have affairs, Harry.'

'Stop talking nonsense.' Grabbing the glass from Evelyn's hand, Harry stormed past his wife and slammed the drink down on the dressing table just inside their bedroom. He wasn't going to bite. She always did this, always tried to push him too far. 'You seriously need to curb your drinking. This shit is turning your brain to mush.

It's making you paranoid. Making you think things that aren't real . . . Look at the state of you, you're a mess.'

Evelyn snapped.

It was Harry's fault she was like this.

She'd spent most of their married life on her own, while he flitted off around the world. He had given her the big house, the expensive cars, but where was he when she was lonely? Where was he when she needed him? And now he had the cheek to say that she was a mess? Like this was all her fault.

'I'm leaving you, Harry.'

Harry rolled his eyes now. He'd heard this one before too. Evelyn threatened it every time they rowed.

'I've packed a bag, and I'm leaving you . . .'

Following Evelyn's gaze, Harry spotted the suitcase leaning up against her dresser.

Evelyn could see the flicker in Harry's eyes as he acknowledged that she really did mean it this time, but before he could say anything, Evelyn couldn't help but twist the knife in some more. 'I've fallen in love with someone else . . .'

Evelyn could see that her words stung him, and she was glad. Finally some real emotion.

'He knows how to make me happy, Harry, how to satisfy me . . .'

Harry flinched.

'Who? When?' Harry's voice was strained. In shock now, Evelyn's words struck him like a physical blow. She'd been cheating on him. All this time, all the accusations, and it had been her that had being doing the dirty on him this entire time.

Standing before him, Evelyn had a look of complete indifference on her face as she confessed her indiscretion. Her eyes flashed anger, yet she had a smirk plastered on her perfectly made-up face. She looked like a stranger, an impostor.

Laughing, Evelyn registered the pain in her husband's eyes; she knew that she had got to him.

'Oh come on, Harry, like any of that matters now. It's been going on behind your back for years. We barely even have sex anymore. You're never here and when you are you're always so tired. And what can I say? I'm a woman, I have needs.' Sneering now, Evelyn shook her head. The look on his face was so pitiful, if she wasn't so full of animosity towards him she would have almost felt sorry for him.

'Don't worry, Harry, I won't tell anyone how you're a champion boxer in the ring, but a flop in the bedroom.' Evelyn smirked now, she was on a roll. 'There's so much more that you don't know, Harry. So many secrets . . .'

Evelyn's next sentence stabbed him like a sharp knife deep in his gut.

Harry stood shocked at the revelation.

He couldn't believe it.

Wouldn't believe it.

Evelyn was laughing now. She knew that her next sentence would finish him off, and she was actually enjoying hurting him. Blurting out what she'd been keeping from him for all these years, Evelyn felt like a weight had been lifted off her shoulders.

Her confession was the final blow.

Clenching his fists, Harry wanted to hurt her then. Just like she had hurt him.

It all happened so quickly.

Looking into her eyes, Harry could see the pure shock on Evelyn's face as she felt herself being pushed backwards down the staircase. He heard the sickening brutal crunch as her head slammed against the wall, breaking both her neck and her fall.

Steadying himself as he clutched onto the banister, Evelyn's last words still ringing loudly in his ears made him feel sick to his stomach.

Fighting back the bile that rose at the back of his throat, Harry stared down in horror to where she lay. Pushed to her death like a straggly rag doll, her lifeless body strewn in a mangled heap at the foot of the stairs, her dress scrunched up around her thighs.

She was dead.

Gasping for breath at the vivid nightmare, Harry Woods threw the damp bed covers off him, and flung himself forwards so that he was sitting up in his bed. His hot, clammy skin was soaked in perspiration.

Holding his chest, he struggled to breathe.

The familiar nightly occurrence that Harry was growing accustomed to was getting worse, much worse. Every time he lay flat on his back his breathing became laboured, and tonight his chest was wheezy as hell.

So much for growing old gracefully.

The only small mercy was that at least his coughing fit had woken him from his nightmare. It was like Evelyn was haunting him. Eyeing the picture of her that sat pride of place on his bedside cabinet, he wondered if maybe he should take it down, tuck it away in a drawer somewhere.

At times it was so painful to look at her that it physically hurt him.

This was Harry's comeuppance, he guessed, this was his karma. His cross to bear.

Every day he'd have to look into the same questioning eyes and feel racked with guilt. Harry felt the tears filling his eyes as his mind went over that fateful day once more. He had replayed it so many times over the years. Again and again inside his head.

The memories were so raw, so painful. Even now, all these years later.

How he'd lied to the paramedics, to the police.

He'd had to. He had to salvage what was left of his family for the kids' sake. For all of their sakes.

And the authorities had believed him. Unquestioningly they had seen his genuine grief and believed every word Harry had told them.

Swinging his legs over the edge of the bed, Harry's breathing was beginning to stabilise. Sitting up seemed to help make him feel less restricted now as he took long shallow breaths deep into his lungs.

Then the wheezing was back, this time with a vengeance. Furiously coughing once again Harry held his hand up over his mouth as he made his way to his en suite.

The red spray of blood shot through his hands, splattering the white marble tiles on the bathroom floor.

It was getting worse and Harry was scared.

During his life, he'd come up against some of the hardest criminals, and the toughest of fighters. He'd buried his wife. He'd lied about it, kept the truth from his own children. All of this and yet he had never imagined in all his days that it would be something like cancer that would bring him to his knees.

When his doctor had confirmed the diagnosis, Harry hadn't batted an eyelid initially. The bloke had clearly got his information wrong. Harry couldn't have cancer. He was fitter than most men twenty years younger than him.

But a second doctor had confirmed it. He'd advised him on the options that were available to keep him more comfortable, even offered his condolences.

Harry had lung cancer, and it was terminal.

He'd been hiding it for weeks. Refusing to have any kind of chemo. Harry was a firm believer of when your time was up, it was up. There was no use in trying to play God and delay things. Besides, the chemo would have only delayed the inevitable, and lessened his quality of life during his final days.

Harry was a fighter.

He would fight this to the end, no matter what.

He hadn't even told Raymond yet. He'd have to soon, though; he wouldn't have a choice.

Leaning over the toilet, Harry spat out another mouthful of blood. Seeing the dark clots clinging to the porcelain bowl, Harry dropped to his knees crippled with fear.

It was taking all his strength not to give in to his fears and cry, but he was so scared. He was getting worse and rapidly.

'Dad?'

Shit, Harry could hear Evie tapping on his bedroom door. He must have woken her. Hearing her feet tread through the room as she made her way to the en suite, Harry pushed the door closed with his foot.

'Don't come in, Evie,' Harry said, shielding his daughter from the horror of his illness. There was no way he could let Evie see him like this. It wasn't fair to put such worry on the girl. As always, he just wanted to protect her, protect them all. 'I've eaten something dodgy, darling, give me a few minutes, yeah?'

Evie waited.

Wiping his mouth Harry pulled his robe from the back of the door before splashing some water on his face. He took a slow deep breath.

'Got a right dicky stomach I have.' Stepping out into the room he could see that Evie was sitting on the edge of his bed, staring at her mum's photo just as he had earlier. Harry smiled. He wondered if Evie could see the startling resemblance, just like he could. How could she not? Evie was the spitting image of Evelyn. She had the same long dark hair and the same piercing blue eyes. It must have been like looking in a mirror for her.

'Don't know what the hell I've eaten. I didn't wake you, did I?' Clutching his stomach, Harry hoped the girl believed him.

'No, not at all, Dad. I couldn't sleep. Think I had too much caffeine today,' Evie lied. She had been listening to her dad coughing for the past twenty minutes, but she didn't want him to think that she had woken up because of him. Evie could see by her dad's solemn expression that there was something wrong. He was doing that thing he always did: plastering a fake smile on his face that didn't quite reach his eyes. Evie could spot it a mile off. She was about to ask him, when they both turned to the window on hearing a car come thrashing down the driveway, before screeching to a halt outside.

'Who the hell is that?' Harry Woods stomped over to the window and peeped through the wooden slats just in time to see Christopher open his car door and impatiently beep his horn.

'What the fuck?'

Pulling open one end of the shutter blinds, Harry opened the window wide and leant out. 'Christopher, what the fuck are you playing at? It's the middle of the bleeding night.'

Harry was fuming with his son. The boy must be out of his mind behaving like this. He and Evie could have been in bed asleep. Should have been in bed asleep. The boy was a fucking nightmare. 'Are you drunk?'

'No, Dad, come down,' Christopher ushered. 'Come on, I've got something to show you. It's important.'

Glancing over to the clock on the desk, Harry looked perplexed. 'What? What could be so bloody important that I need to see it at this time of night?' Harry paused, eyeing his son suspiciously.

The boy looked on edge, like he'd taken something again. Harry knew that Christopher was becoming more and more out of control but he didn't know how the fuck he was going to get the boy to rein it in. Nathan was ready to all but wash his hands of his brother, and

Raymond had told Harry that he needed to be firmer with the boy. But Harry knew that it was his fault Christopher had turned out the way he did. He'd always trodden on eggshells with Christopher, unwilling to talk about that day all those years ago.

Maybe Harry broaching the subject would only dredge up the unwanted past? Who knew?

It didn't help that Christopher's constant struggle with drugs was proving to be a battle that he wasn't winning. Then, he guessed that was just Christopher's way of coping. He shouldn't be so hard on the boy. It wasn't his fault. Harry should have done better by him.

'You need to go to bed, Christopher, we all do.' Shouting down, Harry didn't get a chance to finish.

'No, Dad, you need to come down. Raymond's on his way too. Come on.' Christopher nodded, trying to convince his father, and Harry could see by the pure craziness in the boy's eyes that once again, Christopher was definitely off his fucking face.

'Why the fuck is Raymond on his way?' If Christopher was dragging him outside for something stupid at this time of night Harry was going to clump the boy one.

'Come out and see for yourself.' Christopher stood up against the bodywork of his car now. Crossing his arms over his chest, he wasn't going to give up.

'Evie love, go and put the kettle on, will you?' Harry sighed as he tied the belt of his robe around him and shoved his feet into his slippers. 'Whatever it is that your brother is up to now, I have a feeling that I'm in for a long bloody night.'

Chapter Thirty-Four

'Hope he didn't wake you 'en all?' Walking out onto the driveway just as Raymond pulled up, Harry shook his head apologetically and raised his eyes to where Christopher was stood.

Raymond looked just as perplexed as he felt. Harry had no idea what the hell was going on.

Opening the boot, Christopher stepped back.

Stretching out his arms dramatically, he staggered as he presented his father and Raymond with the contents of the boot.

'Fuck me.' Peering into the boot, Raymond couldn't help but laugh.

Curled up in a ball, with his hands bound together tightly with rope, and a thick band of black gaffer tape wrapped around his mouth, was the elusive Terry Stranks.

'Here, the slippery fucker's only got the imprint of a fucking size eleven boot on his forehead. What the fuck have you done to him?' Shaking his head in wonderment, Harry could say what he liked about Christopher; as much of a loose cannon as he could be, the boy never did things by halves. Delivering Terry to them in this state had Christopher's spectacular style stamped all over it.

Literally.

'Well, I got him here, didn't I? If you wanted a special fucking delivery then maybe you should have rung Parcelforce.' Christopher felt smug.

The entire police force and half his dad and Raymond's cronies had been out looking for this waster, yet he had been the one to finally reel the bastard in. After a week of Nathan giving him a wide birth, and his dad looking down his nose at him too, Christopher was convinced that now he'd served up Terry to them, he'd more than redeemed himself.

'Where did you find him?' Raymond asked.

'He was at Destiny's. I left my wallet there . . . Caught him trying to get in the side window. Don't worry, no-one saw us.'

'He looks a right fucking mess,' Harry said as he took in the sight of Terry's scrawny frame. It wasn't just the damage Christopher had done in getting him here either. Terry looked like a tramp. He was filthy dirty and he'd lost a lot of weight. He looked awful, but then being trussed up like a caged chicken in the back of Christopher's motor could do that to a man, Harry figured. 'You sure no-one clocked you?' he asked, pleased that Terry realised the severity of the situation when his eyes finally flickered open. Conscious once more, Terry stared at the three faces peering down at him, his eyes wide with fear.

'Yeah. I'm sure. There was a light on downstairs though, so maybe Kelly heard this fucker breaking the window. He'd barely made it inside when I got hold of him. No-one was around when I shoved him in the boot.'

'Jesus Christ, did you call him too?' Harry asked as Nathan's Range Rover pulled into the driveway.

'Well, yeah, I thought you'd need some backup. You know, thought we were going to sort him out.'

Christopher turned and clocked his brother as he jumped out of his motor. The scowl on his face spoke volumes. He couldn't resist. 'Managed to tear yourself away from your bird then?'

'What's happened?' Nathan bit his lip. He and Cassie had almost been asleep for the second time tonight when Christopher had called, and Nathan had been tempted to leave the call to ring off onto his voicemail, especially seeing as Christopher had already rudely interrupted their evening only a couple of hours ago. He'd answered, purely for the fact that he couldn't guarantee that Christopher wouldn't take it upon himself to come back for another visit if he didn't. Now he'd been dragged out of bed, and Cassie had the right hump. She was right too: tonight should have been about them. But once again Christopher had sabotaged his plans.

'This had better be fucking good, Christopher, 'cause I really am on the fucking edge with you . . .' Stepping nearer, Nathan could smell the strong smell of rum; Christopher was paralytic.

'Have you been driving in this state?' Nathan turned his nose up, then without waiting for his brother's answer he turned to his dad angrily. 'Why do you let him get away with this shit, Dad? Look at the state of him, he's a fucking lunatic.'

Sensing the tension between the boys and Harry, Raymond quickly butted in. 'Look who your brother rocked up here with. Caught him trying to break into the bar. Looks like Christopher's come up trumps for us . . .'

Christopher grinned at Nathan, ignoring his brother's narky tone. He wasn't expecting his brother to pat him on the back, or give him any well earned praise, but he had thought that Nathan would have at least looked a little bit impressed.

Instead, he just looked thoroughly pissed off. Probably because he'd just been dragged away from his precious girlfriend.

'What's it got to do with me?' Seething now, Nathan had already told his dad that he wanted out of the family business, and looking at the state of Terry all trussed up in the back of Christopher's motor, this was definitely business that Nathan did not want to get involved in.

'Well, I thought you'd want to help out. No-one knows he's here,' Christopher said, smugly. 'So we can sort this mug out and no-one will be any the wiser.'

Hearing Terry's muffled pleas from behind the thick tape that had been stuck firmly over his mouth, Christopher shook his head at the bloke. 'What's the matter, Terry? You need a piss or something?' he mocked nastily. 'If you shit in my motor I'm going to make you fucking eat it.'

Turning back to his dad he added, 'Fuck me, he don't give up, does he? What shall we do with him?'

'Don't worry, Christopher, you've done enough. Leave him with me, yeah.' Harry was insistent. Nathan was right. Christopher reeked of alcohol, and unable to stand up properly without swaying on the spot, he was so far gone that Harry just wanted him out of the way. 'Why don't you go and get your head down, yeah? You've done enough . . .'

Christopher stared at his father, catching the familiar sharp tone that he often used with him. So familiar in fact, that Christopher listened out for it.

His dad always treated him like he was some kind of half-witted cunt. Like he didn't have the brains to carry anything through without step by step instructions. Even now. Christopher could have presented Terry to his father with a fucking pink bow wrapped around him and still he wouldn't be impressed.

'Okay. If that's the way you want it.' Trying to keep his cool, Christopher turned to his brother. 'The windows are all smashed in at the bar. Do you want me to come and give you a hand sorting it out?'

'No, leave it. I'll sort it myself.' Nathan couldn't even look him in the eye. The fumes that were coming from his breath were so strong, Nathan was surprised that Christopher was still standing. His eyes were fucked from the coke.

'Right.' Christopher shrugged. He watched as his dad and Nathan both shared a look. Then his temper kicked in. They thought he was a first class cunt; he could see it in their eyes. 'What was that look for?' he asked, incensed.

'You did good, Christopher. But we'll sort it now. Go on, get to bed, mate.' Raymond pacified. Christopher was so off his face on drugs that he didn't even realise how erratic he was being. He was talking fast and his eyes were flickering quickly as he fidgeted. He was a fucking state. Harry was right: they were better off dealing with Terry without him. He knew what he would be capable of in this state. Christopher had done good up until now; him bringing Terry here like this worked out in their favour. No-one knew he was here. Not the police, not Kelly, no-one.

Christopher in his drug induced condition would be no use to anyone, and none of them wanted to give him the opportunity to fuck things up.

'But I want to help . . .' Stung by the rejection, he could see that they were all looking down their noses at him. Like he was nothing but an embarrassment to them all.

'I said we'll sort it,' Harry said. His words final.

Christopher stood in silence and stared at his father. He was being dismissed.

'You make me fucking laugh.' Christopher sneered at his dad now. 'Looking down your nose at me. You all do. I know what you think. You think I'm a fuck-up. Well, I am, aren't I, Dad? Why don't you tell them why, eh?'

'Christopher! That's enough. You're off your head. Watch your fucking mouth,' Raymond warned the boy now. Christopher was so inebriated with the drink and the drugs that he clearly didn't realise what he was saying. Raymond could tell by the look on Harry's face that if Christopher dared to open his mouth tonight and start spouting shit about the past, Harry wouldn't think twice about lamping him one. Or worse.

'Ahh that's right. Don't tell anyone. Yeah, yeah . . . I remember. Mum's the word . . .' Christopher was almost falling over now, as he staggered over to the boot of his car. 'I'll fuck off then, shall I? I'm clearly not needed.' Gritting his teeth, Christopher was sick and tired of being treated like a mug. He was good enough to serve the bloke up, but not good enough to be trusted to do anything else. 'Get this fucker out of my motor then, the dirty bastard smells like he's just shat his pants.'

Raymond could see that Christopher was goading for a row, and he just wanted Christopher out of here.

He could also see by the look on Nathan's face that Nathan knew Christopher had been referring to something, and Raymond really didn't want this all coming out now. Not tonight. Certainly not like this.

Grabbing Terry roughly by the arm, Raymond yanked him out of the boot. Restricted by the ropes bound around his hands, Terry lost his balance, falling forwards onto the driveway.

Getting in his car, Christopher slammed the Audi R8 into reverse, almost hitting one of the oak beams of the carport, before tearing out of the drive like a man possessed.

'What the fuck was that all about?' Nathan asked warily. Drunk or not, Christopher seemed pretty convinced that he had something on their dad. And Raymond had acted way too defensively when he'd tried to shut him up.

Seeing Raymond and his dad exchange looks, Nathan couldn't be arsed to find out. Whatever his brother had done now, he didn't care.

'Fuck knows.' Raymond shrugged, then turning to Harry he added, 'Touchy fucker, that son of yours. Must get it from you, Harry.'

Harry smiled. Inside he was fuming.

He had seen by the look on Christopher's face that he had been way too close to talking. Seven years Harry had tried to keep the past buried, and Christopher, after another drug and booze riddled night, had almost given it all up. The boy couldn't be trusted. Not in the state he was in. He had always acted like the world owed him something and Harry could see that he was getting worse.

It didn't help that he was off his nut again too.

As much as both his boys had tried to hide Christopher's addiction, Harry wasn't a fool. Only a moron would get inside the ring coked out of his brain and fight. The boy was out of control.

'Take him round to the barn, Raymond,' Harry instructed.

'Gladly.' Raymond nodded. He hated Terry with a passion, and tying up this loose end would be a pleasure. Harry should have done away with the bloke ages ago. It would have saved them a world of aggro if he had.

'Can you give him a hand, Nathan? I'm going to get some clothes on.'

Nathan nodded. He was here now, so he may as well stick around. Cassie had probably gone back to sleep now anyway and, knowing how knackered she'd been, he didn't want to disturb her again tonight.

Walking back across the driveway, the only thing on Harry's mind was sorting this mess out once and for all.

Terry was the only broken link in the chain.

Everything Harry had worked for up until now – the house, the cars, the money – it was all for the kids. It was their security, all that he had to give them after he had gone. Harry couldn't risk Terry Stranks jeopardising all of that.

Coughing once more, Harry clutched his chest.

Harry was a fighter – always had been, always would be.

He was going to fight this cancer with everything he had.

And if he wasn't going to let this cancer bury him, there was no way in hell he'd let Terry fucking Stranks bury him either.

Chapter Thirty-Five

Lifting her freezing cold feet from the cold ceramic tiled floor, Evie tucked them under the breakfast bar stool and wrapped her hands around her mug of hot chocolate, though that too had gone stone cold. Unsure of how long she'd been sitting there, Evie felt beyond tired, but all the while her dad, Raymond and Nathan were out in the barn with Terry, she knew that there was no point going to bed as she wouldn't sleep.

Her dad had fobbed her off with some story about just having a chat with Terry, but Evie wasn't stupid. She'd been stood at her dad's bedroom window, secretly spying on them, peeping out from behind the venetian blinds when Raymond had dragged the man out of the boot. Shocked, Evie had gasped out loud to herself. She knew who the man was. It was Terry. Evie had seen his picture in the football style frame on Billy's bedside cabinet. But, unlike in the photograph of him hugging his son like he didn't have a care in the world, Terry didn't looked anywhere near as smiley tonight. Evie could see why. He had his hands and feet tied together, and even from the distance Evie had been standing at, she could tell that the man had already taken a battering.

She'd known for a while that the rumours about her dad were true. Seeing him in action now, unperplexed as Terry lay like a wounded animal on the driveway, Evie wondered exactly what her dad was capable of.

She knew that she should be tougher than she was, but just the idea of what they might do to Terry made her feel physically sick. He was Billy and Miley's dad. Kelly loved him. Placing her hand over her mouth to stop herself from throwing up, Evie had run into her dad's en suite.

The sight of her father's blood splattered tiles had made her already weakened stomach heave. She violently retched until there was simply nothing left to come up except watery green bile, the acidity burning her throat.

Then she'd heard her dad come into his room.

She'd heard him walk around the bedroom, getting dressed; he'd been completely unaware that she was crouching down behind the bathroom door.

Realising that she was leaning in something wet, she'd lifted her hand up and seen that it was covered in blood – her dad's blood. She had felt like she was going to gag again. Clamping her other hand over her mouth, she'd stopped herself.

Silently, she had listened to her dad as he padded out of the room and down the stairs.

Standing up quickly, Evie had almost run to the sink, scrubbing the blood from her hands.

She had cried. Something was dreadfully wrong with her dad. He was ill. He must be.

Now, sitting alone in the kitchen, Evie was still trying to piece it all together.

Her father was doing what he always did and keeping whatever it was from her. He was hiding the fact that he was ill. From her at least. Then maybe none of her siblings knew? But more than likely he was just keeping it from her.

Her dad had always been like that. Especially after her mother died.

Evie was the youngest, the weakest.

Her dad had tried to keep her as sheltered as possible, only telling her what he had to. He didn't even want her to know about his business dealings, though that itself was a joke. Evie knew all about her dad's criminal ways.

In fact, she'd had them rammed down her throat at school by the delightful Madeline Porter and her horde of disciples.

Evie didn't have a clue what to do now.

If she confronted her dad, he'd only lie.

Maybe she could talk to Kelly.

It was the middle of the night, but she had said any time, and Evie knew that there was no way that she would go back to sleep now.

She was worried sick about her dad.

If she went round there now, Kelly would soon put her mind at ease, Evie was certain.

It was important after all.

Pulling out her mobile phone, Evie dialled for a taxi.

She needed answers.

If her dad wouldn't tell her what was going on, maybe her sister would?

Chapter Thirty-Six

'Well, Lizzy, how are you?'

Sitting at the back of the breathtakingly beautiful church, Lizzy Adams had her head down and her hands clasped together. Caught up in silent prayer she'd been unaware that Father Michaels had even been standing next to her until his softly spoken voice had jolted her out of her morbid daydream.

Unable to stop herself from shaking, Lizzy looked up and gave a weak smile in acknowledgement of the priest's presence, cursing herself for not having more strength to hide her worries as she did so.

She'd been coming into this church for almost a year now, and Father Michaels always knew when Lizzy had something on her mind. He could tell just by her face that she was troubled, and offering the young woman a sympathetic smile in return, he nodded understandingly as he took a seat next to her, joining her in prayer.

He knew that it was better to wait patiently and give Lizzy the opportunity to talk about her troubles if she so wished, rather than push her for information, though he had learnt at his peril not to press Lizzy into talking if she wasn't ready to, otherwise she would only clam up. Father Michaels could always see the pain in Lizzy's eyes; like so many others that found their way through the church's door and frequented the parish, she was a lost soul.

His door was always open to those less fortunate, and situated near Soho Square, the church over the years had turned into a sanctuary for London's needy. A place for the homeless, alcoholics, and sex workers to frequent in their time of need, whether it was for a hot mug of tea, or just a friendly ear to listen to their woes. Father Michaels treated every single person exactly the same. Regardless of what path they had chosen to walk in life, no matter what their circumstances. They were all children of God in his eyes and they all deserved his help and guidance just as equally as the next.

Craning her neck, Lizzy stared up at the spectacular ornate ceiling, decorated with the extravagant golden design. She tried to pluck up the courage to find her voice. She needed to tell someone what was weighing on her mind. Father Michaels was the only person in the world that she trusted with her life.

St. Patrick's Church was the only place in Soho where Lizzy ever really let her guard down. In here, she didn't have to pretend to be anything other than herself. She didn't have to pretend to be strong, or void of all feeling.

In here she was safe. The place brought her peace.

Providing safety from the streets. Soho was just a magical illusion dragging people in with the false promises of its seductive bright lights. The same lights that she had been drawn to herself when she had first arrived here as a runaway, at just fourteen years old. Young and naive she had foolishly believed that Soho was a place where she could be in control of her own destiny. She'd seen how the other girls had survived. How they had made working in the strip clubs and brothels look so easy, so glamorous. Dolled up to the nines in their sexy outfits, tempting men who passed by to step inside, Lizzy had thought that it would be easy money. That the women were in control.

She'd soon learned that once she gave herself up to one of those places, there was no control. It was very much a man's world.

The provocative lights of Soho that had once blinded her with awe were artificial, used simply to cleverly mask over the darkness that went on in Soho's flesh-pots. For every girl that sold her body, her soul, there was always a man lurking somewhere behind the scenes and cashing in on her. It was the ugly truth of how it really worked. Lizzy knew that now.

'I'm scared, Father . . .' Lizzy's voice trembled as she spoke and she hung her head, unable to look the priest in the eye. Just one kind word tonight might make her crumble. She needed to speak, to make sense of what she had seen. She owed at least that much to her friend.

'I'm a terrible person, Father. I've done a terrible thing.'

'I'm sure that whatever it is, Lizzy, it won't feel anywhere near as bad once you say it out loud. Keeping your troubles in is what causes the pain, my girl.' In his time here at the church, he'd seen and heard it all. He doubted anything could shock him anymore.

'I saw something terrible happen to someone, Father. Someone was killed. Murdered.' Lizzy felt the tears come now. Pouring out of her just like her words. 'And I didn't tell anyone.' Lizzy looked the priest in the eye now, she had to. She needed to gauge his reaction, to see his disgust at her. She was a bad person. A disgusting person. All the bravado she put on whilst working the streets was just an act. When it came down to it, when she should have protected her friend she had been weak and pathetic. She'd only thought of herself.

Father Michaels held her stare, but his face said nothing. Nodding, he prompted her to continue.

'I was supposed to be working, but I was in a bit of a state. I was lying in the underpass down by the river, at the embankment. I was out of it. I'd just done . . . Well, you know.' Father Michaels knew that Lizzy was a drug addict and although he had never once judged her for that, Lizzy felt dirty saying the word 'heroin' in church. 'I wasn't sure if he'd seen me at first as it was dark and I was lying on the floor. But I saw this man with my friend. He looked like a normal punter at first. He was a bit rough with her; some of them are. But then out of nowhere he just went crazy. He was biting her and punching her.' Lizzy felt sick as the painful memory played out in her head once more. She remembered her friend Paige's tiny frame as he had attacked her. How tiny she had been compared to the huge man who towered over her. Paige hadn't stood a chance.

Lizzy couldn't get the scene out of her head. Haunting her, it replayed over and over in her mind. How she'd been lying in the underpass, comatose by the hit that she'd earlier shot into her veins. She had thought that the screaming she could hear was a strange echo in the back of her mind at first. It had sounded as if it was coming from a million miles away, not just thirty feet. Finally focusing in on where the sound had come from, she had seen that the person making the desperate screeching sound was her friend Paige. She was in trouble. Real trouble.

Lizzy hadn't been able to do anything about it. The shit she'd injected was so potent that she could barely talk. She was barely able to move.

But she could see.

Lizzy's eyes had zoned in on the huge man as he assaulted Paige.

In a wild fury he savagely attacked the girl, beating her to a pulp. The brutal attack had lasted just minutes. Then he'd taken his huge hands and wrapped them tightly around Paige's neck, squeezing the last bit of life out of her. Lizzy had been sickened. Distraught, she held back her own scream, only a tiny noise escaping as she tried desperately to remain unnoticed. She was petrified.

'He killed her.' Lizzy gulped down a sob that was caught in the back of her throat, the words physically choking her as she spoke.

Then, shaking her head, she couldn't say the words that sickened her. Not out loud, not to Father Michaels. Lizzy had thought she was tripping out at first. Like the drugs that were surging around her body were dodgy. They were fucking her head up and making her see stuff. Sick stuff that wasn't real. As Lizzy had watched the man pound away at her friend's dead body, she was soon left beyond a doubt that the depraved act she had just watched was very real indeed. What that man had done to Paige's dead body was an image that would never leave her.

'Then he dumped her in the river as if she was just a bit of rubbish.'

Lizzy cried now, unable to stop herself. Every time she closed her eyes the visions of Paige's lifeless body being dragged to the wall and thrown mercilessly into the water haunted her. Paige had been cast aside like she had been nothing. No-one. Like she had never even existed.

Taking the girl's hand, Father Michaels took a deep breath as he regained his composure. He was shaken up by Lizzy's words, there was no mistaking that. But ultimately he needed to be there for Lizzy now. That was all he could do, all he could offer.

'It's worse than that, Father.' Lizzy sobbed. 'As he walked off, he looked right at me. Over to where I was lying. Hiding down in the shadows, I thought I'd been out of sight. But he saw me, he looked me straight in the eye.'

A few of the working girls had disappeared over the past few weeks and Father Michaels had warned anyone that came in here to be vigilant. To stick together. If there was a nutcase on the loose, a murderer, and Lizzy had witnessed one of his brutal attacks, then she might now be in grave danger. He needed to try to persuade her to go to the police.

'You were scared, Lizzy. But you can make it right now. You've told me, that's the first step. You need to tell the police.'

Nodding, Lizzy knew that she had to. She had no choice. She hated the Filth. But she owed it to Paige. As long as her friend's body was floating in that cold dirty river, she'd never rest in peace. Lizzy wouldn't either.

'He's been following me, Father.'

She'd seen his blacked out Audi again tonight. It was the second night in a row that she had seen it parked outside Soho Square.

At first she had managed to convince herself that it had just been a coincidence. Now, with an uneasy feeling in her stomach, Lizzy wasn't so sure.

'I couldn't see through the tinted glass, but it felt like someone was in there watching me.' Her heart had been pounding inside her chest as she walked past. She had thought that maybe he would open his door and drag her inside the car. She'd been petrified.

'You need to go to the police, Lizzy. You could be in danger.'

Lizzy nodded. 'I will, Father. I'll go first thing in the morning. I promise.'

Lizzy meant it.

Lizzy had seen the man's face, seen the man's car. Now he was following her.

She was certain of it.

Father Michaels didn't have to state the obvious; she already knew that she was in danger, real danger.

Chapter Thirty-Seven

'Why the fuck did you run?' Pushing Terry down so that he was sitting on one of the large boxes in the middle of Harry's barn, Raymond stood over the man like he was his personal guard, as he waited for Harry to get dressed and join them. Venting off, Raymond wasn't expecting an answer, which was just as well because Terry's mouth was still firmly secured with the thick gaffer tape that Christopher had administered.

Terry didn't seem to get that, though, because the muppet was still trying to make muffled pleas. Raymond knew why Terry had run. Because the bloke was a coward. He wouldn't have lasted five minutes in prison. They knew that, and he knew it too.

Even so, Raymond had to give it to the bloke, he was really trying to stand up for himself now. He seemed desperate to make himself heard. Either that or the stupid prick just didn't know when to quit.

Ignoring Terry as he wiggled about like he had worms crawling round inside his arse, Raymond whistled at the piles of neatly stacked boxes. 'Bleeding Christ, what's your old man been buying now?'

Nathan shrugged. Stood against the back wall, he couldn't take his eyes off Terry. He knew that he was a waster. He'd heard about the way he treated his sister, but Nathan also knew how much Kelly loved the man. As much as he didn't want to be any part of this tonight, he was almost too scared to leave. He didn't know what his dad was intending to do, but he figured that he'd better stick around for a bit longer just in case things got out of hand. As for the boxes, Nathan didn't have a clue. 'Fuck knows, Raymond. Could be anything. You know Dad, he could sell ice to the Eskimos.'

Raymond nodded. Whatever this shipment was, it was bound to be a great little money spinner. Harry always had his finger on the pulse when it came to importing the latest craze from the States, and he always managed to get hold of stock just in time for the UK's high demand. Be it designer watches and handbags, Ugg boots or e-cigarettes, Harry made a fortune on the mark-up when he sold the goods on to his eagerly waiting buyers. The best thing was, it was all legit. 'Woods Enterprises' was Harry's 'front'.

Harry ran it meticulously, only importing genuine, top-notch merchandise. Despite having a few men working down at customs and excise for his Holland shipments, Harry always paid the import duty in full on these goods, and made sure that his accountant worked his magic on the rest. Everything here was completely kosher.

They'd been ploughing the drugs money through the company undetected for years.

The dynamics around the whole enterprise really impressed Raymond. Even when the police had come sniffing around here looking for Terry the other week, Raymond had watched as they poked around; the idiots had actually thought that they'd hit gold by uncovering some sort of an illegal goods den.

After all the years of trying, they thought they had finally caught Harry Woods out. As if he would be so stupid as to have a barn full of evidence that could get him nicked at the back of his house this whole time. The Plod really were something fucking else.

Stamping his legs on the floor, Raymond turned back to Terry. 'Fucking hell, Lairy Bollocks. Calm down, will you? Harry will be here in a minute and I'm sure you can have your say then.' Kicking his leg to stop the noise, Raymond glared at Terry.

Terry continued to stamp his feet on the floor, lifting his knees and slamming his legs down. Raymond kicked the man once more. This time harder.

'Calm the fuck down,' Nathan chimed in now, getting fed up with Terry's erratic behaviour. He could see that Raymond was coming close to really losing it with the bloke. Terry must have a death wish to keep this shit up.

'Here he is.' Raymond almost sounded relieved to see Harry walk in a few minutes later. 'Tell you what, Harry, it's a good thing that Christopher brought him in. You might be right about him blabbing – even with a gob full of gaffer he's still trying to fucking have his say.'

Walking over to where Terry was sat, Harry stared down at the man with hate in his eyes. 'What did my little girl ever see in you, eh? You're nothing but a snidey piece of shit.' Harry could feel himself getting worked up as he spoke. He had years of hate and venom pent up inside him. He hated Terry, had done since the day he'd first met him. Especially the day he'd first met him. Thinking he'd be meeting some adolescent spotty teenager, Harry had been temporarily floored when he'd been faced with this pompous looking prat. Terry was almost the same age as he was for fuck's sake. By the time Harry and Terry had been introduced, it was too late. Harry had seen the look on Kelly's face. His girl was already smitten. Christ knows why, though, he had thought at the time. Terry Stranks thought he was some kind of a wide boy. It must have been the bloke's tacky gifts that he'd wooed her with, because it sure as hell wasn't the poncy floral shirts that had caught Kelly's eye. He looked like a first class cunt. It was like he'd styled himself on some seventies porn film. He was cheap and brash, and Harry had been able to see that the bloke was nowhere near good enough for his Kelly.

Not even close.

Kelly had met the bloke at a bad time. She had been grieving, just like they all had. While she had grown closer to Terry, she and her dad had drifted further apart.

Now, seven years later, Harry couldn't contain himself any longer.

This bloke had taken his daughter from him.

Had kept his grandkids from him.

All in the name of love.

What a fucking joke. Terry had slept with half the hookers in London behind Kelly's back, most of whom Raymond had known. As Raymond had confirmed, Terry was a proper scumbag. He liked the girls he messed about with to be young enough to be his granddaughter, let alone his daughter.

'Go on then, you gobby cunt, say your bit. You're obviously desperate to. Trust me, there ain't nothing you can say that's going to make me change my mind about you. You are a fucking no-mark. Always have been and always will be. And you have been dragging my Kelly down with you for far too long. She'll thank me for this one day, when she's finally cottoned on herself and found a decent man.' Harry roughly yanked the tape off Terry's face, enjoying the fact that it ripped his skin painfully as he did so, and then he pulled his head around sharply to the side.

Terry turned his head back.

Finally he was able to speak.

'If anything has happened to my kids I'm going to kill that numbskull son of yours,' Terry spat now, his mouth bone-dry from the tape.

Harry raised his eyebrows. He'd expected Terry to beg and plead, maybe be a bit cocky.

'What do the kids have to do with this?'

'If Christopher hadn't been so busy using my head as a fucking football, he might have realised that I wasn't the one who was breaking into that poxy bar . . . Someone else beat me to it.' Terry glared now. 'I was trying to help your daughter – my wife.'

Harry stared at Terry, then at Raymond. He was confused.

If Terry was just trying it on with this spiel then he was doing a pretty convincing job of it. Harry, having already underestimated Terry once, didn't want to take any chances in falling for it again.

Raymond shrugged. He wasn't sure if Terry was being straight with them or not either.

Then, Christopher had looked like he was on another fucking planet tonight, and the way the kid had been acting lately, Raymond wouldn't put anything past him. Maybe he had been so off his rocker on gear he hadn't realised what was going on when he'd caught Terry creeping through the window. He guessed it was an easy enough mistake to make. Easy even if you weren't coked up to your eyeballs. Christopher would have been so preoccupied with scoring points by being the one to dish Terry up to them on a platter that he could have easily missed the bigger picture. Let's face it, Raymond thought to himself, Christopher wasn't exactly the sharpest knife in the drawer even when he wasn't snorting gear.

'What's to say that you're not just making this shit up?' Harry questioned Terry now, searching his eyes to see if he could spot Terry lying.

'The way I see it, Harry, you ain't got no choice but to believe me. Kelly is in big trouble and so are my kids. The divvy cow always thinks she knows best. Must be a Woods trait.' Terry's eyes welled up as he continued.

'Knows best about what?' Harry narrowed his eyes now.

'She never paid the fucking O'Sheas, did she? Pocketed all that money you gave her for herself.' Terry was crying now, but he didn't care. Even with snot dripping out of his nose, and Raymond and Nathan staring at him open-mouthed, he didn't give a shit. The drama of the past few weeks was catching up with him now. The O'Sheas, being on the run, Harry. It was all too much.

All Terry wanted was normality once again. He wanted his wife and his kids.

He wanted his life back.

'I know you don't give a flying shit about me, Harry, and that's fine with me. But I'm begging you with my life, please untie me. Jimmy and Micky are animals, Harry, and from what I heard tonight, before Christopher fucking did me over, Kelly is in big trouble.'

Chapter Thirty-Eight

'Terry?' Kelly could tell right away by the tall, slim silhouette that the person lurking behind the oak beam wasn't Terry.

Reaching for her phone, she picked it up to dial Nathan.

'I don't think so, Kelly.' The figure stepped out from the shadows in the corner of the room and Kelly's heart almost stopped as she recognised Micky O'Shea. 'Put the phone down.'

Turning to hear another noise at the opposite end of the room, Kelly should have known that Micky wouldn't be alone. His brother Jimmy O'Shea was here too. Gripping a baseball bat in his hand, he tapped it on the oak floor as he walked towards her, making the same noise that Kelly had heard when she was upstairs.

Whack, whack, whack.

Instantly she recognised it as the noise that had woken her.

Kelly could see by the look on his face that Jimmy was enjoying her reaction to their little surprise visit.

'I take it that hubby's not home then?' Micky ran his finger down the front of Kelly's dressing gown, pulling it open and exposing her nakedness. 'That's a shame, ain't it? Looks like you'll have to do for now then, eh?'

Kelly stood frozen in fear, shivering as Micky's eyes roamed her body, her heart pounding once more.

This was all her own fault. All her own stupid doing.

She knew she had played a dangerous game when she had upped and left the house without paying the O'Sheas what she owed them. She had stupidly thought that because she was back with her family, they would leave her alone. Even if they did manage to track her down, surely they'd find out who her dad was? She had figured she'd be free to take the money and run. No-one would mess with Harry Woods' daughter.

Now she was realising what a grave mistake that assumption had been.

The O'Sheas had tracked her down. They looked majorly pissed off.

'Left your place in a bit of a hurry, didn't you?' Jimmy sneered as he took some glasses from the bar and poured some whiskey for himself and his brother. 'Bit rich, ain't it? You doing a runner and stiffing us for the money that you owe us. After we so generously helped you out. Fancy ending up in a swanky gaff like this too, eh? Nice little setup – you've really landed on your feet, haven't you, Kelly?'

Kelly didn't know what to say; for once she was so scared that she was momentarily lost for words. The kids were upstairs asleep, and she was just praying that they would stay that way. She would take whatever it was that these two bastards were going to do to her; her only concern right now was keeping her kids as far away from it all as possible.

'Funny thing, you doing a runner,' Micky added. 'You left us with no choice but to do a bit of digging about. And we heard that you were here, and that this was Nathan and Christopher Woods' place. Well let's just say it didn't take a rocket scientist to work out that you were their sister.' Micky sneered. 'And more to the point, that you were the famous Harry Woods' daughter.'

Micky curled his lip in contempt as he spoke. This bitch had given them the runaround for long enough. What she and her fuckwit of a husband had been doing borrowing money off them when Harry Woods had money coming out of his ears, Micky had no idea. He'd done some poking about and word was that Kelly had fallen out with her old man years ago. She was clearly back in the fold now, and Micky and Jimmy had a feeling paying Kelly a visit tonight was going to work out extremely lucratively for them both.

Holding out the brooch that he had taken from Kelly, Jimmy sneered. 'Didn't you even want your mum's brooch back, Kelly?'

Kelly eyed the jewellery in Jimmy's hand.

Of course she had, it was all she had left to remember her mother by. But Kelly had chosen to let it go. Jimmy would have never given it back to her even if she had asked for it. Even if she had paid him what she owed. He was just tormenting her.

'Let me guess? Your old man gave it to your mum as a gift?' Jimmy stuck up his bottom lip, impersonating Kelly as she began to cry. 'See, I got a friend who deals in this kind of thing, and as it turns out this brooch is one of a kind. Worth a fortune, only it's hotter than a Mexican's fart. It was nicked from a jewellers over in Mayfair a few years back. So I'm going to bet that your dear dad was involved. Giving his missus knock-off goods as presents – who said romance was dead, eh?'

Jimmy shoved the jewellery back in his pocket before continuing, 'Your old man doesn't like us very much, Kelly. He's been cunting us off to half of London.' Micky drank his drink down in one, enjoying the burn it gave him in the back of his throat. 'He thinks that we're just small fish. Refuses to work with us, don't he, Jimmy?'

'Apparently so.' Jimmy nodded, as he continued to tap the bat on the floor.

Kelly flinched as Micky leant down, and stared her straight in the eyes. The smell of his putrid sour breath as he pushed his pockmarked scarred face up against hers made her want to gag. 'But your old man is exactly that, ain't he? Nothing but an old man. A has-been. See, we've heard this little rumour that he's stepping down; he's set tongues wagging all over London. Sounds to me that your old dad must be losing his edge. And if he is taking a step back from a good earn, me and Jimmy think that it's only right he gives someone else a fair turn.'

Kelly flinched again as Micky leaned in closer.

'Wonder what your daddy would say if he could see you now, eh? Wouldn't think we were so fucking insignificant then, would he?' Micky grinned with malice as he roughly pulled Kelly's lank hair tightly around his fist, and pulled her sharply towards him, causing her scalp to burn in pain. 'It would be a shame to let Jimmy loose with that bat. Makes a right fucking mess, he does. Caved someone's skull in with it last week for a lot less than what you fucking owe us. Now, we ain't going to ask you again, where's our fucking money?'

Chapter Thirty-Nine

Getting in the motor, Harry pulled out of the driveway like the antichrist. The wheels of his silver Bentley screeched as he rammed his foot down hard on the pedal.

'Fuck me, Harry, go easy, mate. We won't be helping Kelly if we're upturned in the fucking ditch.' Raymond held onto the door, as Harry continued to drive erratically, sending Nathan and Terry flying against the back doors.

'I swear to God, Terry, if this is some bullshit fabricated story, no matter what happens, even if Kelly never forgives me, I will fucking annihilate you.' Harry was fuming.

If what Terry had said was true then Harry was going to cause a shitstorm for those two blokes, two-bit cunts who went around bullying people for money.

Harry gripped the steering wheel tightly. He was fuming with Kelly now. She'd put herself in real danger. If she had no intentions of paying them, she should have said. Harry would have dealt with it for her. Like he'd offered.

They weren't the type to just let stuff like that go. They were greedy. That combined with them being under the illusion that they were a force to be reckoned with was not a great combination.

Especially for Kelly. Micky and Jimmy O'Shea were nothing but a pair of money grabbing cunts, and he'd obviously hit the nail right on the proverbial head, because what the pair of them thought they were playing at by breaking into the bar and threatening his daughter, he didn't know. What he did know was that they were clearly asking for trouble.

'I ain't making it up, Harry. You'll see for yourself when we get there.' Terry's stomach was in knots as he spoke. None of them knew what exactly they were going to see when they got there – that was half the problem.

By the time Harry had taken Terry's gag off and let him speak, his Kelly had been alone with those animals for near on an hour. After their threats last time, who knew what they were going to do next?

'The O'Sheas ain't got no backup to take you on, have they?' Nathan asked his father. 'I mean, they must know that you're going to be gunning for them?'

Although Nathan knew that he'd have to help his sister, there was no questioning that he wished to God he'd never answered his brother's call, and was still wrapped up in bed with Cassie. Wedged in the back of the car next to Terry, and on their way to face a couple of shifty loan sharks, Nathan had well and truly broken his promise to her to stop the criminal work. But if Kelly and the kids really were in trouble, he couldn't just walk away.

Cassie would understand.

'Well, whatever their reasoning they have fucking made a grave mistake. This is going to be the most costly twenty thousand pounds those fuckers have ever tried to rinse out of someone.'

'It was ten grand.' Terry shrugged. 'Kelly rounded it up . . .' Under the circumstances it was only fair that Harry had the correct information before he was faced with Jimmy and Micky. The amount of money that they owed didn't really matter now, but

Terry didn't want Harry to look like he didn't know what the fuck he was talking about.

Harry shook his head.

That bloody girl. He'd given her everything, and still she wasn't content. He'd never say it out loud, but she was more like her mother than any of them. Evie might have been the image of her in looks, but Kelly had her selfish traits down to a fine art.

'You don't think they've heard about you dropping the Holland deal, do you?'

Raymond stared at Harry. They both shared a knowing look. It had to be something like that. Why else would the O'Sheas suddenly find their bollocks to do something like this. They were cunting him off because word had got out about him stepping back. He wasn't even officially out of the game yet and people were already treating him like a mug. Like he was too weak to stand up for himself.

The O'Sheas clearly had no idea who they were fucking with. Messing with his family was one step too far.

Slamming his foot down, Harry was on the warpath. When he caught up with the O'Sheas he was going to take great delight in making an example of the pair of them.

Stepping back or not, no-one, but no-one, threatened his family.

Chapter Forty

Stepping out of the taxi onto the path, Evie was now having second thoughts about coming here.

When she'd left the house she had felt determined. But during the silent journey over here in the back of the cab, doubt had crept in and she wondered if she was doing the right thing by burdening Kelly with it all.

Besides, it was the middle of the night. Kelly may have said that she could come to her any time she needed to, but Evie very much doubted that she had meant that in the literal sense.

Spotting the light on in one of the downstairs windows, she guessed Kelly must still be up. Maybe now was as good a time as any, though she was wary of upsetting her sister by laying her worries about their father on her. Kelly had enough to deal with at the moment.

Evie wouldn't mention the fact that she'd just seen Terry over at their dad's house.

Terry's whereabouts were none of Evie's business, and her dad would most definitely not thank her for sticking her oar in.

Walking up to the door, Evie got her key out, but wavered over the lock.

She could just go back home and pretend that she hadn't seen the blood spattered bathroom. That she hadn't heard her dad lie awake half the night coughing his guts up.

Maybe she should ask her dad outright, but she knew that he'd only lie to her.

He was as stubborn as a bull, and he'd do anything to protect his kids from something like that.

If he was ill, really ill, she just knew that he would try to shield them from it for as long as possible.

Evie might be opening up a whole can of worms by coming here, but what choice did she have? Kelly might be able to help. She might know what's going on. Turning her key in the lock, Evie pushed the door open and stepped inside.

'Kelly?' Evie narrowed her eyes.

Kelly was perched on a chair opposite, over by the bar. Her face was stained with streaks of thick black mascara, smeared all down her face like she'd been crying.

Evie's heart went out to her. Her poor sister looked a right state. Sitting here in the middle of the night, crying to herself, over Terry no doubt. 'Kelly, are you okay?'

Kelly didn't answer. Instead she was staring at her strangely. Her eyes wide, as if she was trying to tell her something.

Evie noticed the upturned furniture, the smashed glass all over the floor. She realised that something was very wrong here.

'What the hell has happened?'

Without warning, two men jumped out from behind the door where they had been hiding. Grabbing Evie roughly, they pulled her forwards.

Jimmy locked the door behind her.

Clamping his hand over Evie's mouth before the girl had a chance to scream for help, Micky O'Shea raised his eyes to Kelly. 'Who the fuck is this then, huh?' he asked, eyeing the kid up. The

251

girl was young, just a teenager, and judging by the terrified look on the girl's face she was hardly a threat. For a moment there when they'd heard someone trying to get in with the key, Jimmy and Micky had thought they'd been busted. They thought maybe Harry or the boys had got wind of them being here.

Harry didn't have a clue they were here, and by the time he did find out, it would be too late.

'Please, leave her. It's Evie, she's my sister. She's just a kid.'

Even through Kelly's anguish she wondered how the hell Evie had got here, and why. It was the middle of the night. Something must have happened. Seeing Jimmy and Micky circle around Evie like sharks around fresh meat, Kelly knew that now wasn't the time or the place to find out. Whatever it was would keep for now. Instead, she needed to try to scare these fuckers off. They needed to stay the fuck away from Evie.

'Is Dad with you?' Kelly asked as her eyes bored into her sister's, hinting to Evie to nod that he was. The O'Sheas had already smashed the place up, and Kelly had said silent prayers that they wouldn't wake up Billy and Miley. She couldn't face the kids coming downstairs and witnessing this shocking scene. They'd be terrified.

Ignoring Evie's unconvincing nod, Jimmy laughed. 'Course he is.' Then, pulling at Evie's handbag, he sneered mockingly. 'Are you in there, Harry? Come out, come out wherever you are.'

Pushing Evie onto the chair next to Kelly, Micky couldn't help but leer. She was a pretty girl, this one. Much nicer than her older, plumper sister.

'So, you must be Harry's baby then? Youngest of the kids, are you?' Micky guessed that this little firecracker would probably be the apple of her daddy's eye.

Evie nodded. She felt scared now. She had no idea who the men that were holding her sister were. They looked dangerous.

'Fuck me, tonight just gets better and better.' Jimmy winked at Micky. The two men, as always, both on the same page. This little bitch rocking up hadn't been part of their plan, but she was a very welcome addition.

Harry would be fucking stewing when he got wind of this.

Fuck the ten k Kelly owed them. It wasn't about the money anymore.

Harry Woods should never have dismissed them.

Because now they had the bloke well and truly by his balls.

Chapter Forty-One

Lizzy Adams picked up her pace. She was scared; she could hear the car creeping up behind her and she didn't even have to look.

She knew it was him.

Walking faster, she could feel the adrenaline surging inside her.

She needed to be sure; maybe she was wrong, maybe it was just another punter, or Rusty. Maybe he was checking up on her.

Turning her head, she almost did a double take.

She felt her skin prickle with goose bumps.

Her instinct had been right. It was him.

In the blacked out Audi.

She'd only just left St. Patrick's. Father Michaels was right: she needed to tell the police. She was going to. She had been planning on going home and trying to get a few hours' sleep first, then first thing tomorrow with a fresh head she was going to go straight down to the police station and tell them everything she knew.

She thought she'd be safe now, thought that because she'd seen the killer lurking around earlier, he would have gone.

Hearing the Audi speed up, Lizzy walked faster. As fast as her chunky black platform heels would let her.

Turning off into Dean Street, she listened as she heard the car follow.

He was fucking with her, trying to scare her. It was working.

She was petrified.

Keeping her eyes forward, looking straight ahead, Lizzy pretended that she hadn't noticed the car as it levelled with her, matching her pace. Her heart beat manically inside her chest, and beads of sweat formed on her brow.

Her legs were like jelly.

How she was still walking she had no idea. All she kept thinking was that any minute now that nutcase could open a door and drag her inside. She felt sick with fear.

Seeing the park gates up ahead, she decided to cut back through Soho Square. She was almost running now, frantically through the park, and she stumbled on the stony path. Managing to regain her balance without falling, she stared over to where the headlights were shining through the bushes. He was still there, still following her. Only shrubs and a metal railing separated them.

Then the lights vanished.

Panicking, Lizzy realised that he'd stopped the car. Turned the engine off. He must have got out.

Alone, she ran as fast as she could. Her heart was beating so hard in her chest that it felt like it would explode.

The exit was just up ahead. Another twenty yards and she'd be out on the road again.

Turning to check behind her, she wanted to make sure that he hadn't followed her into the park. Her eyes couldn't focus in the darkness. She felt so terrified. Every tree, every plant swayed in the light breeze, unapologetically, throwing out shadows to confuse her.

The park by day was normally so busy, so vibrant. Now, in the dead of night, it was eerie.

Lizzy started to cry. Heavy sobs shook her; she was terrified for her life. She needed to get away from him. He was a monster; she'd seen what he'd done. What he was capable of. Father Michaels was right, she should have gone to the police. Now she might not get the chance.

Hurtling out through the gate, she could see the alleyway opposite. If she could make it there, she might have a chance of escape.

She could lose him.

Her legs felt like lead weighing her down as she ran. Like her body was purposely going against her, and making the few hundred metres seem like a mile.

She couldn't hear the car, or anyone following her now. Into the alleyway, out of view from everyone. She had made it. Standing up against the wall, she finally let herself breathe a sigh of relief.

Then he grabbed her.

Chapter Forty-Two

Pulling up just down the road from the bar so that they wouldn't be seen by anyone inside, Harry turned off the lights and the engine and turned to Nathan.

'Stay here with him, just in case he's spinning us some kind of line. Me and Raymond will go and see what's what, okay?' Terry had barely spoken a word since Harry had untied him and shoved him in the back of the car, and if Terry did try to kick off, Harry knew Nathan would knock seven shades of shit out of him. He might not be a fighter in the ring, like himself and Christopher were, but he still had the same blood, and Terry was no match for Nathan.

'Seriously, Harry, I know you think I'm talking crap. But what would I be gaining from it? An hour of extra time before you work out what you're going to do with me? Do me a favour! My fucking wife and kids are in there. Let me come in with you.'

Terry shook his head as he spoke. He'd known this would happen. He'd known that Harry wouldn't believe him. He could tell the bloke until he was blue in the face, and still Harry thought he knew best. It was obviously where Kelly got it from.

'No chance,' Harry said. Something told him that Terry was telling the truth, and if he was, if Kelly was in real danger, the last thing Harry needed was Terry strutting around like an irate numpty, getting in the way. Whatever was going on here, he and Raymond would sort it out.

'Please, Harry, think about it. Safety in numbers and all that. The O'Sheas are scumbags but trust me, they are vicious fuckers, Harry, they don't play by the rules. You have no idea what you could be walking into.' Begging now, Terry couldn't just sit outside like a fucking spare part while those savages were inside with his family. He could see that Harry wasn't listening.

Ignoring Terry, Harry knew he was more than capable of dealing with those two fuckers. They were nothing.

'Will you be okay out here?' Harry asked Nathan, as he held out his pistol, nodding at him to take it. Terry couldn't fight himself out of a paper bag, but Harry wouldn't put it past the bloke to try to pull a fast one if he had to. 'Don't let him out of your sight, okay?'

'Yeah, no worries.' Reluctantly, Nathan did as he was told. Watching as Raymond and his dad got out of the car, and made their way around to the boot to get the other guns, he had a really bad feeling about this.

'You ready for this?' Grabbing the shotgun, Raymond passed Harry his Glock.

'Yeah. Terry said it was the side window that he'd tried to go through. He said he'd almost got in undetected, so I say that's our best bet. Then maybe we can suss out what the fuck is going on and take these fuckers unawares.'

Raymond nodded in agreement.

Then together they made their way down the walkway that ran along the side of the bar.

'Please, the kids are upstairs. You can't do this.' Kelly was crying now. Begging the O'Sheas to listen to her. Her hands were tied tightly behind her back, securing her to the chair, just like her sister next to her.

All they could do was watch in horror, as Micky O'Shea held up the jerry can and doused the bar in petrol.

'Fucking place is going to be alight in seconds with all this fucking fancy wood everywhere. It's going to be like the most expensive bonfire party you lot have ever been invited to.'

'Oi, watch my fucking shoes, Mick, I don't want to go home fucking stinking of that shit.' Jimmy jumped out of the way, as the liquid hit his shoe. He wiped the leather on a clean small section of carpet that had been missed, and shook his head at Micky. His brother was a clumsy cunt sometimes. As always, he couldn't help himself, going overboard and saturating everything in fuel. The place reeked.

Seeing the two women crying, Jimmy grinned nastily. The girls could put on the water works all they liked; it wouldn't get them anywhere with him. In fact, all it did was get on his tits. He was getting a headache just listening to the pair of snivelling cows.

'Don't worry, girls, I'm sure that someone will hear your screams and come to your rescue. Let's leave it down to fate, yeah? Whatever the outcome, whether you get out of here alive or not, your dad will have got his warning from us.' Jimmy smirked now. 'As soon as I strike a match, your 'Destiny' will be out of my hands. So shut the fuck up with your whinging before I fucking gag the pair of you,' Jimmy threatened before walking off.

'It's going to be alright, Evie. I promise you . . .' But even as Kelly whispered the words to her trembling sister, she knew herself that it was far from alright. No-one knew that the O'Sheas were here.

If this place did go up in flames, their only chance of getting out of here would be if passers-by came to their aid, and in order for that to happen, they'd have to see the fire and the smoke first. Judging by the amount of petrol Micky had just splashed about the place, the chances were that it would be too late by then.

Kelly could have kicked herself for being so greedy now. This was all her fault. She should have just paid the money that she owed these bastards and then none of this would have happened. Now all she could think about were the kids upstairs, and how she'd put them both in danger with her selfishness.

For the past hour she'd done nothing but pray that Billy and Miley stayed upstairs out of the way. She didn't want them to come down here and see the O'Sheas terrorising her as they set about smashing the bar up. Now, she was scared they wouldn't wake up, that they'd die from smoke inhalation, or worse from the flames.

These bastards didn't give a shit about her or the kids. All they cared about was scoring points with her dad.

'You done?' Jimmy asked as he watched his brother.

Micky nodded as he shook the container, sprinkling the last of the petrol over the velvet booth under the main window.

The place would go up in seconds and the two girls wouldn't stand a chance. Even if they screamed, no fucker would be able to get to them in time. The whole place was soaked in fuel. Once he and his brother left, they'd probably have minutes, if that.

Jimmy O'Shea was sick of trying to claw his way up the ranks of London's criminal underworld. It was about time that people started showing him the respect he deserved. Sorting out Harry Woods was the perfect place to start.

The bloke really rated himself. He refused point blank to work with 'the likes of' him and his brother, and Jimmy had stewed over Harry's dismissal for far too long.

Now he'd heard on the grapevine that Harry was thinking of stepping back from it all. Harry would leave the market wide open to the Turks if he did, and Jimmy wouldn't stand a chance of cutting any kind of a deal with those wankers. Those fuckers kept to their own.

No, the only way that Jimmy was going to be able to worm his way in with any of the bigger gangs was to make a name for himself. Show every fucker within fifty miles of London what he was really capable of.

Harry Woods was big time. He'd been round the circuit for years, and he was well respected. Jimmy wanted to be the man that brought Harry to his knees. He wanted to crucify the bastard by getting to him through his daughters. Take away the man's fight, then take away his business. Harry would soon take notice of who the fuck he was then.

They all would.

No-one would ever dismiss him or his brother again.

Taking one last swig of the whiskey his brother had poured him, Jimmy O'Shea had it all worked out.

Watching this place burn to the ground was going to be a fucking pleasure.

Chapter Forty-Three

The girl was like a wild animal. Her sharp nails were clawing at his eyes, gouging strips of skin from his face. She was a third of his size, yet she was fighting with everything she had. Fighting for her life. He'd been amused at first by the girl's strong spirit and determination. The girl's frame was so skinny and slight, and her strength had impressed him for a few seconds. He hadn't expected it. Now, scratching, and tearing at his skin, the girl's resilience was wearing thin for him and Christopher was beginning to lose his fucking temper.

'You stupid little bitch.' Grabbing the girl roughly, Christopher yanked her arm up high above her head and pinned her up against the brick wall.

'Get off me,' Lizzy screamed. Hoping that someone in one of the houses nearby would hear her shouts for help, she belted her voice out as loud as she could. Tucked away down the alleyway, hidden from sight, she wasn't holding out much hope of anyone coming to her rescue.

Shutting the girl up, Christopher slammed his hand over her mouth. The temptation of wanting to hurt the girl, really hurt her, was overpowering him. He needed to shut the bitch up. Good and proper. So she couldn't tell anyone anything. Wrapping his hands around her throat, he pressed hard as he watched the look of horror wash over her terrified face.

Her skin was pale, and up this close to her he could see scabs on her chin that she'd tried to cover up with cheap make-up. She looked every bit the skanky druggy that she was.

She was nothing to him. Just worthless scum.

Squeezing harder now, he could see the flash of understanding in the girl's eyes as the realisation of what he was about to do hit her. He was going to kill her. Just like he had her friend.

Brutally, violently. Without remorse.

He despised whores. Dirty little bitches, selling their bodies to men for money.

No morals, no fucking shame.

His aversion to them was conflicting. As much as his mind was repelled by women, his body was also drawn to them. He hated that he sometimes couldn't control that need.

It sickened him that as much as he loathed how cheap and nasty women could be, at the same time he wanted to touch them, taste them, feel himself inside them.

How they had that power to make him feel weak.

To want them.

Then he only hated them even more.

Christopher could feel the same torment building inside him now as he continued to squeeze the girl's throat. He could feel the power building up inside him.

The girl was getting weak.

Seeing the man's evil eyes flicker with hate, Lizzy tried to scream, but his hands were so firmly locked around her throat that no sound came out.

She was struggling to breathe in air now. She had a strange feeling: sucking in desperately through her mouth and nostrils, her lungs remained empty, deflated. Wheezing, she was getting weaker.

But she wouldn't give up. She couldn't. She wasn't ready to die.

Bringing her leg up, Lizzy had no other choice but to impact her knee as hard as she could into the man's balls.

It worked. Expelling a sharp breath, the man doubled over in pain. Letting go of his grip, he fell forward in agony, pressing up against her as he did.

Crammed between the wall and the man's huge frame, she wriggled away, desperate to break free from his grip. But when she was barely two footsteps away from him, he yanked her head back sharply, pulling her by her hair and slamming her back up against the wall.

He was enraged.

Like the devil himself, his eyes ablaze with fury, he head-butted Lizzy with full force, straight in her face.

Lizzy's head whacked against the bricks as her nose exploded. Blood cascaded down her face, down her clothes, covering both her and her attacker. Then she fell. Disorientated, her ears were ringing, her vision blurred. She slumped to the floor.

All the while, she was aware that if she allowed herself to slip into unconsciousness she'd never wake up. He'd kill her.

So she fought to keep her concentration. Focusing on anything she could just so that she didn't black out. She needed to keep her mind focused. She could feel the icy coolness of the concrete beneath her. There was a sharpness digging into her leg, like she'd landed on a stone. She kept her mind on that. On the sensation of the cold floor beneath her.

Crouching down, Christopher stared the girl in the eyes. She was a feisty bitch this one, she put up a brave fight. It was a fight she wasn't going to win. His balls throbbed in pain and in neediness.

Grabbing her by the throat, he could feel himself getting hard this time. The violence always did this to him. He felt suddenly powerful, insatiable.

His eyes were going to be the last thing this girl would ever see. His body would be the last thing forced upon her.

Lizzy was vaguely aware of the man pulling her legs apart, still gripping her by the throat with one hand. She tried to stay awake, but her head was throbbing in agony and she could feel herself slipping.

Maybe if she closed her eyes for a few minutes, then the pain would go away. Maybe if she just gave in to oblivion, her ordeal would soon be over.

Then she thought of her beautiful friend Paige. Her best friend. Now missing, her dead bloated body lost to the Thames.

Lizzy wasn't ready to die.

Unable to fight her attacker off, Lizzy reached her hand around underneath her thigh, grimacing as she felt the damp patch of urine. She was so frightened that she hadn't even realised that she'd wet herself.

She could feel her jeans being pulled down. He was yanking her legs out of them, all the while pinning her with one of his huge hands up against the wall.

Crying, she felt desperate. She didn't want to die like this.

She couldn't.

She felt the sharp object that was poking into her leg. It was a shard of glass from a broken bottle. It was far too small to do any damage, but Lizzy continued to feel around the floor near to her, her hand searching the pavement frantically for anything she might be able to use. Desperate now, she was running out of both options and hope fast.

The man continued to squeeze at her throat. His other hand was on her knickers now. Yanking them roughly over to one side, he was pushing himself on top of her, crushing her already struggling lungs as they fought for air.

His eyes never leaving hers, he was silent now. Just staring into her eyes completely mesmerised by her fear and panic. He was just waiting for her to give up and die.

Then he could take her. Like he'd taken her friend.

Feeling something cold and sharp, Lizzy grabbed the object with her hand. It was the rest of the bottle. Holding one end, she faced the jagged glass out, ready to strike. Lurching forward, she stabbed her attacker repeatedly in the face with it.

Christopher let go of her throat, and put his hands up to protect his face. He was too late to shield himself from her final blow.

Hearing an awful popping sound as a large shard of glass penetrated his eyeball, slicing through it, Christopher recoiled backwards. He screeched in agony at the excruciating pain that exploded inside his head.

Gratefully breathing a huge gulp of air deep into her lungs, Lizzy got up onto her feet, taking her chance. Disorientated and covered in blood, she ran for her life.

Chapter Forty-Four

'I'm coming,' Cassie shouted, as she stifled a yawn and threw the covers off her. Jesus Christ, Nathan had only left a couple of hours ago; the way he was banging on the door you'd think he had been gone for a year. Maybe it was time to give him a key. After all they were technically family now.

Padding down the hallway to let him in, she glanced at her mobile. It was almost 4 a.m. Shoving her phone back into her pocket, she was surprised that Nathan had even bothered to come back seeing as it was so late. He'd seemed so pissed off when he'd got the call from Christopher earlier, dragging him out of bed. He'd said that he'd see her tomorrow, that he didn't want to disturb her again. Now he was knocking at the door, she was secretly glad he had.

She hadn't really slept since he'd left anyway; too excited, she'd lain awake thinking about him and the baby. She could still see the smile on his face as the news had sunk in that he was going to be a daddy. He had been genuinely happy, just as she'd hoped he would be.

'If this is your idea of an early morning wakeup call, Nath . . .' Opening the door, Cassie's smile faded and she let out a shriek. Christopher was leaning up against the door, covered in blood, and holding his face.

'Move out the fucking way.' Staggering inside the flat, he pushed Cassie roughly as he made his way through to the lounge.

'Oh my God, what's happened? Where's Nathan? Is he okay?' Cassie's hand was over her mouth. Taking a quick glance outside her front door, she saw that Christopher was alone.

'Christopher, where's Nathan?' Closing the front door, her heart lurched inside her chest as she realised that something very bad must have happened tonight.

'How the fuck do I know where Nathan is? What about me? My fucking eye's hanging out of my head.' Christopher moved his hand away to show her his injury and he could gauge by her reaction how bad it must be.

Heaving at the sight of his now mangled eyeball, Cassie tried to remain calm. There was just so much blood. His face was spliced open, and the blood was trickling down his hand, and all over the floor.

'Jesus Christ, what happened to you?'

Christopher didn't bother to answer; instead he ignored her as he emptied out a baggie of cocaine onto the coffee table then, squatting down on the floor next to it, he leant over and inhaled, not even bothering to sweep the pile of white powder into any form of a line.

Leaning his head back on the seat of the chair behind him, he breathed in heavily as he waited for the drug to kick in.

He couldn't see anything out of his eye. Nothing. The throbbing pain inside his skull was becoming unbearable. He didn't know how he'd even managed to drive here, to stay conscious through the agony.

He just needed something to help take the pain away.

To help him cope again.

That bitch had fucked him up good and proper. His eye was gone. She'd blinded him.

He was royally fucked.

For the first time in his life, no matter how much gear he snorted, he was struggling to gain back any sort of control.

'I don't think that you should be doing that, Christopher, you need to get to hospital.'

Leaping up, wired now that the drug was starting to kick in, Christopher squared up to Cassie, staring her hard in the face. 'What the fuck do you know about what I need? You don't know jack shit about me.'

Christopher paced around the room. Newly energised, he was raging with himself for not sorting the girl out the first time round, when he'd seen her down at the river. Leaving a witness had been foolish, but he hadn't given the skanky druggy much credit at the time. She had looked so out of it, he hadn't been worried. Afterwards, when his paranoia had kicked in, that's when he had started to worry. So, he tracked her down, started to follow her.

He'd been right to. He'd seen the way she had looked at him, at his car.

She remembered him.

She knew what he looked like. What he'd done.

He needed her gone.

She'd go to the Old Bill for definite now, he was sure of it. It wouldn't take them long to catch up with him, and if she led them to that other girl's body, he'd be over. Especially once they linked up the other girls that had disappeared.

'Fuck!' His temper getting the better of him, he kicked the TV right off the stand, watching it smash loudly on the floor. He felt like a caged animal. Like he was trapped. Paranoid that any minute now the police would turn up and arrest him.

Holding her hand over her mouth, Cassie tried to stifle her whimpering. She'd never seen Christopher like this. He was always crazy, always unhinged. Nathan had told her how he thought he was slowly getting worse. Nathan had said how, fuelled by drugs, his brother was becoming out of control.

He was right.

Christopher looked like he had lost the plot. Stomping around the room now, mumbling to himself, Cassie was watching in horror as Christopher psyched himself up into a frenzy. The last thing Cassie wanted to do was give him any reason to attack her.

She had to think about the baby, and try to keep calm.

'Christopher, whatever it is that has happened, I can help you.' Despite her voice shaking as she spoke, Cassie somehow remained composed. She was in work mode; she was trying to stay detached.

'What the fuck can you do, huh?' Christopher sneered. 'You're a fucking cunt just like the rest of them. Fucking women. Ruin everything.'

Christopher was riled. All he could think about was that fucking bitch running to the police. He felt stupid, weak – all the things he had fought so hard not to feel. He felt them all at once. Suffocating him.

Then he flipped out.

Needing to vent, he started smashing up everything around him: the table, the ornaments, the dining chairs. Caught up in his blind rage, he was like a man possessed.

Petrified, Cassie ran for refuge. All she could think about was the baby.

She needed to protect herself.

She needed to protect her baby.

She didn't know what had happened tonight, but whatever it was, Christopher was completely out of his mind.

Locking the bathroom door, she dragged the wash basket over and wedged it under the handle. Not that it would offer much protection, but there was nothing else in the room. Huddled down in the corner, under the sink, she listened as Christopher continued to tear up her flat in his rage. Smashing glass, stamping on things.

There was nothing she could do but pray that one of her neighbours would hear the commotion and call the police. Or that Nathan would come back.

Then, she remembered. Her mobile phone, it was in her pocket. Fumbling awkwardly with shaking hands, she dialled Nathan's number.

She wasn't sure if he'd even pick up. If he was even okay.

It just rang. No answer.

Listening to the ring tone, she suddenly realised that the ruction in her flat had stopped. The loud destruction had quickly turned to eerie silence and Cassie, unaware of what Christopher was doing now, wasn't sure which she found less disturbing.

Placing the phone back in her pocket, she listened hard. Maybe he'd left? Maybe he'd burnt himself out? She thought about getting up to see. Then she decided to wait a few more minutes, in case he was just temporarily preoccupied, shoving more shit up his nose.

The flat was so quiet now that the only sound she could hear was that of her erratic breathing, and her racing heart.

There was a noise.

Something outside in the hallway. Quiet now, but like someone was there.

Then came an almighty bang, as Christopher's foot burst through the bathroom door. Snapping the wood clean off its hinges, and sending the washing basket flying, the door slammed hard against the wall opposite.

Cassie's scream echoed loudly, as she held her hands up above her head to protect herself.

'Christopher, please, think of your brother, think of Nathan.'

Her words were no use.

Crying now, she held her stomach protectively as Christopher ignored her pleas.

Grabbing her viciously by her hair, he dragged her up onto her feet.

Chapter Forty-Five

'Don't lose your head, Harry. We need to be careful, and suss out whether they have weapons.' Raymond could tell that Harry was ready to explode. Crouching down in the dark corner, Raymond could see the girls clearly from his position. If he could, then Harry, squashed down behind him, must be able to as well. They looked a right state, but they were unharmed at least.

The O'Sheas were still here, standing near to where Kelly and Evie were sitting, tied to their chairs. Harry's face had gone a deep puce colour and he was holding his chest, enraged that the two men had the nerve to even think about scaring his two daughters like this. And what the hell was Evie doing here anyway? She was meant to be at home; he thought that she'd gone back to bed.

Harry scanned the bar.

Micky, the tall lanky fella, was holding a baseball bat, while the short porky one, Jimmy, had a gun. He and Raymond were both armed. Against the two men, they'd come out on top, he was sure. He couldn't do anything until the O'Sheas moved away from his girls. There was no way that he could risk either of them getting hurt.

'I'm going to check upstairs, Micky. Make sure the kids haven't heard these two whiney bitches making a racket down here. I'll be two minutes tops.'

Micky nodded. The girls were tied up, and he had hold of Jimmy's bat, so his brother could take all the time he wanted to. Especially if it meant that he'd get a few minutes alone with the pretty younger girl.

Walking over to where they sat, Micky ran the bat up Evie's leg, enjoying himself as Evie shuddered at his suggestive movement.

'You cold, darling? Want me to warm you up?' Leaning down, he grabbed her chin in his hand, pulling her face upwards so she was forced to look at him. She was a beauty alright. It was just a shame that they weren't able to stick around and have more fun with the girl, but he knew that Jimmy had strong opinions on fucking about with the women they dealt with. It wasn't something that he condoned. It was the only way the two of them differed when it came to work.

Jimmy kept business as exactly that: business. Whereas Micky liked to have his fun.

Leering at Evie's chest, the way her pink blouse gathered between the buttons, he just couldn't resist. Jimmy was upstairs. Having a little look at this young one's tiny pert titties wasn't going to hurt anyone.

He wasn't going to touch her or anything.

'Once the fire gets going it's going to get awfully hot in here.' Micky licked his lips as he leant in and started fumbling with the girl's shirt.

Evie squirmed, trying to shake him off but too restricted to move. The rope was cutting into her hands as it was. Her hands tied behind her back, she couldn't stop the man.

'Please, no,' Evie cried as Micky slipped his fingers inside the gaps of her shirt, gripping between the buttons and roughly pulling the material apart. As he ripped Evie's top open, the tiny buttons fell to the floor. Screaming as the man pawed at her, Evie was scared about what he'd do next.

'Get the fuck off her.' Kelly kicked her feet out. She tried to catch his leg, but he was a couple of feet away, and she couldn't reach him.

Raymond had been pulling Harry back up until now, but seeing this cunt roughing Evie up, Raymond was seeing red himself. They couldn't just sit back while that filthy animal was touching Evie like that.

Jimmy was upstairs – now was their chance.

Rushing out of their hiding place, Harry pointed the Glock directly at Micky's head.

Micky, hearing the noise, turned towards the sound behind him. He'd been so caught up in the girl that he looked genuinely shocked to see the two men standing there.

'Put your fucking gun down now, and don't say a fucking word. Or I'm going to blow your brains all over that fucking wall behind you.' Harry meant every word of it too.

Seeing Evie and Kelly tied up and crying was one of the most despicable, frightening sights he'd ever had to endure. They were his babies, his children. This scumbag deserved to die for even thinking about harming a single hair on either of their heads.

Micky lowered the gun to the floor. Slowly he stood back up and raised his empty hands up into the air.

'Move out the fucking way.' Harry nodded to Micky, and pointing the gun he shooed him away so that he could get to his girls.

Micky moved to his right. He still had his hands up in the air, while Raymond kept his gun on him the entire time, unwavering. He wanted to shoot the bloke there and then, but with the kids asleep upstairs, he didn't want to alert Jimmy O'Shea that he had company.

'Kelly, Evie, darlings, it's going to be okay.' Crouching down on the sodden floor, and placing his gun down, Harry pulled Evie's top back around her as he tried to cover up her exposed bra. The girl looked petrified. 'It's okay, sweetie. I'm going to sort these bastards out. You're going to be just fine.'

Untying Evie's hands as he spoke he wrapped his arms around her, tightly hugging her to him. Protecting her. Just as he had always done.

'What the fuck are you grinning at?' Raymond asked as Micky looked straight past him, with a snidey smirk on his face. Then turning to see what Micky was looking at, Harry saw that Raymond was faced with Jimmy. He was standing directly behind him, pointing a gun at his head. He must have sneaked around the back way.

'What's this, a family group hug? Very cosy. Get up!' Jimmy sneered as he ordered Harry to get back up onto his feet. All the while, keeping his gun aimed at Harry's armed sidekick.

'You're making a fatal fucking error, Jimmy, my man.' Harry gritted his teeth as he spoke. 'What the fuck do you think you're playing at?' Standing up, Harry looked down at his gun, on the floor next to Micky's. He'd have to be quick if he was to reach one of them before Jimmy reacted. Too quick. It was impossible.

And Jimmy could see it too.

'Don't even fucking think about it,' Jimmy shouted. 'This was going to be your warning, Harry. Tonight you were going to learn a little lesson about who you can and can't fuck with. But don't worry, all is not lost. Now you're here you may as well join the fucking party. Tie him up, Micky.'

Following Micky with his gun, Raymond debated whether to just shoot the gangly cunt. If he did it quick enough, he might just have enough time to turn and shoot Jimmy too.

Harry's stern look said it all, though. Raymond needed to do as he was told. The girls were here. They couldn't risk putting them in any more danger.

Dragging another chair over, Micky pushed Harry roughly down onto it and then, after tying his hands with the rope from the reel that he had in his pocket, Micky stood back, glaring at Raymond now, defiant.

He might still be armed, but he was outnumbered.

'You,' Jimmy ordered. 'Drop your gun too.'

Raymond took a few seconds to think about this. He could blow a hole in Jimmy's stomach the size of the bloke's head if he wanted to, but it was too much of a risk.

Having no choice but to do as he was told, Raymond bent down and placed the shotgun on the floor.

Jimmy laughed. This was too easy. It was obviously true what everyone was saying about Harry losing it. The bloke was nothing but a has-been. Him and his sidekick. No wonder he was stepping back from it all.

⌣

Seeing his mobile flash up with Cassie's number, Nathan debated whether or not to answer it. Right now, cramped in the back of the car with Terry, while his dad and Raymond were inside the bar with shooters, wasn't the best timing in the world. But Cassie wouldn't ring him unless it was important. The fact that she was calling him at all, at this time in the morning, sent alarm bells ringing in his head. 'You, keep your mouth shut, yeah. Don't try anything funny,' Nathan warned Terry before he answered.

'Cass?'

Immediately, he pulled the phone back away from his ear as the piercing screech belted out from his mobile, almost deafening him.

Nathan thought that there was some kind of fault on the line. Then he realised it was screaming.

Cassie was screaming.

'Cassie? Are you okay? Talk to me . . .' Nathan could feel the colour draining from his face as he spoke. It sounded like she was in pain. Like she was hurt, scared. He'd only left her a couple of hours ago, and she'd seemed fine then.

Then Nathan thought about the baby.

They'd only just found out that she was pregnant. What if something had happened?

'Cassie! Is it the baby? Is the baby okay?'

Terry, who had been sitting quietly up until now listening to the drama unfold, could tell that Nathan was now well and truly preoccupied with whoever this Cassie bird was on the blower, and not one to miss an opportunity, he was getting himself ready to make a run for it.

Leaning forward in his seat, Nathan was frustrated now. Shouting Cassie's name, he just wanted her to tell him that she was okay. All he could hear was screaming.

Then, in the background, he heard a man's voice.

The man was shouting, and Cassie was crying.

Racking his brains, Nathan tried to recall whether Cassie had told him about anyone who may have been hanging around her, an ex-boyfriend, a neighbour.

Whoever it was, he sounded angry. Cassie sounded really scared.

'Cassie baby, talk to me . . .'

Straining to listen now to the man's words as he bellowed in the background, it suddenly dawned on Nathan that the voice was familiar.

It was Christopher. He was sure of it. Positive, in fact.

What the fuck was Christopher doing at Cassie's? More to the point, why was she crying? Christopher sounded strange, demented almost.

It sounded like he was hurting her.

Pulling at the door handle, Terry took his chance at escaping and jumped out of the car. Almost falling onto the pavement in his hurry to get away, he scuttled towards the alleyway like a man possessed.

Nathan reached out to make a grab for him, half-heartedly putting up some kind of protest, but he was too slow. And right now, babysitting Terry was the least of his priorities.

He couldn't take in what he was hearing.

He didn't understand what was going on.

'Cassie, I'm on my way,' Nathan shouted as he too jumped out of the back of the car and got straight into the front. His dad had left the keys in the Bentley's ignition, and without a second thought, Nathan started the car up and sped off.

His only thoughts were Cassie and his baby. He needed to get to them, and fast.

Chapter Forty-Six

Crouching down on the seat, Terry could smell the strong fumes of petrol, and he could see the jerry can that had been discarded on the floor.

He could also see the four chairs that Harry, Raymond, Kelly and the younger girl were tied to. There was no sign of the kids, so at least that was something. Kelly looked awful, her make-up smeared all down her face, and her eyes puffy from where she'd been crying. She looked petrified. Seeing her in such a state, Terry's heart went out to her. All his anger from earlier, when he'd first set his sights on this place, was now gone.

It was like now, with her and the kids at risk of being hurt, Terry had his priorities well and truly tested. Kelly had given him everything, and all he'd ever been to her in return was a complete cunt. Cheating on her and taking her for granted. These past few weeks of sleeping in dingy squats, and rummaging in dustbins for scraps of food to survive had been the loneliest he'd ever endured.

Talk about learning the hard way. Kelly and the kids were his life. He realised that now. Seeing her like this, he felt his blood boil. It was about time that he stepped up and started acting like the husband she deserved.

But if even Harry couldn't sort the O'Sheas out, then how the hell was he going to?

———

Harry's hands were tied firmly around his back, his eyes glaring at Jimmy, flashing with anger. Micky was a first class prick; it was clear to see which man was the monkey and which was the organ grinder here. Jimmy was the man shouting the orders, and this was all down to him. Micky was just the brainless idiot going along with it all.

They were both fools to think that they were going to get away with this.

Staring over to Evie, he could see that she was petrified too. She was a clever girl, though. He had to hand it to her. She had her hands behind her, as if they were still tied.

His gun was on the floor in front of her. All she had to do was reach down and get it, and they would have some kind of a chance of getting out of here.

He could see the fear in her eyes. She was so terrified she looked like she could barely move.

He'd string the O'Sheas up for this when it was all over.

Feeling the rattling start in his chest again, he tried to clear his throat. The small raspy tickle set him off, and soon the tickle in the back of his throat was a loud hacking cough.

Tied to the chair, Harry was exposed.

Choking now, he could taste the metallic tang of blood, and turning his head to the side he spat out the phlegm, hoping that Kelly and Evie wouldn't see the blood.

'What the fuck?' Micky jumped back as Harry gobbed a mouthful of the red mucus onto his trousers as he aimed for the floor.

'Harry?' Raymond could see by Harry's face that what he had just witnessed wasn't new to his friend. He was coughing up blood, a lot of it. But going by his now calm exterior, he was trying to do his best to pretend that spitting blood was normal. Harry seemed unfazed by it, like it had happened before.

'Leave it.' Harry quickly dismissed his actions, embarrassed that he now had no control over his obvious indisposition.

Jimmy, quick to pick up on Harry's weakness, could see it too. He could see in Harry's eyes that the bloke was sick. He twigged just as Raymond did.

This was why Harry Woods was stepping back. He was ill.

Really ill.

'I've got fucking blood all over my leg.' Micky stared at Harry accusingly, as if Harry had purposely spat some kind of contagious venom at him. 'I could get fucking AIDS from this!'

Jimmy shook his head. Micky really was a bloody idiot sometimes. But right now, with an audience watching, Jimmy couldn't be arsed to explain to Micky what the chances of that happening were.

'Go and get yourself cleared up, Micky.' He nodded towards the men's toilets. 'Hurry the fuck up.' Then turning back to Harry, he grinned. 'You don't look too good, Harry. Coughing up blood, that can't be good.'

Harry looked away, but not quickly enough.

'Don't tell me you're about to kick the bucket?' Jimmy laughed.

The way Harry's eyes flickered, Jimmy could tell that his words had hit him. He knew that he was right on the money. Harry Woods was dying.

This was just getting better and better.

'Dad?' Kelly felt sick at where the conversation was going. 'What the hell is he talking about?'

'Oh, sorry. I take it you haven't broken the news to your kids yet? Ah well, it's out now, isn't it? Looks like I could be doing you a favour tonight after all. By putting you out of your misery.'

Then Jimmy really laughed. This was fucking priceless. It really was.

'The only one who's getting put out of their misery tonight is you, Jimmy, and trust me, when I get my hands on you, you're going to wish you were never born. You and your brother are just a fucking joke.' Harry was fuming now.

He couldn't even look Raymond or the girls in the eye now. He hadn't wanted his illness to come out like this. 'You're a fool, Jimmy, if you think anyone will want to do business with you after this. You're nothing, no-one. The O'Shea brothers, a couple of faces? Do me a favour, you two are no more than a couple of cunts.'

Harry had Jimmy's full attention now. Rendered silent, the bloke was seething at Harry's words. He was still pointing the gun at him, but Harry no longer cared.

'What's the matter, Jimmy, truth fucking hurting?'

Harry's mocking had the desired effect. Jimmy was no longer so cocky, nor was he thinking straight. His ego was getting the better of him. Harry could see it in the bloke's eyes.

All Harry had to do was keep him talking. Keep his attention.

'To be fair, it's more Micky that most people cunt off. Your brother holds you back, Jimmy. He ain't anywhere near as smart as you . . .' Harry continued. 'Though that don't fucking say much. Even the Turks wouldn't work with you and they fucking have crack heads doing their running for them. You're a joke, Jimmy, a walking talking joke. But you seem to be the only one who hasn't realised that.'

Harry kept talking. He could see Terry creeping up behind Jimmy ready to strike, and he knew that all he had to do was keep Jimmy's attention. Keep the man talking, and then maybe they'd have some kind of chance of getting out of here in one piece.

Just a few feet away now, Terry was almost ready to pounce. He was unarmed, though, so he was going to have to grab him unawares. Try to wrestle the bloke's gun from him.

It wasn't much of a plan, but it was all he had and he had to at least try, for Kelly's and the kids' sake.

Evie, Kelly and Raymond, all aware of what was going on, kept their eyes down. Not wanting to give away the fact that Terry was almost on Jimmy. Harry was playing a blinder with keeping Jimmy's attention.

Treading carefully, scared that his feet would squelch, he tip-toed on the petrol sodden carpet. Just a couple more steps. Inches away now, he was almost on him.

'Jimmy, behind you.' Coming out of the bathroom, Micky's face twisted in anger as he pointed his hand to alert his brother that Terry was closing in on him. Terry was unarmed, and Micky knew that his brother would have his back. Micky launched himself at Terry.

Watching as his brother and Terry Stranks rolled about on the floor, Jimmy released the safety off his gun. As soon as he got a clear aim he was going to take a shot at Terry. The slippery bastard had come out of nowhere. It was Terry's fault that any of them were here in the first place. If Terry and his stupid bitch of a wife had just paid up what they owed, Jimmy and Micky would have walked away ages ago. None of this would ever have happened.

Watching as the two men started fighting, Jimmy shouted at Micky. 'Fucking hell, Micky. Move out the way and I'll deal with the fucker myself.'

Punching out, Terry whacked Micky straight in the face, his clenched fist impacting hard with Micky's mouth, sending his tooth tearing right through his bottom lip.

Micky tried to hit back, but Terry was getting the upper hand. He whacked Micky again, sending him sprawling backwards, then, before he had a chance to register what was happening, Terry grabbed a fistful of Micky's hair and whacked his head off the floor.

Jimmy took the shot.

Terry moved, yanking Micky up roughly by his hair. The bullet Jimmy fired skimmed past Terry, tearing into the back of Micky's head.

Blood spurted out of Micky's mouth. Instantly he was dead.

Hearing a treacherous howl fill the room, Jimmy took a few seconds to realise the noise was coming from him.

He'd shot Micky.

He'd shot his brother.

Pulling the trigger again, he shot at Terry. He'd just made him shoot his brother. Jimmy wanted him dead.

Terry screamed in pain as the bullet penetrated his shoulder.

'Put your gun down.' Turning around Jimmy almost laughed at the sight of the young girl standing before him, her hand trembling almost as much as her voice as she pointed her dad's gun straight at his head.

Jimmy sniggered. 'I've seen scarier fucking cartoons, love. Do me a favour and sit back down, yeah? This will soon be over.'

Taking the lighter from out of his pocket, Jimmy knew that all he had to do was flick the switch and the whole place would go up in minutes. He'd have enough time to drag his brother outside, he was sure.

As for the rest of them, their fate would be left down to this girl, and there was no way she'd be able to get them all untied and out of here in time.

'Put it down,' Evie shouted. Squeezing the trigger just a few millimetres, she stared him dead in the eyes. It was all on her now.

'Okay, okay,' Jimmy said as he lowered his gun to the floor.

'Evie.' Seeing Jimmy's finger move on the trigger, as he pretended to put his weapon down, Harry called out to warn his daughter.

The shot rang out loudly in the room. Desperate now, Harry threw himself in front of Evie, bringing the chair he was tied to crashing down with him.

Then another shot rang out.

Then Kelly's scream filled the room.

Evie was standing as if in a trance, with the gun hanging down at her side, staring at the floor where Jimmy was splayed out in a pool of dark thick blood.

She'd killed him.

Except she hadn't been quick enough. Next to him was her father, motionless on the floor, with blood seeping out from his shirt.

Harry had taken the bullet that was meant for his daughter.

Chapter Forty-Seven

Taking the stairs two at a time, Nathan couldn't have run faster if he'd tried.

The distraught phone call from Cassie had been cut off on his way over here, and when he'd tried calling her back, she hadn't answered.

Nathan was worried. Something was wrong. Really wrong.

Reaching Cassie's flat, Nathan placed his hand on the already ajar door as he cautiously pushed it open.

'Cass?' he called as he trod carefully down the hallway, apprehensive about what he might be walking into. He listened, but the flat was silent.

Only a few feet inside the doorway, he could already see the mess and destruction. The flat looked like it had been ransacked. Everything was smashed and broken. Glass crunched beneath his feet as he walked, and there was mud all over the place, from where Cassie's favourite yucca plant had been thrown across the room. The large ceramic pot was broken into pieces on the floor.

With a sinking feeling in his stomach, Nathan continued to make his way through the flat, scared at what he might find.

It looked like Cassie had been burgled.

All he could think about was the baby. He prayed to God that they were both okay.

Stepping over chunks of splintered wood, remnants of what used to be the coffee table, he made his way back out of the lounge and along the hallway towards the bathroom.

'Cass?' he called again.

Then, stopping dead in his tracks, Nathan felt the bile rise up in the back of his throat as he looked down at the blood stained carpet. Feeling dizzy and nauseated he held onto the door frame, peering into the small bathroom. The door was completely off its hinges. Like it had been kicked in. And there was more blood on the floor.

Cassie's blood?

Following the trail of blood back out and along the hallway – slowly, apprehensively – Nathan made his way to the kitchen. All the while, he was consumed by the sense of utter dread about what he was yet to see.

He somehow managed to swallow down the sick, watery substance that was beginning to rise up at the back of his throat.

What the fuck had happened here? Where the fuck was Cassie?

Stepping near to the kitchen doorway, Nathan could hear something. It sounded like laboured breathing, like someone was close by, gasping for breath. Almost unable to look, Nathan forced himself to walk those extra few feet into the kitchen. Steadying himself as he saw her, Nathan's hand shot up to his mouth. On the floor in the corner of the room, surrounded by more blood, was Cassie.

'Cassie!' The relief Nathan felt as he saw her there, crouched in the corner rocking Christopher in her arms, was overwhelming.

Cassie looked up at him, but she was crying. Tears were cascading down her face. She didn't look scared or frightened as she had sounded earlier, she just looked sad. She was cradling Christopher in her arms, rocking him backwards and forwards. As Nathan's gaze left hers and met his brother's, he was sickened at what he saw.

The blood had been Christopher's.

His face was a mess. Like it had been carved up. Sliced open in several places, his skin was covered in congealed blood. And his eye; Nathan could barely look at it. Bulging, mangled, it looked like it was coming away from its socket.

He was mumbling the same words over and over, and Cassie was trying to soothe him. Her arms around him, she was comforting him. And Christopher was letting her.

For the first time in his life, unable to find any kind of control, Christopher had finally broken. He was numb. Void of all feeling. He'd burnt himself out, exhausted from his violent outburst.

Cassie had seen it in his eyes, and using her years of experience as a trained nurse she had managed to calm Christopher down. Soothing him with her words of reassurance, she had talked him down from his outburst.

She could see that Christopher wasn't just unhinged and out of control. He was suffering a mental breakdown. Coaxing him onto the floor and cradling him in her arms, Cassie had been surprised at Christopher's sudden unexpectedly subdued mood.

He'd been angry before, but that was Christopher's mask. She could tell that he was scared, confused. He was like a small injured child, allowing himself to be rocked back and forth into a calmer state of mind.

'What the fuck has happened?' Nathan asked. He shook his head, trying to take in what he was seeing, but the scene before him was just too surreal.

Nathan looked at Cassie, but she just shook her head. She couldn't find any words to explain to him what had just happened. All she knew was that Christopher was in a really bad way. She'd managed to calm him down, to sit with him, but so far the words that had come out of his mouth as she waited for the paramedics to turn up hadn't made any sense. He kept talking about girls. Saying how he'd hurt them.

'He's off his head, Nathan, I've called for an ambulance. I don't think he knows what he's saying. He keeps mumbling about hurting girls? He said he killed them?' Cassie whispered.

Then Christopher stared up at him too. His face looked grotesque, his eyeball protruding from its socket and his skin covered in dry blood. And he was whimpering. Nathan stared at his brother in shock, as Christopher suddenly looked very small and very frightened.

He looked like a broken man.

'I do. I do know what I'm saying.' Christopher may have appeared to be a million miles away as he stared into space, mumbling to himself, but he was very much right here with them the whole time. Listening. 'I'm sorry for what I did to the girls. I'm so sorry. I killed them.'

'What did you do, Christopher?' Nathan bent down now, desperately trying to control his urge to be sick at the sight of Christopher's mangled face. 'Tell me, Christopher. You can trust me, you know you can. We're brothers, yeah? Tell me who you killed.'

Christopher let out a weak smile. Then a wail, from deep inside him. Everything that he'd held in for all these years – he couldn't do it anymore.

'You won't love me anymore if I tell you . . .' Christopher had snot running down into his mouth as he spoke now. He was a mess. The drugs, the drink, it had all fucked with his head.

'Tell me.' Nathan held Christopher's gaze.

Nathan could hear the sirens directly outside; the paramedics would be here in just a few more minutes. Worried that Christopher might lose consciousness, Nathan needed to keep his brother talking.

'I hate them and it's all her fault.' Christopher gulped now.

'Whose fault?'

'Mum's. She ruined everything. She made me the way I am. It's her fault that I hate women. Nasty cunts the lot of them. You can't trust them, Nathan. You can't trust any of them.' Christopher was snivelling now. His head was so sore that everything throbbed. He just wanted to go to sleep and make everything go away.

'Christopher, Mum's dead. She didn't ask to die. You can't blame her because things haven't worked out the way that you wanted them to. She loved us. How can you talk about her like that?'

Christopher shook his head. He spoke with great sadness now, finally able to tell his brother the truth about everything. 'Our mother was a lying, cheating whore, Nathan.'

Nathan stared now, biting his tongue. His face gave nothing away but he could feel the knot of anger forming inside his own stomach at his brother's words. Still, he tried to remain as calm as possible. He couldn't even comprehend what his brother was saying. It was wrong, shameful. None of it made any sense. Their mother was a beautiful, caring woman. Her death had been tragic.

'She was leaving him. Said she was going to take Evie with her. Said that she didn't love him anymore. That she'd been cheating on him. Cheating on him for years, Nathan, not just a one-off.'

Nathan was sure that Christopher was wrong now. He was obviously in shock, traumatised from his injuries, or high on gear. Probably both.

Listening to Christopher spouting crap about their mother was hard to take in, but Nathan needed to keep Christopher talking, he needed to keep him conscious until the paramedics got here.

'You must be wrong, Christopher. How come this is the first I'm hearing of it? Dad would have told me. I know he would. Come on, mate, you've had a nasty shock. You're not making sense.'

Christopher looked up now, staring Nathan straight in the face. Finally he was able to tell the truth about that fateful day. Finally someone would listen to the secret he'd been forced to keep.

'Dad told me not to tell you. He told me not to tell anyone. Not a single living soul. He said that it would destroy our family.

That we must keep it a secret. He made me promise.' Christopher cried now.

The image of his brother's huge, beefy frame shaking as he sobbed made Nathan feel uneasy. Christopher never showed any emotion other than anger. Crying was alien to him.

'You should have seen her, Nathan, she was nasty, evil. Her face was all twisted with venom. She was taunting him, trying to hurt him. But she was the one who got hurt in the end. Pushed to her death, she soon stopped laughing then.'

Shaking his head, Nathan still didn't know what Christopher was talking about. He really was a mess. The drugs, his temper; it was all too much. Even now, surrounded by blood and chaos, he was still spinning them all a line, stirring the shit pot, fucking with them like he always did.

'Pushed to her death? What are you talking about? Mum fell. It was an accident, Christopher. You're wrong. How would you even know any of this?'

Nathan exchanged looks with Cassie. He wondered if it was normal for Christopher to be so disorientated. He wasn't making any sense.

Christopher shook his head, then taking a deep breath he said sadly, 'I was there.'

'You were there?' Nathan said incredulously. 'What? You heard Mum confess that she had been having an affair, that she was leaving, did you? Then you saw Dad push her down the stairs? You saw him kill her? It's a bit far-fetched, Christopher . . .'

'They didn't realise that I was home. I was in my bedroom. I'd snuck back in to get some of my WWF wrestling cards to swap with Riley James down the road. The next thing I knew they were shouting and screaming at each other. Well, Mum was. I went out onto the landing when I heard what she said to him. She crucified him, Nathan.'

Standing behind his father, Christopher had huddled against the wall. Only eleven years old at the time, Christopher had watched as his father slumped forward. His body language had said it all, he was defeated by the awful revelation that his mother had made. He'd looked like he'd had the air knocked out of him.

Nathan stared at his brother, unsure now of what he was trying to say. For a story that Christopher was making up, it seemed very detailed.

Nathan wanted to believe that Christopher's words were a complete load of rubbish, but he sounded almost convincing.

'I just saw red, Nathan, when she said what she did about Evie. She ripped Dad's heart out.'

'What's it got to do with Evie?' Nathan shook his head now, adamant that his brother was wrong. He was disillusioned, messed up.

'Ask Dad.' Suddenly Christopher was unsure of his words. Once he said them out loud he knew that there was no way they'd ever be unsaid.

'I'm asking you.'

Christopher shook his head once more. 'She'd been having an affair, and Dad was crying, begging her to tell him that it wasn't true.'

Nathan felt sick again, trying to think back to the day that his mother had died. To how their father had been. Nathan just couldn't recall anything other than their father grieving. It had been an accident. Their dad had told them that it had just been an accident. He couldn't have lied, surely?

He loved their mother. He didn't want to believe what Christopher was saying, but something deep inside him was making him feel that maybe, just maybe, Christopher was telling the truth.

Cassie felt it too. She placed her hand around Nathan's shoulders now, gently trying to pull him back up as the paramedics pounded at the front door.

'Dad said I wasn't allowed to tell anyone. Look at the state of me. Keeping it all inside of me is fucking my head up. I can't do it anymore. I fucking hate her. Why did she do it? Why did she lie? She ruined everything.'

'What did she lie about?'

'You should have seen her, Nathan. She was so vile, so nasty.'

Nathan stared now, silent. Waiting for Christopher to finish.

'Evie isn't Dad's daughter, Nathan. Mum was cheating on him. For years apparently.' Christopher stared at Nathan now. His face was deadly serious and Nathan knew that he was telling him the truth. 'She laughed in his face when she told him. Drunk out of her mind, she actually laughed when she told him. I hated her for what she was saying. For doing that to Dad. To all of us.'

Christopher glanced up now, and stared his brother straight in the eyes.

'So I pushed her. I ran at her and pushed her head first down the stairs.' Christopher had finally said out loud the words that he'd been suppressing for so long. 'I killed her, Nathan. It was me. Dad tried to cover it up so that no-one would ever find out what I'd done. Uncle Raymond took me away and Dad lied to everyone. He tried to protect me. Protect all of us.'

The paramedics came in then and Nathan stepped aside, letting Cassie's comforting arm slip from his shoulders.

Holding onto the kitchen worktop Nathan steadied himself as the ambulance crew tended to Christopher, while his brother's words rang in his head.

Christopher had killed their mother.

Their dad had covered it all up.

And Evie – poor Evie.

Leaning over the basin, Nathan threw up.

Chapter Forty-Eight

'So the O'Sheas broke into the bar, not knowing that Harry Woods and his daughter Evie were here babysitting?' Having raced to the scene of the crime, Detective Chief Superintendent Porter felt like a dog with a bone on hearing the news of the fatal shootout in the Woods family's bar. Finally Harry Woods had left a trail of his own dirt for everyone to see.

Except the words coming out of Officer Mansell's mouth were implying otherwise.

'So you're telling me that Harry was the victim in all of this?'

Mansell nodded. 'They've just taken him to the serious trauma unit over at St. Mary's. He's in a bad way, Guv; Jimmy shot him. The bloke was like a man possessed. Killed his brother, shot Harry and Terry and then turned the gun on the girls.'

Porter's ears pricked up. 'Terry? As in Terry Stranks? What was he doing here? Were the Woods hiding him all along?'

'No, Guv. He turned up just seconds before me. I saw him try and negotiate with Jimmy, but like I say, Jimmy was a man possessed. He weren't having none of it. I could see by Kelly Stranks' reaction that it was the first time she'd laid eyes on her husband. My guess was that he'd been laying low watching the pub. Kelly seemed genuinely shocked to see him. He must have been hanging about outside when he heard the commotion, just like I did.'

Porter frowned. The story was a bit too cut and shut for his liking. It was almost like Mansell had it rehearsed. Porter had had his suspicions about the officer's involvement with the Woods family for a while now; still, with no evidence that Harry had Mansell in his pocket, what could he do about it?

Rubbing his fingers through the stubble on his chin, Porter stepped carefully around Jimmy's and Micky's bodies, which were still splayed out on the petrol sodden floor, covered with sheets.

'So you were here the entire time?'

Mansell shook his head. 'No, Sir. Only for the last part, when Jimmy opened fire. I saw it all, Sir.'

Porter frowned. He was slowly coming to the realisation that Harry Woods was going to somehow dig himself out of this mess once again and there was nothing that he could do about it. It irked Porter that Harry always seemed to get away with things. The bloke was like Teflon: nothing stuck to him.

Porter tried to make sense of the crime scene, as he tallied up what the officer in front of him was saying. 'So you were the first officer on the scene?' Porter asked suspiciously, as he eyed up Mansell's civilian clothing, noting that the officer wasn't in uniform.

'Well, technically I'm off duty, Sir. I was only walking past when I heard the commotion. I'd parked up down the road to get a kebab, see? I had the late night munchies.' Watching his superior officer crouching down as he lifted up the black sheeting that covered Micky O'Shea's lifeless corpse, Mansell repeated his prepared story.

'Late night munchies? It's almost breakfast time!' Standing up, Porter eyed Mansell. He'd been dubious of Mansell's loyalty to the force for a while now. But this story was something else altogether, and Porter knew that his suspicions were right. Mansell was in Harry's pocket, he was sure of it.

'I know. But my wife's had me on this strict diet, you see. I was up late watching some films, thought that I'd pop out and treat myself while the wife was asleep. What she doesn't know won't hurt her, you know how it is.' Mansell knew that his reason for being in the area was lame, but there was no way that Porter could prove otherwise.

'No, I don't know how it is, actually.' Porter glared at Mansell. 'So, you were just walking past? Bit of a coincidence, wouldn't you say?' Porter eyeballed Mansell now.

Mansell shrugged. Even if Porter personally didn't believe him, so what? He had no proof that he was lying.

'Well, coincidences do happen,' Mansell offered before continuing. 'And it's a good job that I did walk by, too. The Woods would have all suffered at Jimmy O'Shea's hands otherwise. The bloke was like a lunatic. The attack was completely unprovoked.'

'Unprovoked?' Porter stared at Mansell questioningly, then raised his eyes.

'The O'Sheas were the only ones with the guns.'

Porter frowned. This was one of the biggest loads of bullshit he'd ever heard.

'I've already questioned Evie Woods; she and her sister Kelly have gone down to the hospital with Harry and Terry. Apparently, according to her, she and her father had been babysitting for the eldest daughter, Kelly, this evening. Kelly's kids are upstairs in bed as we speak. Slept through the whole thing, luckily. Kelly called one of the barmaids in to keep an eye on them before she left. Anyway, Evie said that she and her dad were just getting ready to leave when the O'Sheas burst in with all guns blazing. Apparently they were trying to turn the place over; they'd heard that Harry Woods' kids owned the place and they were after the bar's takings. They didn't realise that Nathan and Christopher never left any money on the premises overnight. So the burglary was foiled from the off. Only, when Harry confronted them both, Jimmy just lost it. Doused everything in petrol and threatened to set light to the place. Micky, having a conscience and knowing that there were kids upstairs, argued with his brother, so Jimmy shot him.'

'Jimmy shot Micky?'

Mansell nodded.

'Over a row about kids?'

Again Mansell just nodded.

Porter was desperate for something on Woods. Anything at all. But already he could feel the case slipping from his grasp. He shook his head and then stared around the room. The place was soaked in petrol, and there was blood sprayed all over the carpet next to where the two bodies lay.

'Whereabouts were you standing? Surely Jimmy would have tried to shoot you too? And if the O'Sheas were the only ones with guns, how did Jimmy end up getting shot?'

'I was over at the window.' Mansell pointed over to the smashed window over by the far corner of the pub. 'I called for backup immediately. By then Jimmy had set the gun on Evie Woods. The girl was terrified. Jimmy was going to shoot her, but Harry was quick off the mark. He picked up Micky's gun off the floor, he threw himself over Evie in order to protect her. They both opened fire. Jimmy shot first and Harry only shot back in self-defence.'

'Self-defence?' Porter stared now.

The story was so far-fetched, and he could almost see the steam billowing out of Mansell's ears as the officer recited the unconvincing version of events.

'So Harry shot Jimmy?'

'In self-defence.' Mansell nodded.

'Hmm.' Porter wondered how much Harry was paying Mansell to make up this load of codswallop. 'And how's Harry now?' Porter asked.

'He didn't look good, Sir. Terry took a bullet to the shoulder, he'll be fine. But Harry, well, like I said, Sir. He doesn't look good.'

'What about Raymond Marks? Was he here too?' Porter was hopeful. He just needed something, a tiny grain of evidence on either of the two men and he could stitch the bastards up. They'd both been running rings around him for far too long.

'Raymond Marks? Why would he have been here? No, it was just Harry and Evie.' Mansell bit the inside of his lip now. Raymond had been the one to call him tonight. Mansell had raced to the bar in just minutes. By then the damage had already been done. Taking the guns, Raymond had left Mansell, Terry and the girls with a story to stick to.

The O'Sheas had attacked them. They were innocent.

Mansell had done his bit now. He just prayed that Raymond hadn't overlooked anything before he fled.

Taking a deep breath, Porter knew that there was a whole lot more to this story. But Porter also knew the score better than anyone: without cold hard evidence, he had nothing to go on. Not unless by some miraculous turn of good fortune they happened upon some evidence that would put either Raymond or Harry in the frame here.

Porter had been silenced by these two crooks for far too long. Tonight he thought he'd finally managed to find some dirt on Raymond and Harry that even they would have problems concealing.

But he'd been wrong.

The fact that Harry Woods and his family were the apparent victims in tonight's attack was too hard to believe. Harry Woods had never been anyone's victim.

'There's one more thing, Guv,' Mansell said as he removed the clear plastic bag from his pocket. 'One of the other officers found this while they were doing the search of the premises and the bodies.

They recognised it straight away as one of the rare pieces that was stolen in the big jeweller's raid in Mayfair a few years back. The one that you were working on.'

Mansell said the words 'working on' with a slight tilt to his voice. If truth be known Porter had been obsessed by that case at one time. That was when his whole vendetta towards Harry had first started.

Holding out his hand, Porter's eyes lit up as he stared at the sparkling green emerald in the centre of the gold brooch. This was one of the pieces that he had spent the last seven years trying to track down. He'd known all along it had been Harry and Raymond who had pulled the robbery off, he just needed firm evidence.

And now he had it. The stolen brooch had at last been found.

'Fucking Bingo!' Porter beamed. Finally a break in the case. He could have hugged Mansell for this. Maybe he'd got the officer wrong. Mansell could have just kept the piece for himself after all. 'Let's hope Harry survives, eh? He'll go down for years for this.'

'Oh no, Guv, you've got it wrong,' Mansell said as he placed the jewel in Porter's hand. 'They didn't find this in Harry's possession, nor was it found in the bar.'

'Well I don't understand. You just said that one of the officers found it during the search of the premises?'

'And the bodies . . . They found it on Jimmy, it was tucked inside his wallet. Turns out that all the time you've been chasing Harry for the robbery, and it was the O'Sheas all along.'

Pursing his lips as he fought his hardest not to laugh at Porter's face, draining of colour, Mansell shrugged. 'What were the chances, huh?'

Chapter Forty-Nine

The bleeping machinery together with the wires and tubes were the only things keeping Harry alive right now. He was getting weak, and he could feel himself starting to slip away. He'd said the cancer wouldn't beat him, and when he'd been shot he'd thought that was it. He'd believed that was how he would die. Taken out in a blaze of glory, by a single bullet.

But it wasn't to be. The gunshot was just a flesh wound. He would have survived.

But the cancer had defeated him in the end.

It had gripped him. Taken over every part of his body so that he could barely move, barely breathe.

Two days he'd been in hospital now, and he knew that they were the last two days of his life.

He felt so weak, it was all he could do not to close his eyes and let death take him. But there was just one more thing that he had left to do.

The doctors had placed him on palliative care, so Harry knew that he didn't have long. He had conserved every last bit of energy so that he could have this one last moment.

He needed to say goodbye to his family. Just the thought alone was painful enough to kill him.

'Help me sit up a bit more,' Harry whispered weakly to Raymond, who immediately started fussing over his friend. Pulling Harry's body farther up the bed, Raymond pressed the buttons on the remote control and raised Harry up so that he was in more of an upright position.

Harry's mouth was dry; he hadn't spoken for hours. He had been waiting for all his children to get here so that he could speak for one last time, when all of the family were finally here together.

All of them except Christopher.

Elevated on the bed, Harry looked at each of his children as they stood around his him.

Harry had one more thing left to do, and it was time. 'Come here, Kelly.' Harry beckoned Kelly to step in closer so that he could hold her hand.

Walking up to her father, Kelly was already beside herself. An emotional wreck, she had been crying since she'd arrived, though her swollen, puffy eyes were testimony that she'd been crying for even longer than that.

Harry held onto Kelly's hand tightly.

'I'm so sorry, Dad, about everything. All those years. I wasted all that precious time. I'm so, so sorry. I love you so much.'

Kissing her father's cheek, Kelly knew that saying goodbye to her dad was one of the hardest things she'd ever have to do. She was riddled with so much guilt, and she wished with all her heart that things had been different. Now, at the end of his life, when time had run out, she'd have given everything she owned just to have one more day with her father.

He'd been right about Terry.

She knew that now.

'You don't need to be sorry about a thing, Kelly. I love you too, my darling. You look after my grandbabies, okay?' Harry smiled weakly. He didn't want to let go. He didn't want to leave his children, his grandchildren, but he knew that the decision wasn't up to him. He had no choice.

Stepping aside to let Evie stand next to their father's bedside, Kelly put her hand over her mouth as she tried to stifle her sobs.

Placing her small hand on his, Evie stared into Harry's eyes. 'I love you so much, Dad. I'm so scared of losing you . . .' Evie cried now, and Harry, unable to stop his own tears, felt them escaping down his cheek.

'Don't you be scared, baby. Do you remember when you were little and I used to read you that book? You know, the one about the guardian angel?'

Evie nodded now. How could she forget? It had been her favourite. So much so, that she had pestered her dad to read it to her every night that he was home for almost a year. She could still recall it word for word even now.

'Well that's what I'll be. I'll be your guardian angel, Evie. I'll never be far away, I promise. I'll be your angel and you will always be my little girl. Always. Just you remember that.'

Unable to speak, Evie lay her head lightly down on her father's chest. Breathing in his familiar smell for the very last time, her body shook as she said goodbye.

Seeing how distraught Evie was, Raymond put his arm around her. Consoling her as much as he could, he led her over to the chair at the end of the bed so that Nathan could have his turn at saying goodbye.

'Dad.' Nathan stepped forward now. At a loss as to what he was supposed to say, he was drained. The last few days had been such a blur, but he knew he had to keep himself together. For the family's sake. Just like his dad had asked of him.

'Remember what we spoke about, Nathan?' Harry whispered now, his body feeling tired, weak.

Nathan nodded.

Until Nathan had confronted his dad about his mother's death, and about Evie, Nathan had thought that maybe Christopher had been lying, maybe he'd been confused. Nathan had hung onto that theory with everything he had. But Nathan had seen it in his father's and Raymond's eyes when he had confronted them both. His father had the excuse of being in pure agony as the reason he could barely look Nathan in the eye as he spoke, but Raymond had nothing to fall back on. And Nathan knew the second that he asked them both that what Christopher said was true.

Just the thought of his mother being murdered pained him down to his core, and the fact that Evie wasn't his dad's daughter, it was almost too much to comprehend.

Harry had begged Nathan not to tell the others. Evie could never find out the truth, it would break the girl's heart. Harry had done everything in his power to try to protect her from ever finding out. He'd even sent her away to boarding school, so that she wouldn't be around Christopher too much. He was always so scared that someday Christopher would tell her. He could be nasty in that way. He got his kicks out of causing misery to people. Harry could say that about his son, because it was true. Christopher was a law completely unto himself. There were times, especially when Christopher was off his face on drugs, that Harry had felt like he was living on a knife edge. It was like Harry's house had been made from cards. All neatly stacked up on top of each other keeping them all safe, keeping them all contained inside, until Christopher, at any given point, pulled one of them out from the pile and brought the whole thing toppling down around him.

'I have your word, Nathan?' Harry asked now.

Nathan nodded, promising his father that he wouldn't tell a soul. It was his dying wish, after all. Besides, Nathan never wanted to be the one to break that kind of news to his baby sister. He wouldn't have even known how to.

The only other person who knew the truth – other than Raymond – was Cassie, and Nathan knew without a shadow of a doubt that he could trust her with his life.

Holding onto his dad's hand now, Nathan's head was wrecked from it all. There was so much left unsaid, so much feeling and emotion swimming around inside him, yet he had been left numb. He was still in shock.

'You've been the man of the house since you were knee high to a grasshopper, Nath, always such a good boy. I didn't tell you enough. Didn't want you to think I was soft.' Harry smiled. His chest whistled as he spoke, his voice quieter now. 'I'm so proud of you, Nathan. So unbelievably proud. Look after your sisters and look after Christopher for me.' Harry blamed himself for the way Christopher had turned out. All he had ever wanted to do was help him. Protect him. He never wanted Christopher's life to be tainted by one dreadful, tragic mistake.

It had been tragic.

Harry knew he'd done wrong now. He should never have made Christopher bury everything deep inside himself. The boy had been tormented by it all. So consumed by hate for his mother, for women. And it hadn't helped that Harry had never once spoken to the boy about it either. He'd been too worried about upsetting the boy by raking it all up. Instead, he'd buried his head.

He didn't want those few stupid split seconds, when Christopher pushed his mother, to affect the rest of his life. All he'd wanted to do was protect him. But in doing so, he'd let him down. Christopher had turned to drugs, and his paranoia had set in.

It had changed him. It wasn't the boy's fault, not really.

Even now, even after everything, Harry still just wanted to protect his kids. No matter what the crime, no matter what the cost.

'Course I will, Dad.' Nathan nodded. He hadn't told his dad everything.

He couldn't.

It was hard enough that his father was going to go to his deathbed worrying about them all as it was. All their dad needed to know was that Christopher had been detained under the Mental Health Act. He was sick, but in time he would get better.

Nathan knew that he owed his dad that slither of a happy ending before he passed. Even though Nathan knew that was far from the truth. Christopher would never get better, nor would he ever be free.

He'd confessed to killing all those girls the police had been dragging out of the Thames for the past few months. Prostitutes who had been beaten, raped, and then cast aside as if they were just rubbish. Christopher had confessed to all the dreadful, depraved things he had done to them. Blaming the torment and guilt that he'd had trapped inside of him for years. He'd developed such an aversion to women, to their mother, that he'd channelled his hate into hurting them.

Christopher was sick. He wasn't right in the head.

Nathan would pretend for his dad's sake that he would look out for Christopher, but the reality was, Nathan would never be seeing his brother again.

Not ever.

He couldn't.

Harry smiled now, relieved that Nathan would do the right thing when he was gone. Nathan was a good kid, a sensible kid. Then, seeing Cassie standing behind Nathan, Harry winked at her.

'You look after this beautiful one too, Nathan. The girl is an angel.'

Fighting back her own tears, Cassie bent down and kissed Harry on his cheek.

'You're going to be great parents.'

Nathan nodded. 'Well, I've learnt from the best, haven't I?' He cried now. He had so much to look forward to. His life with Cassie, and the baby. Yet his dad wouldn't be there to share any of it with him.

It was heart-breaking.

Stepping up now, Raymond bent down and kissed his best friend on the forehead. A rare sign of affection for the man that he'd spent the past forty-five years being best mates with; they'd been friends since the age of ten. They'd been inseparable. Done everything together. They were as close as brothers and Raymond was going to feel the void that Harry left behind him just as much as the kids were.

To him, they were family.

'You look after my babies, Raymond. I'm counting on you.'

Raymond nodded, squeezing his friend's arm. He had already promised that he would, and it was a promise that he intended to live by. He owed so much to Harry. More than his friend would ever know. Looking after the kids was the very least he could do.

It was an honour.

Picking up Harry's oxygen mask as he heard the dull rattle in the back of Harry's throat, Raymond tried to place it over his friend's mouth. But Harry, being such a stubborn sod, refused to take it.

Shaking his head at Raymond, until his friend placed the mask back down on the trolley, Harry nodded at his friend. It was time.

His chest felt like it was being crushed now. He could feel the fluid building up in the back of his throat. His breathing laboured, Harry took one more look around the room. His beautiful babies. All his money, all his possessions, none of it meant jack shit.

Unlike so many people that don't realise it until it's too late, Harry felt blessed to have always known that his family had meant everything to him. Worth more than any amount of money or jewels.

Family is all any of us have at the end of the day, and Harry's family were the only thing of any real value that he was leaving behind.

They were his precious gems, his jewels, his everything.

Closing his eyes, with his children and best friend at his side, Harry Woods slipped away.

Chapter Fifty

'Daddy!' Billy and Miley chorused as they ran towards their father and playfully jumped on the end of his bed.

'Hey, my two little rascals. I've missed you.' Terry smiled at his two children as he pushed himself up into a sitting position, hugging them with his good arm. He hadn't seen his kids for weeks and just the look of excitement on their faces at seeing him made his heart swell.

Watching as Kelly walked into the room seconds later and nodded at the police guard who stood in the doorway, Terry's smile grew.

She looked stunning.

Kitted out in a designer dress and having lost a few pounds, Terry felt like he was seeing his wife again for the very first time.

'Kelly? You came.' Leaning forward he grimaced as the searing pain shot through his left shoulder.

Kelly didn't smile back.

She looked heartbroken. Terry could see the dark shadows under her puffy eyes, that she had tried to conceal with make-up, and he knew that she'd been crying.

'I heard about your dad, babe. I'm so sorry.' Raymond had already paid Terry a visit. He'd told Terry about Harry's passing and had a word in his ear about what he was to say to the police about the incident at the bar. Terry knew that he had no choice but to comply.

Now that Harry was no longer around to keep Raymond on a tight leash, Terry was shit scared of what the bloke would do to him if he didn't.

Terry had agreed to take the rap without causing any grief. The drugs, the assault on the porter – he would hold his hands up to it. And in return, Raymond would let him live.

Apparently Harry and Raymond's bent copper, Mansell, was on the case of smoothing over the O'Sheas' shootings with his superiors, so hopefully there would be no reprisals for any of them about that.

As soon as his shoulder was healed Terry knew that he was looking at a lump in prison. And he would do it. If it meant that Kelly and the kids would still be waiting for him when he got out, and Terry could put all this behind him, then so be it.

'I'm not staying. I just brought you a bag of clothes, some wash things and stuff.' Kelly shrugged, standing awkwardly at the end of the bed. The last few days had left her feeling numb. Her voice was stone cold towards him, and considering he'd just been shot trying to help in rescuing her, Terry's intuition was telling him that his wife knew all about him hooking up with Raymond's tart that night he'd pretended to be mugged. He wouldn't have put it past Harry to make sure that Kelly knew all about it before he'd popped his clogs.

Terry knew that another lie wasn't going to wash with her this time. He needed to tell her the truth. Tell her the truth and then beg for forgiveness, so that they could start again.

'Pull up a chair, Kel? Please, just give me a few minutes, yeah? Here, kids, do you want to go down the corridor to the vending machine and get yourself some sweets?'

Screeching excitedly, Billy and Miley jumped off the bed and waited for some money.

'You haven't got a couple of quid, have you, Kel? I'm skint . . .'

Fumbling through her handbag, Kelly found some money and handed it to the children.

'Stay together, and I want you both straight back here,' Kelly warned as the kids ran from the room.

Sitting down next to her husband, Kelly had had so much to say before, but suddenly everything that she had felt about Terry up until now just diminished into nothing. All the feelings of anger, hurt, betrayal; she didn't feel anything.

'I'm sorry for what I did, Kel. That girl meant nothing to me. None of them ever have. It's you I love. I've been a fool. Please, Kel, let's start again. I can get through a term in prison if I know that you and the kids will be waiting for me. Please, Kel, just say that we can give it one more go.'

Kelly shook her head. Looking down at the floor, she realised that she couldn't even look Terry in the eye. Laid out in the hospital bed, pleading for her forgiveness with that pathetic look on his face, Kelly, for the first time ever, felt nothing towards him.

Her father had died. Christopher was sick. Really sick. All those murders he'd committed. She couldn't get her brain around it. How could her own brother be capable of such heinous acts? How could none of them have realised? The whole family were in shock and Kelly didn't have the energy to deal with Terry now too.

'You and the kids are my everything, Kel. Things will change from now on, I promise you, babe.'

'Of course things will change, Terry. You can't go off getting your leg over with a load of young tarts in prison, not unless you start batting for the other team.' Keeping her tone nonchalant as she spoke, Kelly no longer cared about her marriage. It had been nothing but a joke from day one. Normally she would have revelled in his apologies, thoroughly enjoying every moment of making him squirm after he'd done wrong by her.

But now, his empty words meant nothing. She'd been living as a single mother for the past few weeks, since Terry had gone on the run, and she'd surprised even herself at how easily she'd coped. She didn't need Terry.

And she certainly didn't love him anymore.

'When I get out we can run the bar together, Kel. Go on a big fancy holiday. Your dad's bound to have left you some money, ain't he? It's got to be a small fortune at least. We'll be laughing, babe.'

Incredulous, Kelly stared at Terry now. Her dad's body was barely cold and already Terry's brain was tallying up how much Kelly was set to inherit.

'Money? Is that all you're thinking about?' Kelly glared at Terry now, and she could see by the solemn expression on his face that he knew he'd said the wrong thing. 'Do you seriously think I'm going to put my life on hold for the next five years while you're doing time, so that when you do finally get out I can fund your gambling and whoring addiction? You must think I'm a right mug, Terry!'

All this time she had put Terry before everyone else, even herself. Her dad had been right all along. Kelly could see Terry with full clarity now.

'I want a divorce.' The words tumbled out of her mouth unplanned, but the second that she said them she knew that was exactly what she wanted.

Terry was a user. He only wanted her now because he had nothing else. No-one else.

'My dad was right about you from the start, Terry.' Kelly stood up. 'And do you know what? I would rather be alone for the rest of my life, than spend five more minutes married to you. You're nothing more than a lying, cheating scumbag. Life is too short.'

Turning on her heel, Kelly walked out of the room. She held her head high as she caught the prison guard's admiring glance. After overhearing the whole conversation, he smiled at her; a small appreciative look at an attractive woman who had finally come to her senses and ditched her lowlife husband.

Terry caught the man's gaze too. 'Oi, that's my fucking wife,' he shouted with venom.

Then, turning her head, Kelly stared Terry right in the eyes. 'Not anymore, darling. Not anymore.'

Epilogue

Running out to the car, Evie jumped in the passenger seat.

'I thought you were never going to come home.'

Raymond, seeing the excitement on Evie's face, couldn't help but laugh. He had actually been dying for a cup of tea, but he knew that the chances of him being able to go inside and have one now were non-existent.

Putting his foot down, he tossed his phone down on the dashboard.

'Well, I might have got here quicker, only my phone kept going off. Some real impatient young one kept sending me text messages every five minutes telling me to hurry up.' Raymond grinned.

Today had been the end of an era for him, but he was feeling surprisingly good about it. He'd just been over at the massage parlour with Molly, and officially signed all the paperwork over to her name. The parlour and the brothel were hers now. Molly had been running those places for him for years.

Raymond was taking a leaf out of his friend's book.

Harry had been on to something when he'd said he wanted to step back, and now, with more money than he knew what to do with, Raymond was following suit. He'd moved into Harry's house, and for now, until the kids were ready to sell it, Raymond was happy to stay there and look after Evie.

She didn't want to return to school. And after she'd finally told him about the bullying she had endured, Raymond had no intentions of making her go back.

Harry's passing wasn't what any of them would have chosen, but Raymond was determined not to have his friend die in vain. This was a new start for them all.

A clean slate.

No more crime.

'Do you think Kelly will have left yet? She'll be all over him like a rash if she has and I probably won't get a look-in.'

Raymond laughed now. Evie's excitement was infectious. He'd promised Evie that no matter where he was, or what time of day or night it was, he would get her to the hospital before Kelly got there. It had been a running joke with the girls as to who was going to be their newborn nephew's favourite auntie, and Evie was determined to be the first person other than Nathan and Cassie to hold the little fella.

Pulling up at the hospital a few minutes later, Raymond was still laughing as he and Evie raced through the corridors of the maternity ward.

———

'Auntie Evie, meet Harry Junior.' Placing the small bundle in Evie's arms, Nathan smiled over at Cassie. Calling him Harry after his father had been Cassie's idea, and the second that she had suggested it, Nathan had thought it was perfect.

He could tell by the look on Evie's face that she thought so too.

'Hello, baby Harry,' Evie cooed. Looking down at the tiny boy, she could see the likeness in his face. His eyes were just like her father's, just like Nathan's. Bending down, she kissed the baby on his plump little cheek, and then seconds later she smiled triumphantly as Kelly walked through the door with Billy and Miley.

'Ahh, typical.' Kelly shook her head. 'Billy couldn't find his trainer, and just as we were leaving Miley needed a wee.'

'Here, have a cuddle with your Auntie Kelly.' Evie offered the baby to Kelly.

'Ahh, Cassie, he is gorgeous, bless him!' Gazing down at her new nephew adoringly, Kelly cooed.

'Guess what they've called him, Kelly?' Evie looked at Cassie and Nathan for permission to tell Kelly. They both smiled back at her.

'Harry Junior.'

'Ahh that's lovely. Named after your granddad.' Kelly turned to Miley and Billy, but before she'd even finished the sentence she was off again, crying her heart out.

'Uncle Nathan, I think you should take the baby off Mummy,' Miley said seriously.

'Yeah,' Billy chipped in, 'she's crying all over him.'

Kelly couldn't help but laugh then. Smiling through her tears at her children, Kelly knew that because of them, she'd get through all of this.

'Your dad would be really proud of you, Nathan.' Raymond walked over and hugged the boy as Harry would have done if he was here. He knew that it was going to be moments like this when the kids really felt Harry's absence the most.

Raymond intended on doing right by Harry, just like he had promised. He owed him that much.

Smiling around the room at Kelly and the kids, and Cassie cooing over the baby, Raymond's eyes rested on Evie. Out of all of them, Harry's death had hit her the hardest.

Staring out of the window now, she looked deep in thought, like she was in another world. She was the image of her mother.

Raymond hated Evelyn.

What she'd done to Harry. How she'd tried to break him.

More than that, he hated himself.

Harry had never found out the whole truth. Evelyn might have been a heartless bitch but she had spared him that much at least.

When Harry had called him that tragic day to tell him what Christopher had done, to ask him to take the boy away so that Christopher could never be implicated, Raymond had been glad to find out that Evelyn was dead. She was a bitter, nasty drunk. After sleeping with half of London, she had been threatening to tell Harry everything. Harry had been heartbroken – his wife was leaving him and the young daughter he adored wasn't his.

Evelyn had spared him the truth about Raymond.

Raymond hadn't loved Evelyn, he'd only ever wanted her out of lust.

Beautiful women had always been his downfall.

And Evelyn had been beyond beautiful. She had been stunning and totally out of bounds: she was Harry's wife.

It had only happened the once, but like they said, once was enough.

Evie was his daughter.

All this time, he'd had to stand back and watch Harry raise her as his own. Raymond could never have broken Harry by telling him any different, so he'd settled for second best – her favourite uncle. And that was all right: kids weren't his forte.

And it quickly become apparent as Evie had grown up that Harry was Evie's hero. They had an amazing bond, which Raymond never wanted to take away from her.

Raymond was determined to do right by his friend now, like he should have done all those years ago. He owed it to Harry, and he owed it to Evie to make this right. And he would, no matter what the cost to him.

Evie would never find out the truth, he would make sure of it.

'Here, Raymond, you look a million miles away.' Nathan laughed. 'Grab us that bag from under the bed, will you?'

Pulling the bag out, Raymond smiled as he peered inside at the champagne and the plastic cups that Nathan had brought in especially.

'Well, if Dad was here, he'd be whipping out the champagne, wouldn't he?' Nathan laughed. 'Can't argue with the Woods tradition, can we now!'

Passing the cups around, Nathan turned to Cassie who was holding the baby in her arms and looking down at their tiny son adoringly.

Raising his glass and with a tear in his eye, Nathan smiled. He could almost feel his father's spirit standing beside him smiling down at his new grandson proudly.

'To my beautiful wife, and our gorgeous son.'

Everyone in the room raised their glasses in union.

'To Harry.'

Acknowledgements

Many thanks to Emilie Marneur for giving me this fantastic opportunity to publish my fourth novel with Thomas & Mercer. The journey has been a hugely exciting one, and I have loved every second of it. Huge thanks to Victoria Pepe for the main editorial work – your ideas and input really helped to pull everything together, and it was a pleasure working alongside you. Huge thanks also to Emma Clements for the great work on the copy-edit. Not an easy challenge I'm sure!

Special thanks to David Gaylor – Peter James' real life 'Roy Grace' – for allowing me to bombard you with questions on police procedures. I really appreciated all your help.

Massive thanks to all of my family and friends for your constant support and encouragement, especially to Danny and my boys; my parents, and my sister. Special thanks to my brother Seán for always trawling through my first drafts and giving me his honest feedback, and also to my bestie Lucy (my #freeagent) – thank you for all of your help and advice along the way. And more importantly for introducing me to gin!

And most of all, thank you to you, the reader. For leaving your reviews, and sending me emails, and for all the encouragement and feedback that you give me on Facebook and Twitter. It means so much.

Without YOU, none of this would have been possible. X

About the Author

Born in Cuckfield, West Sussex, Casey Kelleher grew up as an avid reader and a huge fan of author Martina Cole.

Whilst working as a beauty therapist and bringing up her three children together with her fiancé, Casey penned her debut novel *Rotten to the Core*. Its success meant that she could give up her day job and concentrate on writing full time.

She has since published *Rise and Fall*, *Heartless* and her latest release, *Bad Blood*.

Printed in Great Britain
by Amazon